MASTER OF HIS FATE

Books by Barbara Taylor Bradford

Series
THE EMMA HARTE SAGA
A Woman of Substance
Hold the Dream
To Be the Best
Emma's Secret
Unexpected Blessings
Just Rewards
Breaking the Rules

THE RAVENSCAR TRILOGY
The Ravenscar Dynasty
Heirs of Ravenscar
Being Elizabeth

THE CAVENDON SERIES
Cavendon Hall
The Cavendon Women
The Cavendon Luck
Secrets of Cavendon

Others
Voice of the Heart
Act of Will
The Women in His Life
Remember
Angel
Everything to Gain
Dangerous to Know
Love in Another Town
Her Own Rules
A Secret Affair
Power of a Woman
A Sudden Change of Heart
Where You Belong
The Triumph of Katie Byrne
Three Weeks in Paris
Playing the Game
Letter from a Stranger
Secrets from the Past

Ebook-only novellas
Hidden
Treacherous
Who Are You
Damaged

BARBARA TAYLOR BRADFORD

MASTER OF HIS FATE

HarperCollins*Publishers*

HarperCollins*Publishers* Ltd
The News Building
1 London Bridge Street
London SE1 9GF

www.harpercollins.co.uk

Published by HarperCollins*Publishers* 2018
1

A catalogue record for this book
is available from the British Library

ISBN HB: 9780008242404
ISBN TPB: 9780008242411

Set in Sabon by
Palimpsest Book Production Limited, Falkirk, Stirlingshire

Printed and bound in Great Britain by
CPI Group (UK) Ltd, Croydon CRO 4YY

MIX
Paper from
responsible sources
FSC C007454

This book is produced from independently certified FSC™ paper
to ensure responsible forest management.

For more information visit: www.harpercollins.co.uk/green

This book is for my husband Bob, my hero,
who has always given me the freedom and space to write
despite whatever else has been happening.
With my love and gratitude always.

CONTENTS

CHARACTERS

THE FALCONERS

Philip Henry Rosewood Falconer, founder of the dynasty; a head butler.

Esther Marie Falconer, his wife and co-founder of the dynasty; a head housekeeper.

Their sons

Matthew, his eldest son and heir; a stall owner at the Malvern Market.

George, a noted journalist on *The Chronicle* daily newspaper.

Harry, a chef and owner of a café, the Rendezvous.

Their grandchildren (Matthew's offspring)

James Lionel, an ambitious young businessman on the rise.

Rosalind, known as Rossi, a seamstress.

Edward Albert, assistant to his father on the stalls.

Their daughter-in-law

Maude Falconer, Matthew's wife and mother of his children; a seamstress.

THE VENABLES

Clarence Venables, Esther Falconer's brother-in-law, great-uncle of James Falconer. Owner of a shipping company in Hull.

Marina Venables, Clarence's wife and younger sister of Esther Falconer. Great-aunt of James Falconer. A noted artist.

Their children

William, eldest son and heir, working at the Hull shipping company.

Albert, second son, working at the Hull shipping company.

Their daughter-in-law

Anne Venables, Albert's wife.

THE MALVERNS

Henry Ashton Malvern, owner of the Malvern Company, a big business enterprise and property company.

Alexis Malvern, his only child and heir; a partner in the business.

Joshua Malvern, Henry's brother and business partner in London.

Percy Malvern, his cousin who runs the wine business in Le Havre.

THE TREVALIANS

Sebastian Trevalian, head of the Trevalian private bank.

His daughters

Claudia, his eldest daughter and heir.

Lavinia, a debutante.

Marietta, a debutante.

His sister

Dorothea Trevalian Rayburn, an art collector and member of the bank's board.

His son-in-law

Cornelius Glendenning, Claudia's husband, a banker.

THE CARPENTERS

Lord Reginald Carpenter, publishing tycoon and proprietor of
The Chronicle.

Lady Jane Cadwalander Carpenter, his wife.

Their daughters

Jasmine, a debutante.

Lilah, a debutante.

PART ONE

The Barrow Boy
London
1884

ONE

J ames Lionel Falconer, commonly called Jimmy by everyone except his grandmother, was out of breath. He came to a sudden stop in the middle of the road going towards Camden Lock. The wheelbarrow he was pushing was heavy and grew heavier by the minute, at least so it seemed to him. He rested for a few seconds, leaning against the barrow, trying to catch his breath.

It was Thursday 12 June 1884, and last month, in late May, he had celebrated his fourteenth birthday. He felt very grown up now. After all, he had been working with his father at their stalls in Henry Malvern's covered market in London's Camden Town since he was eight. That was part-time until he was ten, when he began to go there every day. He loved the haggling, the negotiating, the wheeling and dealing about prices, just as much as his father did.

His father called him 'my clever lad', which pleased Jimmy. He admired his father, endeavoured to emulate him. Matthew Falconer, who was thirty-seven, dressed neatly to go to work, and so did Jimmy. His father never forgot to ask his regulars how members of their families were, and neither did Jimmy. It had been inculcated in him.

Even his grandmother, Esther Falconer, had noticed, since his early childhood, how he copied his father in most things. It frequently brought a smile to her face, and sometimes she even gave him a threepenny bit for being a good boy. She told him to save it for a rainy day. He did. He paid great attention to her.

Straightening, blowing out air, Jimmy picked up the two handles and started pushing the barrow once more. He walked at an even pace, knowing that this main road got a bit higher after it branched off on both sides.

He stayed on the main road, puffing a bit harder, perspiring; it was a warm day. He was almost at the market when he experienced a sharp, stabbing pain in his chest, and came to an abrupt stop, startled by the intensity of the pain.

Holding onto the handles of the barrow tightly, he kept himself upright even though he thought he might fall over anyway. Slowly, the pain subsided. He was still short of breath; sweat covered his face. He couldn't imagine what was wrong with him. What had just happened?

'Jimmy! Jimmy! Are you all right, lad?'

He recognized Mrs Greenwood's voice and turned around. She was a neighbour, a cook who worked in a big house in a terrace near Regent's Park.

'I'm fine,' he answered, and he did feel better. Whatever the pain had been about, it had gone away. He just felt a bit warm on this sunny day, and breathless.

When she arrived at his side, Mavis Greenwood peered at him intently, her warm, motherly face ringed with concern. 'You stopped suddenly, and looked a bit odd. I can't help thinking something is wrong.'

'No, it isn't. Not really. I just got out of breath and felt hot.'

She nodded. 'Let's not complain about the weather. It's been raining cats and dogs for days.'

Jimmy laughed. He liked Mrs Greenwood. She often brought them some of her baked goods, as she called her marvellous concoctions, and he was especially partial to her gooseberry tart.

'Where's your dad, Jimmy? He shouldn't let you push this barrow. It's almost bigger than you.'

He grinned at her; then his face quickly changed. His expression sobered as he explained, 'Dad's taken Mum to see Dr Robertson. She says it's just a cold, but me dad thinks it might be bronchitis, or – worse – pneumonia.'

'Oh, I do hope it's not, lad. They're serious illnesses.' Placing her handbag on top of the sack covering the contents in the wheelbarrow, she got hold of one of the handles. 'Come on then, Jimmy, take the other handle, and I'll help you push this to the market.'

Jimmy was about to refuse her help, but changed his mind at once. It would offend her. He did as she said, grabbed the other handle, and together they pushed the barrow, keeping in step with each other.

When he had first rented a stall at the Malvern Market, Matthew Falconer had made up his mind to be successful – and he was. The owner, Henry Malvern, soon took an interest in him, realizing what a good merchant he was, and when a new stall became available, it had been Matt who'd been given the chance to rent it. He did.

The Malvern was one of the few covered markets in the area, and because of its glass roof and stone walls, it was protected when the weather was bad. This meant the stalls were open to the public all year round; every stallholder appreciated this.

Jimmy and Mavis Greenwood pushed the barrow through the big iron gates, to be greeted by Tommy, the caretaker, who lived in the gatehouse. Then Jimmy and Mavis headed towards the area where the two adjoining sheds were located.

Once the shed doors were unlocked and folded back, Jimmy opened the doors of the storage rooms, which were like two small shops. Mavis Greenwood helped him to pull out the wooden sawhorses and the planks of wood which made the stalls when put together.

As she assisted Jimmy, she wondered how Matt Falconer had expected his son to do this alone. It baffled her but she remained silent. She knew it was best to mind her own business.

Once they were finished with the stalls, she picked up her handbag from the barrow, smiled at Jimmy. 'And what treasures are hidden under that old sack, then?'

Jimmy pulled it off and showed her. 'Copper kitchen utensils me dad got at an estate sale last week. From a big house up West.' He pointed to a few items.

'Look at 'em, Mrs Greenwood. Copper moulds for jellies, blancmange, salmon mousse; all the things you no doubt make at that big house where you're Cook.'

She nodded and picked up a few items, looking them over carefully. 'Lovely pieces, Jimmy, I've got to admit. How much is this mould then?' she asked, taking a fancy to one.

'Dad forgot to give me the price list, but you can have it for sixpence. I think that'd be about right.'

'Sixpence! That's highway robbery, Jimmy Falconer!'

'Oh! Well, perhaps I made a mistake. A threepenny bit? How does that sound, Mrs Greenwood?' He gazed at her, smiling. After all, she had helped him to get there. She deserved a bargain.

Mavis opened her handbag and took out her purse. She handed him the coin, gave him a big smile, and put the mould in her bag. 'Thank you, Jimmy. You've been very fair. Now I'd better be getting off or I'll be late for work.'

'Thanks for helping me, Mrs Greenwood. Can I ask you something?'

'Anything you want, but best make it quick, lad.'

'Can you have a heart attack at fourteen?' he asked, staring intently.

She stared back at him and exclaimed, 'Don't be daft, Jimmy!

Anyway, you're as fit as a fiddle. You must be or your dad wouldn't expect you to push that heavy barrow up here.'

Once he was alone, Jimmy began to arrange the copper moulds on the stalls, following his father's instructions to always put tall pieces at the back, graduating them down in size because the buyer's eye would look at the first grouping and then move their eyes up to the taller items.

He worried about his mother as he did this task almost by rote, also wondering where his father was. How long would it take at the doctor's? Now and then he turned around, looked down towards the gates into the market. It was still quite early, and stallholders were already there, doing the same job as him. Thoughts of Mrs Greenwood intruded, and he felt a sudden rush of guilt. She had blamed his father for his predicament on the road, but it was his fault. He had filled the wheelbarrow too full, piled in far too many moulds and a variety of additional items. He must explain that the next time he saw her. He didn't want his father to look bad in her eyes.

Jimmy had just finished arranging the wares on the stalls when he spotted his father coming through the iron gates, hurrying towards him. His first instinct was to rush forward, but he restrained himself, as he had been taught from an early age – control yourself, be dignified. And so he waited.

Matthew Falconer approached his son, smiling, and drew the boy close to his body for a moment. 'She's got a very heavy cold,' Matt explained, at once noting the worried expression in Jimmy's blue eyes. 'She's back home in bed. The doctor gave her some good cough mixture. She's to stay in bed, be kept warm and given lots of liquids.'

Beaming at his father, filled with relief, Jimmy said, 'I'm thankful it's not bronchitis or pneumonia.'

'You can say that again. I'm as grateful as you, Jim. Now, I want you to go to your grandmother's. I need her to give you a bottle of her raspberry vinegar concoction and some camphor bags, as well as any special advice she has. Lady Agatha won't mind you going, if she's still there. Your grandmother told me the family is going to France for the next two months, leaving today.'

The boy nodded. 'I'll go now. Shall I take the things home to Mother?'

'Yes do, my lad. Grandmother will no doubt give you a sandwich and perhaps some food to take home for your mother.'

'But what about you, Dad? We forgot to make our snacks before we left this morning.'

'Don't worry about me. The pie man usually comes around hawking his goods at one o'clock. I'll manage.'

'I'll come back, after I've given Mother her lunch.'

'No, no, don't do that! It's not worth it for an hour or two in the late afternoon. Stay at home, look after Rossi and Eddie, and make sure they have something to eat. Now, off you go.'

Two

J ames walked out of the Malvern, without a backward glance, feeling happy for various reasons. He was glad his mother did not have some deadly illness and that she was safe at home in bed. He was relieved his father had lost that worried look. Matthew had been whistling when he left the stalls. And he was thrilled to be going to see his grandmother.

He hurried along the road, wanting to get there as fast as possible. His grandmother, Esther Marie Falconer, was the most important and influential person in his life. As he was in hers. That he knew to be an absolute certainty, because she had told him so. Although she was careful, discreet, not wanting to hurt his siblings.

James loved his parents, emulated some of his father's mannerisms and way of dressing; he loved his sister Rossi, now twelve, and his little brother, Eddie, who had just had his ninth birthday. And then there was his wonderful grandfather, who kept an eye on them all. Philip Henry Rosewood Falconer had taught him a lot, especially about geography and the rest of the world. He had even given him a globe on a stand, which James treasured.

Nonetheless, his grandmother was at the top of his list. She was his guiding light; she had taught him to read and write by the time he was four. When he had gone to school in Rochester at that age, his first teacher had been truly impressed by his ability and his intelligence.

James realized, as he headed down the road leaving Camden behind, that it was as busy a morning as usual. There were crowds of men hurrying up to the Malvern, who were obviously stallholders, and women, too, customers out for a bargain.

Mornings and evenings were generally hectic during the week, the streets filled with men and women going to their workplace, and then returning home at the end of the day.

Some of the men waved to him, and he waved back, smiling hugely. These were the stallholders who had their setups near theirs. James had a genial nature and a ready smile. He liked people and made friends easily. In turn, they were attracted to him because of his charismatic personality and handsome appearance.

His grandparents were in service near Regent's Park, and it was not too far away. James knew he would soon be there, once he had crossed Chalk Farm Road. He was headed in the direction of Marylebone.

He liked Marylebone and knew a lot about the area. His grandmother had told him that the region had been planned and developed by the great Regency architect, John Nash, around 1818, and that his overall architectural scheme had included Regent Street, Regent's Park, and the beautiful terraces and streets of elegant townhouses close to the park.

It was there that Philip and Esther Falconer lived, in one of those formally designed John Nash townhouses facing Regent's Park, belonging to their employers, the Honourable Arthur Blane Montague and his wife, Lady Agatha Denby Montague, daughter of Lord Percival Denby, the Sixth Earl of Melton.

Esther Falconer had been born in the Yorkshire village of

Melton, which was not very far from the great northern seaport of Hull. At twelve, Esther had been pretty, clever and ambitious, and through her mother's connection to Lady Agatha's aunt, she was given a job at Melton Priory.

Esther had been trained to be a lady's maid, specifically to look after Lady Agatha, the Earl's youngest daughter, who had then been sixteen. At seventeen Lady Agatha had come out as a debutante, had been presented at Court, and had her first Season in London.

Esther had been with her mistress ever since. Forty-four years, to be precise. Over the years she had risen in the ranks; now she was the head housekeeper at Lady Agatha's current residences in London and Kent, and proud of her position.

Philip Falconer, a Kentish man, had also gone into service. He had started out as a junior footman, aged sixteen, in the employment of the Honourable Arthur Blane Montague at the latter's country manor, Fountains Court in Kent. He had also worked at the Regent's Park house which Mr Montague had purchased several years before his marriage to Lady Agatha.

Esther and Philip had met at this beautiful Nash house in London, where they had soon fallen in love. They had been married from the house and had lived there ever since. Their employers valued them far too much to let them go. Lady Agatha had transformed a set of rooms at the back of the house into a flat for Philip and Esther. It was still their main home, although they had the same kind of quarters at Fountains Court in Kent where their three sons had been born and brought up.

Esther was crossing the back hall when she stopped abruptly. Somebody outside was repeatedly banging the brass door knocker so hard it sounded like thunder.

Rushing to the service door, she opened it to find herself face to face with her favourite grandchild.

Momentarily taken aback though she was, she instantly smiled, reached out and drew him into the house. Then the smile slipped when she asked swiftly, with a small frown, 'Is there something wrong? Why are you here in the middle of the day, James?'

'There's nothing wrong, Grans, not really. Mum's ill. Dr Robertson says she has a heavy cold, and he gave her a bottle of medicine. He said she should go home to bed. That's where she is now. Dad sent me for some of your raspberry vinegar concoction, as he calls it. Oh, and some camphor bags.'

'I understand,' Esther said, her sudden anxiety dissipating. 'I'm sure the doctor's right. Unfortunately summer colds are hard to get rid of, James.' Putting her arms around him, she hugged him to her. He hugged her back, then stepped away, and said, 'I'm sorry if I frightened you, Grans.'

'I'm all right. Though I thought you were about to break the door down with your knocking.' She gazed at him, her eyes roaming over his face. It had been only ten days since she had seen him, and yet he looked more mature; he was now an inch taller than she was.

Staring back at her, he asked softly, 'What is it? Why are you looking at me like that?'

Esther shook her head and a faint smile crossed her face. 'You've changed a bit, and you seem to be, well, more mature. You might be only fourteen, but you are growing up rapidly.'

He smiled at her, and then laughed. And she was dazzled by him . . . the even white teeth, the natural charm, the most stunning blue eyes, filled with sparkle and life. Women are going to fall at his feet, she thought.

Brushing incipient worry to one side, she now said, 'Let's go down to my parlour and I'll tell Cook to make the raspberry vinegar concoction. She'll also make you something to eat.'

Esther led James down the long corridor where her parlour

was located, Philip's office, as well as the kitchen and the wine cellars. Showing him into her room, she went to the kitchen to speak to Cook.

Left alone in the parlour, James went and sat in a chair near the window. He liked this room. It was comfortable, nice to be in and full of light.

There was a fireplace, a sofa and chairs, and his grandmother's desk. She had once explained that it was Georgian, a very good antique piece which Lady Agatha had given her. Basically, the room was an office where Esther did her menus, her household accounts and other paperwork, but she could also relax here between her many duties.

His grandfather's room was a few doors down the corridor. It, too, had a desk, and was full of books, mostly about wine and the vineyards of France.

Philip Falconer had become an expert on wine over the years, and Mr Montague had allowed him to create a wonderful cellar.

James knew how lucky the whole family was, because of Philip and Esther Falconer. Their very long service in the Montague household protected them all. His father and two uncles worked and made decent livings, but there was, most importantly, the reassuring knowledge that the older Falconers were there for them, should they need help of any kind. Lucky indeed.

People giving over their entire lives to one aristocratic family was not unusual, but James knew his grandparents were kept on also because they were excellent at what they did. In a sense they had become part of the family, were often given many small privileges which were much appreciated. James's grandparents had many perks because the Montagues thought so highly of them. His grandmother had recently confided that Lady Agatha had told her that she was not the best, but better than the best, and so was Philip. Esther had sounded very proud and pleased when she recounted this to him.

James looked across at the door as it opened and his grandfather came in, a huge smile on his face. Jumping up, James ran to him. They embraced and Philip kissed his cheek before releasing him.

'What a nice surprise to see you, my boy. I notice that you've shot up since I last saw you.'

'That's what Father says.'

'Your grandmother told me your mother's not well; that's why Matthew sent you for the raspberry vinegar. He's all right himself, isn't he?'

James nodded. 'Fighting fit, he says.'

Philip seated himself on the sofa, and James took the chair opposite. 'Has Lady Agatha gone away then?'

Philip smiled, knowing how much James enjoyed the way Her Ladyship fussed over him. 'She has indeed, with the Honourable Mister and Miss Helena and Master William, plus two maids, the valet, and enough baggage to fill two coaches. Gone to the Riviera to enjoy the sun and the festivities by the sea. They will stay in Nice and then progress to Monte Carlo. They will return in September, unless the Honourable Mister wants to come back in August for the grouse season.'

Esther arrived and announced, 'Let's go to the staff dining room and have a bite of lunch.' Beckoning to them, she went on, 'Cook has made a cottage pie, and she's now preparing another one for you to take home, James, and an excellent chicken soup for your mother. Nothing like chicken soup to cure a sore throat.'

Philip and James followed Esther as she hurried down the corridor and into the staff dining room, where they sat down together. They would have it to themselves for the next hour, while the other staff cleaned the house and went about their duties.

For a long time Esther had wanted to discuss the future with her grandson, eager to know if he had any special plans about his work. This was a great opportunity to bring up the subject.

Turning to look at him, her pale green eyes filled with love, she began. 'I've been meaning to ask you if you intend to spend your life working at the market with Matthew on the two stalls. Or whether you might have other ideas, perhaps?'

Taken by surprise, James stared at her, his eyes wide, his expression quizzical. He did not answer for a moment. Finally, he said, 'I don't know, not really.'

'It has occurred to me, from time to time, that you love architecture, and I know how intrigued you are about John Nash and his Regency buildings. Grandpa and I would be prepared to send you to school to be trained in architectural drawing, if you want that,' Esther announced, and sat back in her chair, looking at him expectantly.

He shook his head vehemently. 'No, I don't want to be a draughtsman, Grans, but thank you for offering to send me to study – and you, too, Grandpapa. That's generous of you.' He was sincere, and this echoed in his voice.

'What about school in general?' Philip asked, leaning forward, his entire focus on his grandson. He was aware James was a special boy, highly intelligent, with the kind of class that was bred in the bone. He also had enormous charm and looks, and he was an achiever.

When James was silent, Philip added, 'There is no pressure from us, James, but think about it, maybe something will come to you. We just want you to understand we are here to support you. The world is opening up for you.'

James nodded, looked at his grandfather intently, thinking how smart he was in his black jacket, pinstriped trousers, pristine white shirt and silver silk tie. The perfectly dressed butler.

His glance was now aimed at his grandmother, also well attired in a long, navy-blue skirt and matching blouse, with a white collar and cuffs. Her luxuriant silvery hair was piled up on top of her head. To him, she was the epitome of tailored elegance.

He knew she was fifty-six, but she didn't look her age. And neither did his grandfather, who was now sixty. They have worn well, he thought, and suppressed a smile, wondering what they would say if he told them this.

Straightening in his chair, taking a deep breath, James decided to tell them the truth about his dreams. He plunged in. 'I want to be a merchant,' he confided. 'By that I mean I want to own a shop like Fortnum and Mason, or an arcade of shops like the Burlington Arcade in Piccadilly. I want to be the most successful merchant in London! In the world!' His voice had risen in his escalating excitement and, as he sat back, taking a deep breath, he realized his grandparents were staring at him in astonishment.

THREE

James loved his grandparents and he would never do anything to upset them, or disrespect them, but he had a mischievous streak in him and he was tickled that he had rendered them speechless for once in his life. He felt sudden laughter bubbling up inside him.

But he realized he dared not laugh, so he swallowed hard and tried to look serious. Taking a deep breath, he repeated, 'Yes, I want to be a great merchant. That is truly my dream.'

'How wonderful it is to have such a dream, James,' his grandfather responded, the first one to break the silence. 'Just as it's important to know what you want to do with your life at an early age. Good for you, my boy.'

'How are you going to make this dream come true?' his grandmother asked, always down to earth and practical. James had certainly aroused her curiosity this morning with his announcement.

'To answer your last question first, Grans, I can't put my plan into operation just yet. I have to wait a couple of years. As for my plan, I really will make it work. And I shall strive very hard to make my dream come true. When I'm the right age.'

A smile of pleasure gleamed in Esther's eyes. 'That sounds very smart of you, and would you like to share your plan with us?'

'Yes, I would . . .' James stopped as Cook came into the staff hall carrying a tray, followed by Polly, one of the young house-maids.

Moving forward, her white apron billowing around her, Cook put the tray down at the other end of the table, brought a white ceramic dish over to his grandmother, and placed it on the table in front of her.

'Here it is at last, Mrs Falconer, the cottage pie, and Polly has brought a bowl of peas, the gravy boat and the plates.'

'Thank you, Mrs Grainger, and you, too, Polly,' Esther said, smiling at the women as they placed the other items to one side of her on the table.

The women smiled back and departed.

Esther served James and Philip, and then spooned some of the pie onto her own plate. It smelled delicious. The crust of mashed potatoes covering the top of the minced beef was browned to perfection.

After a mouthful of pie, James put his fork down and went on, 'About my plan . . . it's quite clear in my mind. For the next couple of years, I want to work with Dad, learn more from him. I'm going to ask him to take me with him when he attends estate sales in the country, or on the outskirts of London, and wherever he goes. I like to watch him wheel and deal, as he calls it. He's an expert, and I must be an expert too. I also want to learn about other things, as well.'

'Such as what, James?' Philip asked curiously.

'The finer things in life. I think I should gain a good knowl-edge about luxury goods, for instance. I need that information to run a store like Fortnum and Mason, and have an arcade full of fancy shops.' James eyed his grandfather, then looked at Esther, his expression questioning.

'Good thinking,' Esther exclaimed. 'Knowledge is Power with a capital "P".'

'I can teach you about the noble grape, and all the great wines of France,' Philip announced with a smile. 'I'd rather like to do that.'

James's young face took on a glow, and he nodded vehemently. 'Oh, Grandpapa, what a wonderful idea! Thank you. When can we get started?'

Philip and Esther glanced at each other and chuckled, amused, yet also pleased that James was so enthusiastic, and bursting to better himself.

It was Esther who now suggested that she should take James on some trips, when he could manage to take time off from his work at the market. 'I'd like you to visit the Burlington Arcade again. I've only taken you there once before, and there are other arcades in London for you to see. And it is mandatory that we make a few trips to Fortnum and Mason. To study every floor and everything sold on those floors. You are correct, James. To be the owner of a shop selling high-class, luxury goods, you must understand the merchandise, your market, and your customers. And all the things they dream about and want to own. You must know their style, their way of living, what they wear and eat and drink.'

'I will love visiting my favourite store.' His blue eyes were sparkling more than ever, and he tucked into his lunch with relish, obviously enjoying it. He was happy he had confided in his grandparents, and thrilled by their positive response.

Esther gave him a loving look and began to eat her pie; Philip studied his young grandson thoughtfully and acutely, assessing him.

The boy was undoubtedly extremely clever, and he had been well brought up by Esther and Philip and his own parents. His mother Maude had seen to it that James read all the magazines and books he gave him, passed on by Lady Agatha, and Maude had helped him with his other lessons over the years.

Matthew had shown him how to dress well, and in a suitable way, and how to take care of his few clothes. Obviously James didn't have a lot of things at his age, but they were always pressed and kept in good condition; his mother darned and stitched so that her family was always well turned out. His father was also teaching him to be the best salesman.

He certainly looks fit and healthy, Philip now thought, and was glad about that. Silently he thanked his employers for keeping him on the staff all these years, and Esther too. He and Esther had always made sure their sons and their grandchildren had good food and were aware of the importance of nutrition for their good health. It enraged Philip when he thought about his country, which was now – in 1884 – the greatest, richest and most powerful nation in the world, and how it treated millions of its citizens. Without a second thought, the government allowed them to starve and live in filthy, foul slums.

It wouldn't surprise me if they rose up and started a revolution one day soon, he thought suddenly, attacking the aristocracy, the gentry and the government. The French Revolution flew into his mind, and he cringed inside, but it was not such a far-fetched idea that it could happen here. Not the way things were.

The lower working classes and the very poor went hungry all of the time. Their daily sustenance was composed of a chunk of bread, and, if they were lucky, a mug of tea. Otherwise, it was water or a glass of ale. The latter was better than it sounded, because at least it wasn't dangerous like some of the water supply. Philip couldn't help wishing there were more men like his master, who was unusually charitable. Arthur Montague had given plenty of money for philanthropy to his eldest son and heir, Mr Roland Montague, who had started a charity with his wife, Catherine. They did a lot of wonderful work to help the poor and the destitute in Whitechapel and surrounding areas in the East End of London.

'If you're finished, Philip, I think we should collect the food from the kitchen – and the raspberry vinegar – so that I can go with James to Camden,' Esther murmured as she pushed back her chair.

Esther's words brought Philip out of his reverie. He nodded and rose. 'That's a good thought, my dear. I'll take James to my office for a few seconds to show him some of my books on wine whilst you deal with Cook.'

Fifteen minutes later, when James and his grandfather joined Esther in the service hall, Philip immediately insisted she take a hansom cab. 'Those two big canvas bags look awfully heavy,' he protested, as his wife made a move to leave with them, one in each hand.

'It's fine; they're not that heavy,' she answered, 'and James can help me with the smaller ones over there.'

James immediately exclaimed, 'I think they are all extremely heavy, Grans, and they're overflowing. Grandpapa is right. We should take a hansom cab.' He did not want a repetition of the experience he'd had with the wheelbarrow. It had frightened him a little. But, mostly, he longed to ride in one of the horse-drawn carriages. He had never been in one before.

Much to James's relief, his grandfather won the argument. He had gone outside and found a cab almost at once. Now he and his grandmother were sitting in it, surrounded by even more bags. 'Since we're taking a hansom cab, I might as well add a few things for Maude,' she had told his grandfather, who had merely smiled knowingly. He told her to give Maude his love and his hope that she would feel better soon.

James sat opposite his grandmother in the horse-drawn carriage, one arm protecting several of the canvas bags on the seat next to him. His grandmother was doing the same thing. He had no idea what was in the extra bags, although he was certain it was food because of the nice smells emanating from them. Apple pie, he decided, and maybe sausage rolls.

After a long silence, sitting with her eyes closed as if in deep thought, Esther opened her eyes and stared at James. 'I'd like to ask you something,' she said in a low voice.

'You can ask me anything, Grans.'

'Have you told your father about your dream to be the greatest merchant in the world? And your plan?'

James shook his head. 'No, I haven't. Only you and Grandpapa know.'

'Don't you think that perhaps you should tell your father your plan for the future? After all, he ought to know that you'll be leaving the stalls in a couple of years.'

'I might be with him longer than that,' James explained. 'I might be seventeen or eighteen. I have to gauge what Mr Malvern will say when I take my proposition to him.'

'Oh, so you have a proposition for him, as well as a dream and a plan for yourself?'

'I do, yes,' James muttered, thinking that she had sounded odd. Sarcastic? That wasn't like her. No, she wasn't being critical. Just curious.

He said, 'I have some ideas that might make the market hall better, just small things, but they would improve the Malvern in certain ways.'

'Do you want to tell me about them?' she asked, now smiling, more like herself.

He shook his head. 'No. I haven't quite worked them out properly.'

'I understand,' Esther said. 'Keep thinking.'

Four

The hansom came to a halt at the corner of the street where Matthew Falconer and his family lived, just off the main Hampstead Road in Camden.

The driver of the cab jumped down from his seat, opened the carriage door, and helped Esther to alight, with James following his grandmother. He and the driver pulled out canvas bags while Esther opened her purse to pay the driver. She did this once the bags were at the front door and thanked him. Small children watched curiously from across the street.

He tipped his cap, thanked her back, and thought to add, 'Nice young 'un yer 'ave there, missus.' He grinned and went back to the carriage, whistling away.

James was searching for the key when the front door suddenly opened. Rossi stood there smiling, with little Eddie peeping out from behind her. 'James and Grandma! I'm so glad you're here.' She opened the door wider and helped them to carry the bags inside.

The house was tall and narrow and not very big, but it did accommodate the family comfortably, and they liked it. There was a cosy, homely feeling about the large kitchen, a room which was the centre of the household.

It had a big open fireplace and an oven with a range, and a wide window looking out into the back garden. A long oak table stood under the window and it was here they had their meals.

Once the canvas bags were safely on the table, Esther hugged and kissed Rossi and Eddie, and said to James, 'I'm just going to pop upstairs to see your mother, and then I'll be back to heat the raspberry vinegar medicine.'

James nodded. 'I'll unpack the bags, and Rossi will help me.'

'I want to help, too,' Eddie said, and James smiled at him and said he could.

Esther hurried into the front hall and mounted the stairs leading to the main bedroom floor. As she climbed, she could hear Maude coughing, and was quite alarmed when she went into the bedroom and saw her daughter-in-law's face. It was ashen and there were dark rings under her eyes. Her light brown hair, always so glossy and carefully arranged, was rumpled and unruly.

'I'm here, Maude,' Esther said, walking over to the bed, anxiety on the edge of her voice. 'Would you like some hot soup or just the raspberry vinegar?'

Her daughter-in-law could do no wrong in Esther's eyes. She had proved to be an adoring wife and mother, and the whole family was devoted to her. To Esther, Maude was the calmest person she had ever known. Maude kept a loving and peaceful household; angry words were unheard of and food was always on the table. The house was clean as a whistle and the children well cared for. Her son was a lucky man. So were her grand-children.

Pulling up a chair, sitting down next to the bed, Esther leaned closer and said in a low voice, 'Are you awake, Maude? I've brought soup, and my concoction.'

'Just drowsing; the raspberry vinegar would help,' Maude whispered, her voice hoarse. 'Is Jimmy with you?'

'He's downstairs with Rossi and Eddie. He came to get me earlier. We had a bite of lunch; then we came straight here. I've brought plenty of food, so you mustn't worry about Matthew and the children being fed. They'll be all right.'

Maude looked up at her, the sparkle in her dark brown eyes dulled by her illness. 'Thank you,' she murmured. 'It's not the bubonic plague, you know, merely a chill and a sore throat. I'll be up and about in a few days.'

'When you're better, and not until then. I'll be back in a few minutes, love.' Esther hurried downstairs.

When she returned to the kitchen, she noticed that the bottle of raspberry vinegar and the jar of chicken soup were on the oak table. Everything else had been put away in the pantry.

'Is Mother very ill?' James asked, his worry obvious.

'No, it's just one of those bad chills, and she's a bit chesty. But she'll be fine. You can go up and see her if you want, or better still, you can take the drink up to her. It'll only take a moment to boil.'

As she spoke, Esther crossed the room, picked up the bottle, and was back swiftly. Standing over a pan on the oven top, she stirred the raspberry vinegar. To this she added sugar and a large piece of butter, which James had brought to her from the pantry.

'Is that all it is?' James asked, sounding surprised, glancing at his grandmother. 'Just those things boiled together?'

'More or less,' Esther nodded. 'But I prepare the vinegar in a special way and put a few herbs into it as well.'

'What are they?'

'That's a secret.' Esther winked at him and poured the concoction into a cup. 'Here it is, my lad. You can take it up to your mother. She must sip it slowly. It's a bit hot.'

James did as he was told, and when he entered his parents'

bedroom he saw at once how poorly his mother looked. Carrying the cup carefully, he put it down on the bedside table.

Hearing the slight noise, Maude opened her eyes, and a smile surfaced when she saw her eldest son. 'There you are, Jimmy.'

'Grans said you're to sip this slowly,' he explained, reaching for the cup. 'Be careful, Mum. 'It's very hot.'

Maude now pushed herself up in bed and took the cup from him. 'I don't know why but this is always helpful, really a good remedy for me.'

'I think Grans put something special in it, but she wouldn't tell me what. She said it's a secret.'

Maude peered at him over the rim of the cup. 'That's strange. Your grandmother usually tells you everything.'

James chuckled. He settled back in the chair, his eyes focused on his mother. Although she looked tired and sick, he remembered his grandmother's words that it probably was only a chill, nothing more serious. Comforted by the thought, he relaxed.

It had been a slow day at the stalls, and Matthew decided to leave early on this warm June afternoon. The market's owner, Henry Malvern, wasn't visiting until the next day; concern about his wife made Matthew hasten his departure, and propelled him down the Hampstead main road.

He didn't even take the barrow with him to bring back goods tomorrow. They had plenty of stock and he had locked it away in the shed with the sawhorses and planks.

The road was full of men who were leaving the market hall and others who worked in companies or factories nearby. The road was filled to overflowing, which surprised him. It was only five o'clock. Most men worked until six or seven, some even later.

Perhaps it's the nice weather after lots of rain, Matthew

thought, as he strode out, moving at a steady pace, not wanting to start perspiring. We all want to sit in our back yards and read a newspaper, or go to the pub for a pint.

The pub. A lot of men he knew made a habit of going for a drink after work – many of them most nights of the week. He didn't. He wanted to be in his home with his Maude and their children. They were his whole world. He wasn't interested in swilling down beer in the taproom or playing darts, and he certainly didn't want to listen to husbands grumbling about their wives, trying to unload their problems on him.

Maude. The image of her face came into his head, and he smiled inwardly, suddenly thinking of the first time he had set eyes on her. Eighteen years ago now.

He had been nineteen and she had been seventeen, and they had bumped into each other in the back yard at Fountains Manor in Kent.

She had explained that she was delivering a blouse for Lady Agatha when she saw him glancing at the small suitcase she was holding. He had asked to carry it for her, and she had agreed. Then he had led her to the back door, ushered her into the kitchen, where his mother happened to be speaking with Cook.

His mother obviously knew the most beautiful girl he had ever seen, had greeted her warmly, and admired the rose-pink dress she was wearing. Within seconds, she had whisked her away, taking her to Lady Agatha in her boudoir.

The sense of disappointment he had felt that day rushed back to him as he increased his pace down the road, needing to get home to be there for Maude. He recalled how he had hung around the yard until the beautiful girl had finally emerged from the house. He had asked her if he could walk her to the main gates. She had looked at him intently, questioningly, and then she had smiled and he had smiled back, floored by her beauty. Those deep brown eyes, set wide apart, full of sparkle and life under perfectly arched brows, the burnished brown hair that fell in curls around her lovely, heart-shaped face, and the slender, lithe figure. She was breathtaking.

He was smitten. And so was she.

A year later they were married. And then came the children. They were happy, loving, devoted, and extremely close, and bonded with his parents and brothers to make a dependable family unit that gave them all a sense of security.

'I'm hungry,' Eddie wailed. 'Why can't I have a sausage roll? Now!'

Rossi looked across at him and explained gently, 'Because we're waiting for Father, and when he gets home we can sit down and have supper together.'

'Will Mumma get up and come down?' Eddie asked wistfully.

'I don't think so, lovey. It's better she rests.'

Eddie jumped off the chair, and said, with sudden determination, 'I'm going upstairs to see her. I want to give her a kiss to make her feel better.'

Rossi put the knives and forks she was holding down on the table, walked across to the pantry and went inside. 'Just this once I'll make an exception. Please bring me one of those plates, Eddie, and I'll give you a sausage roll to keep you going.'

Running over to the oak table, Eddie took a plate to Rossi in the pantry, a beaming smile on his face. His sister placed the roll on it, then admonished, 'Don't gulp it down . . . eat it slowly.'

'I will.'

'And what else do you say?' Rossi stared at her young brother.

'Thank you,' Eddie replied, and carried his plate to the end of the table, far away from where Rossi was setting the places for supper.

At this moment James came back into the room, carrying the cup. 'Mum's fallen asleep at last. The rest will do her good.' He took the cup to the sink, and turned to his sister. 'I see you gave in to Eddie's nagging. But he probably is hungry, Rossi. It's getting late.'

'I know, but he has to learn to be patient.'

'I don't want to be a patient,' Eddie cried. 'Then I'd be in hospital.'

'Patient also means being able to wait for something, without making a big fuss,' James explained, and went to sit next to the nine-year-old. 'I could eat one of those myself, but I'll wait till Dad gets home.'

Eddie adored his older brother, and he looked up at him and smiled, offered him the sausage roll. 'Have a bite. I don't mind sharing it with you, Jimmy.'

Shaking his head, James put his arm around the younger boy's shoulders. 'Our grandmother brought us a cottage pie and chicken soup and, as soon as Dad arrives home, we'll tuck into it.'

Rossi exclaimed, 'Perhaps I'd better put the pie in the oven now, Jimmy, and the chicken soup in a pan on top of the range. What do you think?'

'That's a good idea. Shall I help you?'

'I'll help, too,' Eddie volunteered, and took a bite of the sausage roll.

'I can manage,' their sister answered, finally finishing the last setting. Suddenly she began to laugh as she walked back to the pantry. 'You and Grandma brought enough food to feed Nelson's navy. There's also a steak and kidney pie in here, and a hunk of boiled ham. Oh, and an apple pie. Not to mention the sausage rolls.'

James laughed with her. 'Grans kept adding things once Grandpapa had insisted we come here in a hansom.'

'I've never been in one,' Eddie said, the wistful tone echoing yet again.

'You will one day,' James murmured.

'When? I want to know when!'

'Never if you don't stop nagging!' Rossi exclaimed.

James said to his sister, 'How was school today?'

'It went well. I taught some of the younger children, as I do these days, and then I had an hour with the sewing teacher. I love sewing and designing things. As you know, I won't be going back after this month. I'll be working with Mum, helping her to fill her orders for the blouses and shawls.'

The three of them jumped and looked startled at the sound of knocking on the door. It was James who immediately stood up, motioned the others to remain where they were.

The knocking started again as he reached the front door. 'What do you want? Who is it?' he asked, having been instructed time and again never to let anyone into the house if they were alone.

'It's me, James. Grandpapa. When your grandmother arrived back, she said your mother needed rest and she sent me to see if the three of you are all right.'

James turned the key and opened the door to let his grandfather in. 'Sorry to keep you waiting.' James explained to Philip, 'Dad has drilled it into the three of us not to open the door unless we know who's there.'

'Very wise,' Philip answered, and he and James walked into the kitchen, where Philip was immediately assaulted by Eddie and Rossi, who threw themselves at him, hugging him.

When he finally became disentangled, he turned to James. 'Shall I go upstairs and look in on your mother? Or is she resting?'

'Perhaps she's still asleep,' James answered, 'I'll creep up and take a look.'

Philip nodded, and allowed himself to be pulled further into the kitchen. Having been taught to be polite, Rossi asked, 'Would you like a cup of tea, Grandpapa?'

He shook his head, and then looked towards the door as he heard the key in the lock turning. 'I think your father has arrived.'

FIVE

Matthew stared at his father, alarm rushing through him. Why was he here? Had Maude become worse? As if reading his son's mind, Philip said, 'I just dropped in to see how Maude is doing, Matt. Although when she got home, your mother told me it was definitely only a chill.'

'And what do you think, Dad?'

'I haven't seen her yet –'

James interjected, 'I was just upstairs, Father, and she's sleeping.'

Relaxing, Matthew walked into the kitchen and opened his arms as his two younger children rushed towards him across the floor. He kissed them both, and then straightened. Turning to James, he asked, 'Has your mother taken the raspberry vinegar?'

'Yes, I sat there while she sipped it and fell asleep. It must have knock-out drops in it, or something like that.'

He's far too bright for his own good, Philip thought, but said, 'Don't be silly, James. It's the cherry juice your grandmother puts in it that makes a person sleepy and soothes a sore throat.'

Matthew walked towards the door, turned to look back at his father. 'Will you have supper with us?'

'I'll stay a bit longer, go up and see Maude after you, but I can't linger. I told your mother I would have dinner with her tonight. We don't often get a chance to do that.'

Matthew nodded, hurried out, flew up the stairs two at a time, and then paused on the landing, took a deep breath and calmed himself before pushing open the bedroom door. He went in as quietly as possible, then realized Maude was awake.

'Matt,' she whispered hoarsely when he sat down next to the bed, and reached out her hand to him.

He took hold of it, leaned closer, his eyes searching her face. She was extremely pale and her forehead was damp. When he tried to kiss her, she moved her head. 'I don't want you to catch cold.'

Smiling at her, he ignored her words and kissed her cheek anyway.

'It seems very hot in here, Maude.'

'I am a bit warm.' she answered.

He jumped up and went to the window. Although it was six thirty, it was still light outside. He opened the top and bottom of the sash window, shaking his head as he did so. Like every Victorian, he suffered from paranoia about his home not having sufficient oxygen. 'I don't understand why this is closed,' he muttered. 'We're all fully aware we must have oxygen circulating through every room. The whole country knows it.'

He walked back to the bed, continuing, 'We mustn't let carbonic acid build up because we don't have proper ventilation.'

Sitting down, he took her hand again and stared at Maude. 'Breathe in, love, you need fresh air. It'll help you get better.'

'It was becoming stifling in here, but I just didn't have the strength to get out of bed to open the window,' she murmured.

'What else can I do to make you more comfortable? Are you thirsty? Do you want a glass of water? Or perhaps some chicken soup? Are you hungry?'

'I have no appetite at all. I think I'd just like to rest here, maybe doze off again. Sleep is the best thing for me right now.'

'Dad's downstairs, Maude. He came to see you.'

'Oh, that's nice of him. Tell him to come up.'

'I will. And I'll get supper going, although I think Rossi has started doing that already.'

A faint smile touched Maude's face. 'No doubt.'

A moment later, Philip Falconer was seated in the bedside chair. His love for Maude was reflected in his eyes; he could only hope and pray that his two other sons, Harry and George, would be lucky enough to marry women like her. 'I felt I had to come by to see you for myself, Maude. Naturally, I trust Dr Robertson's diagnosis and Esther's opinion. On the other hand, I do worry about the entire family. And I just can't help being concerned about you, after that terrible bout of bronchitis you had last year.'

'I know that, Dad,' she answered, using the name she had called him since her marriage to Matthew. 'This time it is just a bad chill. I'll be better in a few days.'

'Do you promise?'

'I do.' She smiled at him, her face ringed with affection.

'Then I shall walk home with a lighter heart. And I know you're in good hands with Matthew and the children to take care of you.'

When he went downstairs, his grandchildren begged him to stay for supper with them. He told them he couldn't, explaining that their grandmother was waiting for him.

'Why didn't Maw come with you?' Eddie asked. He had never been able to say grandmother. Only Maw came out of his mouth as a small child, and that she had been ever since.

'Maw is busy working on that rag rug she's making for you,' Philip said. Kissing the three of them and walking over to his son, he took Matthew's arm, and led him into the hall.

33

'Maude will be all right, Matt, just make sure she gets plenty of liquids, and don't let her leave that bed for a few days. Oh, and keep the room cool, as you have it now.'

'I will,' Matthew replied, and gave his father a questioning look. 'Is there something special in that raspberry vinegar Mum takes?'

Philip couldn't help laughing. 'No. Just cherry juice, as I told James.' He eyed his son, amusement still flickering on his face. 'Fancy you asking me that at the age of thirty-seven. Has anybody in this family ever died after drinking it?'

Matthew joined in his laughter. 'Oh, Dad, you are a card. There's nobody like you.'

Philip drew his son closer and gave him a bear hug. 'Have a good night, son,' he murmured and left, closing the door quietly behind him.

It was a nice evening and Philip decided to walk back to Regent's Park.

His thoughts lingered on Maude. His lovely daughter-in-law was more frail than she looked, and had a tendency to catch cold easily. Bronchitis had felled her last winter, and in consequence they fussed over her – perhaps too much. Also, a sick member of a family was a drain on everyone. Fortunately, he and Esther could afford to pay for a doctor, but most of the Falconers' street couldn't, which was why staying healthy was so important. They all tried to protect themselves from germs as best they could.

He was reassured by the doctor's opinion. He did not want his son a widower or his grandchildren motherless. It was all too common and with heartbreaking results.

He knew how lucky he was in so many different ways. He had been blessed with kind, loving, good-hearted parents, who had set him on the best course when they encouraged him to go into service.

His father, Edward Falconer, had owned a small grocery shop in Rochester, Kent. His parents, his brother Tom, and he had lived in a flat above it. Being rather crowded never ever bothered them, since they were a loving family and enjoyed each other's company.

It was his mother, Olive, who had recognized he would make a good butler if he had the correct training. She knew he was efficient, well organized, had good manners, charm and a special way with people.

It was she who had suggested he visit Fountains Manor nearby to seek employment. He had done so, and had been taken on immediately by the Honourable Arthur Montague, who was struck by his politeness, pleasant voice and good looks. He had risen through the ranks with ease and rapidity, learning about wine, food and clothing in order to improve himself.

Philip had always thought that his eldest, Matthew, took after his own father in wanting to be a salesman, and had rented stalls. Now James was following in their footsteps. But his dream was not of a little shop in a country town or stalls in a market, but a grand emporium like Fortnum and Mason – catering to the rich.

Hearing James's plan today had given Philip genuine pleasure, and Esther as well. There was no doubt in their minds that their grandson had a prodigious intelligence; he was clever, smart, had enormous ambition and drive. These two particular characteristics were essential to success. Anyone aiming high who did not own them was doomed to failure. Whether he could achieve such a lofty dream was another matter, though.

As Philip walked along, striding out at a brisk pace, he decided he would select some of his books on the red wines of Provence for James to read. That was how he would begin to teach his grandson – lead him into the wonderful world of vintage wines.

After a while Philip had to slow his pace. There were too

many people on the streets tonight. Men and women hurrying home after a long workday; couples were strolling along in a more leisurely fashion, obviously out for an evening of entertainment at a restaurant or the music hall.

Philip loved London, thought of it as the capital of the world. They had a Queen-Empress in Victoria, the aging widow, and Britain was the richest and greatest nation on the planet. Yet he hated the fact that this age of Victoria, momentous in so many ways, was also a hungry and deprived age. Millions of its citizens went to bed with empty bellies.

Gladstone, Disraeli and Salisbury – politicians all – raged and argued in Parliament about the terrible conditions, but did nothing positive to change the game as far as he could see. Certainly there was nothing much he could do either, except to help a friend in need from time to time. And this he did whenever he was asked. His conscience ruled his head and his heart. And at night he prayed for better days ahead for the common people of England.

That night James found it hard to go to sleep. He felt calmer about his mother and knew the doctor had been correct. She had caught cold, and it was nothing worse. What kept him awake was the sudden worry about his father – how would he react when James told him about his dream? Now he had confided in his grandparents, he thought he would have to explain to Matthew that he did not want to work on the stalls at the Malvern forever. He had ambitions of his own . . . of being a merchant prince. Even his grandmother had brought that matter up to him as they had been driving over to Camden Town in the hansom cab. He didn't want to upset his father, but he knew within himself that he would have to follow his dream. It was like a burning flame inside him.

Knowing his father the way he did, understanding that he was a fair man, one who saw everyone's point of view, James was sure he would not object to his leaving the stalls.

Not yet, of course. He would have to be seventeen or eighteen before he could think of moving on. Could his father manage without him? Would he use Eddie? He would need help. Perhaps he could hire somebody.

He tossed and turned in his bed, his mind whirling with dire thoughts. How would he approach Mr Henry Malvern? The owner of the Malvern Market was a pleasant man; he usually came over to speak to his father, and always had a word for him. But James was smart enough to know that this didn't mean a thing. Mr Malvern was pleased at how well his father ran their stalls, had made a success of them, but that didn't mean Mr Malvern would give him a job at the Piccadilly office just like that. Why would he? Why should he?

And there was another thing. He was a working-class boy. Might Mr Malvern think he was stepping out of his place? Maybe. Maybe not.

An education was what he needed. James had been to school. He could read and write very well; he knew his geography and English history. And he was a dab hand when it came to arithmetic. The teachers had told his parents he was gifted and an excellent pupil.

Yet he still needed to know more. Knowledge was power; his grandmother always said that. It came to him in a flash. He would speak to his grandfather, who was going to teach him all about the noble grape and the great wines of France. That's how Grandpapa had put it. And lend him books about wine. He knew his grandfather would be pleased to lend him books about many other things as well. There was a big library at the Nash house in Regent's Park.

Lady Agatha would surely agree to lend him a book or two. Or three. He would take care of them, handle them with respect.

He let out a long sigh. *Books*. That was his answer for gaining more knowledge. He had to work hard in the next few years, bettering himself in every possible way he could. When he eventually went to see Mr Malvern, he had to be absolutely acceptable in every way.

That was the new goal of James Lionel Falconer. Having found the answer to his problem, he relaxed and soon fell asleep. He would awaken the next morning with new determination to be the best. And, later in the week, he would take a deep breath and tell his father that he had to follow his dream.

PART TWO

New Horizons
London/Kent
1887

Six

Alexis Malvern stood in front of the cheval mirror positioned near the window in her bedroom. She studied herself for a moment, turning to one side and then the other, and decided she would pass muster.

At twenty-five, she knew her own mind, and some time ago she had given up wearing crinolines, except for very special evening occasions. She felt they were too cumbersome for her and the life she led. Instead she favoured the crinolette hoop, made of steel and cotton, a framework worn under the back of the skirt only. This meant that the skirt of a gown was slim at the front and the sides, with a big bustle at the back, supported by the hoop tied around the waist.

This afternoon her gown was made of a rich cream silk. It had a high neck, long slender sleeves and a tight bodice that accentuated her slender waist. From the waist down, the front of the skirt was flat, with pleats at each side, which, in turn, became the bustle.

Her clothes were designed by Madame Valance, a Frenchwoman, who was everyone's favourite at the moment. Her clothes were elegant and stylish and not as flamboyant and flashy as some of the other fashion designers in London.

Walking over to the bed, Alexis picked up the hat which had been made to match the gown. It was a cream silk bowler, but more of an oval shape than round like the kind men wore. Trimming the rim of the hat were lengths of knotted tulle tied in a bow at the back.

Placing it on top of her auburn curls, Alexis tilted it to one side, set it at a jaunty angle, and stuck a hatpin in for safety. Now she was ready to leave at last.

Picking up her reticule, she walked to the door. She paused for a moment in the corridor, knowing she ought to go to her father's study to say goodbye.

But she was reluctant to do so. There had been a breach in their relationship that troubled them both, and it had now gone on far too long. Perhaps this afternoon was the right time to heal that breach, and get them back to their normal relationship. But how would she begin? She stood there, thinking, knowing it was the proper thing to do, if only she could find the right words.

Although she did not know it, her father was having similar thoughts as he sat at the desk in his study. He wondered if he should go up to her room to speak to her and attempt reconciliation. Not that they had really quarrelled, and they were polite and civil with each other on a daily basis. Yet there was a coolness on her part, and he was hurting from it.

Henry sighed under his breath, rose and walked across the room, looking out at the garden, ruminating about the problem. It was Saturday 30 July 1887, and a glorious day, filled with sunshine. Yes, he wanted her back very badly, loathed her emotional withdrawal from him.

Henry Ashton Malvern was not exactly a self-made man. Rather he had taken his father's small and rather badly run property business and turned it into a flourishing enterprise. And a big moneymaker. He had become an extremely wealthy man.

His older brother, Joshua, was his full partner in Malvern and Malvern, but did not have any ambition, no dreams of glory like Henry always had. It was Henry who had been the driving force behind the business, just as his daughter was now. She was so like him in many ways.

She was Henry's only child, the third member of the Malvern team, and had worked by her father's side from the age of sixteen, having refused to go to finishing school in Switzerland.

Her mother had died when Alexis was eight years old, and it was Henry who had raised her. She would often tease him and say that he had brought her up to be a boy. She was intelligent, hardworking and smart.

Alexis was his sole heir, and one day the business would be hers. She knew every aspect of it, and now, at twenty-five, she could take control of it if needs be. He had never known anyone more talented at business than his daughter; he had great respect and admiration for her.

Quite aside from this, Alexis was a rather beautiful young woman, with her auburn hair, deep green eyes and English-rose complexion. Because of her looks and her charming manner, she had had many suitors over the last few years. None of them appealed to her; also, she was wary of marriage, knowing that a husband would be the head of the family and would perhaps take control of her inheritance and the business. Frightening prospects to her.

And so, a few months ago, she had told her father that she would never get married, and had given him the reasons why. The prospect of not having a son-in-law or grandchildren appalled Henry. He also worried about the future of Malvern and Malvern after he was dead and Alexis grew older. Who would be her heirs?

A long and difficult discussion had ensued, and had brought about this breach in their loving relationship, a situation both of them genuinely hated. Nothing like this had ever happened; they felt isolated from each other.

There was a light knock at the door and, as Henry swung away from the window, Alexis walked into his study. He couldn't speak for a moment. This afternoon she was breathtakingly lovely. The cream silk gown was a wonderful foil for her natural colouring, which appeared more vivid than ever and was most arresting.

'Do you have a moment, Papa?' Alexis asked, closing the door behind her, walking towards him.

'Of course I do,' he answered. 'I was about to come and find you, before you left for your ladies' tea. I hope you told Bolland to have the carriage ready for you.'

'I did, Papa. Not that I'm going very far, only to Delia Talston's house in Belgravia, but I can't very well walk through the streets in a cream-coloured dress. It'll soon be dirty.'

'And, I might add, looking the way you do . . . very comely, indeed, my dear.'

A faint smile crossed her face, and she sat down on the edge of a chair. After a moment, she said, 'I've been wondering how to start this conversation, Papa, and decided just to . . . well, blurt it out. So, I want you to know that, first of all, I'm sorry for my coolness and that there's been a distance between us. Truly, truly sorry, and I apologize for hurting you. I would like us both to forget about our . . . disagreement, shall we call it? Let us put it behind us, be close again, as we've been all of my life.'

'I want that more than anything in the world, Alexis. Thank you for taking the lead. I was wondering myself how to broach the matter to you a few minutes ago. You see, I've come to understand that you must live your life the way you wish. After all, it is your life, not mine. You must be happy and fulfilled, and if the business is enough for you, then so be it. It is your choice.'

'Thank you, Papa. It's not that I have anything against men, you know. I rather like them, enjoy their company. But I can't become someone's possession or have another person rule me. I need my freedom and I need to work in a business I love. I'm not cut out to be a housewife.'

Henry chuckled and held out his hands, pulled her to her feet. Automatically, she went into her father's arms. He held her close for a moment, relief suffusing him, and he kissed her cheek, then released her.

Walking across to his desk, he said, over his shoulder, 'I know you and Delia wish to launch that charity you dreamed up together last year, and that's what this tea is all about today? I'm right, aren't I?

'Yes, you are,' Alexis answered, staring after him, wondering what he was getting at.

He looked across at her and showed her an envelope. 'There is a cheque in here which I wrote two weeks ago. I want to be the first to make a donation to your charity and wish you great success.'

Crossing the room, Alexis, accepted the envelope. She looked at the cheque. 'Papa! How generous of you. Thank you, thank you so much.'

Delia Talston greeted Alexis in the peach-coloured drawing room of her townhouse, a smile of approval on her face. 'You look quite divine today, Alexis. No wonder men fall all over you. I would too, if I were a man.'

Alexis laughed. 'I should wear cream all the time, since it

seems to engender compliments. I see I'm the first, so let me give you this before the others arrive.' Opening her reticule, she handed the envelope to Delia. 'Look inside. It's a cheque from Papa.'

Delia raised a brow as she took the envelope from her. 'Have you two finally reconciled? Oh, I do hope so.'

'Everything is back to normal. I apologized to Papa just before I left, and he handed me the cheque. You'll see he made it out two weeks ago.'

'And he's been so generous! How wonderful of him. Richard gave me a cheque this morning for five hundred pounds, and my father did the same last week. We now have a good sum for our kitty, because of other small donations I've received. Please thank your father, and I shall write him a note.'

'I think we're off to a good start.' Alexis sat down on the edge of a chair, and glanced around. 'I've always loved this room since you painted it peach a few years ago. It has worn well, I must say.'

'Become too worn, I think. I was wondering the other day if I should create a new look.'

'Oh no, don't do that. The peach has grown mellow and warm; on a day like this, the room is so welcoming with the sunshine streaming in on us,' Alexis observed.

'The Persian's somewhat tired,' Delia murmured, glancing down at the large burgundy rug patterned in cream and moss green.

'Leave everything alone!' Alexis exclaimed. 'Anyway, you won't have time. You and I both are going to be rather busy—'

Alexis broke off as Parker, the butler, opened the door, announcing, 'Mrs Clive, madame.'

Delia stood up and went to greet Vera Clive, an old friend, who shared her feelings about the plight of poor women in London.

After kissing each other's cheeks, Delia escorted Vera into the room.

Alexis stood up, thrust out her hand. 'It's a pleasure to meet you, Mrs Clive.'

'And you too, Miss Malvern.'

At this moment, Parker returned once more, leading another young woman to the drawing room. He announced, 'Miss Trevalian has arrived, madame.'

Once introductions had been made, the four elegant women sat down in chairs grouped near the French doors. These stood open, showing a view of the summer garden and allowing fresh air to circulate in the room.

Delia looked at her friends. 'Welcome. I'm so happy you are here. And before we start speaking about the project, I did want to inform you that Miss Malvern's father has made a very generous donation, my husband and father have also donated, and I've garnered another significant amount made up of smaller donations from members of my family. So not a bad start, wouldn't you say?'

Vera Clive nodded. 'My husband has given me a cheque for five hundred, I'm happy to tell you. And it is a very good start indeed.'

'Thank you, Vera, and please thank Rupert on our behalf,' Delia said.

Claudia Trevalian spoke up. 'And I am giving the same amount, Delia.' She opened her reticule, took out an envelope and passed it to Delia.

'Thank you. How generous you've both been.' Delia placed the envelopes on an occasional table next to her chair. Her eyes swept over her friends, and she began. 'Last year Alexis told me a story that so appalled and disturbed me, I immediately agreed with her when she said she wanted to do something to help abused women. Mostly living in the East End. To start a charity, in fact.'

Glancing at Alexis, who sat opposite her, she continued. 'Will you tell Vera and Claudia the story please, Alexis?'

'Of course,' Alexis said. 'As you are no doubt aware, my father owns the Malvern Market in Camden. Last year, he went on one of his regular visits to the market to meet with stallholders, and one of them – Jack Holden – approached him. He wanted to know if my father knew of any safe shelters for women in distress.'

Alexis paused for a moment, shifting on the edge of the chair. 'My father did not, and he asked Jack Holden why he needed this information. Seemingly, a neighbour of the Holdens had come to their home late one night seeking help. She had been so badly beaten that they knew they had to get her to the nearest hospital at once. Which they did. The poor woman had been attacked violently by her husband, and for such a long time that she had massive internal bleeding. Sadly, she died in the hospital later that week. Mr Holden's startling comment to my father that abusive husbands were 'two a penny', and that they exist all over different areas of London, shocked Papa. He recounted all this to me, and so I went to see Mr Holden to gather more facts. I decided there and then I was going to find a house and turn it into a refuge for these distressed and helpless women.'

'That is very commendable of you,' Vera Clive remarked. 'You can count on me to help you.'

'And I would also like to volunteer,' Claudia said. 'Can we perhaps look for the right place together?'

'I found the house six months ago,' Alexis explained. 'And I bought it. The interiors needed a great deal of work, and I had to add baths. And also water closets. I can only say thank goodness for Thomas Crapper and his products. I bought his WCs, which work well.'

'That must have been a very expensive operation,' Vera said, a frown furrowing her brow. 'Perhaps we should give you some of the money we've donated to help with these costs.'

'No, no, I don't need it, but thank you for the offer. You

see, Malvern and Malvern, our family company, does a lot of building in the course of the year. And I was able to negotiate some excellent deals with the building firms we constantly use. I have a legacy from my late mother and I paid for the refurbishing of the house with some of that. I think she would have approved.'

'The good news is that Alexis now has the house ready,' Delia interjected. 'And we have found a good woman who will be in charge of it. She is helping us to put together a staff of five women, three of whom will live there with her. She's called Madeleine Thompson; she will be the manager of the house.'

'Well, you've certainly done an awful lot already. When can we see the house? And what can we do to help?' Claudia asked.

'I can take you to see the house any day next week,' Alexis said. 'It's in Whitechapel near Commercial Street. Just round the corner, before you come to Whitechapel High Street. There is plenty of room there. It's simply furnished, and this just occurred to me – if you're thinking of throwing any pieces away, consider the house first.'

'Oh, goodness me! I have several comfortable chairs and a sofa I want to get rid of,' Vera said. 'I'll arrange for them to be taken over whenever it's convenient for you.'

'Thank you very much,' Alexis said. 'You see, Delia and I don't want the funds we've raised to be used for purchasing furniture and the like. Rather we need the money to pay for food, medicines, and Mrs Thompson's wages, of course.'

'What about the other women who will work there?' Claudia asked. 'Will they be paid also?'

'The three who will live in are former battered women and in need of a roof over their heads – a safe place to live. Since they have that, we will be paying them only a small amount of money, but they will get all of their meals,' Alexis told them. 'They too want to help women who have suffered.'

Delia said, 'There's another thing you can do, Vera, and you too, Claudia. Discarded clothing would be most useful, especially coats, cloaks, shawls, skirts, and blouses. Nothing too fancy. And even undergarments. When the women come to the house, they will literally have nothing at all with them except the clothes they're wearing.'

At this moment, Parker arrived in the doorway and looked across at Delia, a questioning expression on his face. She merely nodded her head, and he hurried away.

'Parker is about to bring us tea and biscuits,' she said, smiling at her guests. 'If you have any more questions, we will answer them. I can't tell you how happy I am that you're willing to join with us. And I know Alexis is as well. All suggestions are welcome.'

Claudia, looking thoughtful for a moment or two, finally asked, 'The two other women who agreed to help . . . are they volunteers?'

'Yes, they are,' Delia replied. 'The three who will be living in will cook and clean, and do everything they can to help the battered women.'

'What happens if they fall ill?' Vera looked from Delia to Alexis. 'Will you pay for a doctor?'

'Yes, we will. And, if necessary, we will send them to hospital. After all, we are a safe house offering temporary protection, and helping the women to get on their feet. We can't look after the sick. If possible, we want them to move on and start a new life.'

Parker and two young maids entered the drawing room, placed several trays on a table nearby. Parker poured the tea and the maids served the ladies, and the butler followed with a plate of biscuits.

Once they were alone again, Vera asked, 'What about bed linen and towels? I can have my housekeeper go through our linen closet. I'm sure we can spare quite a lot of items.'

'That's very kind of you,' Alexis nodded. 'Delia and I did the same thing, and Delia's mother paid for some beds.'

Delia said, 'This is all turning out very well, and I think it goes without saying that we will literally take anything you can give—'

'Or cadge,' Alexis cut in, happy that Delia's friends were so enthusiastic.

SEVEN

Alexis and Claudia sat together in the drawing room, chatting amiably about the charity. Vera had taken her leave, rushing off to be with her ailing father, and Delia had excused herself and gone up to her boudoir to pen a note to Henry Malvern, to thank him for his cheque.

It was money that Claudia was now speaking about, and this did not surprise Alexis. She knew very well who Claudia was – the daughter of Sebastian Trevalian, head of an ancient bank dating back a century at least. It was as famous as the renowned, longstanding Coutts.

It struck Alexis that her understanding of money was no doubt in her blood. 'The amount donated is an extraordinary beginning,' Claudia went on. 'A veritable fortune, in fact. But I believe we should think further ahead and continue to raise money. Now. For the future. We mustn't rest on our laurels.'

'I agree with you. Money so easily slips away. Very fast.'

'I will ask my father for a donation, and I'm sure he will supply a cheque immediately. I will also attempt to find other sources. We ought to build up a large amount of cash. In reserve, so that we are never caught short. Don't you agree, Alexis?'

'I do, and I feel very strongly that we should not waste the cash by buying items we can source elsewhere. Rather, it should be kept for medicines and good, nutritious food. In the six months it took to renovate the house, Delia and I managed to cadge enough furniture, crockery, and kitchen utensils to make the house functional and relatively comfortable to live in. And, in fact, every single thing was donated by our families and friends. Or bought for us by them.'

Claudia chuckled. 'I shall have to learn to cadge, and I think I might be rather good at it. I'll start with my sisters and cousins.'

'That's usually a good idea. I think you'll find that those you ask will be glad, even relieved, to have somewhere to send items they no longer use, but don't want to hoard away in cupboards.'

Claudia said, 'One thing I forgot to ask you earlier: how many women will the house accommodate at one time?'

'Twelve comfortably,' Alexis replied. 'We have six bedrooms. Delia and I placed two single beds in each room. But at a pinch those rooms could take a third bed, if necessary. There is also a large upstairs parlour that would quite easily convert to become a small dormitory. That would hold about four women and several children. You see, some women may well bring a child with them, or more, afraid to leave them behind. Our aim is to have twenty beds eventually. To give them shelter and safety, and that includes a few children. But we can't become an orphanage. No one can live there for long: there are too many others waiting for a place.'

Claudia stared at her, a look of shock registering in her eyes. 'Is it that bad? Is there such a lot of physical abuse among poor women?'

'Oh yes. And even among the rich, if the truth be known,' Alexis responded. 'But wealthier women generally have families

53

to run to, or loyal friends who will help them escape their husbands and their situation.' Alexis shook her head, and added quietly, 'Class doesn't define abusive men, Claudia. I am afraid they are everywhere in society. In all classes and creeds.'

Sitting back in the chair, Claudia snapped her eyes shut, not saying a word.

Watching her closely, Alexis saw that her face had turned pale, and she seemed upset. After a moment, Alexis asked in concern, 'Are you all right? Can I help you?'

Opening her eyes, sitting up straighter, Claudia said, 'I'm fine. I was just remembering something . . .' A great sigh escaped her. 'I had a friend who once confided in me, told me her husband abused her, and very brutally. At times she had to remain at their country house until her bruises faded and she had recovered her equilibrium.' There was a pause. Unexpectedly, Claudia's eyes filled with tears.

Reaching out, Alexis touched her arm. 'You are upset. What can I do to help you?'

Blinking back the tears, Claudia endeavoured to recover, to collect herself. Her voice was sad when she said, 'I was remembering something, suddenly understanding how wrong I once was. About a friend. You see, I didn't believe her. He was such a good-looking man, full of charm and grace, a true gentleman, an aristocrat of impeccable lineage. It just didn't seem possible . . .' Her voice trailed away and she shook her head.

'Just because a man is a born gentleman doesn't mean he isn't also a cad. And a dangerous cad at that! I can think of a number of worse words to use to describe those bad men.' Alexis's voice had raised an octave in anger.

Claudia took out a handkerchief and patted her face. 'I wish I had believed her. She was reaching out to me. She wanted my help. And I abandoned her. How awful of me. But I never saw any physical damage.'

'Because she had waited until her wounds had healed.' Alexis leaned forward, and asked, 'I hope nothing terrible happened to her. I hope she didn't die.'

There was a moment of silence before Claudia whispered, 'She did. But not by his hand . . . She took her own life.'

'Then she *did* die by his hand! He drove her to it.' Looking at Claudia intently, Alexis saw she was still upset. Her eyes were moist again. She said, 'You mustn't blame yourself, or feel guilty. We are all in charge of our own lives, Claudia. Character is destiny . . . it is who we are inside ourselves that leads us to live the lives we do. Our character makes us who we are.'

A look of comprehension crossed Claudia's face. 'I see what you mean. Nonetheless, I should have helped her get away from him.'

'She should have left him, sought help from someone else. Or did he keep her cloistered away?'

'I don't know. She stayed in the country when he'd hurt her badly. She told me she couldn't show herself in that condition in London society.'

For a moment Alexis was silent, realizing how violent the man must have been. She couldn't help wondering who he was.

Claudia levelled her gaze at Alexis. 'Why on earth does a woman stay with a brutal man?' She sounded genuinely puzzled, frowning.

'I don't know.' A thoughtful look crossed Alexis's face. 'What I do know is that a woman living in poverty is extremely vulnerable. She has nowhere to go, probably not one single person to help her. And if she has children, it becomes more difficult, complex.'

Claudia simply nodded.

Alexis shrugged her shoulders, lifted her hands helplessly. 'As for women of our class, despite the scandal of leaving, why they stay I'll never understand. Could it be that they still love the man, despite his wickedness? It's a mystery to me.'

'And to me, Alexis. I have learned a lesson this afternoon. I shall never disbelieve a friend again, if she comes to me with a similar story. I shall pay attention and I will do something.'

'I feel the same way.'

'I know you're not married,' Claudia stated, half smiling at Alexis. 'Neither am I. That is because I haven't met the right man. But I hope I will do so one day. I would like to have a husband and a family. I love children.'

'Yes, I'm not married,' Alexis said, relieved that Claudia had recovered from her sadness about her friend. 'And, frankly, I don't expect I ever will be. My business career is more important to me than anything else . . .'

Alexis stopped short, suddenly wondering why she was confiding in Claudia, whom she did not really know. Then she realized that she had felt drawn to her the moment they had met.

'Your reputation as a brilliant businesswoman precedes you, Alexis. You inspire other women who would also enjoy being in business, but are not allowed to work.'

'What about you? Would you like to be a banker, following in your father's footsteps?'

'No, I wouldn't. But I would like something to do, which is one of the reasons I want to be involved with your charity. By the way, does the safe house have a name yet?'

'It does. Delia and I decided to call it Haven House, because that says exactly what it is – a haven for women who need to be safe.'

'I can't wait to visit it next Tuesday, and when will it be opened? When will women be able to come there for help?'

'It's really ready now, and Delia and I will make it known to the local churches and hospitals that we are there to give shelter,' Alexis explained, and looked at the doorway as Delia walked in.

Delia joined them near the window. 'I can see that you have hit it off. I knew you would. In fact, I'm sorry I didn't ask you to become involved with the charity before, Claudia.'

'So am I, but here I am now, ready, willing and able to do whatever I can. Wouldn't it be possible to go and visit Haven House regularly, Delia?'

'Of course, we'd love that. Alexis and I believe that the women will appreciate our interest in them. We fully intend to drop by whenever we can. Of course, they may be a bit shy at first.'

Claudia looked from Delia to Alexis. 'I had a thought when I was on my way here earlier. I'd like to share it with you . . .' A questioning look crossed her face.

'Please do tell us.' Delia smiled encouragingly.

'I was wondering what I would actually do if I visited the shelter. It suddenly occurred to me that I might be able to teach the women something during their stay. I came up with the idea of taking some books. I thought perhaps there might be some women who can't read.'

Alexis exclaimed, 'What a clever idea! It's just wonderful, Claudia. And there are bound to be many women who never went to school before it became compulsory.'

A smile spread across Claudia's face, and she began to discuss the kind of books she would collect, how she might bring a carpenter to build bookshelves in one of the communal rooms with their permission.

As she sat listening to her, liking Claudia more and more, Alexis saw the strong family likeness between her and Delia. Their mothers were sisters, making them first cousins. Margot, Claudia's mother, had died some years ago, but Delia's was still alive and had helped with the charity.

Both women had the same burnished, glossy brown hair and dark eyes. Pretty women, they were well groomed and smartly dressed. She knew that Delia was just thirty because she had attended her birthday luncheon. But she had no idea how old Claudia was . . . younger than Delia, about twenty, perhaps, not much older than that.

Each of them was wearing a gown by Madame Valance. Her

unique style was easy to recognize and it was obvious to Alex that they also patronized the French designer.

Delia had chosen a deep-rose-coloured silk gown, with long sleeves, a square neckline and a sweeping bustle; Claudia was dressed in a purple silk jacket with a cleverly cut skirt which matched. It was a straight skirt, with side drapes, but no bustle. Alexis thought it was chic, and decided she would order something similar. She liked the idea of skirts without those cumbersome bustles that she no longer tolerated.

Delia broke into her thoughts, when she said, 'You are certainly giving us a very sharp once-over, Alexis. And the answer is yes. We are clients of Madame Valance.'

Alexis laughed. 'I was actually admiring you both. And I have suddenly had a serious thought. We must be simply dressed when we are at Haven House, wearing plain clothes.'

'Nothing like these gowns, nothing fancy. That's most important,' Delia interjected. 'They would be upset, I think.'

Claudia was in agreement. 'We have to show them respect and kindness, and we mustn't appear to be superior or patronizing.'

'Correct,' Alexis said. 'Plain clothes, plain talk, too, and very good manners. We must also have a lot of patience. These women who are so much in need must never be made to feel inferior.'

EIGHT

As they took their leave of Delia, Alexis turned to Claudia. 'I have my carriage waiting, and I'm certain you do, too. But, if not, I would be happy to take you to your home.'

'How nice of you, Alexis, and thank you. I'm going to visit a relative with my father. He said he would come for me, and I'm sure his carriage is already outside.'

It was. As Alexis and Claudia left Delia's house, she saw it at once. Her father was standing outside on this glorious sunny afternoon, leaning against the carriage door nonchalantly smoking a cigarette. As soon as he saw them he dropped it, stubbed it out with his foot. Then he began to walk towards them, a smile on his face.

After greeting his daughter in an affectionate tone, he said, 'Won't you introduce me to your friend?'

'Of course, Papa.' She looked at Alexis. 'I would like to present my father to you . . . Sebastian Trevalian. Papa, this is Alexis Malvern.'

Sebastian bowed slightly, offering her his hand.

'Good afternoon, Mr Trevalian. I am very pleased to meet you,' Alexis murmured, taking his hand.

'The pleasure is all mine, Miss Malvern,' he responded, staring at her with great intensity. He was still holding her hand in his, struck by her vivid beauty: her luxuriant auburn hair, deep-green eyes, and English-rose complexion. She was stunning. A beauty. No, a great beauty, and extremely elegant in her cream gown.

Startled by her father's attention to Alexis, even puzzled, Claudia cleared her throat several times.

Glancing at his daughter, noting the surprised expression on her face, he immediately let go of Alexis's hand and took a step back. 'Wherever it is you are going, Miss Malvern, we will take you there.' Turning, he put a hand under her elbow and began to walk her to his carriage.

'Thank you, Mr Trevalian,' Alexis said, 'I have my carriage here, but such a kind offer on your part.'

Claudia said swiftly, 'I'm so glad we met, Alexis, and I look forward to visiting Haven House on Tuesday.'

Taking hold of her father's arm, still amazed by his fascination with her new friend, she made to lead him in the direction of their carriage. He shrugged her off gently, an amused look settling on his face.

'I shall escort Miss Malvern, help her into her carriage,' Sebastian announced firmly, and did just that, with Claudia staring after him, more and more surprised.

After stepping up into her carriage and seating herself, Alexis rolled down the window and looked at him, her attention held by his pale-grey eyes.

'Thank you,' she murmured.

Sebastian stared back at her for a long moment, before saying, 'I do hope we shall meet again, Miss Malvern. Soon. I shall have Claudia give a small supper. You will come, I hope?'

Alexis found herself saying, 'I would enjoy that,' and then she wondered why she had accepted so quickly.

He nodded politely, and as he turned away she noticed the small smile playing around his mouth.

Her carriage moved forward, the horses snorting, the driver urging them on. Alexis leaned back against the leather seat, thinking about Sebastian Trevalian. His behaviour had been a bit odd. No, not odd. Very male. She knew he had been surprised by her appearance. And he had been attracted to her. Very much so.

With a little jolt, she understood that Claudia had been startled by her father's behaviour. And she wished she had not accepted his invitation with such alacrity. It might look too eager. And she didn't have the slightest interest in him. None at all.

And yet her thoughts stayed with Claudia's father as the carriage rolled on towards Mayfair. He was undoubtedly one of the handsomest man she had ever set eyes on. It was his silvery-grey eyes, translucent and clear, that were so arresting and compelling.

His colouring was very fair, his light brown hair filled with blond streaks. There was no doubt that he was an Englishman, although his face had strong lines. It was sharply chiselled, with a Roman nose, a masculine jawline and generous mouth. He looked too young to be Claudia's father. Her guess was that he was only forty.

Oh bother, what does it matter, she thought, as the carriage finally pulled up at her front door, at the bottom of Chesterfield Hill on the corner of Charles Street. Why am I thinking about him? I'm not going to supper. I'll never see him again.

But she was wrong.

Alexis crossed the marble-floored entrance foyer and noticed that the library door was half-open. She hurried forward.

Her father was sitting in a chair near the fireplace and imme-diately jumped up, putting the book he was holding on a nearby occasional table.

'There you are, my dear. I hope you had a good afternoon and that all went well.' His smile was welcoming.

She kissed his cheek, and went and sat on the edge of the chair opposite his. He also seated himself again.

'Yes, it was a great success, Papa.' Opening her reticule, she took out the envelope, explaining, 'Delia has written to you about your donation.'

Henry Malvern took the envelope, opened it and read the note. He passed it back to his daughter, so she could read it for herself. 'She expresses herself very well,' he murmured.

'And it is indeed a very generous gift to us. Thank you again, Papa. Delia's husband donated and so did Vera's, and Claudia Trevalian the same amount. We've suddenly got a nice cash reserve.'

'You do indeed!' he exclaimed. 'Is your friend Claudia Trevalian by any chance related to Sebastian Trevalian?' he asked, an interested expression on his face.

'Yes, she is his eldest daughter,' Alexis answered but, noting the curiosity, seeing an eagerness in her father's eyes, she said nothing else.

Henry leaned back in the wing chair and was silent for a moment or two, wondering how well his daughter knew Claudia. Unable to resist, he finally asked, 'Have you known Claudia a long time? Is she part of the charity?'

Although she knew where this was leading, Alexis understood she had no option but to continue the conversation. 'No, not an old friend, I met her today. She's Delia's cousin, and yes, she really wants to be genuinely involved, from what she said. She's come up with the idea of teaching some of the women to read and has offered to pay for bookshelves and bring books.'

'How remarkable! And it's an excellent idea. I'm certain a lot of those women never went to school. So now you're all set to open Haven House, aren't you?'

'We are, Papa, and Delia and I will probably do so next week. We want to get the word around first, so that people know of its existence.'

'I will tell Jack Holden and some of the other stallholders when I go to the Malvern on Monday. They'll spread the word. Good news travels as fast as bad news, you know. And how old is your new friend?'

'Claudia? Oh, I'm not sure – about twenty, I think.'

'Yes, that sounds right. Her mother died when she was quite young . . . ten years ago, if I remember correctly, when Claudia was ten. And I must say Sebastian has done a wonderful job of bringing up his three girls. With the help of nannies, I've no doubt, but he's been a spectacular father, devoted to them.'

Before she could stop herself, Alexis said, 'You sound as if you know him.'

'I do, but not in the sense of being a friend. He's a nodding acquaintance, shall we say. We're members of the same club.'

Alexis merely nodded, not wishing to be drawn into a conversation about Sebastian Trevalian. But her father had other ideas, and her heart sank when he began to speak.

'Trevalian's the most eligible man in London, from what I hear. Only forty or so, a widower with a fine reputation, no scandals about women. Handsome, rich and available. No wonder women fall at his feet.'

'Oh really,' Alexis muttered, 'Have you seen them actually doing that?'

Henry began to laugh. 'No, of course not; no one means it literally. It's just a saying. They do flock around him, though, according to some of the other club members. A few of the men wonder why he's never remarried, others don't. They think he enjoys his bachelor life to the hilt.'

Alexis sat very still on the edge of her chair, not liking the way she was feeling. Her chest had tightened, and she was suddenly uneasy. Obviously Sebastian was one of those men-about-town they called playboys. Why do I care? It doesn't matter to me what he does.

She knew she must remove herself from her father's presence for a while, otherwise he would go on and on about Claudia's father. Single men drew him like a bee to honey. He was always on the lookout for a good, upstanding, available man. For her. Even though he knew she was not interested in becoming involved with any of them, and certainly marriage was out of the question. For her.

She stood up, clutching her reticule and the envelope, which she passed back to her father. 'If you don't mind, Papa, I am going to go to my room and change my clothes. I thought I would wear one of my house gowns for supper. They are much more comfortable.'

'Yes, my dear, do go and change. And I shall continue to read *David Copperfield*.'

'Yet again,' she said, smiling at him. He looked about to speak, and she cut across him and said, 'I do know it's your favourite book of all time. It was even Dickens's own favourite.'

'Do you always have to have the last word?' he asked, his eyes loving.

She brought her fingers to her lips, shaking her head. Then she blew him a kiss and disappeared.

Within minutes, her lovely maid, Tilda, was in her room helping Alexis undress. First she undid all of the little buttons down the back and helped her out of it. Alexis removed her small hat. Then Tilda began to unlace the tight corset which went over her torso and down over her hips. Once the corset was removed, two different petticoats came off, then the half-hoop which was tied around her waist. The last things to be removed were her knickers, the chemise across her chest, and finally the garter belt and silk stockings.

Naked, Alexis slipped on the silk robe Tilda held out to her and tied it, turned around to look at her maid, and thanked her profusely.

'What a relief it is to get these undergarments off,' Alexis said. With a smile and another word of thanks, she went into the adjoining bathroom as Tilda began to hang up the gown.

Feeling free at last, Alexis stretched her arms above her head; she bent low, touched her toes, then she waved her arms in the air and reached for the ceiling. She did these exercises every night, the moment her garments were removed. They were very constricting.

Once she felt suppler and free, she leaned forward, gazed at herself in the mirror above the washstand. There was no doubt in her mind that she did look rather nice this afternoon . . . how hard he had stared at her. When she had looked at him through the carriage window, he had held her eyes, devoured her with his. She had been unable to look away. His eyes were so translucent she felt as though she were looking deep into his soul. Something had been said without words . . . a message had been sent.

She turned away from the mirror swiftly. Why was she thinking about Sebastian Trevalian? She must dismiss him from her thoughts.

Returning to her bedroom, she found it was empty. Tilda had put her clothes away and disappeared. Before leaving, her maid had closed the draperies and placed a small quilt on the chaise, so that Alexis could take a rest before supper.

She lay down, covered herself with the quilt and closed her eyes. But she did not fall asleep. Her mind turned and turned . . . about the charity, her new friend Claudia, and Claudia's father.

Why had he stuck in her mind? Because of his extraordinary

eyes, and what they had told her so eloquently. That he desired her, wanted to be with her, aimed to get her. She could not allow that to happen. Sebastian Trevalian might be the most handsome man she had ever met, but he was also the most dangerous.

NINE

C laudia Trevalian loved Aunt Dorothea, her father's sister. She was a very special woman, rather unique, and she had been kind to them all after their mother's death, extremely caring. Claudia's two younger sisters, Lavinia and Marietta, loved her as much as she did, and their father adored her.

At this moment Thea, as she had always been called, was sitting with Sebastian near the bay window in the parlour; Claudia was at the other side of the room, seated near the fireplace. Even on this late afternoon in July, the weather had already cooled, and the fireside was a warm and welcoming place to relax.

Although Aunt Thea was a widow and well taken care of by her husband's considerable estate, Claudia was aware that she was a shareholder in the family's private bank, which her father ran. His sister was also on the board of directors and had been for years. Of course she was. Her father protected those he loved.

Close together, chatting animatedly, Claudia saw them objectively for a moment. Anyone would know they were brother and sister, so alike were they in appearance. Although Aunt Thea had brighter blonde hair and pale blue eyes, their features were similar, cast no doubt.

Dorothea Trevalian Rayburn was fifty years old, but did not look it. Her husband, Martin, had died fifteen years ago in a riding accident. He had been thrown by a new stallion he was attempting to break and train. It was an instantaneous death; he broke his neck in the fall.

Aunt Thea had once told her that she was glad it had been so quick and that he had not been left wheelchair-bound for life. 'He wouldn't have been able to tolerate that,' Aunt Thea had explained, 'being such an athletic man, a hunting-shooting-fishing man.'

Claudia saw the truth in that, but then she was down-to-earth, just like her aunt. She glanced around whilst her father and aunt went over more bank papers.

As always, she admired the way Aunt Thea had furnished the room in light pastel colours. The upholstered sofas and chairs were filled with cushions and were comfortable, and there weren't too many small occasional tables. But Aunt Thea's were tall tables, chosen to accommodate the crinolines the women wore. Because of their height they didn't get knocked over.

Her thoughts went to Alexis, who had been dressed in a tailored gown, the kind she herself now preferred. The purple suit she was wearing today was the most comfortable outfit she owned, and she decided there and then that she would have another one made by Madame Valance. Alexis. Her image hovered in her head. She had liked her the moment they had met at Delia's house earlier, had thought her quite beautiful. No wonder her father had looked at Alexis twice. That she understood. What had puzzled her was his blatant moving in on Alexis, the way his eyes had been riveted on her the entire time she was with them.

Turning in the chair, Claudia stared at the fire, watching the flames flying up the chimney. She was remembering how, when they were in their carriage, finally coming here to Kensington, her father had been silent, looked preoccupied, gazing out of the window most of the time. Hardly speaking. And she had noticed he appeared to have been genuinely affected by Alexis, which was something she had never ever seen happen with any other woman before.

In fact, there had not been many women around him since her mother's death. He had certain women friends of long-standing, whom he invited to join him on special occasions or to go to events, but she was aware they were merely friends. If he knew any other women, with whom he might have more intimate relationships, she did not know about them . . .

'Claudia, here we are.' His voice brought her out of her thoughts as he strode across the room, followed by her aunt, who said, 'I'm afraid I've neglected you, my dear,' and sat down in a nearby chair.

Claudia smiled at her. 'It's nice just being here in this lovely room, Aunt Thea. And I think I've spotted a new painting, haven't I?'

'You have indeed,' Thea answered, and immediately rose, beckoning Claudia to follow her.

Sebastian said, 'It's the John Everett Millais you mentioned to me, isn't it?'

'It is indeed.'

The three of them stood grouped in front of the painting on a side wall. It took pride of place, hanging alone, without any other paintings to crowd in on it.

'What a beautiful little boy blowing bubbles,' Claudia said, staring at the painting, her face full of smiles.

'It is called *Bubbles*, my dear. The perfect name, I think,' Thea replied. 'The artist started it in 1885, and finished it in 1886. I was so happy to acquire it.'

Sebastian stared at the painting for the longest moment, before saying, 'Millais is the best of the current painters, in my opinion, and his attention to detail is quite amazing. I think that if I touch the boy's trousers, I'll actually feel the velvet, it's so realistic. And congratulations, Thea, I know how much you longed to own this.'

'I did. And I'm going to let it hang alone, Sebastian. I think it needs space, nothing competing with it.'

'I know what you mean,' Claudia said. 'People make their rooms far too cluttered these days, in my opinion. They hang too many paintings on one wall, then they add a palm tree in a brass pot, and soon you can't move in the room, or know which painting to look at.'

They both laughed and agreed, and Thea said, 'I haven't offered you any refreshments. Won't you have something before you leave?'

Sebastian shook his head. 'No, thank you. Reviewing the bank papers took longer than I expected. I have a guest arriving at the house very shortly, and we must leave now, I'm afraid.'

Claudia hid her surprise, wondering who he was expecting, and merely smiled. She moved closer to her aunt, kissed her cheek. 'My congratulations, too, and I'd like to talk to you next week, if I may? About a charity I've become involved with.'

'Then you must come for lunch. Any day you prefer?'

Once they were in their carriage and driving to Sebastian's house in Grosvenor Square, Claudia spoke out.

'Who are we expecting, Papa?'

'My dear friend, Uncle Reginald,' Sebastian answered, settling back against the seat, crossing his long legs. He was taller than many of his friends.

'Did you invite him for supper, Papa?'

'Yes, I did. However, I have a feeling he may wish to go to

the club, although I would prefer to remain at home. I must dine alone with him if we stay. It was my understanding he needs to discuss something private with me.'

Claudia nodded. 'Whatever you wish, Papa, that is fine.'

Sebastian looked across at his eldest daughter, responded in a warm voice, 'You always say that, and have ever since your mother died. I don't know what I would have done without you by my side, Claudia, over the past ten years.' He shook his head almost wonderingly. 'I've leaned on you a great deal; perhaps made you grow up far too quickly by sharing some of my problems with you.'

'I wanted to be by your side, to help you if I could, Papa. And so did the others, but they weren't old enough then.' She began to laugh. 'And I don't mind if I've become more grown up. And I am twenty now, Papa. Don't forget that.'

His quirky smile played around his mouth for a moment, but he remained silent, looked out of the window for a while. Then he brought his gaze back to her. 'How old is she?'

Claudia had known he would discuss Alexis with her, and she was prepared for his questions. 'Delia told me she is twenty-five.'

'Oh, I thought she was older.'

'She doesn't look it, not to me.' Claudia frowned as she spoke.

'Nor to me. But I've realized exactly who she is whilst we've been at Thea's. She is extremely well known. Works with her father and has a reputation for astuteness and acumen. So twenty-five, not much older than you.' He turned his face to the window, looking out, remained silent, tautness in his shoulders.

When the silence had dragged on far too long, Claudia decided to open up the conversation again. 'Papa, I need to speak to you.'

He swung his head to face her. 'What is it?'

'It's about Alexis. I've never seen you behave like that, ever in my life. You were . . . startled by her . . . caught up in her. Actually, I think the best word I can use is mesmerized.' Claudia sat back, watching him, hoping he wouldn't close himself off, like he so easily could when he did not want to discuss something.

He sighed. 'Mesmerized, eh? Is that how I seemed to you, Claudia?'

She merely nodded.

He was reflective for a moment. Finally he spoke. 'I was stunned by the vividness of her colouring and her beauty. And then something strange happened I felt . . . I don't quite know how to describe how I felt . . .' His voice faltered.

'Attracted to her? Happy? Joyful?' Claudia suggested, aware he couldn't find the right way to describe his reaction.

'No, none of those. What I experienced was a sense of excitement. Yes, that is the best word to use. Excitement. And a rush of . . . need. No, not need. Something else. Something a man feels for a woman. Those are the emotions she evoked in me.' He shrugged. 'And naturally you are correct; I did have a strong reaction to her. You said I was mesmerized. Perhaps. I do know I was blinded for a moment or two and conscious only of her.'

'Has that ever happened to you before, Papa?'

'No, never. I'm sorry if I embarrassed you.' His smile flickered momentarily.

'You never felt that about Mama?'

'It was different. Your mother and I grew up together, Claudia, as you well know. Our families were very close. From the age of fourteen, our parents were quite certain we would marry. And we did. We loved and adored each other. Margot was the perfect woman for me, and we knew each other so well. Just imagine, we were both only twenty when you were born.' A sigh trickled out and he blinked.

Acutely attuned to her father, after their unique closeness of the last few years, she spotted the sadness in his eyes, which had grown moist. He coughed behind his hand, and sat up straighter on the carriage seat.

Taking a deep breath, wanting to change his mood, Claudia plunged into the deep end. 'You want to see her again, don't you?'

He didn't answer.

His daughter knew he was debating how to respond, always the discreet and careful man – sometimes over-cautious.

'Yes.'

'Then you must do so.'

Sebastian gave her a swift look. 'I did tell her I wanted her to come to supper and that I would ask you to arrange something. I said soon.'

'How did she reply?'

'She said she would like that.'

Claudia gave him a huge smile. 'I think Miss Malvern might well have had the same reaction to you as you had to her.'

'Perhaps,' he said, that caution now entering his voice.

Claudia said, 'We are home, Papa.'

He glanced out of the window and saw that his carriage had already entered the square and was pulling up outside his grand townhouse.

Did this woman Alexis Malvern preoccupy him so much that he hadn't noticed where they were?

Ten

When Sebastian and Claudia went into the house, they were immediately greeted by Lavinia, who was seventeen, and Marietta, fifteen. Both girls were excited to see their father and Claudia.

They rushed over to them, only slowing down when they reached Sebastian. Smiling with pleasure, he pulled them both into his arms and hugged them. Once he had released them, answered a few questions about Aunt Thea and how she was, he explained, 'I'm afraid I've got to hurry. I must change my clothes. Uncle Reginald will be arriving imminently.'

'Can we say hello to him?' Marietta asked, who loved company and was quite socially inclined for a young girl. She was filled with charm, whilst Lavinia was more reserved, a bit aloof.

'He'll be delighted to see you, Marietta, and you too, Lavinia,' Sebastian answered, edging away, conscious of the time.

'And I think he will like to say hello to me, too,' Claudia murmured, smiling at her sisters indulgently.

Leaving his daughters standing in the middle of the elegant

entrance hall, Sebastian ran up the staircase, and headed down the corridor to his bedroom.

As he entered, Maxwell, his valet, emerged from the dressing room. 'Good evening, sir,' he said, and went to help Sebastian out of his black frock coat.

'I'll take the waistcoat off as well, Maxwell,' Sebastian said, and did so. 'I've no reason to change my tie, or my black trousers. However, I will put on one of my smoking jackets. I will be dining at home this evening.'

'Much more comfortable, sir. Which one do you prefer? The burgundy, the blue or the dark green?'

'The blue. Thank you. Please excuse me for a moment.' Sebastian hurried into the adjoining bathroom, where he washed his hands, patted his face with a clean cotton towel, then picked up a silver-topped brush and smoothed his hair back. He glanced at himself, and couldn't help thinking he looked tired, but he simply shrugged away the thought and returned to his bedroom.

Maxwell helped him on with his deep-blue velvet smoking jacket, which had a tie belt with fringe at each end. 'Thank you,' he said, with a nod, and left the room.

Claudia was waiting for him in the library, standing near the blazing fire. 'So you will be having supper at home, Papa.'

'Yes. I believe Reginald will prefer it, and frankly, so do I.' He joined her at the fireplace, and stood with his back to it, warming himself. 'It's turned chilly, don't you think?' he said, glancing at Claudia.

'It has. But perhaps you're also hungry, Papa. I know we had a nice lunch together with the girls, but it's now six o'clock. I can ask Mr Bloom to bring in caviar and toast. You always enjoy that, and I know Uncle Reginald does.'

He laughed. 'What a grand idea. Tell Bloom not to mess it up with additions I don't like, such as chopped onions and chopped boiled egg. Caviar must be eaten as it is, with just a squeeze of lemon and the toast.'

'I know. You taught me that when I was about twelve. Shall I ask Mr Bloom to open a bottle of champagne? Dom Pérignon?'

'I believe I taught you well, my Claudia,' he answered with a nod.

She offered him a glowing smile. 'Do you want me to plan a supper for next week? So you can invite Alexis?' Before he could answer, she rushed on, 'I was thinking of Thursday.'

'Who would we invite?'

'Not Aunt Thea, as much as I love her, and not Delia and Richard. I think Alexis has to be with people she doesn't know, and certainly not any family.'

'You must be there!' he exclaimed. 'I absolutely insist.'

'I intend to be, Papa. I thought we could invite Uncle Reginald and Aunt Jane, and Mark Brewster and his nice sister Evangilina.'

'Good thinking on your part,' Sebastian responded, suddenly feeling rather proud of his intelligent and clever daughter. 'With the two of us we will be six, and with Alexis we'll be seven. Should we make it eight by inviting someone else?'

'No. We don't need too many guests, Papa. You want to talk to Alexis, get to know her, don't you?'

He began to chuckle, and before he could answer her, the butler tapped on the door and entered. 'Lord Reginald has arrived, sir.'

'Thank you, Bloom.'

The butler stepped aside, and Sebastian's best friend walked in, smiling broadly when he saw Claudia with Sebastian. 'My favourite girl!' he exclaimed, walking over to the fireplace. After kissing her on each cheek, he turned to Sebastian and took his outstretched hand.

'Glad you're here, Reggie.'

'Glad to see from your smoking jacket that we're dining at home. Not only is it much more private than our clubs, the food is better. You have the best chef in London.'

'If you'll excuse me, Papa, I will go and speak to Bloom. And, by the way, you will be having roast leg of lamb for supper.'

Sebastian's eyes followed her as she glided across the room, thinking how well she had turned out. What a lovely young woman she had become!

At the doorway, she said, 'Oh, Uncle Reginald, Marietta and Lavinia wish to greet you later on.'

Lord Reginald smiled at her. 'It will be my pleasure, my dear.'

Once they were alone, Sebastian sat down and Reginald followed suit. He reached into his pocket, took out a gold cigarette case, and opened it.

'Oh, do you want to smoke, Sebastian?' He offered the case.

'No, thank you anyway. What I do want is for you to open up to me. What is troubling you?'

After lighting a cigarette, taking a puff, Reginald said, 'I wanted to discuss some business – and we will. But it's Jasmine. She has not been feeling well, and has developed a nasty cough. Jane took her to see Dr Stoppard, who says she has to stop wearing very tight corsets.'

Frowning, focusing on his friend, Sebastian asked, 'Wearing corsets is making her ill? But every woman wears corsets. And seemingly the tighter they can make them with the lacing up, the better. Or so I'm given to understand.'

'That tight lacing is the root of the problem!' Reginald exclaimed. 'It is compressing her ribcage, which has become smaller and smaller, and apparently that's not healthy.'

'What treatment does the doctor suggest?'

'Jasmine has to stop wearing corsets, or rather, tightly laced corsets. And that's where the problem is. Jasmine wants to have a tiny waist like the other debutantes – the tinier the better, apparently.'

'I'm sorry about Jasmine's health issue, Reggie, but surely her mother can make her see sense?'

'She's trying to, but these girls . . .' Reginald broke off, shaking his head. 'They are so competitive with each other, it's unbelievable.'

'Can I help in any way? Actually, I don't see how I could.'

'I believe Claudia may be the one person Jasmine will pay attention to, and I was hoping you would ask her to come and call on us. Sometime next week. Perhaps she could help our daughter.'

'I shall do that. I must also talk to Claudia myself about this tight-lacing problem. I don't think Claudia approves of it, now that I'm discussing the matter with you. I vaguely remember her chastising Lavinia and Marietta about it a few weeks ago.'

'Thank you, Sebastian, I really appreciate your help, and if anyone can talk sense into Jasmine, I believe it will be Claudia.'

'We are like brothers, you and I, Reggie,' Sebastian suddenly said. 'Just imagine, we were boys at Eton together, then at King's College, Cambridge. We've spent our lives in each other's pockets, and we've never had a cross word.'

'An extraordinary friendship, yes, indeed we've had that.' He puffed on the cigarette and, changing the subject, he went on, 'I had a meeting today with George Havermill. He wants to buy my newspapers. Offered a very good price. What do you think?'

'Consider it, if you really do want to sell. Or start something new. Maybe I should take a look at the deal he's offered you.'

'I'd like your advice.'

'And I would like yours.'

'What about?'

'A woman.'

It was obvious from his expression that Reginald was taken aback. 'What kind of woman?'

'I'm not sure I know how to answer that, Reggie.'

'Well, what I mean is, are you interested in a woman with whom to have a friendship, one of those lovely ladies who accompany you to events? Or are you speaking about a woman with whom you wish to be . . . well . . . intimate?

'Neither.'

'Oh, I see,' Reginald began, and stopped abruptly when Bloom came in carrying a silver tray, followed by a footman with a silver bucket containing a bottle of Dom Pérignon.

Once the champagne had been poured into crystal flutes, and the caviar passed to the two men, the butler and the footman took their leave.

After clinking glasses, Reginald said, 'Do you realize you've never discussed women with me since we were very young men – fifteen, or thereabouts? So naturally I'm a bit surprised. Who is she?'

'A woman I met today. This afternoon, and very briefly. I must see her again.'

'And you knew at once?' Reginald asked, his surprise obvious in his tone of voice.

'I did. It was the most extraordinary thing. I was instantly struck by her looks, bowled over really. So much so, that even Claudia noticed and was taken aback.'

'She was with you at the time?'

'Yes. She had been at a ladies' tea with some other women, at Delia's. A meeting to do with a charity they are involved with. I went to fetch her, so she could accompany me to my sister's house, and the woman was with Claudia when they left.'

'And what did Claudia say to you?'

'She didn't say anything until much later, after we had left my sister's, when she mentioned that I'd had a strong reaction to her companion. She asked me why.'

'And you told her what?'

'That I wasn't sure. But I'd had a rush of feelings: excitement, a sense of need, perhaps desire. Claudia told me I had appeared to be mesmerized.'

'Mesmerized. That's a strong word, old chap.'

'I said I'd felt blinded, conscious only of her. Anyway, she's in my head, Reggie, and I can't wait to see her again. Only then will I understand myself, my reaction to her.'

'She must be quite a stunner to affect you in this way. I know it's not happened to you before. You would have told me, wouldn't you?' Reginald raised a brow quizzically.

'Of course.' Sebastian took a sip of champagne. 'I've never had any secrets from you.'

'So who is this woman who has you so rattled? What's her name?'

'Alexis. Alexis Malvern.'

Reginald gaped at him, stunned into silence. After a split second, he exclaimed, 'There can't be two women with that name. You must be referring to Henry Malvern's daughter, aren't you?'

'I am indeed. Do you know him?'

'He's a member of one of our clubs, Savile's. And we chat occasionally, but I can't say I know him well. He's a powerful man, very wealthy, and all of his businesses are extremely successful.' Reginald chuckled. 'It is well known that his daughter is his only child and heir. She works in his business, but then I'm sure you know that.'

'I had heard of her, and her business acumen. However, she is also extremely beautiful. And she is a mere twenty-five.' Sebastian grimaced. 'Too young for me, I think.'

'No, not at all. You're only forty. I would certainly like to meet her.'

'Glad to hear that, Reggie. Claudia is planning to give a small supper here next week. We hoped you and Jane would accept our invitation.'

'Wild horses couldn't keep me away.' Reginald lifted his flute of champagne and took a sip.

ELEVEN

James Lionel Falconer was now seventeen and a striking young man, not only because of his chiselled good looks, fair complexion and deep blue eyes, but because of his height. He was just under six feet.

None of the other Falconers was as tall, and, in fact, most people in general were much shorter than him.

Aside from these physical assets, he was naturally charming, had a congenial nature, and was also thoughtful to others, and kind. He owed these latter traits to his grandmother, Esther, who had taught him a lot of things when he was young. She had made sure he had excellent manners and behaved with politeness and decorum at all times. And to everyone, whoever the person was.

As she looked across the Falconers' kitchen at him, Esther felt a swell of pride. There was no one quite like James that she knew of, anyway, and that included the children of her employers, Lady Agatha and the Honourable Mister, as her husband called Arthur Montague. To Esther, her grandson was quite unique, but then they had tried to give him the best of everything to ensure that he could follow his dream. James was as ambitious and driven as ever, and looked to the future with great hope. Esther did not worry. He was going places. It had been ordained.

As if he was aware she was staring at him, James swung his head and smiled at her. 'Uncle Harry's doing very well here, Grans. He's the best chef around.'

'I know that,' Esther answered, laughter in her voice. 'I taught him, you know.'

Harry said, 'That's why I will be forever grateful to you, Ma. For putting me on the right track when I was a little boy. And one day I'll have my own restaurant, you'll see.'

'You're not doing so badly now, Harry,' Esther pointed out. 'You have a very nice little café in Marylebone, and it's been successful ever since you started making snacks to go with the coffee.'

Harry nodded. 'It's still really only a coffee shop, though; not really a café, even.'

'The right time will come,' Esther said, and looked down at the fine cotton shirt she was making for James, and plied her needle once more.

Rossi, now fifteen, was sitting beside her doing exactly the same thing. She said, 'I agree with Grandma. I know we'll enjoy the supper tonight. Everything smells delicious, Uncle Harry.'

He waved the wooden spoon in the air, laughing. He was intent on a pot on the range. 'Thanks, Rossi,' he answered without turning his head, concentrating on the food on the stove, stirring the pot.

Harry, with James as helper, was preparing supper at his brother Matt's house in Camden. It had become a ritual in the summer: Saturday night supper for the entire family cooked by Harry.

July, August and September were the months that Lady Agatha, her husband and two younger children were on their annual sojourn in France, and sometimes Italy. Their absence meant that Philip and Esther were free to join them.

It was looked upon as a special family affair; the supper gave them a chance to catch up on things and enjoy each other's company. George, the middle brother, usually arrived a bit late; he was working on a newspaper these days and often had to do Saturday duty. But he always made it in time for the second course.

After looking in the oven, peering at the leg of lamb, basting it, Harry asked James to start making the mint sauce. 'And mind you chop the mint very fine,' he added, glancing at his nephew. 'Then you can start preparing the base for the gravy, please. The ingredients are next to that basin over there.'

A moment later, Maude walked into the kitchen, thinking how welcoming it looked with the fire blazing up the chimney, but the light in general was a bit dim.

She had gone upstairs to change and had put on what she called 'my best dress', which she had made herself. The colour was unusual, a deep lilac that was almost mauve. Tailored and stylish, it fell to her ankles and had long sleeves. A cream lace shawl-style collar and cuffs gave the silk dress a certain elegance.

Maude had swept her dark glossy hair up in a twist, and on the crown a pile of curls was held in place by tortoiseshell combs. Her wedding ring was her only piece of jewellery. She was thinner these days, still prone to winter colds, like the nasty one she had suffered some years back, which had scared them all, but healthy.

Esther nodded in approval, and exclaimed, 'Maude, here you are at last, and it was well worth the wait. You do look lovely, my dear.'

'Thank you,' Maude said, moving gracefully into the large kitchen. She headed for a chest of drawers, took out a box of Swan Vesta matches and went to the gas lamps on the walls. These she lit, one after the other.

'That's better. I can now see you all,' she announced. The

kitchen had instantly taken on a rosy glow as the lamps flickered brightly.

'It was growing dim in here,' Harry told her. 'Come and see my leg of lamb. Gorgeous, ain't it?'

Maude joined him, looked into the oven, and agreed with him that she had never seen one better.

For once Esther ignored Harry's use of slang; she had been correcting his speech for years, often to no avail, and had now given up. She was more concerned about his life in general. He was already thirty-one, and there was no sign of a woman in his life. She wished he would meet someone, start courting and eventually marry. She wanted her two other sons to be settled, and the sooner the better. As for George, who was thirty-three, he seemed to be married to his newspaper.

There's nothing I can do about any of it, Esther thought, a sigh escaping. She stuck the needle into the fine cotton shirt carefully, folded it neatly, and then put it in a linen bag at her feet. Standing, she took the bag into the parlour across the hall. Observing her grandmother, Rossi did the same, and followed her.

'We had better light the gas lamps,' Rossi said, as she entered the small sitting room. 'It's gloomy in here.'

'Yes, I'll do that,' Esther answered, and found the matches. Instantly the parlour looked more welcoming with the gaslights burning, and the two of them returned to the kitchen.

Rossi made for a cupboard, took out two white tablecloths, and her mother helped her to spread them on the long oak table. Once they were in place, Rossi, Maude and Esther went to the china cupboard and began to take out plates and dishes. Within a short time, they had set ten places at the table, added glasses and cutlery. They put candlesticks down the middle of the table, and added the white candles.

'Ten of us again?' Esther murmured, turning to Rossi.

'Yes. Denny Holden will be arriving shortly. You see, he just loves our suppers. He says he has never seen anything like them, or tasted such delicious food. He's from a small family, Grandma, and I know he loves to be amongst boisterous us. Anyway, he and James have been close friends for years, working together on the stalls.'

Maude said, 'There's not a boy I know in these parts who's nicer than Denny. It cheers him up to join us. His mother's a bit poorly at the moment.'

Esther nodded. 'I like Denny. He's very polite and . . . well . . . rather reserved. In any case, it's always rewarding to do someone a good turn. I like his father. Jack's a decent man.'

Almost on cue, there was a knock on the door. Rossi ran to open it, to find Denny standing on the doorstep. She gave him a quick once-over and smiled inwardly. He had undoubtedly made a huge effort to dress appropriately, and was wearing a dark suit, a white shirt and a tie. The suit looked stylish, of the moment.

'You look very smart,' she whispered as she drew him into the house.

'It's a new suit,' he whispered back. 'Pa bought it for me at one of those shops which sells suits put together like this. I think they're called ready-made.'

When they walked into the kitchen together, James waved, then hurried over to Denny, greeted him warmly. For his part, Denny said hello to everyone, and James announced, 'It's getting a bit crowded in here, and Uncle Harry does need to concentrate on the food. Let's go into the parlour.' They all agreed, and James led the way.

As they were settling down in the chairs and on the sofa, Eddie came running in, a happy smile on his face. He was followed by Philip, who was also smiling.

Rushing over to Maude, Eddie said, 'Grandpapa mended my easel, Mum. It works again. I can paint tomorrow!'

'I knew he could fix it for you, Eddie.'

Eddie, who was now twelve, leaned against the arm of the chair, and looked up at his mother, his happiness reflected on his young face. He was never far from her side.

Philip took a seat on the sofa next to his wife, and said, 'I only needed a screwdriver. A few of the screws had come loose.'

Esther nodded. 'I'm happy it was easy. Eddie is quite talented, you know, good at drawing. He's given me several of his paintings.'

Rossi, as always, jumped up first when she heard the knocking on the front door. 'Uncle George has arrived!' she exclaimed, and she was correct. George stood there holding bunches of flowers in his arms, and grinning at her.

'Oh my goodness!' Rossi cried, staring at the profusion of flowers as she took him into the parlour. George handed a posy to Rossi, Maude and his mother. The three of them thanked him profusely, and after greeting them all, he said, 'I'll just go and see my brother the chef.' James went with him.

Whilst George was talking to Harry, James went back to his small duties as his uncle's helper. He had finished the mint sauce, had remembered to add the sugar to it. The base for the gravy was almost ready to go into the meat pan, once the leg of lamb came out.

James was slicing the loaf of bread when the sound of a key in the door told him that his father had arrived home from the Malvern. Now the entire family was here, and soon the supper would commence.

When Esther and Maude led the others into the kitchen to start supper, they both glanced at each other and smiled. Now they knew why Rossi had suddenly disappeared, after taking George's flowers from them. These were now arranged in small vases down the table. Salt, pepper and sauces had been put here and there, white napkins were at each place, and two bottles of red wine had been uncorked and stood on the chest in order to breathe.

'You did a lovely job,' Maude said, smiling at her fifteen-year-old daughter.

'Thank you, Mum, but it was James who helped me and then he opened the red wine, as per Grandpapa's instructions earlier.'

'Certainly the table looks perfect and the smells emanating from the range are mouthwatering,' Esther remarked as she sat down, thinking that Harry had probably outdone himself tonight.

Within a few seconds, a stack of soup dishes stood next to Maude's place where she sat at one end of the table; suddenly Harry was there carrying a huge tureen, followed by James with a ladle. Harry placed the tureen on the other side of Maude.

'Please serve the soup, Maude,' Harry said, and took an empty soup dish from the pile, put it in front of her. He picked it up when the soup was in the dish and took it away. Then it was James's turn to serve a bowl of soup, then Matt, and so on, until everyone had a bowl and was dipping into their mulligatawny soup, declaring it delicious.

Empty dishes were whisked away, and the next course was ready to be served: thinly sliced leg of lamb, individual Yorkshire puddings, roasted potatoes and cauliflower. It was Harry who put four gravy boats on the table, two at each end, and also glass dishes of mint sauce. Matt carved the huge roast lamb, which had been put in front of him. James and George helped by carrying covered tureens of vegetables to the table, along with a huge platter holding ten individual Yorkshire puddings. And Denny, who had wanted to help, had been assigned the task of walking around the table offering the sliced bread to the diners.

Matt served the meat on plates in the same way Maude had ladled out the soup, and everyone helped themselves to the vegetables on the table, once the lids had been swiftly removed by James, Harry and George.

Once a full plate sat in front of every person, James and his grandfather went around the table pouring the wine, but Rossi and Eddie were only allowed a thimbleful in a glass of water.

Everyone enjoyed the food and being together, and there was much laughter and jokes and serious talk between George, Matt and their father about current politics. And George's Fleet Street gossip about former prime ministers such as Disraeli and Gladstone was entertaining. But it was Rossi who surprised them all when she announced, 'I like Salisbury best,' referring to the present prime minister.

This comment led to more discussion, but soon amusing stories about the latest actresses on the London stage and other celebrities took over, as a more colourful subject than politics.

After chatting for a while and then clearing the dishes, Harry, George and James brought out clean plates. Harry presented the family with their favourite dessert. His very special plum pudding with Mr Bird's 'magic custard', as he called it.

James was by nature a fast walker, but he slowed his steps tonight in order to stay in line with his grandfather. Philip walked between Harry and himself, and following on behind them were George and Denny on either side of his grandmother.

After supper they had relaxed for a while, drinking tea and continuing to chat, until Esther announced she and Philip had to leave. They were extremely conscientious, and never stayed away from the Montague home near Regent's Park for too long. They were in charge when the family was in France for the summer, and did not wish to neglect their duties. Philip considered them to be the custodians of the Honourable Mister's property.

His uncle George was staying the night with them, as he often did, since Sunday was his day off from the paper. James knew George enjoyed this break and the chance to spend time with Philip, and especially Esther, who spoiled him.

He and Denny had decided to go along for the walk after Harry had invited them to come to his café for coffee and cakes.

They had been intending to spend the rest of the evening at Tango Rose, a bar just off the Strand. But the three-mile walk from Camden to the bar seemed such a long way all of a sudden. So James had accepted his uncle's invitation. Denny was disappointed because he liked one of the barmaids, but James was now relieved, wanted to avoid the place. Harry had told him earlier that Tango Rose was full of bad people, and they should stay away, must never go back.

James shivered slightly as they walked along. Even though it was July, it had turned cool, and the thought of a hot cup of coffee was most appealing. They were not too far away from their destination, already entering the district of Marylebone where Harry's café was located on the High Street.

When they finally arrived, Henry exclaimed, 'Here we are then! Are you sure you won't come in for a cuppa, Mother? What about you, Father?'

'Another time, son,' Philip answered, hugging Harry, who in turn hugged his mother and his brother, and James followed suit. He said goodnight to his grandparents, as did Denny.

Once they were inside the café, James was happy they had come. Secretly, Harry was very proud of Café Rendezvous, and took them to a table near the window, explaining, 'You'll be surprised how late we stay open. People flock here after they've been to the theatres or the music halls. Give me a minute or two, and I'll send over a waiter with coffee and cakes.'

James nodded, and once they were alone, Denny said, 'When Harry talks about this place, he makes it sound like a hole in the wall. But it's nice, ain't it?'

'It is, yes, and the people here look as if they're enjoying themselves. Harry's done a grand job, but I know deep down he wishes it were a proper restaurant.'

'As yer grandma said, that day will come.' Denny sat back, a reflective look crossing his face. After a moment, he said quietly, 'Thanks for tonight, Jimmy. Yer all make me feel real welcome . . . it's a change from our 'ouse . . . Dad's so worried about me mum.'

'I know.' James reached out, touched Denny's arm, wanting to console him. 'It's difficult for him, and for you, too, and Nancy. How is your sister, by the way?'

'Doin' awright, and she comes over when she can. She likes the woman she works for.'

At this moment, the waiter arrived with a tray, placed cups of hot coffee and plates of small cakes in front of them. 'Selected by the boss himself,' the young man said, gave them a bright smile and walked off.

James liked the atmosphere in the café. It was filling up with more customers, and the overall mood was friendly and certainly lively. Surrounded by the chatter, laughter, and clatter of the place, James sat back and relaxed, noticing as he did so that unexpectedly Denny appeared less tense. It struck him that Harry had been right to bring them here. It was, after all, a much safer place to be than in the bar called Tango Rose.

TWELVE

As they entered the vast, elegant entrance hall after a convivial dinner, Sebastian took hold of Lord Reginald Carpenter's arm and turned him gently. Lord Reginald now faced the double staircase that floated up to a huge window on a landing, and Sebastian said, 'That's him up there. Staring down at us. I look like him, don't you think, Reggie?'

'You do indeed. In fact, the resemblance is quite remarkable. It might very well be a portrait of you, not of your grandfather.'

Laughter bubbled up in Sebastian's throat and he nodded. 'True. Except he was my great-grandfather, and I was named for him. I've probably inherited other characteristics from him, not only his looks.'

'What do you mean?'

'I've never told you about him before, but he was killed in a duel over a woman. And I've been rendered brainless by a woman I spent three minutes with. Let's face it, my old friend, that's not exactly normal, now is it?'

Reginald half smiled and steered Sebastian towards the library, where he knew Bloom was waiting to serve them a nightcap. Walking into the room together, Reginald murmured, 'We'll speak about that matter when we have drinks in our hands.'

The butler hurried forward. 'What will be your pleasure, Your Lordship?'

'A Napoleon, please, Bloom.'

Looking at Sebastian, the butler said, 'Will you have the same, sir?'

'Not tonight, thank you, Bloom. I rather fancy a Bonnie Prince Charlie.'

Bloom inclined his head and went over to the drinks table to pour the cognac and the liqueur into the correct glasses. Sebastian walked over to the fireplace and Reginald followed him, a thoughtful expression lurking in his eyes.

'It's turned bloody cold,' Sebastian murmured, standing with his back to the fire. 'I can't believe it will be August Bank Holiday this coming Monday. August, and it's cold.'

'*Tempus fugit*,' Reginald responded.

'Indeed. Time flies. And yet time is . . . endless.' A sigh escaped him as Sebastian continued, 'I was rather horrified a while ago, when you were speaking to Claudia. I hadn't realized that women have been hurt, physically injured, for years by all that tight corseting.'

'I was partially aware of it. However, I only lately realized just how bad it is, because of the problems we're having with Jasmine. I am delighted Claudia has agreed to come to visit us on Monday afternoon. I think my daughter will listen to her, rather than to her mother. You know what young women are like.'

'As a father I do, yes.'

The butler brought the two glasses to them on a silver tray. Reginald took the balloon of French cognac and Sebastian the small wine glass filled with Drambuie, a liqueur of Scottish heritage, supposedly a favourite of Bonnie Prince Charlie's when he lived in Scotland as a fugitive. Hence its nickname.

The two friends touched glasses and sat down in the wing chairs facing the fireplace. The library had a mellow feeling to it on this Saturday evening. The logs burned brightly and the gas lamps added to the soft glow which pervaded the room.

It was filled with mahogany bookshelves and comfortable, rather masculine sofas and chairs. These were upholstered in varying shades of red, which repeated the reds in the Persian carpet. It was very much a room planned and designed for a man. In fact, Sebastian spent most of his spare time here, often working at the large Georgian partner's desk near the window, or reading in front of the fire.

Both men were at ease with the long silences which often settled between them; they had been close since their early schooldays at Eton. They sipped their drinks, now caught up in their own thoughts for a while. But eventually Reginald swung his dark head and looked at Sebastian, cleared his throat, yet still remained silent.

'So go on, old chum, tell me that you agree with me . . . that I have no brains.' Reginald did not reply, and Sebastian looked over at him and added, 'I'm bloody well daft in the head! I met a woman earlier today, was with her for only a few moments—'

'And you can't get her out of your head, can't stop thinking about her, want to see her again as soon as possible. Now. Immediately. At once.'

Staring at his most trusted friend, Sebastian could only nod his head for the moment. He took a swig of the Drambuie, and finally said, 'That's exactly how I feel.' He frowned. 'How did you guess?'

Even as the words came out of his mouth, Sebastian remembered an incident which had happened to Reginald about ten years ago, and said in a low voice, 'The Frenchwoman. That's how you felt about her, isn't it?'

'Yes. Fortunately for me, and my marriage, her husband suddenly arrived from Paris and took her off to Scotland to shoot grouse. And that was the end of that. The affair that never happened.' Reginald shook his head wonderingly. 'But when I really do think about meeting her, and recall that incident precisely, those emotions come rushing back. But you're not married, and neither is Miss Malvern, so you don't have the problem I did.'

'That's correct. But I've been given to understand that she is not interested in men, and—'

'That's only hearsay. I've heard she's not interested in marriage. But that doesn't mean she might not want to have a "dalliance", shall we call it?'

'I doubt that very much, from what Claudia has said. Or do you know more about her than you're saying?' Sebastian raised a brow.

Reginald shook his head, grimaced. 'I don't know any more than you do, and I wasn't suggesting a sexual dalliance. I meant just going to dinners and events with a man, or to the theatre; having male companionship. I wasn't impugning the woman's character.'

'I know that, Reggie.' Sebastian stared into the fire, thinking of the last ten years: the loneliness, the solitary life he had led . . .

Reginald leaned forward towards him and said in a low voice, 'What you've been feeling tonight is not unusual – nor is it daft at all. You're a perfectly normal, forty-year-old heterosexual man. You saw a woman you were instantly taken with, wanted, desired. All normal feelings. And I know better than anyone else how lost and lonely you've been these many years.'

'So what shall I do?'

'You've done it already.'

Sebastian frowned. 'What do you mean?'

'You're giving a supper on Thursday of this coming week. You invited her. You invited me to come with Jane.'

'I know that,' Sebastian answered. 'I mean, how do I get through the next few days?'

'I don't know.'

Reginald sat thinking for a moment or two, and then exclaimed, 'Why don't you tell Claudia to ask her for tea tomorrow? Tell Claudia you want to give Alexis a donation to her charity. I bet it would work. Nothing ventured, nothing gained, as our school master used to tell us.'

Sebastian couldn't help laughing at his reference to their teacher, and then he said, 'Very clever of you to think of that, Reggie. I don't know why it didn't occur to me.'

'I do,' Reginald responded swiftly, grinned at him. 'You've been very busy pondering other things.'

'You're right, I'm afraid. My mind has been elsewhere. I shall write a cheque for her charity, and I'm happy to do so, actually. It's a good cause.'

'Make sure it's a large one,' Reginald said, and lifted the brandy balloon to his mouth. Then he grimaced and looked across at Sebastian. 'Listen, will Claudia go along with this . . . plan?'

'There's no question in my mind about that. She has longed for me to become involved with someone, has actually encouraged me to think about getting married again. But I'm not sure about my other two girls. Claudia is very close, thinks like me and is wise beyond her years. Simply put, she wants me to be happy.'

'And so do I, my very dearest friend. Count me in. I'll become your other collaborator, do anything I can to help you snare this particular lady.'

Sleep eluded him.

He spent endless hours twisting and turning, and finally, in frustration, he got out of bed. Pulling on a dressing gown and putting his feet in his slippers, Sebastian left his bedroom.

It was dark as he walked along the corridor, but once he came to the landing, brilliant moonlight shone through the huge glass window at the top of the double staircase, lighting his way. And what a moon it was. A perfect silver orb. A night for lovers, he mused, as he went downstairs, across the hall and into the library where the fire still flickered in the grate.

Lovers. What a thought! He hadn't had a lover for years. Lowering himself into a wing chair, he leaned back and closed his eyes. Margot had been his love and his lover. How he had grieved for her, missed her, his lovely wife.

There had been one entanglement, of a sexual nature, and it had lasted two years. Yet it had been on and off, in a sense, since the lady in question was married and not always in his immediate vicinity.

Had they been lovers? Not really, not in the truest sense. 'Sexual partners' might be a better way of describing their secret relationship. He had ended it because he had come to realize that his emotions were not involved, only a certain part of his body.

There was no cure for grief. You simply lived with it . . . until the years blurred the many images and remembered occasions. Memories lasted.

And the loneliness became a part of life, to be dealt with courageously, by filling one's days with work, events, children's needs, birthdays and Christmas, and summer holidays at the house in Kent.

He sat up straighter and opened his eyes, a smile flickering on his mouth. He would take her to Kent. She would love the house the way he did. He just knew it in his bones. Instinctively. She. Her. Alexis. A young woman he had only just met, and briefly at that, but whom he could not erase from his mind. And her image was there with him wherever he was in this house, like a ghost haunting him, tantalizing him.

Why? What was it about her? His daughter had said he had

appeared to be mesmerized by Alexis. And that was true. Or perhaps blinded by the light and beauty that shone out of her was a better way of describing it. And thrilled, excited, and suddenly full of life, wanting to take her hand, run with her, be with her alone. Intimately.

Suddenly, unexpectedly, he knew what it was that she did to him. She made him feel alive for the first time in years – those years he had sleepwalked through, alone.

This knowledge sent a shiver down his spine and he knew the truth and what to do. He must follow his instincts and make her his. Permanently. This was a woman who could give him what he needed to be a whole person again. And he would give himself to her completely, in a way he never had before. He and Margot had been closely woven together, but to be honest he had always held part of himself back . . . kept it hidden.

He believed and with great certainty that with Alexis Malvern he could open his heart and mind, could let her become a part of him. He smiled to himself. How wonderful it felt to be . . . *alive*.

Thirteen

The attack was sudden and so unexpected that neither James nor Denny had time to think. On silent feet, three men had sprung as if from nowhere on Chalk Farm Road and had surrounded them. Two grabbed hold of them in vice-like grips.

James struggled hard in an attempt to free himself, shouting to Denny, 'Get away. Run. Run.'

But Denny was smaller and weaker than James, and his captor was a heavyset man with strong arms. There was no way he could escape. He was truly trapped, a goner in his mind. He was afraid. He thought he was about to die.

It was James who finally struggled free, managing to punch the man, who had grabbed him, on the jaw. He leapt over to the bruiser who was still clutching Denny and attempted to wrest his friend away, but it was to no avail.

Nonetheless, James didn't give up, pulling at the man's shoulders, punching him on the arms, shouting, 'Let him go. He's only a boy. Whatever this is about, take me instead. Stop hurting him. Let him go, for God's sake!'

James did not see the man with the cricket bat creeping up

behind him. But he felt the heavy blow when the bat struck his shoulders. As he went down and hit his face on the ground, James knew he and Denny had not had a chance. That was his last thought before he lost consciousness.

The bruiser still holding Denny shouted, 'Bring that there bloody bat over 'ere, let's do 'im in too. Come on, 'urry up. The coppers on the beat will be 'ere soon.'

Denny was so terrified and also surprised when the heavyset man let go of him that he froze on the spot. Before he could take one single step, he was hit across the back with the cricket bat, went down heavily. Twisting slightly, he hit the back of his head on the road and passed out.

'Let's scarper,' one of the attackers cried. 'That bleeding moon is like a bloody great lamp. We'll be seen and caught.'

'We won't! Let's mek sure. Do the job right. Let's give 'em a kicking job. Our boots are strong enough to kill a bloody bull.'

The two other men followed instructions, and the gang of three set to work, their hobnail boots hitting James's ribs, legs and thighs. Denny's body got the same brutal treatment. The men only stopped when they felt tired themselves.

The moon was high in the night sky and bright, flooding the road with light. The thugs took off, running down a side street, making their way back to Marylebone, where they had started to follow their targets.

Once they were hidden in a dark alley, the man with the cricket bat said, 'We can tek it easy. These two buggers are out cold, mebbe even dead.'

'Use yer loaf, Fred. We gorra get away from 'ere. Let's flit ter the docks. Saturday night the coppers go two at a time on rounds,' the bruiser muttered.

'Yer bloody right! Let's scarper afore we're caught.' The three of them began to run, putting distance between themselves and their victims.

* * *

It was well over an hour before James and Denny were discovered. It was Constable Tony Roy and Sergeant Mick Owen who spotted the two bodies on Chalk Farm Road as they did their rounds.

They usually partnered up on Saturday nights in the summer months. There were plenty of drunks around, often intent on disturbing the peace. Violence was common, pickpocketing the norm. There were frequent robberies, and some thieves even targeted shops and houses, breaking in to steal valuables.

'If it hadn't been for the full moon, we might have easily missed these two,' Constable Roy said. 'Chalk Farm Road is usually as safe as houses. During the week I often give it a miss.'

'I know, and it's a good thing you happened to glance down here tonight,' Sergeant Owen shot back.

Both policemen knelt down and turned over James's body, and then Denny's, and Constable Roy said, 'Let's look in their pockets. I hope to God that they have identification on them.'

They didn't. But both young men had money on them and each had a key in a trouser pocket.

'Not a robbery gone wrong then,' the sergeant said, frowning. 'They've been badly beaten. There's a lot of blood.'

'A helluva lot of it, I'd say.' Constable Roy glanced at his partner. 'Malice aforethought? At least that's my opinion.'

'I agree with you. This was a most purposeful crime. The attack was obviously planned, and cleverly. These two nice-looking lads were targeted and followed. But why? What's this criminal attack all about?'

The constable stood up. 'I don't know, but it was brute force. Strange they weren't robbed – unless something else was taken. I'll go for an ambulance, Owen. You stay with the lads. I'll be as quick as I can.'

'Make it fast. The smaller one has a bad head wound; blood's still oozing.' Sergeant Owen was now standing, and he looked at the constable with keenness, and added, 'We've got to make sure they're taken care of properly. And then we've got to try to catch the bastards who did this. Put them away.'

'We will do exactly that,' Constable Roy answered, and was gone, running down the road.

Miraculously, Constable Roy returned within the hour, riding in the horse-drawn ambulance along with two ambulance men.

When he jumped down from the ambulance and ran over to Sergeant Owen, he noticed at once how white he was and how anxious he looked.

'Thank God you're here,' Owen said. 'These boys need help. As soon as possible.'

The two ambulance men who followed Roy carried a litter. They put it down, lifted Denny onto it, and took him into the ambulance. A moment later they returned for James. The two policemen followed behind and rode along with them all in the ambulance.

'Which hospital?' Sergeant Owen asked.

'King's. It's the best for head wounds, which they both have.' The constable shook his head and peered at Owen. 'As we agreed earlier, this was a deliberate attack. And it was murderous. Whoever did it was out to kill. And I can't help wondering why. They look like ordinary, everyday young men, nicely dressed. I just can't figure out a reason for such an attack.'

'Neither can I. But somebody was out to do harm.' Owen rubbed his chin, and glanced at his partner. 'I don't recognize either of them, from around here, I mean. Do you?'

'No, I don't. And of course it was a deliberate beating. I just hope it's not too late, and that the doctors can save them.'

Senior Nurse Peg Nolan had worked at King's Hospital all of her adult life, after she had finished her training to be a nurse.

When she was a young girl, she had been inspired by Florence

Nightingale, known as the Lady with the Lamp, who had organized a unit of field nurses during the Crimean War. They had saved the lives of many British soldiers at Balaklava in 1854, after the doomed charge of the British Light Brigade against heavy Russian fire. Tennyson's poem 'The Charge of the Light Brigade' had always been one of Peg's favourites.

Peg loved nursing and making people well, and she was beloved by all of the staff at the hospital after her long service there. She was the top night nurse and preferred the late shift because it gave her enough time to enjoy her married life and her daughter. She went off duty at six in the morning, was home in bed by seven, and up and around her house at two o'clock, with the whole afternoon and half the evening ahead of her.

Tonight had been much busier than usual, and it was always hectic at weekends. She was well aware why this was, and told beginners to look out for Saturdays, when people went out on the town, so to speak, and somehow managed to get themselves injured.

Now, at three in the morning, she was taking bandages out of a cupboard when a young nurse came rushing down the corridor. 'Nurse Nolan, I need your help!' the girl exclaimed, as she came to a standstill, and out of breath.

'Aren't you Nurse Jean Riley?'

The girl nodded.

'You are assigned to Senior Nurse Clapton?'

'Yes.'

'Then perhaps you ought to be asking her for help. I wouldn't want her to think I'm trespassing on her territory.'

'I know that, Nurse Nolan, but Nurse Clapton is in surgery with Mr Perdue, who is at this moment extracting a bullet from a man's head. A self-inflicted wound. She's not available.'

Peg nodded. 'I understand. So how can I be of help?'

Nurse Riley said, 'I'm sure you know that two young men were brought in about eleven thirty last night, very badly beaten and with head wounds—'

'Oh yes, I heard. Is the problem to do with them?' Peg cut in.

'Not a problem, really. One of them has finally awakened, and that's important for Mr Perdue to know and also the policemen.'

Peg frowned. 'Are they still here? It's three in the morning.'

'They are. They wouldn't leave. Nurse Clapton told me that. Their shifts have ended but they need to know who those boys are. They didn't have any identification on them.'

Peg groaned and threw the young nurse a pained look. 'Naturally. I will come and speak to him, find out who he is. Where is Mr Frayne? I believe I would like to have a surgeon with me when I see the young man.'

'I don't know. But I can go and find him for you, Sister.'

'Take me to the young man first, and then scoot around and seek out Mr Frayne . . . I really would feel happier with a doctor in the room.'

Nurse Riley led Peg to the other end of the corridor, opened a door and ushered her into one of the small emergency rooms. Peg thanked her, sent her off to find the surgeon, and then walked over to see the patient.

The young man stretched out on the bed stared at her through the brightest blue eye she had ever seen. The other eye was covered by heavy bandaging, which went across part of his forehead and then wrapped around his entire head. One arm was in a splint, resting on top of the sheet.

He said in a tired voice, 'I'm alive then?'

'You certainly are. Thankfully. A junior nurse came to fetch me because the senior nurse who has been attending to you is in the operating room with your surgeon at the moment.'

'I understand. I just woke up. Is my friend all right? He got attacked with me.'

Peg couldn't help thinking what a lovely voice the young man had, so cultured, a fine voice indeed. An actor's voice. She said,

'I don't know about your friend, but I will find out for you shortly.'

'Thank you, Nurse. Could I have a drink, please?'

Peg walked over to the bed, reached out for the glass of water on the nightstand, and suddenly drew back, staring at him intently. She knew him. She simply couldn't remember his name.

'I'm Nurse Peg Nolan,' she said. 'You look familiar to me. What is your name?'

'James Falconer, and I recognize you. Isn't your aunt Mavis Greenwood?'

A smile spread across her face. She nodded and the smile grew wider. 'She is indeed, and she's known you since you were a little boy. In fact, she lives near your parents in Camden.'

She leaned over him and helped him to take long swallows of the water, and then put the glass back on the nightstand.

'How are you feeling, James?' she asked, her eyes sweeping over him.

'Not great. Sore. All over. A broken arm, as you can see, and there's something wrong with my left leg. Otherwise I'm fine.' He tried to grin with no success.

Peg nodded and laughed. 'At least you're not dead.'

'About my friend. Can you find out, please?'

'I will indeed. And I will get a message to Mr Perdue that you are awake, and I will also tell the two policemen who brought you in. I believe they've waited to find out your identity, and what state you're in.'

'Thank you very much,' James said as she hurried towards the door.

'That's my pleasure. I'm just happy you're alive.'

The two policemen arrived before the surgeon. Peg showed them into the room and departed, leaving them to do their job.

It was Constable Tony Roy who spoke first, introducing himself and Sergeant Mick Owen. 'We were the ones who found you, Mr Falconer, and got you both here to the hospital as fast as we could.'

'Thank you very much. I believe you came along just at the right time,' James responded. 'How's my friend Denny doing? The nurse didn't know anything.'

'He is still unconscious, I'm afraid,' Constable Roy said, 'and he has other injuries. He's been looked after very well.'

'Will he be all right?'

'We think so . . . we hope so,' the constable answered. 'The doctors will give you the best information. What's his full name, by the way?'

'Dennis Holden. We all call him Denny. His father is Jack Holden, and he has stalls at the Malvern, like my father, Matt Falconer.'

Sergeant Mick Owen said, 'Is Philip Falconer a relation of yours, by any chance?'

'He's my grandfather,' James replied. 'I think someone has to be in touch with my parents in Camden, let them know I'm in hospital. They'll be worried when they discover I didn't go home last night. And Denny's father needs to be informed.'

'We'll deal with it immediately,' the sergeant said, and added, 'I know your grandparents, Mr Falconer. They are employed by Mr Arthur Montague, and Philip and Esther Falconer are fine people.'

'We need to ask you a few questions,' Constable Roy interjected. 'Did you know the attackers? Why do you think you were assaulted in this manner? With such violence.'

'I didn't know them, and neither did Denny, I'm sure of that. I don't have the slightest idea why we were attacked. All I can add is that – from the glimpse I got of them – they were rough types: bruisers, my father would call them. English, not foreigners, up from the docks. And they were brutal, as you just said.' James grimaced. 'I can't imagine why they attacked us, because we didn't have much money on us. Nor anything else valuable. And when you check around, you'll discover Denny and I are law abiding, have never been in trouble.'

'We've no doubts about you and your friend. As for robbery, that was certainly not the reason. They didn't take what bit of money you had between you. No, this is a puzzle. And they aimed to do a lot of damage, even kill you.' Constable Roy shook his head. 'Why? Do you have any enemies? Is there anyone you've quarrelled with? Offended?'

'No, none of those things. I'm baffled, and I know Denny will tell you the same thing when he wakes up.'

'Where were you coming from last night?' Sergeant Owens asked. 'Had you been out on the town? Drinking? In any bars?'

James said, 'Can I begin at the beginning?'

'Please do.'

The sergeant went and brought a small chair from across the room, and then fetched another one. The two police officers sat down, and the sergeant nodded. 'Please, tell us everything, Mr Falconer.'

'In the summer, on Saturday nights, my father likes to have a family supper. That's when my grandparents can join us because the Honourable Mister and Lady Agatha are in France. My father's brothers usually come too, and last night I invited Denny.'

James reached for the glass, took several swallows of water, and continued. 'After supper was over, at about eight, my grand-parents were ready to leave. My uncles also decided it was time to go, and we walked along with them. Uncle Harry has a café on Marylebone High Street, and he invited us to join him there for coffee and cakes. We did.'

'What about your grandparents and your other uncle? Did they go with you to the café?' the constable inquired.

'No, they didn't. My grandparents went home to the Montague

house near Regent's Park, and Uncle George accompanied them. He's a journalist and works on *The Chronicle*.'

'What time did you leave your uncle's café?' Sergeant Owen asked.

'About ten o'clock. Denny and I headed straight for Camden. But we never got there because we were jumped by the three men. You know the rest, sir. It's a mystery to me.'

'And to us. But we'll get to the bottom of it, don't you worry. We're going to leave you in peace for now. Let you get some rest. And we'll make sure your parents and Mr Holden are informed where you and Denny are. And I personally will go and see your grandfather later this morning.'

'Thank you, Sergeant Owen.'

Fourteen

Matthew Falconer paid their local 'knocker-upper' two pennies a month to be awakened every morning at five o'clock, seven days a week. The man walked along the street carrying a lamp and a long stick, with which he tapped the upstairs windows of his customers.

When Matt heard the tapping this morning he was out of bed at once, moving quietly, not wanting to disturb Maude, who was sound asleep. He took off his nightshirt, dressed quickly, and went to the washstand to shave, comb his hair and clean his teeth.

Once he was downstairs he found the Swan Vestas and began to light the gas lamps. He then added paper and wood chips to the low fire which had burned all night, and filled the kettle with water, put it on the stove.

He was taking a cup out of the cupboard when there was a light knocking on the front door. He set the cup down on the table, frowning, wondering who it could be calling on him so early on a Sunday morning.

Matt unlocked the door and stiffened when he saw the two

policemen on his doorstep; he swallowed hard, wondering what they wanted. For Matt, two coppers visiting him was not a normal sight.

Before he could say a word, Constable Roy said, 'Good morning, Mr Falconer. I'm Constable Tony Roy and this is my partner, Sergeant Mick Owen. We need to speak with you.'

'What about? Has something happened?' Matt asked, his voice rising.

Constable Roy nodded. 'Your son has been injured, Mr Falconer. Can we come in, please?'

Matt felt a tightening in his chest, and he paled as he opened the door, allowing the policemen to enter the small hall. Finally he managed to say, 'Jimmy's not home?' He glanced at the staircase. 'I thought he came in late, after we'd gone to bed. I was just about to wake him up.'

'He didn't get home, I'm afraid,' Sergeant Owen said in a low voice. 'Let's go into the kitchen, shall we? And we'll tell you everything we know.'

Matt nodded, now unable to speak. His mouth was dry as bone. The cold chill that swept through him seemed to flow out of his body to fill the room. He shivered as he pointed to the chairs around the long oak table, and sat down; the policemen followed suit.

Matt felt as if he'd just been hit in the chest. He pushed the words out, when he asked, in a shaking voice, 'Where is Jimmy now? How badly is he injured?'

'He's at King's Hospital, and he has some serious wounds. We found him and his friend unconscious on the Chalk Farm Road last night. But I'm happy to inform you that he is now awake. We've spoken to him. He appears to be lucid.'

Matt gaped at the police officer. 'Lucid? That tells me Jimmy has head injuries. Whatever happened to him?' He was afraid for his son, shaking inside.

'He does have minor head injuries, but the surgeon, Mr Perdue, told us he will be all right. Let me reassure you he will recover, be his old self in time. As for what happened, he and his friend Dennis Holden were attacked by some men. Your son said you would call them "bruisers". We were doing our rounds at eleven thirty when we saw them passed out.'

'My God! I can't believe this! Who would want to harm them? It doesn't make sense. How is Denny?'

'His wounds are a little more severe. He was still in a coma when we left the hospital to come here.'

Matt closed his eyes, shook his head. After a moment he opened his eyes. 'Have you been to tell Denny's father?'

'Not yet. We will see Mr Holden after we leave here,' the sergeant explained.

Constable Roy, leaning closer to Matt, said quietly, 'We don't know who did this, Mr Falconer. Your son told us he didn't recognize them. There were three men who apparently appeared from nowhere and assaulted them on Chalk Farm Road.' The constable paused before adding, 'We've no lead, no witnesses, nothing to go on.'

The sergeant now asked, 'Do you know anyone at all who would want to hurt your son and his friend?'

'No. Jimmy's a good lad, works hard with me on our stalls at the Malvern Market. He's a lovely lad, very popular, and Denny's the same. He works with Jack on their stalls. Could it have been a robbery?'

'No. They both had a bit of money on them and it wasn't taken,' Constable Roy answered.

'What time do you think this happened?' Matt's voice was still shaky.

'Around ten thirty.' Tony Roy sat back, and continued, 'Your son told us he and Denny went to your brother Harry's café. Your parents and your brother George continued back to the Montague house near Regent's Park.'

'That sounds right. Harry mentioned to me he was going to

invite Jimmy and Denny to have coffee and cakes . . .' Matt broke off. After a moment, he exclaimed, 'This was obviously planned, wasn't it?'

'That's what we think,' Tony Roy agreed. 'And, if it was planned, what was the reason for the attack? Can you think of anyone at all who might want to get even with you? Want revenge?'

Matt shook his head vehemently. 'I can't. Because we haven't done anything to anyone. Nor has Jack Holden, for that matter, I'm sure. He's a good chap.'

'To say it's a mystery is an understatement,' Mick Owen muttered. 'Attacking two young men so violently for no reason whatsoever doesn't seem right to me. There has to be more to this. Something we're not seeing.'

'I agree, but I can't hazard a guess.' Constable Roy looked at Matt. 'Is there anything from the past? Something that happened years ago maybe?'

'Absolutely not.' Matt rubbed his eyes with one hand, and then suddenly sat up straighter. 'I wonder if someone holds a grudge against my father, Philip Falconer.'

'I doubt it,' Mick Owen exclaimed. 'I've met your parents and they're fine people. I can't imagine anyone being set against them.'

Matt nodded. 'I agree. There is one thing I do remember, though – not about the past, but more recently. My brother, Harry, told me that Jimmy and Denny have been going to a bar near the Thames . . . Tango Rose. I think that's the name. Harry warned them off last night, told them it was a bad place, full of bad people.'

'That's a start. We'll go and see the owner. He may remember the lads and, more importantly, anyone they might have been with, or mingled with,' Mick Owen replied.

'What's happened?' Maude, fully dressed, walked into the kitchen, a look of immense apprehension flooding her face when she saw the police.

Matt jumped up and brought her to the table, introduced the policemen. It was Constable Roy who told her why they were there and what had happened. She collapsed against Matt's chest and began to weep. But, eventually, she controlled herself and sat up, wiping her wet cheeks with her hands.

Maude looked at Constable Roy. 'When can we go and see our son?' She stood up, her face anxious. 'I want to go now. At once. Seeing him will make me feel better and it will help Jimmy too. Perhaps we should take Jack Holden with us. What do you think, Matt?'

'Yes, we must go to King's Hospital, and take Jack with us. I'd better rouse Rossi and Eddie, hurry them on, so they can come with us. And you'd better make a bit of breakfast. Then we'll go.'

'And we'll take a hansom cab, or a brougham, if Jack's with us,' Maude answered, in a voice that told everyone at the table there would be no argument about that, whatever the cost.

FIFTEEN

S ebastian Trevalian stood at the soaring window in his
library, staring out at Grosvenor Square. It was filled with
bright sunlight on this Sunday morning, but he knew it
wasn't a warm day.

When he had been dressing earlier, his valet, Maxwell, had
told him looks were deceiving. Funny weather this summer,
Sebastian muttered to himself, as he turned away and walked
over to his desk.

He was a little edgy and nervous today, but the moment he
sat down and stared at the papers on his desk, he felt a sense
of calm overtaking him. He loved his work, took his responsibilities as head of the family bank seriously, and finally he relaxed
as he read some of the documents.

Half an hour later, he glanced up when there was a knock at
the door, and Claudia came into the room. She had a broad
smile on her face. As she glided across the floor, she announced,
'I've invited Alexis for tea this afternoon, Papa, and she has
accepted. I for one am very pleased, and I'm sure you are.'

'I'm delighted,' he responded, and, rising, he walked towards her and put an arm around her. 'Let's sit in front of the fire, shall we? Much cosier.'

Every large mansion in London had fires burning in all of the main rooms, without exception. These vast, very grand houses were elegant and impressive, but not the warmest places to live in, at any time of year. Once seated in front of the hearth, he looked at his daughter, a questioning expression on his face. 'How did it all come about?'

'I wrote Alexis a note, inviting her to tea, because you wished to know more about her charity. I said you would like to give a donation. I told her in the note to simply say she would come or would not come, and that Gerald would relay the message to me verbally.'

'And he returned here and the answer was yes?'

She nodded. 'I like Gerald by the way, Papa. He's a good footman, very diligent.'

'How much should I give to the charity, do you think?'

'That's really up to you, Papa. Shall I show you the list of donations?'

He nodded. 'I don't want to upstage her father. So what time is she arriving?'

'Around four o'clock. Is that all right with you?'

'Of course it is.' A smile flickered. 'I can hardly wait.'

She laughed, and then stared at him intently, her face solemn. 'Papa, there is something I must discuss with you, if I'm not interrupting your work.'

'The papers are not important; they're only small things I'm dealing with. Anyway, it's Sunday, a day of rest. Supposedly. You sound serious, Claudia. What is this about?' He looked at her curiously, his eyes narrowing slightly.

'I think we need to invite another person to the supper on Thursday. We are seven, and the table is unbalanced. Actually, we need another man, although I suppose another woman would do at a pinch.'

'I could ask my cousin—'

'Oh no, no, Papa, we said no family members to gawk at Alexis. I have just the right man to invite. Cornelius Glendenning.'

'Well, why not? He's a rather nice chap, good looking, and he's well brought up. Smart enough not to start flirting with Alexis.'

'Oh, he'd never do that, not Connie . . .' Her voice faltered, and she sat back in the chair, realizing she was growing red in the face. She had given herself away without intending to do so. She was mortified.

There was something about the way she had said the man's name that made Sebastian look at his daughter more intently. After a moment, he said softly, 'Claudia darling, you're blushing. Are you growing close to Cornelius, and he to you?'

When she was silent, appeared slightly embarrassed, he leaned across and took her hand in his. 'You and I have supported each other for years. Surely you can confide in me about something that appears to be important to you.'

There was a moment's silence. Claudia compressed her lips together, then she nodded. 'As you well know, Mrs Glendenning has invited me to many events this year: dances, teas, luncheons, and a garden party in June. Her eldest son Cornelius has always been present. We got to know each other . . . and . . . well . . . we have a very special friendship now.'

'I have no objection to Cornelius coming, none at all,' Sebastian told her. 'I shall welcome him into the family home.'

Claudia's face was radiant, and she stood on her tiptoes and kissed his cheek. 'Thank you, Papa, thank you very much. You've made me extremely happy. And Connie will be happy, too.'

'I hope he's overjoyed,' Sebastian responded, smiling at her, full of love for this young woman who had been so strong and devoted to him after her mother's death. He suspected she liked Cornelius Glendinning far more than she was telling him. And the Trevalians had never liked or condoned arranged marriages.

They had always believed a marriage had to be made out of true love. Perhaps at last Claudia had met the right man.

In mid-afternoon, after lunch, Sebastian went up to his bedroom, wishing to be alone. His daughter had taken him by surprise. He was glad that she had set her sights on a man from a family he knew well. Cornelius was about twenty-seven or twenty-eight; he didn't consider him too old for Claudia, who, at twenty, was mature for her age. An old soul. They were a good match, and he'd never heard any gossip about Connie, as she called him.

Now he had come to understand that she hadn't meant to mention her friendship with this young man until after the supper on Thursday, when he would have seen their interaction together.

Sebastian smiled to himself. The words had slipped out of her mouth when he had mentioned the word 'flirting' in relation to Connie. Her sudden flustered appearance had given her away. He had often wondered when she would meet a proper young man and make the right choice. It appeared that she had finally done that. It had caught him unawares, but then Claudia was lovely, from a renowned family, and one of the most eligible and desirable young women in London.

Walking across the floor, he went into his dressing room, opened a cupboard door and unlocked the safe inside. He took out several leather jewellery cases and instantly found the one he was looking for.

Opening the case, he stared down at the single strand of diamonds, a necklace he had given to Margot after Claudia's birth. He had intended to pass it on to his daughter on her twenty-first birthday, but now seemed the appropriate time. He would give it to her if she and Cornelius Glendinning became engaged. He replaced the cases, locked the safe and went back to the bedroom.

He seated himself at the bureau plat, an elegant French writing desk he had bought at an antique shop years ago, where he often worked on personal papers. He would write a cheque for the charity from his personal funds, then he realized he did not know the name of the charity Alexis had started. Claudia had not told him.

Alexis Malvern. The image of her had not left his mind since he had helped her into her carriage. Yesterday. Was it only twenty-four hours ago? It seemed much longer to him. Nothing like this had ever happened to him before. He had been captivated by her at first sight, could hardly wait to see her again, and had endured a restless night thinking about her.

Reggie's idea of inviting her to tea today to talk about the charity had been seized upon this morning after breakfast, when he had told Claudia of Reggie's suggestion. She had acted on it at once, writing a note and sending the footman, Gerald, to the Malvern house in Charles Street. This was only a few minutes away from Grosvenor Square.

He glanced at the small carriage clock on the bureau plat and saw that it was already three thirty. In half an hour she would arrive here. He couldn't help wondering how he would react when he saw her. Perhaps he had simply imagined there was something magical about her . . .

Maxwell knocked on the door and entered, disturbing his inner thoughts. 'Do you wish to change your clothes, Mr Trevalian?'

Sebastian stood up, walked towards his valet. 'Do you think I should? I rather like this suit . . . whoever invented the new "lounge suit" should be congratulated, don't you agree, Maxwell?'

'I do, sir, and it's ideal for tea on Sunday.'

SIXTEEN

It was the butler who opened the front door and ushered Alexis into the grand entrance of the Trevalian mansion in Grosvenor Square.

After he had helped her to take off her cape, she turned around and was startled to see Sebastian Trevalian on the landing at the top of the double staircase, standing in front of the large window. Caught in a ray of sunlight, he was elegantly dressed.

Her breath caught in her throat. What a handsome man. For a split second she wanted to leave this house, run far away, and put distance between them. But she knew she could not leave. She had come for tea. And so she must stay. But not for long. She would leave as soon as she could. She sighed. No, she wouldn't. She had come because she had wanted to see him again, be in his company, be with him, get to know him better.

He raised his arm, moved his hand in greeting.

Alexis Malvern responded in the same way.

She watched him closely as he descended the stairs, an expression of admiration settling on her face. He was wearing one of the fashionable lounge suits many men currently favoured, though of a more casual style. Even her father had bought several lounge suits for himself. Sebastian's consisted of the loose-fitting jacket, double-breasted and worn open, in silver grey, a pale grey waistcoat and grey-on-grey checked trousers that were fuller and fell down over the front of his shoes.

As he stepped into the hall, she walked across the floor to meet him. He thrust out his hand. She took it. He held it tightly in his, and said, 'I'm so glad you were able to come, Miss Malvern.'

Her mouth was unexpectedly dry, but she managed to say, 'It was kind of you to invite me, Mr Trevalian.'

They stood gazing at each other for the longest moment, neither of them able to look away; green eyes locked on translucent grey.

It was Sebastian who blinked and let go of her hand. 'Come along,' he said, firmly guiding her towards the library. 'We always have tea in the blue room; however, I need a few moments alone with you, regarding the donation I want to make to your charity.'

'Thank you for caring, for doing this,' Alexis answered, and felt his hand holding her arm as he led her into the library. She glanced around swiftly and noticed at once how well decorated it was, with the mellow antiques and the play of reds that dominated the room making it so warm and welcoming.

'It is my pleasure,' he said. 'And from what Claudia has told me, it is a good cause.'

He looked down at her and a fleeting smile crossed his face. 'Come, sit here.' He indicated a chair at the other side of his desk.

She nodded, did as he asked, and he went around his desk and sat down opposite.

'Does the charity have a name?' As he spoke, he took the cheque out of his coat pocket, placed it on the blotter in front of him. 'How shall I make it out?'

Now, sitting face-to-face to her, he was relieved the desk was between them. She was perfection this afternoon, wearing a pale green silk dress and jacket, the colour emphasizing the green of her eyes. Her auburn hair, piled high in the latest style, was a burnished crown of curls on top of her head.

The same emotions he had experienced yesterday were flooding through him once again. He longed to take her in his arms and hold her close to him, to kiss her, love her.

'The charity doesn't have a name,' Alexis murmured. 'But I thought about that last night, and decided it should be called Haven House. You see, I hadn't expected to receive money from anyone, and yet at the tea Delia held I received several large cheques.' She told him the amount.

'That's a small fortune!' he exclaimed. ' My goodness, how remarkable!' He shook his head. 'It can't just sit in a bank account, you know. Money has to be made to work . . . to make more money.' He looked at her keenly, and added, 'But then you of all people should know that. Your reputation as a business-woman precedes you, Miss Malvern. From what I have heard, you are extremely clever.'

'Thank you for the compliment, Mr Trevalian. I think you should make the cheque payable to Haven House . . . I will make that the name of the charity.'

Sebastian picked up a pen. He had already filled out the rest of the cheque upstairs. Once the name was written, he lifted his head, leaned across the desk and handed it to her.

'Thank you for your generosity,' she said, taking it from him.

'Do you have a bank account for the charity?'

'No, because I've been using my own money for the last year, to get it going, to become an entity.'

'I can open a bank account for you at Trevalian Brothers, my own bank, if you so wish.'

Momentarily taken aback, she stared at him, her eyes wide with surprise. 'Thank you, so kind of you.' She leaned over the desk the way he had, and gave him the cheque back. 'I will give you the other cheques later, to be deposited with your bank.'

Sebastian sat back in his chair, a reflective look in his eyes. After a few seconds, he said, 'I have a suggestion to make. I could invest the money on behalf of the charity, and that would help your funds to grow.' When she was silent, he exclaimed, 'Well, perhaps not . . . I see your hesitation.'

'No, no, I'm not hesitant! I was just surprised that you would do that for me.'

He seized the moment. 'I'm glad you answered that way, because I would be doing it for you, not for the charity, although it is a worthwhile cause.'

She looked at him, her face suddenly solemn. 'I know that.'

'I am happy you do. Also—' He broke off as Claudia came into the library.

'Hello, Alexis!' she exclaimed walking across the room. 'Would you please come to the blue drawing room? And you too, Papa. It's almost tea time.'

Alexis walked through the entrance hall with Claudia, leaving Sebastian behind, who had paused to speak to the butler.

As she was led into the blue drawing room, the first thing she noticed was that the blue room wasn't really blue at all, but rather a faded bluish-grey. The walls were painted this soft colour and matched the silk draperies at the two windows and the carpet. Several chairs and sofas were upholstered in varying shades of blue. No doubt it was these pieces that gave the room its name. But it was a charming room and not over-cluttered, like so many rooms could be.

A painting hanging at the far end of the room soon caught her eye as she glanced around. She turned to Claudia and exclaimed, 'What a lovely painting that is . . . the garden scene.'

'Yes, it is, and it's at Papa's house, which is in the background. Come and look at it more closely.' The two young women walked down to the end of the room, where the painting hung above an antique chest.

The rendition was of an old house, and in the foreground was a stunning garden filled with masses of blue flowers, including delphiniums, irises and cornflowers. Here and there were pink rose bushes and, to one side, a weeping willow tree. A blue sky with drifting white clouds floated above the house, which appeared to be very old.

After gazing at the painting for the longest moment, Alexis asked, 'Where is the house, Claudia?'

'In Kent,' Sebastian answered, and she felt the light touch of his hand on her shoulder. 'In a village called Aldington, near Romney Marsh.'

Claudia said, 'I shall go and ask Bloom to serve tea. Excuse me for a moment, Alexis, Papa.'

Left alone, Sebastian continued, 'It is a very old farmhouse, dating back to the last century – 1790, something like that. I actually bought it for the land that stretches to the Marsh, about a hundred and forty acres. But I'm afraid the house itself was a ghastly mess.'

'So you had to renovate it?'

'I did have to rebuild parts of it, and add rooms. Some of the restoration parts I did myself.'

'You did! I can't even imagine that. You're far too elegant to be on a ladder.'

Sebastian laughed, amused by her comment, enjoying her forthrightness. 'Give me a bag of nails, a hammer and some planks of wood, and you'll soon know what a good carpenter I can be. I enjoy working with my hands.'

His words startled her. She couldn't visualize him doing carpentry, but she believed him and laughed with him. 'When did you buy it?'

'Seven years ago. I was looking around Kent, wanting to be near the Marsh, and came across it quite by accident. I needed to occupy myself at weekends, wanted a project. And *voilà!* Suddenly there was the old farmhouse that needed an overhaul, and much love to go into its restoration.'

'And what about the garden? Did you create that as well?'

He shook his head. 'No. That was done by a very talented gardener. However, Claudia and I did suggest various flowers, the ones we liked, and the colours we wanted. In particular, I needed lots of blue in that garden.'

Stepping closer to the painting, she asked, 'Who painted this, Sebastian? I don't see a signature.'

'There isn't one.' He smiled at her. 'It was painted by a friend of mine, who is rather shy about his talent as an artist. There are a few more of his paintings at Goldenhurst Farm. Perhaps, no, I hope that you will visit us at the farm one day soon.'

She nodded and looked directly at him, unexpectedly without any words to say, held by those compelling clear grey eyes, lost in them.

'I want you to see another painting. One I love as much as my friend's gift to me. You missed it when you entered the room, because it's behind us, hanging over the fireplace.'

As he walked her down to the fireplace, she knew instantly that this was very special indeed. It was a painting of a young girl with a parasol in a garden, and as they drew closer she realized at once who had painted it.

'It's a Renoir!' she cried, gazing at the painting in awe, genuinely thrilled by its beauty.

Sebastian was delighted she knew about art. 'So you like Renoir? Other Impressionists, too, I suppose?'

'I do indeed. I like Monet very much. I believe it was the title of his 1872 painting that effectively gave the movement its name.'

'That's right – his *Impression, Sunrise.*' He was looking at her intently, had to use extreme self-control not to go and embrace her, hold her close. He started to say something when he abruptly stopped.

Claudia was coming back into the blue room, followed by an unexpected guest. There he was, his best friend, Reggie, grinning from ear to ear.

'I hope you don't mind me barging in, old chap, but I was in the vicinity and couldn't resist dropping by. Can I cadge a cup of tea?'

'Of course. Come and meet a friend of Claudia's.' Turning to Alexis, he said, 'I'd like to present Lord Carpenter . . . Reggie, this is Miss Alexis Malvern.'

The two of them shook hands, and Alexis smiled at him with her usual grace. Sebastian was delighted to see that his friend was quite bowled over.

Claudia said, 'Come along, Uncle Reggie. Sit down with me for a moment. I need to speak to you about Jasmine.'

Sebastian stepped over to the window, then looked back and beckoned Alexis to join him. She did, walking across the room swiftly. 'Don't mention the garden painting. It was Reggie who painted it. As I told you, he is rather shy about his art.'

'I wouldn't have mentioned it anyway, Mr Trevalian.'

He said in a low voice, 'You know what happened between us yesterday, don't you?'

'Of course I do.'

'Tell me what happened. I want to hear it from your mouth, so there are no misconceptions between us.'

'We . . . made a connection. We instantly saw something in each other that we liked, that we wanted from each other. I realized you wished to see me again, and I felt exactly the same way.'

Her answer thrilled him. He felt that rush of excitement, that overwhelming desire, and that wonderful sense of being fully alive. 'So, are we going to have a . . . friendship, Miss Malvern?'

'Alexis. And yes, we are going to be . . . friends.'

'Call me Sebastian. Mr Trevalian sounds like an old man, like my father . . . Sebastian, please.'

She made a *moue*, and asked in the same low tone he had used, 'Is it all right to call you by your first name in front of Claudia?'

'It is indeed. In front of anyone you wish. It is my name, after all. What else would you call me?'

She knew suddenly that he was teasing her, and she replied, 'Why Mr Trevalian, of course.'

He grinned. 'Do you by any chance speak French?'

'Yes, I do. I wouldn't go to the finishing school my father had selected for me in Switzerland. I did agree to take French lessons in London. I had a good teacher. Why do you ask?'

'I'll tell you later.'

SEVENTEEN

For all of her life, Esther Falconer had believed that things happened by chance . . . both good things and the bad. They just happened, and that was that, as far as she was concerned. Life either came up hard to hit you in the face or it came up soft and gave you something beautiful.

But she no longer believed in chance happenings, not now, after the horrendous attack on her golden boy, her beloved grandson James. He had been targeted on purpose along with his friend Denny. No question about that.

She would never forget how shocked and frightened she had been when Sergeant Mick Owen and Constable Tony Roy had arrived at the Montague residence on Sunday morning, earlier in the week.

Her fear for her grandson's life had permeated every cell of her body. Even after Sergeant Owen had endeavoured to reassure her and Philip that he would be fine, that fear had lingered. Yes, James might well live, she had thought on that horrific morning, but would he be brain damaged? Or facially disfigured? No one could really answer that. The entire family had rushed over to King's Hospital: his parents and siblings first, then she and Philip; later his uncles, George and Harry. Everyone had visited every day to comfort and console James. It had been five days of anxiety for them all. Now it was Thursday, and on Friday, the old bandages would come off and new ones would go on. The healing process had begun. This thought helped her to relax. She believed he would be as good as new.

Esther was sitting next to James's bed, her sewing in her hands, although the needle was still. Her grandson was sleeping, breathing gently, at rest. He was now in one of the main wards in the hospital, with screens around him for peace and quiet, and also privacy. Two detectives from Scotland Yard had been to see him, following up on the policemen Roy and Owen, who had found the boys on Chalk Farm Road. Unfortunately, there were no leads, nothing to go on. Seemingly it was a dead end.

Why?

That was the question which haunted Esther. Why had someone wanted to harm her grandson and his friend Denny Holden? Innocent boys, minding their own business, never in trouble. Jack Holden had asked her that on Sunday and every day since. She had no answer for him or for herself. It was a mystery.

An image of Jack Holden's face came into her mind, and a slight shiver passed through her. On Sunday, he had looked stricken, white with shock, anguish making his body taut, tension surrounding him like an aura. His Denny was in a coma, and Jack feared for his son's life.

Esther had attempted to comfort him, wanted to help him get through the ordeal. He had no one else. His wife was ill, and his daughter, Nancy, was in service and had not been reached. Thankfully, she had finally been contacted and was now with Jack, supporting him as best she could. But she was just a young girl, with little experience of life – not much to draw on.

A sigh escaped. Esther leaned back against the chair, her

thoughts whirling in her busy mind. Sunday had been the worst day. Then, slowly, things had settled down, and the news for them had been good . . . James was improving on a daily basis. Jack Holden was beside himself, his pain a palpable thing. Philip was spending time with him at this moment, hoping to ease his suffering.

'Grans?'

At the sound of James's voice, Esther was on her feet. She went to her grandson swiftly and stared down at him. 'Do you need something, James?'

'A drink of water, please.'

Esther reached for the glass, propped him up, and helped him to hold the glass. He drank half of the water in the glass, obviously thirsty. 'That's better,' he said, smiling at her.

Placing the glass on the nightstand, she returned to her chair, pulled it closer to James and sat down. 'How are you feeling, my boy?'

'All right, really, Grans, but I'm still a bit stiff. My whole body aches.'

'The doctors believe you will come out of this all right, James. Be as good as new, one of them said.'

'That's what they told me earlier. How's Denny? I'm worried about him.'

'He's still in a coma, but apparently that's not uncommon under the circumstances after that kind of beating. They think he'll be out of it soon and that he'll be fine.'

'I hope so. He's not as strong as I am, you know. I often call him Tiddler, just as a joke, because he is shorter, smaller than me.'

Esther nodded. 'That's true, but I want you to know he will get the best of treatment when he comes around,' Esther assured her grandson. 'Now, I need to ask you a question regarding Denny. You told me yesterday that you went to that bar, Tango Rose, because Denny liked the barmaid there. Sergeant Owen went to speak to her . . . she's called Milly Culpepper, I believe. Is that the girl you mean?'

'Yes, that's her. Very pretty. A blonde girl with a nice manner. They really liked each other, she and Denny, I mean.'

'Sergeant Owen told me she's not married, so it can't be a jealous husband who attacked you both. However, does she have a boyfriend? A young man who might be interested in her?'

'Not that I know of, Grans. She met with Denny several times, just the two of them. They hit it off, you see.' James fastened his good eye on his grandmother, and asked uneasily, 'Do you think she lied to Denny? Do you think we were attacked because of her?'

'I don't know. No one knows. But Scotland Yard is going to investigate her. She might not have been telling Denny the truth about being unattached.'

'Oh my God!'

'Don't be upset. Let the police do their work. You and I have other fish to fry.'

'What do you mean?'

'I have a plan for you, James, a wonderful plan that we shall put into place when you are feeling better. I'd like to tell you about it.'

'Tell me, Grans. I'm all ears . . . I can't wait to be up and about and out of here.'

Leaning forward slightly, Esther said, 'I am going to take you away from here, far away from Camden and up to Hull. It is there that you will recuperate properly at my sister's house on the High Street. Great-Aunt Marina and Great-Uncle Clarence will look after you, and I shall be able to stay two weeks. When you are up to it, you will go and work with their son William at their shipping company. You will learn a lot from Clarence and William, which will serve you in good stead when you return to London.'

'It's a good plan, Grans, but when will that be? When will I return to London?'

'In about a year from now. Your illness is a good reason to stop working with your father on the market stall. You'll come back strong and whole, and you'll have learned a lot. Then you can put your own plan into operation. The plan you have about working for Mr Henry Malvern at his Piccadilly office.'

James began to laugh. 'If I could clap my hands I would, Grans!' he exclaimed weakly. 'I'm thrilled you think I can still have a plan and make it work.'

'Of course you do, silly boy. You are not a defeatist. You are a winner . . . winners always go up and up and up! And I wager my last shilling on you. I know in my deepest heart that you will always be the winner, James Lionel Falconer. You see, that's what I trained you to be.'

EIGHTEEN

By the time of Thursday supper, Alexis was well aware she was totally besotted with Sebastian Trevalian, just as he was with her. They had hardly been apart since Sunday afternoon.

This had been easily facilitated by their sudden business relationship. At his suggestion he had become her banker and financial advisor for her charity, Haven House. It was a means to an end. A morning meeting in his office inevitably led them to lunch at a restaurant, and another in the afternoon prompted not only tea but also supper at his Grosvenor Square house.

A great deal had been conveyed between them, obliquely, by innuendo, and often quite outspokenly. They knew exactly where they stood with each other, honesty being the byword of their budding relationship.

He had told her she had turned his life upside down, and she had shot back that he had not only turned her life upside down, but inside out as well. He had merely smiled that enigmatic smile of his, made no response.

It was true. All of her past beliefs, plans, ideas and decisions about her life, men and marriage had been blown away, gone forever from her mind.

So many thoughts about him ran through her head tonight. She was seated next to him in his elegant dining room at the Grosvenor Square mansion. Surrounding them were his daughter Claudia and the guests they had invited to the Thursday supper, which she knew full well had been done especially for her.

Lord Reginald, whom she had met before, and his wife Lady Jane, Cornelius Glendenning, Mark Brewster and his sister Evangilina were the other guests. Just eight. Exactly the right number. They obviously knew each other well, so that conversation between them was easy and relaxed, and there was a certain friendliness towards her. She felt welcomed, accepted by his friends.

Alexis was pleased she was sitting next to Sebastian for a variety of reasons. Her body was close to his; she could breathe in the scent of him, his cologne. He frequently put his hand lightly on her knee or nudged her foot under the table. And twice he had placed her hand on his knee.

She realized he had planned the table seating, knowing that if they faced each other they would be unable to conceal their feelings for each other. He had told her that only Claudia and Sir Reggie knew how smitten he was with her, and that Reggie would never betray a confidence, not even to his wife. So their secret was safe.

There were other secrets in this room. Alexis smiled to herself. Claudia was to become engaged to Cornelius in the very near future. He had asked Sebastian for her hand in marriage two days ago, and Sebastian had agreed. Alexis thought he was not only a good-looking young man, but had charm and a certain gentleness about him. She had liked him the moment she had met him.

The last secret was one that both excited and frightened her. Sebastian had asked her to go with him to Kent, to spend a week at Goldenhurst. Claudia and Cornelius would come for a weekend 'as cover', he had said. And then they would spend the rest of the time trying to work out their future together. He had also explained that his two other daughters were going with his sister, Dorothea, to her shooting lodge in Scotland, which was an annual holiday for them. He had lowered his voice when he had finished that in Kent they would be alone for most of the time, except for the servants, and would hopefully get to know each other fully.

Alexis had already told her father that Claudia had invited her to spend a week at the Trevalian country home in Kent, and that she had accepted. She couldn't help noticing the gleam in her father's eyes when he had asked who else would be there. She had shrugged and answered that she had no idea. She had been astute enough to add that Sebastian Trevalian would not be present because he would be abroad. The white lie had been a necessity to throw her father off the track.

Sebastian broke into her thoughts when he turned to her and said, 'You're very quiet, Alexis . . . I do hope you're enjoying the evening.'

She nodded, offered him a warm smile. 'I've been thinking and listening, very happy being here . . .' She broke off, slipped her hand under the table to touch the side of his leg.

He said, 'That makes me happy.'

Leaning into him, she murmured in a low voice, 'You never did tell me why you asked me if I spoke French?'

'I wanted to know if you knew what a *un coup de foudre* meant?'

'Literally "a bolt of lightning", meaning "love at first sight",' she answered, looking into his lovely grey eyes, not caring if anyone noticed.

He gazed back at her. 'That's what happened to us, isn't it?'

'It is,' she answered, feeling her heart swell inside of her. She knew he loved her.

* * *

Sebastian made his own rules in life, liked to be in control of the world he occupied. One of his genuine dislikes was the social habit of dividing the men and women after a lovely dinner. Suddenly the men went off to smoke and drink a port or brandy, and the ladies were left to their own devices in another room.

He had never quite understood why that was, and had abandoned this peculiar separation of the sexes when he owned his own home. Those friends who had partaken of supper were led into a drawing room where they enjoyed an after-dinner drink together, and the men smoked if they so wished. He wanted the companionship, laughter and enjoyment of the meal to continue on without disruption.

And so on this particular Thursday evening, everyone flocked into the blue drawing room, where Bloom served nightcaps to the men, cordials to the women, and coffee to those who enjoyed it. There was more conversation, hearty discussion about all kinds of things, from current politics to the latest play in the West End, and a certain amount of gossip.

Sebastian liked this chance to speak longer to his friends, share confidences and ideas, and he moved around the room in a leisurely way, a brandy balloon in his hand.

Alexis watched him closely, thinking how handsome he looked. He favoured the colour grey in many of his clothes, and tonight he wore a dove-grey suit, beautifully tailored and obviously an expensive item from Savile Row. The colour suited him, and the cut of the jacket made him look slimmer and taller than he already was. There was no question in her mind that he was the most elegant of men.

It was Lord Reginald who intruded on her thoughts, when he sat down next to her on the sofa. 'May I join you, Alexis?'

'Of course,' she answered quickly, smiling at him. 'I was glad to hear from Claudia that your daughter, Jasmine, listened to her and has promised to stop lacing herself so tightly.'

'Indeed she has, and her mother and I are truly grateful.' He laughed lightly. 'That was quite a brilliant idea you had, suggesting that Claudia should tell Jasmine that tightly bound waists were out of fashion and the crinoline was as dead as a doornail. That now, the chicest gowns are plain, simple, and without a bustle.'

Alexis laughed with him, and explained, 'It wasn't an invention on my part, Lord Reginald. It happens to be the truth. I for one am very pleased. I like this new style in gowns.'

Lord Reginald nodded and sat back, turning towards her slightly. In a low voice he said, 'He means a lot to me, you know. Don't break his heart, will you? I couldn't bear it.'

Momentarily startled at this intimate comment, Alexis stared at him for a moment, and then answered softly, 'I love him with all my heart and soul, and may God strike me dead if I hurt him in any way. Which I won't, I promise you that.'

'I think I know that already, my dear. I've worried about him for years . . . he has lived a lonely life, that I can attest to, I'm afraid. You make him happy—'

'What are you two chatting away about?' Sebastian asked, stopping in front of them. 'I do hope you're telling her nice things about me, old chap. I'd appreciate it if you sang my praises to her . . . all the time.'

Alexis said, 'He was doing just that, although no one needs to tell me what a wonderful person you are. I've known that since the moment I met you, Sebastian.'

Smiling, his eyes now leaving her face, Sebastian sat down on the arm of the sofa and touched her shoulder gently. Looking at Reginald, he said, 'Tell my lovely friend what a surprise she's going to have when she sees Goldenhurst.'

Eyes lighting up, Reginald exclaimed enthusiastically, 'Oh yes, you are indeed, Alexis. It's a most unique place. Right in the heart of Kent, near the Romney Marsh. And the gardens will take your breath away.' Giving Sebastian a quick glance, he asked with a certain eagerness, 'When are you planning to go there?'

Sebastian shrugged lightly, almost dismissively. 'I don't know yet. It's not really been planned, although I have told Alexis quite a lot about the farm.'

'If you want company, I'd love to join you . . .' Reggie began and stopped abruptly when he saw the look of horror on Sebastian's face. 'Ah, I see. Of course.' A smile spread across his face. 'You wish to show your little gem to Alexis on your own. I do understand.'

Sebastian couldn't help laughing, and rising he toasted the two of them with his cognac and moved across the room to speak to Cornelius, who would one day be his son-in-law. He liked the young man Claudia had chosen, and hoped Cornelius loved her the way he loved Alexis.

NINETEEN

S ebastian went to Kent on Saturday morning, and he took Alexis with him. They went alone. Claudia and Cornelius would follow later in the day.

It was important to Sebastian that he show Alexis the farm alone, without others present, because it meant so much to him.

In a sense, he wanted her to fully understand the work and effort he had put into it to make it what it had become. His haven. He needed her to love it, to enjoy it as much as he did. For a very simple reason. He intended to make her part of his life forever, and they would share that house. It would be their haven.

They drove to Kent in his brougham because he liked the four-wheel, box-like carriage with the driver on the outside. It was roomy, comfortable, and could easily carry four people if necessary.

The two of them sat next to each other on the back seat, facing the way they were going. Occasionally they looked at each other and smiled, held hands, and chatted about his friends she had met on Thursday evening. She told him how much she had liked Cornelius Glendenning, and he had looked pleased, then quizzed her a little about his daughter's future husband.

As usual, the time passed quickly when they were together. At one moment she said, 'I've never been to Kent before, but it looks as if we are going towards the Thames estuary.'

Sebastian glanced at her, nodded, 'That's right. We're actually heading for the Strait of Dover. And on the way to Maidstone – which, as you no doubt know, is the county town. Eventually we'll be crossing the North Downs, which are very chalky, and then the Weald. As I told you, Aldington is the little village where Goldenhurst sits. It's not far from Romney Marsh – I think you'll love the Marsh as much as I do.'

Turning towards him, she now looked at him intently and asked, 'Why do you love Kent so much?' She was genuinely curious to know everything about him, desiring to understand this complex, unique man.

He did not answer her, sat staring out of the window. His silence prompted her to press him. 'Does it have to do with your childhood? Does it go back in time?'

'No, it doesn't. Well, not really,' he finally answered. 'I fell in love with the place when I was eighteen. I went with a school friend to visit his family home, a manor near Maidstone. There was something about the Kentish landscape that was so beautiful, I was utterly captivated. The sky appeared to be high-flung and soaring, a giant stretch of blue, and the land-scape was truly pastoral, such lush meadows and fields, the glorious woods. I remember feeling very calm there, somehow . . . content. I think that's the best word to use. I felt contentment.'

'So why didn't you buy a house there before? I mean, earlier in your life?' she asked, frowning.

'Because I have a family home near Cirencester, in Gloucestershire, one which has been in the Trevalian family for several hundred years. I inherited it on my father's death, and I do go there quite frequently. It is a huge part of my heritage, and I grew up there. However, this farm is mine.'

'And you've created something very special, I expect,' Alexis murmured, and reached out, took his hand in hers.

He inclined his head, smiled at her. 'How well you already know me. I turned it into a special place, where I could be entirely myself, if you will. I relax there, potter around, and lead a more casual lifestyle.'

'I'm sure it's very different from a grand stately home; that's something else altogether. And what is it called, your big grand house?' she wondered out loud, laughter echoing in her voice.

'Courtland Priory, but everyone refers to it as Courtland.' He chuckled and squeezed her hand. 'I shall take you there soon, and you of all people will understand how I feel about it. You see, it's rather a grand place and we'd have to be ever so proper.'

She laughed with him, loving the way he teased her, and rested her head against his shoulder. He looked down at her, and said, softly, 'I'm so happy you wandered into my life – and so unexpectedly. It was exactly at the right time.'

Halfway to Goldenhurst, Sebastian opened the wicker hamper his housekeeper had prepared, and they shared a selection of small tea sandwiches filled with smoked salmon, cucumber, tomatoes, egg salad and ham. There were slices of fruit cake, and two whisky flasks filled with hot tea.

As they ate the sandwiches, Alexis confessed, 'I didn't know much about Kent, so I looked it up in my encyclopedia. I hadn't realized how really ancient it is: that the Romans were there and built many roads, and that there was an Archbishop of Canterbury long before the Conquest.'

'That's right, and there were so many different races plunging across Kent at different times: invaders and plunderers. As you're well aware, Dover is the gateway to the Continent.' He sat up suddenly, his eyes sparkling. 'You know, my darling girl, I shall take you to see the most wondrous place in the world—'

'And where's that?' she cut in. 'In Kent, I expect.'

'Correct. The white cliffs of Dover, of course, which are something to behold.'

It was when they were finally approaching Aldington that Alexis asked quietly, 'Do you have a lot of servants at Goldenhurst, Sebastian?' She suddenly felt self-conscious, arriving without Claudia, and ahead of the others.

'No, I don't. I don't want to be top heavy with people in the house. Enough to be respectable! There is the housekeeper, Mrs Bellamy, a housemaid Eliza, and Broadbent. He's . . .' Sebastian lifted his hands in the air, shrugged and started to laugh. 'I think I can best describe him as . . . a general factotum. He's a butler, a valet. He does everything, actually, and loves every moment of it. Naturally, he rules the roost. But everyone secretly loves him, despite his bossy ways.'

'And do you think I will feel the same way?' She eyed him coquettishly.

'I do. Broadbent will be happy to serve you in any way he can.' A small sigh escaped. 'Talking of being top heavy with people, I do have quite a few gardeners. However, when we arrive, you'll understand why.'

Before she could reply, Sebastian took hold of her arm tightly and exclaimed, 'Look, over there, the gates to my farm! We'll be there in a few minutes. It's a long driveway, but rather charming I think – bluebell woods like you've never seen.'

TWENTY

T he gates to Goldenhurst were quite plain, made of black iron with no ornate decoration at all. Alexis realized it would have been easy to ride on without noticing them, they were so understated. Immediately she understood that he had done this on purpose.

The driveway up to the farm was somewhat statelier in comparison. The woods on either side of the wide gravel road were lush with trees, but no shimmering bluebells in sight – it was the wrong time of year.

Sebastian was silent as the carriage rumbled on up the drive, and so was she. The self-conscious feeling she had experienced minutes ago was slithering through her yet again. She felt decidedly odd to be arriving on the arm of Sebastian Trevalian, and not with his daughter Claudia.

What would the staff think? How would they perceive her? Anyway, why did it matter really? She supposed they didn't care; otherwise he would not have put her in such an awkward position. He was too much the gentleman to do that, expose her to criticism.

He broke into her thoughts when he said, 'Well, here we are. It is a rather odd-looking place, I must admit.'

The carriage had come to a stop not far from the front door. She hardly had a chance to look out of the carriage window before the door was opened by Hamm, Sebastian's head driver. Hamm helped her down the steps, with Sebastian following swiftly after her. Through the corner of her eye she noticed a pond not far away, off to her right, with ducks floating on it, swimming in circles.

What she also saw was an ordinary series of buildings linked together to create a plain, old-fashioned farmhouse. He had said it was built in the seventeenth century, and it did indeed look old. Nonetheless, there was no architectural merit to it. That didn't matter to her, because he loved it, and therefore she would too.

'So, what do you think?' he asked, walking over to her.

'It's plain, as you said, but I love the tiled roof; because it's quite low and elongated, it has a sort of . . . Tudor look to it.' When he made no response, she murmured, 'That's what I think, anyway.'

He smiled inside. Trust Alexis to come up with the fanciful idea of Tudor, to make him feel better. He said, 'I bought the farm for the land: one hundred and thirty-nine acres, to be exact. Wonderful land, as you'll soon see, and also for the views of the Marsh. And, on a clear night, the lights on the French coastline. But come along, you must meet Mrs Bellamy and Broadbent, who are waiting on the front steps.'

Taking hold of his arm she pulled him back, asked in a worried voice, 'Who do they think I am?'

'Miss Malvern,' he answered, a brow lifting in obvious surprise.

'I mean in relationship to you.'

'They know you're a friend of Claudia's, who'll be arriving later. I am also their employer, and it's not their place to wonder about anything I do, or anyone I bring here.'

When she was silent, he smiled down at her and added softly, 'Please don't worry about any judgments being made about you. They don't care. You're my guest and they'll treat you like the lady you are.' He glanced across at Hamm, already handling the baggage. 'Broadbent will help you, Hamm, and I won't be needing the carriage again today. Look after the horses and take the rest of the day off. Settle down in your quarters.'

Hamm nodded. 'Thank you kindly, sir.' He touched his cap, and smiled at her.

A moment later, Sebastian was greeting Broadbent and Mrs Bellamy, and introductions were made. Mrs Bellamy was a slender, middle-aged woman with a kind face. She was dressed in a deep-blue dress with a white collar and cuffs. Broadbent, a small, wiry-looking man, wore the typical butler's uniform.

'I'll help Hamm with the luggage, sir, if you'll excuse me. It won't take long. Then I will be at your service.'

Sebastian nodded and led Alexis into the house, explaining to Mrs Bellamy, 'I am going to show Miss Malvern around the house and the grounds. Then we might have something to eat, Mrs Bellamy.'

'Yes, sir. I understand. I have made several light dishes, which would be appropriate at this hour. I shall be in the kitchen if you need me, Mr Trevalian.' With a small nod, she disappeared down a corridor.

Once they were alone, Alexis glanced around. They were still standing in the square front hall. It was painted a rich cream and was furnished with an antique mahogany carved-wood table and two small carved hall chairs to match. The wood floor was dark and highly polished and, as she looked beyond the entrance hall, she saw that the wood flooring continued on into a gallery. This was also painted cream to match the hall, creating a sense of space.

Taking hold of her arm, Sebastian led her forward. 'I had this gallery built by joining two small rooms together, so that it led

143

right up to the barn. That was a separate building when I bought the farm. The barn is now part of the house, what I call the Great Room – a big living room, actually.'

A moment later he opened the door that led her inside. Alexis caught her breath in surprise. It was indeed a Great Room, with a fireplace at each end and a wall of windows facing the gardens.

The walls were painted the same cream, which made a wonderful backdrop for a collection of beautiful paintings.

The dark wood floor was bare except for two cream rugs placed in front of each fireplace. Several large cream sofas and comfortable armchairs were arranged in groupings, but the room was empty otherwise.

'How wonderful!' she exclaimed, as her eyes swept around the room. 'And so unlike most rooms these days. No clutter, no plants, no photographs.'

He laughed. 'I like rooms which are spacious to *look* spacious. The staircase over there leads to the family quarters, bedrooms, a parlour and bathrooms. And,' he went on, 'this is my library.'

He opened a door near the fireplace, and guided her into a medium-sized room with a huge window overlooking the blue garden. It was entirely panelled in light-coloured wood, which she thought was pine. When she looked at the shelves she noticed how the books and art objects had been mingled very effectively.

'This is the room you built, isn't it?' she asserted, turning around, smiling at him.

'How did you guess?'

'You indicated you had worked with wood and could build bookshelves, and *voilà!*' She waved her hand at the wall of shelves and saw the flat-topped writing desk with a chair, a sofa and two chairs in a circle near the fireplace. 'And it's another lovely empty and spacious room.'

'The interiors are much nicer than you might expect when you first see the outside, aren't they?'

'They are indeed, and it makes me think about clearing out half the furniture in my own room at home.'

Taking hold of her hand, Sebastian led her over to one of the French doors, which opened onto a long terrace and the garden.

'Here it is,' he said, as they went outside, waving his hand at the beds of flowers. 'This is the part Reggie painted, and if we walk over there, you'll see the miles of low-lying Marsh. Some of it is well below sea level. It makes it look as if the far-off sea is floating high up in the sky. All an illusion, of course.'

Alexis understood now why he loved this part of Kent, where he had made a quiet haven for himself. And she was flattered he had wanted her to see it, to share it with him. He had made that patently clear in the last few days.

She had set out on a path with him and knew she had no alternative but to take that walk, accept where it led. There was one certainty in her mind and heart. She loved this man to distraction and wanted to be with him. Deep within herself, she suspected that they would become lovers in the next few days and she wanted that. She was not bound by the conventions of the age in which she lived. She was an independent woman with her own fortune, and thankfully the freedom to do what she wanted. She was mistress of her fate.

They walked through the gardens, which were truly beautiful and in full bloom. They had been landscaped by his favourite gardener, who was creative and inventive.

'Her name is Magdalena Ellis,' Sebastian told her, 'and she planned them to look like separate rooms, as she calls them. Each one is very different, as you can see, and I really enjoy them.'

'That was a clever idea, and they are lovely,' Alexis responded as she glanced around, taken by the beauty of the areas. There were also flowering bushes and a rose garden at the far end of the garden, and beyond that an orchard.

Taking hold of her hand, Sebastian led her across the sloping lawns to a higher spot. 'Look around you, Alexis: all you can see are flowing pastures and meadows, acres of them, and wonderful trees. Not a building in sight.'

'It's a panorama of green, and there's nowhere quite as beautiful as the English countryside on a bright August day like today.'

'Only too true.'

'Do you farm these fields?'

'I don't, but I lease some of them to local farmers and they are happy. It gives them a living.' He turned to her, and said, 'Listen, Alexis, do you hear it?'

Surprised, she shook her head. 'I can't hear anything.'

'That's right. There is no sound. You're listening to the silence, my darling girl. No noise at all out here, except for the twittering of the birds at times, and occasionally the patter of rain or the wind in the trees. Now perhaps you understand why I have found a certain contentment here.'

'Yes. I do. It's a great change from the hustle and bustle of London.'

'Do you think you could share it with me? My life out here?'

'Yes, I do. On Saturday and Sunday, I suppose you mean. I do have to go to work, you know.'

He chuckled. 'And don't forget that I run a bank, a financial empire. Of course, I mean at the end of the week.'

'Do Lavinia and Marietta enjoy being here?'

'Not as much as Claudia. They like to go to Courtland Priory, because there's much more social activity there.' He paused, and glanced at her. 'Claudia decided not to come this afternoon after all. Connie will arrive later on . . .' He let his voice trail off, his grey eyes fixed on hers intently.

'She wanted us to have time alone, didn't she?'

He nodded.

'I'm glad. I want to be alone with you, Sebastian. Don't you feel that way also?'

'You know I do.' Taking hold of her hand, he led her back to the gardens, and steered her to an arbour just beyond the massed blue flowers. They sat down together. He paused before speaking, and he continued, 'I'm playing for keeps, you know. This is not some fleeting affair I'm embarking on with you. I want you to be my wife. Will you marry me?'

'Yes, I will. I want you to be my husband.'

'A big change in your thinking, eh?' He grinned at her, and there was a look of happiness in his eloquent grey eyes.

'That's because it's you I've fallen in love with.' Her face filled with radiance. She leaned into him, and murmured, 'You're my first love.'

'And you are my greatest love,' he answered. He took her in his arms and kissed her fully on the mouth for the first time. She clung to him, kissing him back, felt a sudden rush of excite-ment as his tongue slipped into her mouth and curled against hers. Instantly their passion soared. After a moment, she pulled away from him. 'Can we go into the house?'

He did not reply, simply jumped up, pulled her to her feet and together they hurried back to the terrace, through the Great Room, and ran up to the floor above.

'We'll go to my rooms,' he said, leading her down a corridor. 'No one will interrupt us in here.' Opening the door, he led her into the parlour and through into his dressing room. After locking the door, he steered her into his bedroom and immediately took her in his arms once again. They kissed each other passionately, their bodies pressed close together.

Alexis suddenly stepped back, took off her shoes and began to unbutton her white blouse, which she took off and threw on a chair. She then unhooked her long wool skirt and stepped out of it and removed a silk petticoat.

Sebastian stood rooted to the spot, unable to take his eyes off her as she disrobed, the heat in him rising. He was mesmerized by her beauty, her auburn hair and ivory skin, the vivid green eyes.

The last garment she removed was her camisole, which revealed her taut breasts. There she stood, totally naked for him, except for a black suspender belt and black silk stockings.

His heart was racing as she began to pull the pins from her abundant hair, so that the auburn curls fell down onto her shoulders. As he walked towards her eagerly, his desire flaring higher and higher, he realized she was a natural redhead.

Within seconds Sebastian had shed his clothes. They embraced, holding onto each other as they moved towards his bed. He looked into her face with wonder, and said, 'You are the most beautiful woman I have ever seen.'

'And you are the most beautiful man,' she answered softly, standing on tiptoe, kissing his mouth lightly.

'Take your stockings off, Alexis. I want to make love to you.'

'I think you should take them off.' As she spoke she sat on the edge of the bed and stretched out her long, shapely legs.

He did as she asked, his hands trembling as he unfastened each stocking, rolling it down her leg, and then undid the suspender belt.

Alexis felt free and unfettered as she stretched out on the bed, opening her legs and her arms to him, her heart clattering in her chest. She was surprised at the moistness between her legs, something she had never experienced before in her life. But then she had never made love before. Oh, how she wanted him inside her.

Sebastian lay down next to her, marvelling at her ivory skin, as smooth as silk, the inviting auburn hair between her legs which he knew he must explore. He kissed her neck, her shoulders, and then slid his mouth onto one of her breasts and suckled her, felt her nipple harden.

She moaned softly, excited by his mouth on her, and then she whispered, 'I want to please you so much. What shall I do?'

Pushing himself up on one elbow, he looked down into her deep green eyes. 'Nothing . . . just seeing you like this gives me pleasure. I know this is your first time, and I am going to love you as you should be loved, and I will give you pleasure first, before we share a special kind of ecstasy that will thrill us both. And I will take precautions to avoid unwanted consequences.'

He was slow and gentle with her, but as a forty-year-old man he was both experienced and a wonderful lover. So much so that she responded to his touch swiftly, so obviously filled with desire for him it quickened his own lust. And there was lust between them as well as true love.

How well suited we are, he thought, as she opened herself up to him. When he parted her legs wider and began to investigate that auburn mound, she stiffened, then relaxed and enjoyed his touching and stroking. When he intensified this, she spasmed quickly and called his name. He knew he could no longer hold back and entered her hard and fast. She gasped in pain, but he kept moving with rapidity. The bad moment passed, and she moved with him rhythmically, her legs going around his back. Their pleasure in each other escalated to a higher level; they reached fulfilment together, and quickly; were overflowing with ecstasy.

And so it began, a union filled with enormous sexual passion and true love. Sebastian Trevalian had never known a woman like her before: one who desired him so much, who responded to him in every way. She thrilled him, made him feel young and alive as he had not been for years.

That week in Kent, even though Claudia and Cornelius soon joined them, they spent a lot of time alone. He showed her his beloved county, including the White Cliffs of Dover. They took trips and walked through his land, and laughed together, became boon companions, sharing so much. He loved her for her quick wit, outspokenness and honesty, as well as her intelligence and great beauty.

As for Alexis, she loved him for who and what he was: a true gentleman, who was kind, considerate and elegant in every way. Sometimes she laughed to herself, thinking of her ideas of the past. She had sworn she would never give herself to a man. And now she had. Except that he was not any man. He was Sebastian Trevalian. Her first love. They would be together forever.

PART THREE

Unique Relationships
Kingston Upon Hull/
London
1888

TWENTY-ONE

James Lionel Falconer had fallen in love. Not with a person but with a town. Its correct name was Kingston upon Hull, although locally it was simply called Hull.

It was a great seaport on the river Humber which flowed into the North Sea, and it had been highly successful for more than a hundred years, trading with the Baltic countries and Russia.

James had been captivated by it immediately. By the cheerful, smiling, friendly people in the hustle and bustle of the busy streets, who were all well fed, well dressed and obviously well employed. There was an air of enormous prosperity about the town, and the people too, and, of course, this came from the shipping industry. It didn't take him long to realize that these happy, pleasure-loving people were hellbent on having a good time. *Money*. That was the secret. Everyone earned a good living. There were many rich families from the Hull merchant class, the owners of the ships, who also were attracted to pleasure and entertainment.

Within the first week of living with Great Aunt Marina, his grandmother's younger sister, James had been to a theatre to see a play, visited a music hall where there were dancers, comedians and even performing dogs. And he had heard about the sumptuous suppers, the balls that went on until four o'clock in the morning, the tea dances, and the card games. Gambling was a favourite pastime in Hull, and there were even gambling clubs.

Great-Uncle Clarence Venables, the husband of his aunt, had told him Hull was a 'City of Gaiety', and James had nodded in agreement, liking this very apt description.

He was staying with the Venables family in their beautiful house on the High Street. This was the best street in town; each house had a long back garden which swept down to the sea. To live here a person had to be in the upper echelons of Hull society. And the Venables family now were.

When Clarence and Marina had first married, he had only been on the lower rungs of his family's growing shipping business. But, after his two brothers died young – one of a heart attack, the other in a train crash in France – Clarence was suddenly and unexpectedly the heir.

Clarence was lucky to have a father who understood he could not mourn too long for his dead sons. He knew he must put his youngest through his paces and train him to run Venables and Sons as fast as possible. Otherwise, disaster might ensue.

Jacob Venables had been well satisfied with Clarence within the year, realizing that his last-born child was intelligent, practical and a true businessman. He far outshone his late brothers and would lead the company into new worlds of shipping, ensuring the future of the business.

Clarence had taken to James at once. When he had arrived with Esther six months previously, Clarence had been impressed by his height, his looks, his manners and his general demeanour. He had not seen the boy for six years. Now James was a young man, and an impressive one at that.

James swiftly bonded with his uncle and made a point of

letting him know about his interest in wine, learned from his grandfather Philip and his many books. Clarence promised him a trip to Le Havre in the not-too-distant future, the next time he went to visit their warehouses.

Esther had stayed two weeks in Hull, enjoying being with her sister and the Venables family, while getting James settled in with them. He was to work with Clarence and learn about the shipping business, and at the same time help Clarence to develop a wine-importing arm.

Before she left, Esther took James aside and said quietly, 'Behave. Don't get into any squabbles or quarrels. Not with anyone. And protect yourself and the women you might take out. Don't forget what your grandfather explained. Also, you must never kiss and tell. Be the gentleman you are. Always.'

He had given his promise, and she had kissed him goodbye at the railway station and gone back on the train to London and her head housekeeper's role at the big house in Regent's Park.

There were moments when James relapsed into sadness when he thought of Denny. His friend had never recovered from his injuries; he had died quite suddenly a few days after James had left King's Hospital. The attack still came back to haunt James, even though it was now April 1888.

Like his grandmother, the word '*why?*' loomed in his mind from time to time. There was no answer. Even Scotland Yard had come up with nothing, and the people at Tango Rose had been of no help. They were as mystified as everyone else.

As best he could, James always tried to put these sorrowful thoughts to one side and attempted to get on with his life. He was to stay a year in Hull, and then he would return to London. He still had his plan in his head and aimed to put it into operation when he was nineteen. He would go and see Mr Henry Malvern and inquire about the possibility of a job at the Piccadilly office of the Malvern Company. By then he would have a year's experience with Great-Uncle Clarence, from whom he expected to learn a great deal.

Within the first few weeks of living in Hull, James had made quite a few friends. He was rather chuffed that people seemed to like him so much. The one person he cared about most was his cousin, William Venables, the eldest son of his great-aunt and great-uncle. William still lived at home because his fiancée Elizabeth had died of a rare blood disease three years earlier. He had been broken-hearted, and had not yet taken up with another woman; he liked the comfort of being with his parents. William was twenty-six, a few years older than James. Albert, the younger son, was twenty-two. Albert was married to a quiet young woman called Anne. They lived in a small house on the outskirts of Hull. But James found Albert somewhat remote, a rather taciturn young man. Their paths did not cross too often, which pleased James.

James and William worked together in the new wine business of the shipping company, and they learned from each other as the weeks went by. They also spent their free time together, attending events, going to dances, parties and the theatre, but only on Saturday and Sunday. They were similar in disposition, putting work before pleasure. James had soon realized that frequent socializing was not his priority.

His mind, as always, was focused on advancement. He had drive, ambition, dedication and determination. His aim was to reach the top. Only then, when he was a merchant prince, would he be truly happy.

For someone as good looking as he was, he was not at all vain, nor was he a dandy. But he had been trained by his grandmother always to look stylish in an underplayed way: neat and clean, and no flash. And so tonight, as he stood in front of the cheval mirror in his bedroom, he eyed himself intently, making sure he looked appropriate for the supper ahead.

Nodding to himself, he stepped away from the mirror, went over to the desk under the window, sat down and wrote notes to his sister and brother, Rossi and Eddie. He did that every Saturday, and also wrote letters to his parents and grandparents, who appreciated hearing from him on a regular basis. He glanced at the date on the calendar. It was Saturday 14 April 1888. He had been here in this house since November 1887. How time flies, he thought as he went back to the mirror, straightened his cravat, and left the room. Six months in Hull. Certainly he had enjoyed every minute.

Tonight his aunt and uncle were giving a small supper, and he was looking forward to it. Afterwards, he and William would go out on the town, maybe to visit a music hall, attend one of the dances, or simply have a few cups of champagne at one of the many bars or cafés.

They lived in a male-dominated culture. All men had strong friendships with other men. In London, he knew the wives were usually left at home to look after the children. Hull was slightly different in that it was a town dedicated to gaiety and fun. Women were certainly needed when it came to the dances, parties and balls. Nonetheless, many men went around in groups, especially those who gambled and frequented the gambling clubs. He did not gamble, and neither did William. They mainly kept to themselves, just the two of them, only occasionally joining with a couple of like-minded friends. James and William had become confidants and would remain close all of their lives.

On the landing at the top of the stairs, James paused for a moment and settled into his jacket, thinking how happy his grandmother would be if she could see him tonight. He looked smart in a quiet way, just the way she wanted him to be. It would please her that he was considered to be quite the gentleman by the hostesses who invited him to their suppers and dances.

How lucky he was to have relatives like the Venables family. His aunt and uncle were warm and loving and William was his best friend. Pretty young women chased after him, and he even had one woman who was extremely infatuated with him. Lucky me, he thought. Just one thing troubled him. He added under his breath: I have a dangerous enemy in these parts; one I must be extremely wary of at all times.

Twenty-Two

William was the only person in the drawing room, standing in front of the fire, warming his hands. He swung around when he saw James out of the corner of his eye, and a huge smile spread across his face.

'There you are, old chap, on time as usual. No one else here yet, though.'

After a quick handshake, James said, 'How did your day go? It was nice for a good ride, wasn't it?'

'Indeed, and I'm going to get you up on a horse one day, my lad, because I know you'd enjoy it.'

James grinned at him. 'One day. Perhaps.'

William stepped closer and said in a low voice, 'Did you know that Mrs Ward is coming to supper?'

Shaking his head, James answered in the same low tone, 'No, I didn't.' He shrugged. 'But why does it matter?'

'I think she's after you. I've seen the way she looks at you.'

James laughed. 'How is that?'

'Longingly. I think she might be a bit predatory, James. You must not get trapped into a relationship with her. She's very important in this town, a rich widow. You wouldn't want any gossip about you.'

'She's not after me. I see her during the week sometimes, to help with her paperwork. She's perfectly nice and not predatory.'

William sighed. 'I feel like your big brother at times. I suppose that's why I worry about you. Anyway, she is ten years older than you, so why would you be interested?'

'Only too true,' James replied, trying not to laugh. The one thing he had never confided in William is that he liked older women. He never had much to say to the younger ones who swooned over him.

At this moment, Marina Venables came into the room to join her son and her great-nephew. As a young woman she had been strikingly beautiful and, even now, at fifty-four, she was still good looking, and stylishly dressed in a purple gown and several strings of long pearls. She had been born with a great talent for painting and calligraphy, and her husband's success allowed her to become a well-established and popular artist whose paintings sold very well.

'James, William, good evening,' she said, as she floated across the floor, a loving smile on her face.

She reminded James of a younger version of his grandmother, and certainly she showed the same kind of affection for him. She was also fair of colouring, as he was, unlike all the other members of the Venables family, who were dark-haired with dark brown eyes.

'Your father will be down in a moment,' she said to William, and went and sat in a chair near the fireplace. She continued, 'It's a small supper tonight. The four of us, Thelma and Vincent Cannon, Phyllidia Jones and Georgiana Ward. I thought it would be nice to invite the two ladies to keep you two company. But I suppose you'll go out after supper, won't you?'

'I'm afraid so, Mama,' William said, and smiled at her.

'However, we'll keep your lady friends well entertained whilst we are here.'

'Good evening, everyone,' Clarence boomed from the doorway, sweeping into the room. He was a well-built man, with a shock of black hair, a jolly face and twinkling dark brown eyes. He was the same age as Marina and was renowned for his cheerful disposition, his ability to get things done swiftly and his generosity, especially to those in poor circumstances, down on their luck.

'I'm glad we're alone for a moment or two,' he said to Marina. Then, glancing first at William and then at James, he continued, 'I have something very special to say to all of you, although it really concerns you, James.'

They were all taken aback and stared at Clarence.

Clarence said, 'James, I am well pleased with you. I have observed you for the last six months and you haven't made a wrong move. You are highly intelligent, have great common sense, and your growing knowledge of wine has been invaluable to us. I want to offer you a permanent position here at the company . . . I want you to make Hull your home. I would make it worth your while.'

James was not entirely startled by this offer, just by its timing. He had seen it coming for a while now, but he could not take it, generous though it was. Yet he knew he could not insult this wonderfully kind man who had welcomed him into his home and his shipping company with open arms. He exclaimed, 'My goodness, Uncle Clarence, what a surprise! And what a marvellous offer on your part. I know you'll understand when I say I do have to think about it and discuss it with my parents and grandparents. I need to consult them.'

'Of course, you do,' Clarence said. 'Think it over, talk to them. Take your time. Mull it over. No hurry.'

'I hope you're going to accept it,' William said, grinning at him. 'I for one couldn't be happier that Papa has made this offer.'

'I second that,' Aunt Marina said, smiling at him, and standing up as Godfrey, the butler, announced, 'Mrs Ward and Mrs Jones have arrived, madam.'

James was relieved the women had entered the drawing room, since it brought the conversation about Clarence's offer to an end. He had no desire to hurt his great-uncle's feelings, but he had his plan, a plan born in his childhood. He was determined to see it through to the end. There was no doubt in James's mind that he would succeed. He would be a merchant prince with a store like Fortnum's and arcades. He was full of self-confidence about his future. He must find a way to gracefully decline. Now he must entertain Mrs Ward, who was coming across the room towards him.

There was no question that she was a most beautiful woman, with a mass of jet-black hair, blue eyes and an exquisite face, finely drawn with high cheekbones, arched black brows and a wide forehead. She had a full, rather voluptuous mouth that he thought begged to be kissed. And yet he had always resisted making any move towards her, attracted though he was.

She was *verboten* as far as he was concerned. William was correct there. And he certainly didn't want any scandal attached to his name. However, deep down he suspected she was infatuated with him, although she had never done anything untoward in his presence, even when they were alone.

'Good evening, James,' she said as she stopped in front of him. She was wearing a delphinium blue silk gown with a square-cut neckline, which showed the rise of her milky breasts. A sapphire necklace, the colour of her eyes, dropped down into the cleft and his chest tightened slightly as he stared at her.

He shook her outstretched hand and then let it go at once. 'It's nice to see you, Mrs Ward. I hope my work was all right. Did your brother-in-law go over the books?'

'He did, indeed, James, and everything was to his liking. However, I need you to work on another set of books.' She leaned closer, and went on, 'I want you to attempt to evaluate the company and the worth of my shares. It's rather urgent. Is there any chance you could spare an hour or two tomorrow?'

'Oh, I'm not sure, Mrs Ward. That sounds like a fairly big task. I don't think I could get that done in an hour. How urgent is it?'

'I want to sell my shares,' she said in an even lower voice. 'As soon as possible.'

He nodded, seeing the sudden worry in her eyes. 'All right. I could come over to see you tomorrow afternoon, around four o'clock, and start on them. But it does sound like a big task, as I said. I wouldn't be able to finish them in an hour, or even two.'

She nodded. 'Getting a start would relieve my mind. I will explain everything when we meet tomorrow, explain the problem. Thank you so much. I shall expect you at four.'

She paused and turned as William came up behind her to join them. After they greeted each other, William said, 'I must compliment you, Mrs Ward. You look beautiful. You should always wear blue. And sapphires.'

James couldn't help smiling, noticing how William's eyes were glued to Georgiana Ward's neckline. But what man wouldn't look at her like that? She was stunning, and she oozed sensuality tonight.

Marina brought Phyllidia over and the conversation turned to the latest play at the Theatre Royal in Hull. And a few seconds later, Godfrey announced the arrival of the Cannons. Now the supper could commence.

Twenty-Three

The sun had dropped behind the horizon and the pale blue sky had faded into grey. Soon the mist would rise across the Romney Marsh, obscuring the trees. It was that time of early evening, twilight, when the Marsh took on an eerie feeling. Sebastian called it dusk, and it was the most magical moment of all, he so often said.

Soon, when the sky finally darkened, the lights on the French coast would be seen twinkling far off, almost matching the bright stars littering the sky.

Alexis turned to Sebastian, sitting next to her on the bench on the rise at Goldenhurst Farm, and took hold of his hand. For a moment he did not respond and then she felt his squeeze. He put his other hand over hers, clasped her fingers tightly.

Softly, she said, 'I'm sorry, darling.'

'For what?'

'Hurting your feelings . . . I think.'

He put his arm around her, brought her closer, and said against her hair, 'You didn't hurt my feelings or make me angry, or even give me a sense of disappointment. I just felt sad; sorry for myself, perhaps, but only for a short moment.'

'I do want to get engaged to you. I do want to marry you. You know that's the truth. I just think if we did all that now, as you said you wanted to earlier today, we would overshadow Claudia's marriage to Cornelius. You are a very famous man, a banker of great repute. I'm not entirely unknown, since I'm the woman who prefers to work rather than marry a man. So we would get written about, don't you think? The newspapers would have a field day.'

His laughter echoed on the cool April air. He bent his head and kissed her cheek. 'If only they knew how you loved this man, oh my goodness, wouldn't they all blush?'

Alexis laughed with him and said, 'Please tell me you understand.'

'I suppose I do. Actually, I'm inclined to agree, if the truth be known. We mustn't steal their thunder.'

'Since we're having a secret love affair, perhaps we could have a secret engagement.'

'What a grand idea! And we might even have a secret marriage . . . that's what Edward the Fourth did. He married Elizabeth Woodville in secret because she wouldn't sleep with him until she had a wedding ring on her finger. On the other hand, you've already slept with me.'

Alexis smiled.

'Let's go inside. It's growing cold and, anyway, I have something I wish to give you,' Sebastian told her.

'What is it?'

'You'll see. Come on.' Rising, he pulled her to her feet and they hurried down to the terrace and through the French doors into the Great Room. He led her across the floor, adding, 'It's in the library.'

Once they were inside her favourite room, the one he had built himself, covering the walls with pine, she understood that something special had already been planned. The fire was blazing in the hearth and there was a bottle of champagne in a silver bucket on a side table.

Clutching his arm, Alexis raised an auburn brow and asked, 'Are we about to celebrate something?'

That small, amused smile slid across his mouth and was instantly gone. 'I'm always celebrating when I'm with you. As I've told you before, I can't get over my luck that you wandered into my lonely life when you did.'

'Thanks to Claudia,' she replied, and stood on tiptoe, kissed him on the mouth. He grabbed her immediately and kissed her properly, then let her go. He strode over to his desk. 'Go and sit near the fire. I'll pop the cork and we'll toast each other.'

She nodded and did as he said. He swiftly opened the desk drawer, took something out and put it in his jacket pocket.

After opening the bottle and filling the two flutes with champagne, Sebastian walked over to the fireside and said, 'Give me your hand and close your eyes.'

She followed his instructions. She felt him slip a ring onto her finger and opened her eyes at once. 'Oh, Sebastian, it's beautiful!' she exclaimed, staring down at the large square-cut emerald ring on her engagement finger.

His cool grey eyes were riveted on hers. 'Do you like it?'

'I love it and I love you. And thank you for it and for surprising me.'

He merely nodded. 'It's the exact colour of your eyes. I made sure about that, you know. Not all emeralds are exactly the same colour. They differ a lot. That one is flawless, by the way.'

Alexis held out her left hand and stared at the ring. She then stood up, put her arms around him and pressed herself close. 'You've been leading me on all day, you wretch, now haven't you? Knowing full well you were going to give me this ring at this very moment.'

'Of course. Let's toast each other, my darling girl, and you are mine now. Well, almost. Only when we're married will I actually feel you will never leave me, that you are truly mine.'

'You know very well I am truly yours now.' When she took the flute from him, she lifted it and touched his glass. 'To my first love, my only love.'

'To my greatest love,' he answered, clinking his flute to hers, happiness flooding his face.

'Let's sit down and enjoy this moment,' Sebastian suggested. 'I told Mrs Bellamy to make spring lamb, since it's at its best right now. We'll celebrate this very special moment with a lovely supper. I do love you so very much, Alexis.'

'As I do you.'

There was a long moment of silence between them as they gazed at each other, their eyes saying so much. It was Alexis who finally blinked, looked into the flames roaring up the chimney, her throat tight with a rush of emotion.

Sebastian took a sip of champagne and said, 'I want to ask you something, although I'm not sure I should . . . well, you don't have to answer, not if you don't want to . . .'

She frowned and shook her head. 'If you think I won't want to answer you, why are you asking me?'

'You're such a clever girl, aren't you? I suppose because I can't help myself. That's my only explanation.'

'So ask me.'

'Do you think Claudia and Cornelius are sleeping together?'

'I'm not sure,' she said immediately, speaking the truth. 'Nothing has ever been said but, if you want my opinion, I believe perhaps they are.'

'Why do you think that?'

'Because most people who are in love, as they are, do have intercourse, despite what you might think about the morals of our times. After all, contraception makes it perfectly safe. Ever since the rubber was discovered and condoms were developed, it's all worked extremely well.'

He burst out laughing and shook his head. 'Is there anything you don't know?'

'Yes, a lot. I've often wondered why condoms are called French letters.'

'I can't answer that. I've absolutely no idea.'

After a moment, Alexis leaned over to him and asked, sotto voce, 'Does it upset you that they're probably in bed together when they're here?'

'I suppose not. After all, they're getting married in June, and I'm sure he's wise enough to take precautions.'

'Well, Goldenhurst is the only place they can share a bed. They can't very well do that when they're in London. Unless they go to a hotel, and Claudia would never do that.'

'You're correct, she wouldn't . . .' He did not finish his sentence, and simply leaned back in the chair, gazed into the fire, his face reflective.

After a few minutes, Alexis ventured, 'I know how you feel – at least I think I do. She's your daughter, just a young girl really, only twenty-one, and fathers can feel strange about a daughter's intimate life . . . I'm sure mine does.'

Sitting up alertly, Sebastian asked, 'Does he know about us? About me?'

She shrugged. 'I don't know, to be honest. I haven't told him, but he might have guessed, although he is aware that Claudia is my best friend, so the fact that I spend time here wouldn't necessarily seem odd to him. And he's met her, of course. That was her idea, by the way. She's rather clever. Anyway, it will please him when he does know about you. He's a great admirer of yours.'

He merely smiled, and after a long swallow of the champagne, he said, 'There's something I want to tell you, and now that we have sealed our troth, as they used to say, I can. I want you to have my child. My children perhaps, I should say. You will, won't you?'

'I want your child more than anything, Sebastian. I want part of you growing inside me. I'm not that dedicated to work that I can't be a mother . . . the mother of your child, your children. As many as you want.'

Amused, he chuckled. 'One will be enough, or maybe two. I already have three. Let's see . . . I now have a great idea: shall we start trying now? Get ahead of the game, so to speak?'

She began to laugh, knowing he was teasing her. Or perhaps he wasn't. He looked suddenly rather eager, ready to spring out of the chair and go upstairs.

'Contraception, until we're married,' she answered firmly.

'When will we get married, Alexis? Give me a date, please.'

'Let's have a September wedding, Sebastian. And a honeymoon in Paris, as you suggested last week.'

'Thank you, darling. Your words make me very happy indeed.'

Sebastian was an early riser, and even on Sunday he was downstairs at the crack of dawn, shaved, dressed and sitting at his desk in his library.

After writing three letters and addressing the envelopes, he took out his leather-bound diary where he made private notations about matters important to him.

Quickly turning the pages, he came to the date of this day. Sunday 15 April 1888. A small smile played around his mouth as he wrote in his distinctive handwriting: *Yesterday I became engaged to be married with Miss Alexis Malvern, who agreed to become my wife. We shall marry this coming September. I gave her an emerald engagement ring which she promised never to take off, and she agreed to bear my children. This is one of the happiest days of my life, knowing I have a future to look forward to with my greatest love.*

Returning the diary to the drawer, he then sorted through the pile of papers he had brought home from the bank. He was sifting through them when a shadow fell across the doorway. He glanced up to see Alexis standing there.

'Why are you up so early?' he asked, pushing back the chair, going over to her.

'I missed you.'

He smiled. 'I see you're ready for our morning walk. Let's go.'

He went out into the corridor with her, took a warm jacket out of the cupboard and slipped it on. After kissing her on the cheek, he took hold of her hand and led her outside.

Sebastian's love of the Kentish countryside, especially his own land, drew him outdoors incessantly. He loved to walk along, admiring the huge, luxuriant trees, the flowering bushes, the gardens which Magdalena had designed with such creativity. The views always gave him a thrill. When he was up on high ground, he could admire the landscape spread out before him, a panorama of beauty that could only be found in England.

The Marsh had always intrigued him since the first time he had seen it. It was so full of mystery and old wives' tales about smugglers and booty and the haunted parts where spirits came out after dark. The rising mists early in the evening and the shining sea which looked high in the sky from lower ground only added to the pleasure he derived. What pleased him so much these days was that Alexis seemed to love the farm as much as he did, and appreciated nature and all the wildlife.

At one moment they stopped, and he turned her around to face him. He said, 'I treasure this land of mine . . . my land, our land, yours and mine from now on. It will be the land where our children will grow up, and, one day, it will be theirs when we leave this earthly paradise.'

Staring at him, looking into those cool translucent grey eyes, she choked up, filled with love for him. Longing for the future he spoke about, her emotions flared, rendering her speechless. She could merely nod and hold him tightly in her arms.

TWENTY-FOUR

Georgiana Ward always sent a hansom cab for James when he was going to her house to do paperwork for her. It arrived at exactly three thirty on Sunday afternoon.

It was the same driver as usual; seemingly she had a special arrangement with the man who was to be available whenever he was needed.

James sat back against the leather seat as the horses began to move, his mind focused on Mrs Ward. He had noticed the worried expression in her eyes last night, when she had mentioned selling her shares. It had alerted him to problems. No doubt there was trouble ahead for her, and, unquestionably, it would be trouble with her brother-in-law. She had spoken about him several times and always in a dismayed, even sarcastic tone. James had perceived that there was great dislike between them. But then that was often the case in families when money was involved.

James glanced through the window as they left the High Street and drove towards the city's outskirts. Mrs Ward's house was on the edge of Hull, standing on a small promontory overlooking the North Sea.

He liked her house, which was a small manor in the Georgian style, and he much admired her good taste. She had used lovely clear colours and antiques from the Georgian period. He thought it reflected her talent for creating warm, comfortable rooms.

Within twenty minutes he was alighting from the cab. Moments later Mrs Ward was opening the front door to him, smiling as she ushered him inside the manor house.

The entrance hall smelled faintly of lavender. As she led him towards the library, he relaxed. It was always cool and quiet here; the tranquillity reflected her disposition.

Once they were in the library, she turned to him, indicated a chair, and asked, 'Would you like a glass of lemonade, Mr Falconer? Or something else?'

'Thank you, the lemonade would be nice, Mrs Ward. It's been quite warm today.'

'It has indeed.' Georgiana Ward swung around, moved lightly across the room, her hips swaying slightly. Her dress was a similar blue to the gown she had worn last night; obviously it was her favourite colour. Several strands of aquamarine beads were looped around her long, swan-like neck, matched dangling aquamarine ear clips. Her raven-black hair, upswept, added to the elegance of her appearance. For a moment, he was awestruck, as she moved around, lithely, with a dancer's grace: going to the desk, picking up several notebooks, bringing them to him, then over to a table, pouring the lemonade.

Once she had handed him the glass, she sat down in the chair opposite, and said, 'Thank you for agreeing to come this afternoon. First of all, I trust you implicitly to keep my confidence, and secondly, I trust your judgement about financial matters.'

'Thank you, Mrs Ward, you can indeed trust me to be silent

about what we discuss, but I'm not sure I can advise you on your financial affairs. After all, I've only ever done paperwork for you, paid your bills, and given you totals.'

'That's true. But you can also read between the lines, I think. I would like you to look at these two notebooks, which my husband gave me when he was gravely ill. He told me that if I wanted to sell the shares in his company, which he was leaving to me in his will, I should wait three or four years before doing that. He said the notebooks would guide me.'

James nodded his understanding. 'And do they do that?'

'Yes and no. He valued the shares highly and put down what they would be worth now, not three years ago, when he was on his deathbed. Recently, I told his brother I wanted to sell the shares and quoted Preston's valuation. Ernest, his brother, disagrees, and he will only pay half the amount.'

'I see,' James said, his eyes narrowing, wondering if the brother-in-law was trying to cheat her, whether her late husband had overvalued his shares, or if the shipping company was not doing as well as he had expected. However, he remained silent.

'Look at the book with the small number one on the first page,' Mrs Ward now urged. 'Then the second one.'

He did as she asked, studying the books carefully, reading slowly, and then rereading certain parts of each book yet again. Once he had finished, he placed the two black leather notebooks on a side table and looked across at her.

'I understand what your late husband did, Mrs Ward. The first book explains the founding of the shipping company and its progress over the years, right up to his illness. The second one is a sort of . . . prediction . . . of what it will become and how the shares will grow in value.' James paused, stared at her. 'That's correct, I'm sure you will agree. Your husband is crystal clear in his writing and assessment.'

'That was the way he was, and from what I know of the company today, it has succeeded as he predicted. Unfortunately, my brother-in-law doesn't agree. He says it's not in the black, it's in the red, and that my shares are now worth much less.'

'My advice to you is to hire a good – no, a great – accountant, one who can be trusted, and a solicitor who is also of good repute. They should sort this out for you.'

'But I want you to do it,' she said quite vehemently, staring at him, her blue eyes flashing.

'I would if I could, but I can't. I work for my great-uncle. I have a busy job and responsibilities. I could never devote the amount of time that would be needed to your problem, I believe. Nor am I really qualified. You need seasoned men, honest men with the right attributes—' He broke off, looking at the window, as lightning suddenly flashed.

Mrs Ward's little white dog, asleep near the fireplace, awakened, started barking, and jumped out of the wicker basket.

The dog ran to Mrs Ward. She patted it and exclaimed, 'Calm down, Polka, calm down.' But the dog kept running around her, still barking, obviously excited and alarmed by the noise.

Lightning bolts flashed over and over again, and behind them, thunder rolled through the air, growing louder by the second. Georgiana hurried over to the French doors and looked out. She saw the sky darkening. Turning to James, she cried, 'We're in for a huge thunderstorm! It's coming off the North Sea. Oh dear, I do hope my sea wall will bear up under it.'

'I can't believe this,' James exclaimed. 'It was a lovely sunny afternoon when I arrived. Now look at it.'

Glancing over her shoulder, she told him, 'This is Yorkshire. One minute it's a lovely day, the next a storm blows in and takes over, creating havoc. You'll see, trees and bushes will be blown down and the flowerbeds destroyed. Nothing's safe in its path.'

Before he could stop her, she opened the French doors and stepped outside, the dog running after her.

James jumped up, instantly filled with alarm as he went onto the terrace. Mrs Ward was running down the garden path, heading for the sea wall.

'Come back!' he shouted at the top of his voice. 'Mrs Ward, come back! The rain is starting.'

Even as the words were leaving his mouth, he knew he had said the wrong thing. It was not merely rain but a deluge. And there was a high wind gathering speed that whipped the rain, turned it into a force to be reckoned with. Sheets of rain drenched him.

When he finally reached the sea wall, Georgiana was clinging to it, the little dog wedged between her feet. 'Can you rescue Polka first?' she muttered, her voice almost drowned out by the thunderclaps.

'I can,' James answered. He bent down and grabbed the little dog that was terrified and trembling. He pushed her down inside his coat, which was buttoned tightly. The dog struggled but he managed to secure her safely and quite suddenly she snuggled against his chest and stopped trembling.

He put his arms around Mrs Ward and tried to pull her away from the sea wall. But for a moment she wouldn't let go, until he yelled at her. 'We must leave. The rain is getting heavier. Come on. We will drown out here.'

With one hand she held onto his arm, and finally brought the other around to grab the back of his jacket. Clinging onto each other, they attempted to make it up the path, swaying from side to side, buffeted by the wind which was already becoming a gale. They almost fell several times, but James was strong and he managed to keep them upright until they finally reached the terrace.

Wrenching open the French doors of the library, they staggered inside and collapsed in a heap on the floor. Their clothes were sodden through, dripping water. But they were too exhausted to move and simply lay there trying to breathe normally, thankful they were safe inside the house.

* * *

It took a moment for James to gather his scattered senses. Then, pulling himself together, he opened his jacket and released the struggling dog. It shook itself vigorously, shedding rain, and ran across to the basket near the fire.

Pushing himself up to his feet, James bent over Mrs Ward and carefully helped her into a sitting position. She looked pinched. Her complexion was almost grey and her soaking wet hair fell down dishevelled around her shoulders.

There was a stricken look in her eyes when she gazed back at him. He asked gently, 'Do you think you can stand up?'

She simply nodded and made a great effort as he brought her to her feet. 'We must go to the kitchen,' she said. 'It's the warmest room on this floor.'

James put his arm around her for support and led her across the library, out into the entrance hall, and down a corridor. The little dog came running after them.

'It is better in here,' James said as they went into the spacious kitchen. There was a large fireplace in the hearth, with a range and an oven on each side. Heat permeated the room. As they drew closer to the fireplace, James asked, 'Is it Mrs Mulvaney's day off?' He was referring to the motherly housekeeper who always made him feel welcome.

'Not exactly,' Mrs Ward replied. 'She prefers Thursday. But her daughter is not doing well, after giving birth to another child. She needed to see her today, and I sent my maid Sonya along to help out. Meg, that's Mrs Mulvaney's daughter, lives at the other side of Hull on the Scunthorpe Road. They were due back at six o'clock, but I don't think they'll make it. Not in this raging storm.'

'I agree. So let me help you undo the buttons on the back of your dress, so you can slip out of it. In fact, I must shed my outer clothes as well.'

After unbuttoning the afternoon dress she was wearing, James moved to the other side of the kitchen, turned his back, and took off his suit and his wet shoes. His shirt, underclothes and socks were also wet, but he decided to keep them on for the moment, not wishing to embarrass her.

Hurrying across the kitchen, Mrs Ward announced, 'I'm going upstairs. My brother-in-law always keeps a few things here. Maybe he's left something behind which you can wear until your clothes dry.'

'Thank you.'

Left alone, James went back to the fireplace, stood in front of it, needing the warmth of the flames behind the fireguard. It seemed to him that the pelting rain had gone right through his clothes and into his body. He was still shaking slightly, as he knew Mrs Ward was. Getting themselves warm and dry was an imperative. Neither of them could afford to catch cold, which so often led to bronchitis, and – even worse – pneumonia, such a deadly and often fatal disease in this day and age.

Once he was feeling drier, James took the kettle off the hob, filled it with water and set it back to boil. They needed hot tea with a shot of whisky in it. That was a good cure-all.

Within a few minutes, Mrs Ward returned. She was wearing a thick dressing gown and dry shoes, and was carrying a man's dressing gown made of wool.

'I'm afraid this is the only thing Leonard left behind. He's not as tall as you, but I think it might fit. The room he shares with my sister Deanna is at the top of the stairs. I left the door open. You can change in there, where you'll have more privacy.'

He nodded, strode out, clutching the dressing gown, and ran upstairs. He saw the open door at once and went in, noticed some shirts and trousers laid out on the bed, and knew they were for a smaller man. In the bathroom he was filled with relief as he stripped off his shirt and underwear and put on the dressing gown, which did fit him, although it was a bit short. Shrugging, he went back downstairs to rejoin Mrs Ward, already feeling warmer.

She was huddled in a chair in front of the kitchen fire. He noticed she still looked pale and drawn. 'How about a cup of hot tea?' he suggested.

'Thank you, yes.' She half smiled. 'I noticed you put the kettle on. Mrs Mulvaney keeps whisky in that cabinet over there. I think a drop of it needs to be in the tea. It'll take the chill out of us.'

TWENTY-FIVE

I t was almost six o'clock by the time James and Mrs Ward
sat down in the beautiful upstairs parlour to partake of their
tea, which, in fact, had become a light supper.

Mrs Ward had gone into the pantry off the kitchen and brought
out a pork pie, a veal-and-ham pie, a leg of lamb and a variety
of cheeses. She had cut slices of the pies and meat for each of
them, placed the cheese on a platter with bread and butter, and
then made the tea. James had carried the tray upstairs, and she
had followed with the bottle of whisky and a bowl of food for
the dog that trotted behind her.

The upstairs parlour was everyone's favourite. It was a long,
spacious room with a big fireplace and four windows overlooking
the North Sea. At one end a piano took pride of place; at the
other, there was an antique desk at which Mrs Ward worked
every day. The centre of the room was filled with a huge sofa
and several armchairs grouped in front of the fire. Although the
room was quite large, it still had a sense of cosiness and warmth.
Mrs Ward usually entertained guests in this rather unique parlour,
which was so welcoming.

Now the two of them sat in front of the fire, eating the food and sipping their cups of tea, which James had liberally laced with whisky.

Outside, the storm still raged and the sky was heavy with dark clouds, the sheets of rain slashing hard against the window-panes. They both knew the weather would not change for a long time and that they were in for the night.

At one moment, James said, somewhat hesitantly, 'I don't want you to think I'm prying, but why have you suddenly decided to sell your shares? You don't have to answer that, if you'd prefer not to.'

Mrs Ward shook her head. 'No, no, it's all right. I trust you. I don't like my brother-in-law. To be honest, he's sort of . . . well, he tried to inveigle me into an affair with him. Much to my utter disgust and revulsion. I want to sell out so that I don't have to deal with him in the future. I must put distance between us.'

'I understand, and I'm appalled he would attempt to start something with you. His brother's widow! It's reprehensible.' A look of shock settled on James's face, and he sat back, staring at her in sympathy.

She said, 'I'm going to leave Hull, James. But again, that's between us. I will put this house on the market once I have sold my shares in the shipping company. I intend to move back to London; my entire family lives there. I've been a little lonely here since my husband's death, I must admit.'

'It can be difficult for a woman who is widowed.' He half smiled. 'Widows and single women don't get invited out too much, do they?'

Georgiana smiled. 'Perhaps I do get a few more invitations than others, because I have a number of good women friends. However, I do miss my sisters and the intimacy of being with family. Deanna and Vanessa do visit me, and I also occasionally get to London. Yet I still feel isolated up here in Yorkshire.'

'I shall be going back to London, too,' James volunteered. 'But that's something I'm not discussing with my aunt and uncle at the moment. Promise me you'll keep my secret.'

'Of course I will. But Marina indicated to me that Clarence had really been impressed with you. I hear he wants you to become a permanent member of the family and take a full position in the shipping company.' A black brow lifted and she eyed him, curiosity reflected in her eyes, the colour of pansies.

'It's a wonderful offer, and I told him I'd think about it,' James answered swiftly. 'But I have a plan . . .' He broke off, realizing he was perhaps telling her too much.

'What kind of plan?' she asked eagerly, obviously interested in him.

'I want to work in a different area, not just shipping, but I'd prefer not to discuss it at the moment. I still have to work it out,' he improvised, holding himself back. He was aware she was infatuated with him, and he found himself tempted by her.

'You are very clever, James, and highly intelligent. I know whatever you decide to do with your life you will be successful. You have ambition and self-confidence, which are most important if you want to make it in this rather hard world we live in.'

'That's what my grandmother has always told me. She and my grandfather have encouraged me to work hard and to reach as high as I can.'

Picking up the whisky bottle, he splashed some liquor into her cup and his, and then filled their cups with tea. 'This is the best medicine in the world, on a cold wet night like this.'

'I couldn't agree more.' Georgiana picked up her cup and took a long swallow. 'Oh, that does feel good! It warms the cockles of my heart.'

James laughed, and then glanced across at the windows as bolts of lightning flashed and there was a long roll of thunder. 'I'm afraid Mrs Mulvaney and Sonya won't be able to make it back tonight, Mrs Ward. I hope they haven't tried and been thwarted, and that they've just stayed with Mrs Mulvaney's daughter.'

'I'm sure they have. Mrs Mulvaney is a very practical woman.'

James stood up and strode across to the windows, peering out of one of them. In the distance, he could see many big ships anchored further down the shoreline, moving hard and bobbing about, but obviously well secured. The sea itself was rough and raging, the waves high.

He shivered slightly and turned around to find Mrs Ward walking towards him.

'You're shivering, James,' she said, as she came up to stand next to him. 'You should come back to the fire.'

'Look out of the window, and you'll shiver yourself,' he replied. 'I'm afraid the storm is more powerful than ever, and God knows what's happened to your garden.'

She shook her head. 'It doesn't matter. Everything can be replanted.' Edging closer to him, she went on, 'Can I ask you a personal question, James?'

'Yes.'

'Do you have a lady friend? Some lovely young woman in your life?'

'No, I don't, Mrs Ward.' A smile flickered on his face, suspecting where this situation was leading and liking the idea. 'Why do you ask?'

'Just curious. After all, you are a stunning young man and everyone says young girls drop at your feet.' Her tone had been teasing and she began to laugh.

He chuckled with her. 'They may drop at my feet, but I haven't picked any of them up.'

'And why is that, may I ask?' Her eyes were riveted on him.

'I haven't been attracted to any of them.'

'Oh, really, and why is that? They must have all been pretty from what I hear.'

'I prefer older women.'

'What's older to you?'

'Twenty-seven, twenty-eight, thirty.'

She was silent, stood gazing up at him, her blue eyes fierce with desire.

'You see, I acquired a taste for older women when I was sixteen. My Uncle Harry introduced me to a former girlfriend of his. He thought I ought to know about sex. Her name was Fiona. She was twenty-eight, and very, very good to me.'

'You're seventeen now, aren't you?'

'Yes, eighteen next month. But my grandfather once told me numbers don't matter and that the only age a man should be interested in is on a bottle of wine.'

'I must remember that.' There was a pause. 'I am thirty.'

'I know.'

'Do you find me attractive, rather than those young girls?'

'See for yourself.'

As he spoke, he took off the dressing gown he was wearing and threw it on the floor, then reached for her, untying the belt of her robe. When she stood before him naked, he pulled her closer, bent his head and kissed her on the mouth. A moment later he placed his hands on her back and drew her into him, closer to his body. They clung together.

'Oh, James,' she whispered against his chest.

'What is it? Tell me.'

'I want you. Desperately.'

After a moment he pulled away from her and walked across the floor.

Startled, she stared after him. 'Where are you going?'

'Mrs Mulvaney might get back after all.' He turned the key and locked the door. 'I don't want to be interrupted.'

Georgiana Ward stood waiting for him, watching him walk back to her, thinking what a wonderful specimen of manhood he was. She felt a tiny prickle of fear, knowing he would entrance her and that she would become besotted with him.

TWENTY-SIX

The entire area of Hull and Humberside had been devastated by the gigantic storm, the worst in years. It had hit on Sunday afternoon and finished twenty-four hours later on Monday afternoon, almost to the minute.

The damage was enormous. Private gardens were destroyed. Public parks, woods, and acres and acres of land were ripped apart by its impact. Homes and public buildings crashed and tumbled down. Worse, many people were injured. It was the biggest disaster in decades.

Now, on Wednesday afternoon, James Falconer was inspecting the large Venables warehouse, which housed a considerable amount of goods for export. He was there at the behest of his great-uncle Clarence.

Within only a few minutes, James began to fear that the warehouse could not be repaired. It was a very old building to begin with, and had suffered too much damage from the storm. Half the roof was gone; windows had been smashed and cracks had appeared on all the walls. As he walked back to the huge open door, hanging on its hinges, it occurred to him that it might not be safe for the men even to be inside the warehouse any more. It seemed to him that there was considerable risk involved since the violent storm. Anything might happen which could kill or cripple them.

Joe Turner, the foreman, was standing outside, leaning against a pile of boxes which had recently been removed from the warehouse. He was smoking a cigarette. 'I can see from yer face that yer agree, Mr James. Repairs won't work. In fact, the whole bleedin' thing can topple any minute.' He shook his head, scowling. 'Mr Albert's gor it wrong. Best we can do is get the bloody building emptied out, save summat.'

'I agree with you, Joe,' James answered, and went and sat down near the foreman on another pile of large wooden boxes. 'Mr William is currently trying to find some empty warehouses which we can rent, but he's not been successful so far.'

'He won't be either – there's nowt around,' Joe muttered. 'He might as well ask the vicar if we can store our stuff in the church, all the good he'll do looking to find space. There ain't none.'

James blew out air. 'I know what you mean. The other shipping companies have all had bad hits and are stuck with damaged warehouses . . . we're all in the same position. Let me just think a moment.'

At the back of his mind, something flickered. James tried to grasp onto it, but he couldn't quite reach it. Something he'd seen, a few years ago . . .

Joe said, 'Can I set the men ter work, Mr James? Get goods out quick like. Bricks can come falling down like snowflakes afore yer knows it.'

'Yes, you'd better do that. I suppose the best way we can protect the goods is to cover them with tarpaulins and arrange for a few guards to keep the yard safe.'

'That's it. Macy's allus in the gatehouse; got his eyes peeled at night. Nobody'll tek owt.' Joe dropped his cigarette on the ground, stamped his foot on it, and added, 'Pity the boss didn't tek a look at this bloody old thing six years ago, when t'other warehouse was given a goin' over.'

Six years ago. That was it. The memory jumped back in his mind, and James exclaimed, 'Barns! That's it. Barns, Joe!'

The foreman gaped at him, frowning. 'Wot are yer saying, Mr James? I'm not follering yer.'

'I'm sorry. I realize I'm not making sense to you. I know where there are some barns we could rent and use to store the export goods. That's the solution.'

'Bleedin' barns in Hull? Yer not serious are yer, sir?'

'Not in Hull, no. But in Melton.'

'Melton? Yer don't mean that there little village, do yer? Yer can't be serious; it's miles from 'ere.'

'No, it's not. It's about an hour. And what does that matter, if the goods are safe and protected?'

The foreman took out a cigarette and struck a match, puffed on his Woodbine for a few seconds. After a moment he muttered, 'Mebbe yer've got an idea, Mr James.'

'I know I do. Where else can we store this merchandise, knowing it's safe and not sitting under tarpaulins, getting wet? I just hope nobody got there before me.'

Observing the excitement on James Falconer's face, and knowing how clever he was, Joe suddenly exclaimed, 'Go get the barns, sir. Nobody's had a better idea. The boss'll be 'appy with yer.'

'Any pitfalls to look out for, Joe?' James gave the old-timer a questioning look.

'Be sure the stuff'll be safe, that yer knows ter do. Check out roofs and walls. Mek sure there's no rotting wood, poor locks. Yer don't need me ter tell yer, sir. That's a certainty.'

James shook his hand and hurried out of the yard and up into the street. Within seconds he had hailed a hansom cab and was instructing the driver to head for the village of Melton. When the driver appeared to hesitate, James said, 'I'll make it well worth your while, and you'll be waiting for me, bringing me back. A double fare, a good deal for you.'

'Aye, it is, sir. Off we go then.' The driver flicked the reins, and the horses set off at a quick trot.

Sitting back against the leather seat, James laughed to himself. Six years ago he had come with the entire Falconer clan to stay at the farm in Melton, which was owned by his grandmother's cousin, Colin Fulton. Grove Farm. That was where he had seen the big barns, which were empty because Colin no longer had use for them. They had been used to store farm equipment. Colin did very little farming these days, having sold a large tract of land for a huge amount of money. James now prayed he wasn't too rich that he might refuse to rent out the barns.

As it turned out, Colin Fulton was happy to see James. He came out to greet him as he was alighting from the hansom cab.

'James! Lovely to see you! Esther wrote and told me you were staying with Marina and Clarence, learning the shipping business. What a surprise. Come on in and tell me why you've arrived out of the blue, so to speak.'

After shaking Colin's hand and greeting him with his usual amiability and charm, James followed Colin into the farmhouse.

He noticed at once that it had been spruced up quite a lot, and there were flowers and other touches that suggested a woman's influence.

And at that moment, a woman did appear, and a rather pretty woman at that.

She smiled at James as she walked towards him, and Colin said, 'This is my wife, Arlette, James. Arlette meet James Falconer, my cousin twice removed.' He grinned at James. 'I think that's what we are, isn't it?'

'I just don't know,' James admitted, shaking Arlette's hand, smiling. He took the seat Colin indicated.

Arlette said, 'May we offer you some refreshment? A cup of tea, perhaps?'

'Thank you, that would be nice,' James answered. As Arlette disappeared, James said with his typical gallantry, 'What a lovely woman, congratulations. You're a lucky man indeed.'

Colin preened a little and sat down. 'I am lucky, yes. She came into my life very unexpectedly, two years ago, and we married last year. She's half French, and she's put a new spring in my step.'

James nodded, then said, 'I thought I detected a slight accent. But I meant it, you are lucky to have found her.'

Sitting back, a small, pleased smile shining in his grey eyes, Colin now asked, 'What can I do for you, James?'

'I want to know if you'll rent out your three barns to me.'

'Why on earth do you want to rent my barns, for God's sake?'

'They're not for me personally, Colin, but for Marina's husband, Clarence.' Without wasting any time, James explained everything about the storm and how he had come upon the idea of driving out to Grove Farm only an hour ago, desperate for a solution.

Colin listened carefully, asked a few questions, and then nodded. 'Normally I wouldn't want to bother with all this, but Marina was extremely kind to me when I was ill, after my first wife died. I owe her one, and I do truly understand your predicament. I bet there isn't a warehouse available within a hundred miles of Hull.'

'I think you've just hit the nail on the head.'

'It's a bit out of the way, though, here in Melton, isn't it?'

'No, I got here in forty minutes with the hansom-cab driver going at a medium trot. Anyway, you're family and so this is a safe place. And that's a truly important point, as far as I'm concerned.'

'From the way you told the story, I suspect you haven't spoken to Clarence yet.'

'No, I haven't, but I hope he'll go along with it. No reason why not. Or is there?' James gave him a concerned look.

'None at all. Let's have a nice cup of tea, and then I'll show you the barns. See what you think, and if they'll work for your purpose.'

On the way back to Hull, James was pleased to realize that they made it into the city in thirty minutes. Alighting at the warehouse, he paid off the cab driver, gave him a generous tip, and went down the steps into the yard.

The moment Joe saw him he hurried forward, and exclaimed, 'Glad yer back, sir. A big piece of t'roof fell off, just missed me. I'd been a goner if Ernie hadn't pulled me away just in time.'

Worry filled James's eyes and he shook his head, took hold of Joe's arm and squeezed. 'Thank God you're all right!'

He glanced around and saw that men were still bringing out boxes and crates of merchandise. They were stacking them next to the newer but smaller warehouse, which luckily had not been damaged by the storm.

'What's your assessment, Joe? How long will it take them to empty the big warehouse?'

'A few hours. I asked Benny Baxter, who manages the smaller one, to lend me a few chaps – and he obliged.'

'Can you finish the job before dark?' James raised a brow.

'Bloody well 'ope so, Mr James. That bleedin' thing will topple by then, mark me words.'

'Right! I'm going to see Mr Clarence and bring him here if necessary. Mr Albert's wrong, I'm afraid. This warehouse cannot be repaired.'

'True. And let's 'ope there'll be no weeping widows later on today.'

When James arrived at the Venables shipping company ten minutes later, he bumped into William who had been hovering, waiting for him.

'Hello, James. I'm relieved you're back. Papa is waiting for you. He thinks you've taken rather a long time.'

'I have. Because I took a side trip,' James replied. 'I'll go right to his office now. You'd better come with me to hear what I have to report.'

'He might not like that. I think he wants to see you alone.'

'Have you found any warehouses to rent?' James asked.

'No such luck.' A morose look settled on William's face. 'There isn't such a thing to be found in Hull.'

'Then you must come along.' James strode out of the office, William at his side, and a moment later he was knocking on Clarence's door.

His uncle called out, 'Come in.'

As he did so, James exclaimed, 'Sorry I took a while, Uncle Clarence, but I had to meet someone. More of that in a moment. My assessment is extremely bleak. The warehouse cannot be repaired. In fact, it could fall down at any moment.'

Clarence Venables sat up straighter in his chair, and nodded. 'As I suspected. It is very old, perhaps ninety years old. This is not good news. What to do?'

Before James could answer, another man stepped forward and joined them near his father's desk. It was William's younger brother, Albert. 'It *can* be repaired!' he exclaimed in a sharp tone. 'Rebuilding is not necessary – it's a waste of good money.'

James, who had not seen Albert lurking in the background, swung around to face him. He said in a steady, impartial voice, 'I beg to differ, Albert. There are huge cracks in the walls, pieces of the roof are still falling off, and Joe almost got hit with debris a while ago.'

Turning to look at his uncle, James said, 'That warehouse has to be emptied as quickly as possible. Men are at risk in there. They could be injured, or – worse – killed. We don't want any deaths on our hands, now do we, sir?'

Clarence nodded his understanding. 'You're correct. We must not take any chances.' He glanced at William. 'So what is your opinion? You went there, too?'

'I have to agree with James, Papa. The warehouse should be demolished. We do have to ensure the safety of our men. To do otherwise would be unconscionable.'

'Joe has borrowed a few workers from the smaller warehouse. He has them helping to move out the merchandise as fast as they can,' James volunteered.

'Come and sit down the two of you, and you as well, Albert. Let's talk about the storage of the merchandise.'

'I haven't found any available warehouses in Hull,' William said. 'I might have to go further afield.'

'What about Scunthorpe?' Albert suggested, 'or Grimsby?'

William snapped, 'Grimsby is on the Humber. It's been as damaged as we have. As for Scunthorpe, it's miles away. York might be better, since it's on the River Ouse.'

'That's not such a bad idea, William,' Clarence responded, nodding. 'You're thinking we should use barges on the river to move the merchandise down from York to the ships on the Humber, which flows into the North Sea.'

'That was my thought,' William said.

'Scunthorpe's closer,' Albert announced, throwing his brother an angry stare.

There was a silence.

Clarence sat back in his chair, his hands steepled against his mouth, a thoughtful expression in his eyes. It was obvious he was pondering the situation.

Clearing his throat after a moment, James said, 'I do have a suggestion, Uncle Clarence. I'd like to tell you about it.'

Blinking, placing his hands on the desk, his uncle stared at him. 'I hope it's better than the ones I've just heard, which I don't really believe will work . . . except York. Perhaps.'

'I hope so,' James answered. 'After realizing how bad the condition of the warehouse was, I asked Joe to start moving the merchandise out as fast as possible. Then I took a hansom cab to Melton.'

Clarence frowned. 'Melton! Why ever did you go there?'

'Because I remembered that there were three empty barns at Grove Farm, which belongs to Colin Fulton, as you're well aware. All of the Falconers stayed there six years ago, if you remember. It suddenly occurred to me that Colin might rent out those empty barns to us. We could store the goods there. They would be dry and safe, and not too far away from Hull.'

'Melton is no good to us,' Albert announced, giving James one of his ugly scowls. 'How ridiculous can you get?'

Clarence said, 'Not so ridiculous, actually.' He focused his attention on James. 'How long did it take you to get to Melton this afternoon?'

'Forty minutes going there, sir, and thirty minutes coming back.'

Clarence gave James a small knowing smile, and continued, 'What were the barns like? In good condition, I've no doubt. But the main question is this . . . was Colin willing to rent them to us?'

'He is happy to rent them out, and they are in good condition, all three of them, Uncle. They're bigger than I remembered, and I know they would hold all of our export merchandise, and also our imported goods.'

'How do you propose to get the stuff there?' Albert asked, his voice sarcastic, a smirk lingering on his mouth.

'By large carts, drays. Moving the goods by land doesn't present a problem,' William cut in. 'I trust James's judgement, Pa. But if you wish, I would be happy to go to Melton. It can be done in half an hour, that I know.'

'Melton,' Albert scoffed again. 'What a stupid idea.'

Clarence, irritated with Albert already, said coldly, 'You'd better not let your mother hear you speak about Melton in such a derogatory tone. Much of her family was born and brought up there.'

This comment rendered Albert speechless, and he sat back in his chair, the ugly expression lingering. The other three men ignored him. All of them knew he was not the brightest and that he disliked James Falconer. He was always on the ready to trip him up or humiliate him in some way.

Clarence addressed James. 'Did you actually make a deal with Colin? Come to terms about the barns?'

'No, I didn't. I said I would have to present the idea to you, get your reaction, and that no doubt you yourself would go out to Melton to negotiate with him. He said he looked forward to seeing you.'

'Then I shall do that right now. We have no time to waste. William, you must come with me. James, I want you to go back to the warehouse and work with Joe to empty out that blasted wreck. And keep the men safe. The latter is the most important thing of all. I don't want any dead bodies.'

'Thank you, Uncle Clarence. I take it you will trust my judgement if I think I should pull all the men out at some point, and sacrifice the goods.'

'Certainly! The men come first with me, as well as with you. Life is sacred. I couldn't live with myself if anyone got injured or died.'

'What shall I do, Papa?' Albert asked.

Clarence held his temper, bit back the sarcastic comment at the tip of his tongue. He said in a steady tone, 'I think you should check out the possibility of using barges from York to the Humber, down the River Ouse. You never know, we might have to use that method after all. It's certainly better than focusing on Scunthorpe.'

'I know the manager of the barge company,' Albert said. 'Shall I go and see him then?'

'Yes, do it now,' his father answered and, pushing back his chair, he motioned to James and William. 'Let's go. We've no time to waste. I want this problem settled by tonight, and with all our men standing.'

Twenty-Seven

Alexis smiled to herself as she stared down at her engagement book, realizing it was a busy afternoon ahead. But then it was Wednesday, the day when she managed to pack in a great number of things after one o'clock.

It was 18 April 1888. She had taken three meetings that morning and, very shortly, she would go down to Whitechapel where Haven House was located. Wednesday afternoon was her time to visit the charity, which had been running for nearly a year now.

Claudia usually joined her, and they stayed there for several hours, helping in the kitchen, speaking to the battered women living there, and going over matters with Madeleine Thompson, the manager they had hired.

Looking at the date, it struck her that Claudia's wedding was only weeks away now. She was to marry Cornelius Glendenning in early June, and it would take place at Sebastian's great stately home, Courtland Priory, which had been in the Trevalian family for several centuries.

It was a beautiful old house, and Sebastian had ensured it

was well kept and well run. He had an efficient staff that followed all of his rules precisely.

The first time he had taken her there, he had made her laugh a great deal, comparing Courtland to the old farmhouse, Goldenhurst, in Kent. It was true they were very different indeed.

Although he kept telling her he enjoyed being at the farm more than at Courtland, she knew that deep down he loved his stately home as much as Goldenhurst. They were very different, that was obvious, but he truly enjoyed living different lives, whatever he said. And she enjoyed sharing them with him.

She glanced at the small clock on her desk and realized she must set off for Whitechapel. Closing the engagement book, she rose and went to the cupboard, took out a dark green wool jacket, which matched her ankle-length skirt. Turning, she glanced at herself in the mirror, fluffed out the jabot of her white silk skirt. She picked up her handbag, her gloves and left her office.

Outside their office building on Piccadilly, her carriage was waiting. Her driver Josh spotted her as she came through the door, and he jumped down from his seat to greet her.

Within minutes she was sitting back, many thoughts rolling around in her head as she travelled through the centre of London. The traffic was heavy, filled with horse-drawn buses, carts and carriages. The pavement was crowded with people rushing about their business. It seemed to her that there was a great sense of urgency everywhere as determined pedestrians traversed the streets and all types of vehicles jammed the roads. Was it busier than ever today? Or was it her imagination?

Attempting to relax, she let her mind wander to her own wedding, which would be in September. She had suggested that month to Sebastian and he had seized on it. She knew he would hold her to it and she wanted him to. It was the right time for them to marry, following in Claudia's footsteps rather than ahead of her and Cornelius.

By the time they had reached the High Street in Whitechapel,

Alexis was completely settled down, her mind calm. She smoothed her dark green jacket, knowing she was nicely dressed but understated. That was one of her rules for Haven House. Delia, Vera, Claudia and herself must always be simply dressed in order not to offend the women.

Claudia was already there, sitting in the office with Madeleine Thompson. Both women jumped up when she entered and came to greet her warmly.

A moment later they were seated, the door closed, discussing the business of the charity. Alexis had good news for them. The funds which Sebastian had invested for Alexis last year had doubled in value and would continue to grow.

'So you don't have to worry about buying medicines, food, and any other small daily requirements the women need,' Alexis finished. 'But I'm still going to cadge lots of things from my friends, and you must too, Claudia.'

Her dearest friend nodded and opened her handbag. 'My future mother-in-law has given me a cheque,' she said with a big smile. She handed it to Alexis. 'Not only that, she's promised to keep any unwanted bed linen and towels for us, rather than throwing them away.'

'How lovely of her,' Alexis said.

Claudia beamed. 'I like her a lot. She's a very nice woman and, of course, she's thrilled Connie is marrying me.'

Madeleine Thompson laughed, and so did Alexis, who then changed the subject and asked, 'How many women are staying here this week, Madeleine? It sounds a bit quiet out there in the communal rooms.'

'We're not as full as usual, Alexis, but that doesn't necessarily mean there's been a drop in marital abuse. Perhaps some women haven't found the courage to come here yet.'

'I understand. However, my father says some of the stallholders at the Malvern Market think the more brutal men are trying to hold themselves in check.'

'Oh, I do hope so,' Claudia exclaimed. 'Will there ever be a day when we can actually close down Haven House? Because of a shortage of women in need?'

'I doubt it,' Madeleine answered, suddenly looking dour. 'There will always be brutes around. Some men might change but not all of them. Now, shall we go over the books for the week? It won't take long; everything's in order.'

Once they had done this, they went out of the office and made their way to the kitchen. The three women, Mavis, Gladys and Doreen, who lived in Haven House and worked there, greeted them cheerfully. Within seconds they were bringing out cakes and jam roll from the pantry, and making a large pot of tea.

Alexis and Claudia enjoyed this part of the visit to Haven House. They got to chat amiably to Mavis, Gladys and Doreen in the kitchen, and share moments of female bonhomie with them.

Claudia knew that it was Alexis who set this wonderful, friendly tone; who made the women feel good, and equal to them. She genuinely admired her friend for doing this. Her quips, her laughter, her small confidences kept the women laughing and listening.

What a gift Alexis has for making everyone feel as if they are the most important person in the world to her, Claudia thought. She smiled to herself, thinking what a wonderful stepmother Alexis was going to be . . . probably like no other in the world.

Later on, when they had talked to some of the new arrivals, both Claudia and Alexis were glad they had come this afternoon. They generally did experience this same sense of happiness that they had given safety and security – and brought hope – to these helpless, battered women.

As she always did, Alexis had dismissed her driver Josh, and she went back to Mayfair with Claudia, sharing her carriage. She was having dinner with Sebastian.

The women chatted about the visit and shared their thoughts

about the success of Haven House. They were encouraged to keep it a financially stable charity. It meant a lot to both of them that they could give back something to women less fortunate than they were.

After that they spoke about the next fitting for Claudia's wedding gown and those for her two sisters Lavinia and Marietta. Claudia had begged Alexis to be the third bridesmaid, but she had declined. Sebastian had backed her in this decision.

A silence fell between them for a short while, and then suddenly Claudia took hold of Alexis's hand, and lowered her voice. 'I want you to do something for me,' she whispered.

'What is it?' Alexis asked, also in a low voice.

Claudia told her, and instantly Alexis froze in her seat.

After a moment, she said, 'No. No, that's not possible. I can't . . .'

A chill swept through her and goosebumps flew up her arms. Someone just walked over my grave, she thought, remembering an old wives' saying. She pushed it away, considering it silly. But the chill stayed within her and she was filled with a strange sense of foreboding.

PART FOUR

The Road To Destiny
Hull/London
1888

TWENTY-EIGHT

Marina Venables sat at the end of her garden, staring out at the North Sea. It was a sunny afternoon in the middle of May and the sea was glorious, almost as smooth as a lake. The deepest of blues were flecked with crests of white.

She was in the middle of a painting of the sea and still held the paintbrush in her hand. She put it down on the palette and sat back in her chair.

Her great-nephew, James Falconer, had entered her head, and she was thinking about him. After the great storm he had managed the collapse of the warehouse, and she was secretly rather awed by how he had led and handled the men. He had saved all of their lives.

Just imagine, she thought, if he hadn't gone outside to take off his jacket and roll up his sleeves and then walked back to the warehouse. He wouldn't have seen that slight movement just under the roof. The men inside, and James himself, would have been killed, buried under bricks and mortar. But he had gone out and he had noticed the imperceptible shift, rushed back inside, yelling at the men to run for it. He had herded them out just in time. James and the crew had stood there, dumbstruck, watching the warehouse slowly move, sway and collapse in front of their eyes.

She was well aware that the men who worked with him liked and respected him. Now he was their hero, and she wasn't a bit surprised.

No wonder Albert was full of hatred for him, but then her youngest son had been mean, jealous and filled with envy since his childhood. William, his brother, could attest to that.

Marina had tried to love her youngest son, but he was so vengeful and unpleasant she now held him at a distance. She had tried her hardest when he was growing up, but never felt close to him.

Her happiest moment had been when he married Anne and moved out. Anne: a lovely young woman who appeared to dote on Albert. Marina had once mentioned their marriage to Georgiana Ward, wondered out loud why it worked. Georgiana had lifted a brow knowingly and laughed. She had said that the rumour was Albert was an artful lover, knew how to please a woman. Sex, she thought. It's always about sex.

Marina sighed, asking herself how she was going to warn James about Albert without causing any embarrassment to him. At the back of her mind, she heard her older sister Esther's voice telling her, when she was ten, that she must always tell the truth. Nothing less would do.

That thought stayed with her when James came walking down the garden path, as handsome and well dressed as always on this Saturday afternoon.

'Here I am, Aunt Marina, right on time,' James said, smiling, walking over to the sea wall and sitting down to face her. 'I hope you've enjoyed painting today. The weather's wonderful, isn't it?'

'It is, James, and I am painting a seascape. Actually, it's for you, because I know how much you've enjoyed everything about the sea: living on the seafront, here in the house, and travelling on the ships when you went to Le Havre with your uncle and William recently.'

'What a wonderful surprise! Thank you so much. How thoughtful of you.'

'I don't want you to forget us,' Marina murmured, looking across at him, her expression loving. 'You won't, will you?'

'Of course not! How could I? You've been so welcoming, kind, and loving to me. But I'm not leaving for some time yet. Unless you're suddenly pushing me out.' He frowned. 'You're not, are you?'

She began to laugh and shook her head. 'No. You can stay as long as you wish. Forever, if you want. That would certainly make Clarence and me happy. He was so sad when you said you couldn't accept his offer.'

'Yes, I know. I explained all my reasons, and he was very understanding, if very disappointed.'

'He told me, and my sister told me about some of your plans made long ago. Esther was very honest with me.'

'Yes, I know.' He cleared his throat. After a moment, he said, 'You had something you needed to talk to me about, Great-Aunt. You mentioned that this morning.'

'Yes, I do.' Marina moved to sit down next to James on the sea wall. 'It's about Albert. He is my son, but I see him through very clear eyes. I always have, since he was a child. He is mean and vengeful, and not a very nice person at all. I've always known it, and I tried hard to encourage him to change when he was growing up. But he didn't listen. I suppose character is bred in the bone. There's nothing I can do with him and his life. However, I do know he has decided that he is your enemy, and surely you know that.'

'Yes, I do, and thankfully, I don't have to see too much of him, Aunt Marina, although he was under our feet last month after the storm.' There was a pause. James turned, sat staring directly at her, his blue eyes piercing. 'What are you getting at?'

'I want to alert you that he has started a rumour about you . . .' She paused, wondering how to continue tactfully. It was a delicate matter.

'Exactly what is he saying about me?' James asked quietly.

'That you are involved . . . in a relationship with . . . Mrs Ward.' There, it was out. She held her breath.

James said in a cool, even tone, 'That's not true. I am friendly with her, as you know. I've been doing a bit of bookkeeping for her at Uncle Clarence's request, and have visited her at her home. But that's all there is to it, Aunt Marina. He's invented this.'

'So you're not having an affair with her?'

Without any hesitation James said, 'No, I am not. And how do I stop Albert from impugning a decent woman's character, ruining her reputation?'

'I don't think you can do much,' Marina replied, filled with relief that she had brought this matter to his attention. 'I suppose you have to rise above it, ignore it.'

'You're correct. However, perhaps you ought to alert Mrs Ward. I think perhaps she should know, too, don't you? She must protect her reputation.'

'I agree. Still, I don't think she can do much to curtail Albert's chatter either.'

James let out a long sigh, knowing his aunt was correct. After a moment he went on. 'I suggested to Mrs Ward a while ago that she come to see you and Uncle Clarence about her need for an accountant and a solicitor. It was regarding selling her shares in her late husband's company. I haven't seen her lately. Did she visit you? Were you able to help her?'

'Indeed we were. Or rather, Clarence was,' Marina answered. 'And she is in good hands. In fact, it is my understanding that they are making excellent progress.'

'At least she will have her financial affairs in order,' James murmured. He reached out and took hold of his aunt's hand. 'Thank you for alerting me, telling me about Albert's venomous lies. I suppose I will just have to . . . rise above it, as you suggest.' A brow lifted quizzically. He gave her a wry smile. 'I don't think I have any alternative.'

TWENTY-NINE

Later that day, as he dressed for the family supper, James's thoughts remained on Albert Venables. How could that vengeful being have found out about his affair with Georgiana Ward? Because that was what it had become. He had been seeing her constantly, in secret, mostly late at night, ever since the storm had thrown them together.

The family knew he did paperwork and kept her books once a week, on Thursday evenings. So perhaps Albert was blowing that out of proportion. Maybe he didn't know anything more than that.

Unless someone else knew and had told him. But who? Mrs Mulvaney, the housekeeper? He didn't think so. She was devoted to Mrs Ward and had worked for her for twelve years, since her marriage to Preston Ward.

Besides, he often came and went late at night when the housekeeper was in bed fast asleep. This aside, she was not only genuinely loyal and caring of her employer, but also desperately needed the job because of her ailing daughter.

Sonya, the maid? He was also certain of her devotion to Mrs

Ward, who had taken her in when she had found her as a child, starving on the streets. Mrs Ward had discovered her sleeping near the dustbins on the outside steps of the cellar at her town-house in London. The Wards had taken her in, taken care of her, and Mrs Mulvaney had trained her to be a lady's maid. She had been with Mrs Ward for ten years. Anyway, like Mrs Mulvaney, Sonya adored Georgiana. She also was in bed asleep when he visited his paramour.

As he slipped on his waistcoat and began to button it, James decided it could only be one of two things. Either Albert was making a clever guess based on the Thursday visits, or he had hired a private detective to follow him. Or maybe Albert himself was tracking him. He immediately dismissed that idea. Albert lived on the other side of Hull, and he was a married man. How would he explain his many absences late at night to Anne, his wife?

He didn't have to, of course. Husbands came and went as they pleased, whatever time it was.

His aunt had actually taken him by surprise this afternoon, because he had not heard the rumours about his being involved with Mrs Ward. Instantly, his grandmother's training had kicked in. He was not born a gentleman, but she had turned him into one, to such an extent that the gentlemanly attributes of an aristocrat were bred in the bone.

So he answered Aunt Marina as a gentleman would. He lied to protect a decent woman's name and reputation, her position in society in Hull. And also in London, for that matter. Gossip travelled as fast as a telegram these days, especially if it were salacious.

He wondered if Georgiana had heard the rumours. Perhaps not. But one thing was imperative. She had to be told. Forewarned. And immediately. It couldn't be tonight. There was the family supper at six o'clock, and afterwards he and William were going to a music hall and later to Restaurant Tamara for a late-night snack. They were both partial to the Russian dishes served there. He could not disrupt these plans. It would look suspicious.

I'll go tomorrow in broad daylight, James thought, and then thought again. Perhaps he ought not to be seen going to her house. At least not alone. William. He would ask William to accompany him and give the reason. He wished to inform Mrs Ward that Albert was spreading untrue rumours about them.

There was a light tap at James's bedroom door, and William put his head around it. 'Do you have a minute, James?' he asked.

'I do indeed. Actually, I was just thinking about you, hoping you would do me a favour.'

'You know I will. Anything you wish me to do. But first, I must ask you if Mama was speaking to you about Albert and the lies he's telling about you to anyone who will listen?'

James nodded. 'She was, and I told her that it was not true. I'm not having a relationship with her friend. As you yourself pointed out weeks ago, why would I? She is an older woman, far too old for me.'

'Exactly! She's thirty. James, that's twelve years older than you – you're not eighteen till the end of May, are you? What about all those pretty young things who flock around you at the dances and parties? You can take your pick.'

'I know. Albert must really harbour a deep hatred for me to do such a thing,' James said in a low, even tone. 'It's vile.'

'It's his character, his nature. He was rotten to me when he was growing up. Jealous. Just as he's jealous of you now. More so, since the collapse of the warehouse. You're a hero to the men, James. One of them heard the rumours and vowed to me that he would attack Albert, turn him into pulp. But I managed to persuade him he might just go a bit too far and kill him by mistake, and that Albert wasn't worth swinging for.'

James nodded, and asked swiftly, 'I hope it wasn't Joe.'

William half laughed. 'Oh no, Joe had murderous intent on

his mind, that is the truth. I talked him out of it and took the carving knife he had in his sack.'

James was genuinely taken aback, and said slowly, 'They care that much about me?' He sounded slightly surprised and puzzled.

'Don't be daft, of course they do. You are their hero . . . Think about it. You saved their lives as well as your own. You prevented their wives from becoming widows.'

James sighed and reached for his jacket. 'I asked your mother what I should do, and she didn't really have an answer. She said I should ignore it, rise above it.'

'I think that is the best.'

'Perhaps I should go and confront Albert. Take him to task. Threaten him with legal action, although I'm not sure about the law in this kind of thing. But surely spreading untrue stories, lying about people, is libellous, isn't it?'

'I don't know, but I could ask our solicitor. In the meantime, don't go near him, please, James. He's nasty. He'll go for you. He's very pugilistically inclined.'

Esther's words rushed into his mind. How often had she told him not to get into any fights for innumerable reasons – not least to protect his looks? So he said quietly, 'I will take your advice, and your mother's: you know Albert better than I do.'

'Take it from me, he's very vindictive. So let's move on. You said a moment ago that you need a favour. What is it?'

'Ah yes, William. Would you accompany me to the home of Mrs Ward tomorrow morning? After church at around eleven. I think I must do her the courtesy of informing her about the lies Albert is passing around – the rumour that we're having an affair. She has a right to know and to protect herself.'

'Very gentlemanly of you, and I agree with you. Anyway, I think it is better to have someone with you. In fact, you shouldn't go there alone ever again. Are you sure my mother shouldn't tell her?'

'No, thank you,' James said, 'I must go.' He had to get to Georgiana before anyone else did, to ensure that she didn't admit to anything.

They went downstairs together and found Marina sitting in the drawing room waiting for them. It was just the four of them for supper tonight. Although everyone in the city had been stoical, hardworking, and had set out to put Hull back together after the devastation of the storm, many of the ship-owners had cut down on their major entertaining and social life for the moment, believing it unseemly.

'So where are you two young blades going after supper?' Marina asked, smiling at her son and great-nephew, thinking how stylish they looked.

'To the musical hall first,' William answered, kissing his mother's cheek, sitting down next to her on the sofa.

James followed suit, kissing her and then taking the chair opposite. 'Later we're going to have a late-night bite at the Restaurant Tamara. We really like it,' he explained.

'I've never been there. Perhaps your father and I will try it, join you one night. What is the food? All Russian?'

'No, no, it's not,' James answered. 'And it's very good. The restaurant is owned by a young couple, Mr and Mrs Paul Daley. They make a mixture of items. Sometimes fish and chips, just to remind everyone they're in a Yorkshire restaurant, but they also like to cater to foreign customers—'

'You would love the caviar and blinis,' William cut in. 'They're my own favourite, actually. James goes for their borscht, a beet soup with a blob of cream in the centre. They also have French items, such as quiche Lorraine and croque monsieur.'

'Quite a selection. You're making my mouth water. I can't wait to go—' Marina broke off abruptly when Clarence came walking into the room rather briskly. She knew at once that he had heard the rumours. He had a face like thunder.

After greeting them cordially, he looked hard at his wife and said, 'Why didn't you tell me about those ridiculous tales Albert is spreading? I can't believe, not for one second, you were endeavouring to protect that idiot.'

'No, I wasn't, Clarence. I only just heard them myself a couple of days ago. Frankly, you've had such a busy time this week; I didn't want to worry you. I was going to tell you tonight.'

'I see,' he said, somewhat sharply for him. He looked across at his son, and then at James. 'You two know, I suspect.'

'Mother talked to me about it this morning and she told James this afternoon,' William replied.

'He's got to be stopped. Once and for all.' Leaning forward, Clarence focused on James. 'He's not going to get away with it. I can assure you of that. He has to be taught that he can't malign people, lie about them. I am going to see him on Monday morning first thing. He's going to get a piece of my mind.'

James said, 'Thank you, Great-Uncle Clarence. My main concern is that he is trying to damage the reputation of a decent woman.'

Marina said swiftly, 'I do hope he listens to you, Clarence. You know what he's like: stubborn and opinionated.'

'Oh, he'll listen all right,' Clarence said in a hard tone. 'I will inform him that if he ever repeats these lies about James and Georgiana Ward again, he will leave my employment. I shall give him the sack. He can go out into the world and fend for himself. No son of mine is going to remain in my employ when he spreads untrue and wicked tales about a respectable woman, and people we care about.'

'Don't be surprised if he doesn't listen,' Marina said again, in a warning voice, knowing how dumb Albert was. 'He's so full of himself; he'll believe he can get another job quite easily because he's called Venables.'

'He might just be foolish enough to think that. However, I don't believe he will like being disinherited, which I aim to do if he doesn't toe the line. And at once.'

'Would you really do that, Papa?' William asked, taken aback.

'Of course, I would, William! No son of mine is going to get away with being a liar. He's also lazy and makes bad business decisions. Frankly, I wouldn't miss him at all. Good riddance to bad rubbish.'

There was a stunned silence in the room, and Marina broke it when she looked at her husband, and asked, 'I couldn't help wondering this afternoon if there were any legal steps James could take? Are Albert's lies considered libellous?'

'Not sure. English libel laws are a bit strange. I could ask our solicitor, but frankly I can't be bothered at the moment. Albert goes; he's out of my will if he doesn't stop spreading these stories. I shall make sure he really does understand that. And now that you've mentioned the law, I shall have Ian McDonald in my office as my witness on Monday. I can assure you, Albert won't like seeing my solicitor present.'

Marina nodded, filling with relief. 'Ian's presence will have the right effect. Albert always has been a little intimidated by Ian – frightened of him, actually.'

Clarence nodded and stood, helped Marina up off the sofa. 'Let's go in for supper, shall we? Let's obliterate Albert and this unpleasant subject from our minds. I want to enjoy our family Saturday evening before you two go off to paint the town red.'

Hull had soon gone back to being a City of Gaiety, once all the debris from the great storm had been removed. Parts of the town had been swiftly rebuilt.

It was a lovely May evening when James and William walked down the High Street after supper, making for the city centre.

As usual it was full of people: groups of men, mixed couples, others walking alone. A colourful mingling of locals and visitors. Hull had catered to the Baltic countries since the early 1700s, when shipping was big business and at the forefront, as it was today. This great northern seaport was always filled with ships moored along the shoreline. Many of them were anchored at the edge of the gardens, outside the homes of their owners on the High Street.

All manner of goods were still traded, exports and imports; many foreign languages mingled with English. It was a grand mix.

James enjoyed being in the middle of the city where the theatres, music halls, shops and restaurants were located. He felt elated to be among the madding crowd, hearing different tongues, seeing interesting faces and unique clothing that often told him whence the wearers came. He had come to understand that he enjoyed the cosmopolitan atmosphere, which gave him a boost, made him feel alive.

Making their way into the Restaurant Tamara, after they had seen the acts at the music hall, James realized that it was an international crowd eating here. Foreign voices lifted into the air, along with the local Yorkshire dialect.

Once they had ordered their food, William glanced around and exclaimed, 'Oh, look over there, James. The Daleys have hired a trio. That's something new.'

'It is, yes, and I rather like it,' James answered, noticing that the three men were dressed in Russian clothes, wearing high-necked white silk shirts with full sleeves, baggy black pants sashed in red silk at the waist. He recognized one of the instruments. It was the balalaika, which sounded like a mandolin. The two other men were each playing violins. 'It makes for a jolly mood,' James said. 'I think they're a clever couple, inventive. The Tamara will soon grow in popularity.'

'Yes, you're right.' William took a sip of water and cleared his throat, and said in a low voice, 'I want you to understand my father means what he says. He'll cut Albert off without a penny and not think twice about it. You see, neither of my parents likes Albert.'

'That doesn't surprise me. He's obviously an irritation. Certainly he brings everything on himself. He can't blame anyone else.'

'Too true. He's not like us at all.'

'So I've noticed. I think the whole world has noticed,' James murmured. 'He bumbles around like he's half asleep or half drunk most of the time.'

William chuckled, and suddenly confided, 'I was once dozing in the library. I must have been about fourteen at the time. Your grandmother Esther came in with my mother. They didn't notice me, because I was in a big wing chair and they went and sat on the sofa. Just like sisters do, they were gossiping about family. I heard my mother say something like, "God knows where Albert came from, Esther. I don't. And I swear to you Clarence is his father."'

'Esther said, "He looks like a Venables. In fact, he resembles his father, even if he doesn't have his father's wit and wisdom."

'Then Esther remarked that she wondered where you came from because you looked like a Falconer but were far too superior to really be one. My mother told her you were like a golden boy arrived from another planet. And they laughed and started speaking about something else. I had to stay put for ages until they finally left.'

James chuckled, 'That must have been a trial for you, because you're very restless at times. And I do realize your father means what he says. That's one of the reasons he's a brilliant businessman.'

Their supper was served. As they ate the finely cooked food, they chatted about the barns out at Melton and how cooperative Colin had been, and touched on a variety of other things.

At one moment, William paused, looked directly at James, and asked, 'What are you planning on saying to Mrs Ward tomorrow?'

James looked reflective. 'I think I must repeat exactly what your mother told me.'

'Will you tell her my father is going to deal with Albert?'

'Perhaps I should, don't you think? To put her mind at ease.'

William nodded, and they both turned to listen to the band once more.

THIRTY

As they stood together on the doorstep of Mrs Ward's lovely old manor house, waiting for their knocking to be answered, James and William eyed each other nervously. They were both slightly apprehensive about meeting with her.

A moment later the door was opened by Mrs Mulvaney. The housekeeper greeted them warmly and with her usual politeness. 'Good morning, Mr Falconer, Mr Venables.'

James said, 'Mrs Ward is not expecting us, Mrs Mulvaney, so I hope she is available. We do have to speak to her about something rather urgently. It is quite important.'

'I'm sure she will be happy to receive you both,' Mrs Mulvaney replied, opening the door wider, bringing them into the entrance hall.

'Excuse me for a moment. I shall go and let her know you are here.'

This wasn't necessary, because Georgiana Ward had heard their voices and was coming out of the library into the hall, a ready smile on her face.

'James, William, good morning! How nice to see you both.'

As she walked towards them, James couldn't help thinking how lovely she looked. She was simply dressed in a white blouse with a high neckline, puffy mutton-chop shoulders and long, tight sleeves. It was worn with a long burgundy skirt cinched at the waist with a black belt. Her raven hair was upswept, her violet eyes sparkling.

He stepped forward, took her hand, 'Good morning. I'm sorry we've arrived unexpectedly, but we have an important matter to discuss with you.'

'That is absolutely fine,' she answered. She turned to William and shook his outstretched hand. He, too, greeted her warmly. There was an expression of surprise and admiration in his eyes. She looked younger than her age, he thought.

Mrs Mulvaney, hovering behind Mrs Ward, now asked, 'Should I serve refreshments, madam? Tea or coffee? Or something cold, like lemonade?'

'Which would you prefer, William? James?' Mrs Ward glanced at them in turn.

They both said that they would enjoy coffee and Mrs Mulvaney disappeared into the kitchen.

Once they entered the library, Mrs Ward took a seat near the fire and beckoned for the two young men to join her. 'The month of May it might be, but these old manors are always so cold, as you well know, William.'

William nodded. 'My mother has all the fires blazing the year round. It's the wind coming off the North Sea, you know. It whistles through the houses.'

She merely smiled at this comment, and then addressed them both when she asked, 'What is this matter you wish to discuss with me?'

James hesitated. 'It's a little delicate. My great-aunt Marina informed me yesterday afternoon that Albert is spreading stories about us. He's telling people we are . . . having an affair. Naturally,

I was shocked when Aunt Marina told me this – appalled, actually, that he would lie in such a terrible way. I vehemently denied his accusation and told my aunt he was not only smearing my name, but – much worse – impugning your good reputation.'

James realized immediately that she had not heard the rumours and that she was genuinely shocked, as she stared back at him aghast. Her eyes flicked to William and back to James. 'Why would Albert lie about you and me? And how do we stop these false stories?'

'I asked my aunt the same thing. She suggested I ignore them, rise above it all. William has said the same thing to me and advised me not to go near Albert, who enjoys physical fights.'

Georgiana was even more startled, and she gaped at William, her face serious. 'How horrendous this is. Does your father know?'

'He does indeed, Mrs Ward. He's just heard the rumours and brought the matter up before supper last evening. He is going to deal with Albert very severely.'

'Oh, I do hope so. I cannot have my reputation tainted.' She frowned, held herself perfectly still, digesting everything that had been said. She had known instantly that James had been the perfect gentleman, had lied to protect her. Because mud stuck. But how would Clarence be able to kill the stories? That was her sudden worry.

Looking directly at William, she asked quietly, 'I am relieved to know your father will chastise your brother, but that doesn't necessarily mean he'll stop his lying chatter, does it?'

'Normally I would agree, Mrs Ward,' William replied swiftly, realizing she needed reassurance. 'Because we all know how incorrigible Albert is. However, my father told us he would threaten to disinherit him, if he didn't stop maligning you and James. It's really about James, you know. Albert is jealous and envious of him. Even more so now than before.'

'I understand. Because James saved the men, behaved with

such valour, and—' She stopped speaking when Mrs Mulvaney entered the library, carrying a tray. After serving coffee to Mrs Ward and the two young men, she departed.

They sipped their coffee and there was a short silence. This was eventually broken by Mrs Ward, when she remarked, 'Your father is a brilliant man. If anyone can put the fear of God into Albert, it is Clarence. I do hope he succeeds, not only for me but also for James, too, who is having such a success in business here. In a certain sense, it would affect me less, now that I think about it.'

'What do you mean?' William stared at her, amazed at her calmness. 'Albert's lies do indeed affect you.'

'Perhaps they would, if I continued to live in Hull, but, as a matter of fact, I have been planning to leave. And for some time now. When I mentioned to James that I wanted to sell the shares my husband left me, he suggested I go to your parents to ask them if they could recommend a good accountant and solicitor. Of course, they did. Your father introduced me to the two men who work with him.'

She sat back in her chair, and finished, 'They now represent me and my interests, and all my business matters are in their capable hands.'

William nodded. 'They will certainly do well by you, Mrs Ward.' Glancing over at James, he remarked, 'You did Mrs Ward a really good turn when you sent her to my parents. Good show, James.'

'Has your brother-in-law bought the shares your husband left you?' James asked, hoping her new representatives had made a good deal for her.

'A negotiation is ongoing at the moment. I am sure that matters will be settled to my satisfaction. Ian McDonald is my new solicitor, and he will also handle the sale of the house.'

'So you don't intend to remain in Hull?' William interjected, sounding surprised.

'No, I don't. My family is in London, and I want to be near them. Originally, I was planning to visit them in June, for Ascot. However, I had a letter only yesterday from my brother-in-law, Leonard, who is married to my sister, Deanna. She has not been well. He asked me if I could come to London sooner.'

'When are you leaving?' James asked.

'Before you both arrived, I was looking at my engagement book for the next week. I don't seem to have anything special coming up. So, I'm hoping to leave this weekend.'

'Never to come back,' William murmured. 'We shall all miss you, Mrs Ward, especially my mother. Does she know you are leaving?'

Georgiana inclined her head. 'Some time ago I told her I was planning to be in London in June, because of the races at Ascot and the Summer Season. Obviously, she doesn't know my plans have suddenly changed today, because of Leonard's letter.'

'Nevertheless, Albert does have to be stopped,' James announced in a firm voice. 'He has maligned us both with his lies. He must be taught a strong lesson. His lying tongue can ruin other lives, and he's a menace.'

William looked at his friend and nodded. 'True. Albert's got away with many bad things over the years.'

Georgiana Ward was silent for a few moments, thinking of her friend, Professor Allan Miller, who was an expert on mental illness. She leaned forward slightly, told them, 'It is possible that Albert will never change. I have a friend who is an expert in the area of lunatics and the mentally infirm, and he has told me some of his theories from time to time. He may have no sense of remorse about what he does; not feel any empathy for other people. Don't you think Albert is like that?'

This question was addressed to William, and he was fast to answer. 'I do indeed! He has to be stopped before he does something even worse than tell lies.'

'That's right,' James remarked, looking from William to Mrs

Ward. 'Clarence will deal with him with great firmness; I've no doubt about that.' Now he smiled at Mrs Ward and, changing the subject, he said, 'I agree with William. Everyone will miss you and your lovely company at all the suppers, dances and balls. Hull society won't be the same without you.'

'What lovely compliments you are both paying me. I am very flattered,' Georgiana answered. Her eyes rested for a moment on James. Her life would not be the same either.

Thirty-One

Clarence, Marina, William and James sat at the best table in the Tamara. The four of them had arrived together to celebrate James's eighteenth birthday.

His birthday was actually on Sunday 27 May, three days away, and he would be spending it in London with the Falconer clan, as he called them. He was excited about the trip home.

But the Venables were family, too. They had wanted to do something memorable for this unique young man who had proved so loyal and hardworking since his arrival seven months ago.

Clarence was a jolly and hospitable host, and he insisted on ordering a bottle of champagne and caviar when they first arrived at the Tamara so that they could toast James in the best way. After this, Clarence and Marina settled down to enjoy the spirited atmosphere, the cheery sound of laughter and enjoyment, and the unusual mixture of people this young restaurant attracted. In many ways, it was a revelation to them.

William was secretly sad to see his young cousin leave. He had suggested they buy him a gift which would convey their appreciation. After much discussion, they had agreed to give him a pair of gold cufflinks, perfect for a young man of style and elegance as he was.

They were gratified by the look of pleasure on his face when he opened the gift-wrapped package and saw them.

When James noticed the musicians entering the room and going over to their designated corner spot, he was immediately excited, and exclaimed, 'Aunt Marina, you love music, so do pay attention to the balalaika, that odd-looking instrument. It sounds like a mandolin. I love it.'

Marina smiled and nodded, and then glanced at William. 'What dishes do you recommend? I know it's your favourite place.'

'It is, and James's, too. He likes the borscht, the beetroot soup, and also chicken Kiev – that's rolled chicken, fried, I think. When you cut into it, butter flows out. But there're a number of local dishes as well. Let's ask for menus.'

These were brought to them at once. After studying it, Clarence said, 'I've decided to have the soup that James enjoys and the chicken you recommend, William.'

Marina discussed certain dishes with James, taking her time, and eventually they had all chosen and ordered. They sat back to relax and finish the champagne. Clarence studied the wine list, focusing on red.

At one moment, Marina leant forwards and said quietly to James and William, 'I'm glad Mrs Ward wrote notes to you both before she left last week. I know she was very appreciative that you had gone to explain things to her. She's such a nice woman, and I certainly hope her sister Deanna is better soon.'

Clarence nodded. 'I thought it was kind of her to invite us to join her in her brother-in-law's box at Ascot. I'm rather regretful we weren't able to accept.'

'She wants us to call on her when we are next in London,' Marina remarked. 'She has taken a lovely house in Mayfair. I said we would let her know in advance when we were planning to go up to town.'

It was William who now asked, 'What plans have your family made for your birthday, James? I'm sure it's something special.'

James began to laugh. 'They haven't told me anything and I know they won't. Rossi and Eddie wrote and told me it's something special, but a huge secret. I'll have to wait and see.'

At this moment, the waiter arrived with the bowls of borscht they had all ordered, and conversation came to an end as they lifted their spoons and dipped them into the beet soup topped with large dollops of thick cream.

'We're being very adventurous, aren't we, Clarence?' Marina murmured when their second course was served. 'This Russian food is delicious. But everyone's selected chicken Kiev!'

Much later that night, sitting at the desk in his bedroom, James was thinking about the evening he had just spent with the Venables family. He had enjoyed it, as they had, and he was touched by their kindness and generosity to him.

It was a relief to see his aunt smiling again, and Clarence now in a better mood. Ever since the revelation about Albert's vile stories, his uncle had been upset and angry. Now that he had solved the problem, he had become more like himself again.

What a joy it had been not to hear Albert's name mentioned tonight. Nor had it been mentioned for several days. Thanks to advice from Clarence's solicitor, Ian McDonald, that very clever Scotsman, the Albert problem had gone away.

Now James couldn't help thinking: but for how long? Certainly several months. He hoped it would be for longer, because in November he would be returning to London permanently. His year in Hull would have come to an end.

A smile flickered on James's face when he thought of Albert's current fate. Clarence had decided to send him to Scotland, on the advice of Ian. He was to visit the various whisky companies, with the idea of the Venables's business exporting Scotch to the Baltic countries.

Clarence had confided that it would take quite a few months to do this, and that Albert was going to be dealing with a lot of tough, very canny Scotsmen, who would easily make mince-meat of him if he stepped out of line. That day in Clarence's office, James had grinned. The memory was stuck in his head.

'Och aye, they will indeed,' Ian McDonald had volunteered, a sudden grin on his face. 'Tough buggers at the best of times, but they have been forewarned to give Mr Albert Venables an extremely hard time.'

Clarence had also laughed then. And James had asked, 'Then what? After his Scottish Highland fling? Are you really going to export whisky?'

'I don't know. I just needed to get Albert out of the way before I strangled him for his stupidity and villainous ways.'

'Perhaps he'll drown in a vat of whisky. That would solve everything,' James said, adding, 'Just like the Duke of Clarence did – though he drowned in a vat of sweet wine, so obliging Edward the Fourth.'

'Ah, no such luck,' William had muttered.

The scene in his head, enacted days ago, faded away, but his mind was still filled with a myriad of thoughts. His eye caught the glitter of gold against the mahogany wood of the desk. He picked up a cufflink, examined it. A perfect, plain oval, but beautifully made and solid gold. He would treasure the gift always. The cufflinks were the most expensive thing he owned at the moment, but it was the kind of understated, elegant item he hoped to own many more of as he built the life he dreamed about.

Unexpectedly thoughts of Mrs Ward slid into his head. He opened the middle drawer of his desk and took out the envelope containing the note from Mrs Ward. William had received one as well, and had assumed James's was the same thank-you note. But it wasn't.

Taking the piece of embossed writing paper out of the envelope, he read it for the umpteenth time.

My dear James:

I want to thank you for being so thoughtful as to come and see me to inform me about those false stories. I am glad you brought William with you to give support. I have also written a thank-you note to him.

Your advice has been invaluable to me, over these last few weeks, especially, and has helped me to feel much better in so many different ways. On another matter, I must add that I will never forget the night of the storm. You rescued me and little Polka, and gave me such amazing care as the weather worsened. Please believe me I shall never forget what you did for me.

When you return to live in London, perhaps you would like to come and see me so that I can thank you properly in person.

I wish you luck in your future endeavours.

Sincerely,

Georgiana Ward

From the first moment he had read the letter, he had understood that anyone would think it was a normal thank-you note. Only he saw the innuendo and read between the lines. She was referring to their lovemaking. How clever she was. She was also indicating she wanted to continue the relationship, no question about that. But did he?

He glanced at the top of the page where her new address was embossed in violet blue. He knew where she lived. She had already given him her London address weeks before, making no secret of her interest.

When Aunt Marina had discussed the rumours about them, asked if they were involved, his upbringing had instantly kicked in. He had lied to protect her honour and her reputation, as any gentleman would. Certainly a gentleman did not kiss and tell.

That code of honour had been inculcated in him by his grandmother since he was a child – it was as if she had somehow injected it into his bones. Esther Falconer had made him who and what he was, and therefore he knew no other way to behave, no other way to live.

Placing the letter in the envelope, he put it back in the drawer. He stood up, walked over to the window, looking out at the sea.

That was one thing he was going to miss: the North Sea. Would he miss her? This woman of the storm? He did not know, and he was not sure whether it was wise to see her again.

THIRTY-TWO

When James came down the narrow stairs of his childhood home and went into the kitchen, he was surprised to see only his mother and Rossi standing there. They were waiting for him, both dressed elegantly for his birthday supper.

He didn't even bother to glance around. The house was empty. Silence reigned.

'Where are Father and Eddie?' he asked, staring at his mother, his puzzlement apparent.

With a bright smile, Maude said, 'They left a short while ago. They had to . . .' She stopped, and then improvised, 'Pick up something for your grandfather. We are to meet them there.'

'And where is there?' James asked, a smile surfacing as he added, 'Oh, I forgot! You're not going to tell me . . . it's a big secret.'

'You'll soon know,' Rossi replied, and picked up her purse.

James raised his eyebrows with a grin at his sixteen-year-old sister, who had grown in the months he had been living in Hull. She was taller, willowy, and prettier than ever, with her shining golden hair and large, pale blue eyes. She was wearing a long pink silk gown, with a boat neckline, puffed sleeves and frills at the hem, which suited her colouring perfectly. 'You look beautiful, Rossi,' he said.

She merely smiled and edged towards the entrance hall. He turned to his mother. There was admiration in his voice when he told her, 'And so do you, Mother. Blue has always been your best colour, and your gown is very stylish.'

Maude nodded, thinking her son seemed to fill the room with his presence. His shoulders were broader, and he looked a little older than eighteen. And, of course, his looks were still startling. Thank God he hadn't been left scarred after the beating he had suffered last year. She said, 'Thank you, James, for your compliments, and now I think we must leave. There is a hansom cab waiting outside, sent by your grandmother.'

If this surprised James, he did not allow it to show. He took his mother's arm and shepherded her into the small hall.

Outside on the pavement, Maude double-locked the door. Then James helped her and Rossi into the hansom cab. He heard his mother tell the driver to go to their destination as he climbed in behind them.

James was amused at the trouble everyone had gone to in order to keep the secret. He had arrived from Hull on Friday night; nobody had given in to his mild badgering, refusing to discuss his party. But they had welcomed him with smiles, their faces filled with joy. He had responded in the same way, happy to be in the midst of the Falconer clan again. There was an enormous amount of love in his family; he considered that to be special and possibly unique. Was there any other family like theirs?

As the carriage went through Camden Town and across Chalk Farm Road, his mother and sister made idle chitchat, including him at times in their meandering thoughts. He replied to their questions and comments, amiable and friendly, all the while glancing out of the window, trying to ascertain where they were going.

It soon became obvious to him that they were not heading in the direction of Regent's Park, but were driving towards the centre of London and the West End.

For a moment, yesterday, he had believed that his grandparents might be giving his birthday party at the Montague home, but Eddie had whispered that this was not so. Then he had refused to say another word, suddenly guilty about what he had let slip out already.

They were going to Mayfair. James realized this before they began crossing Oxford Street, and soon they were pulling up outside the Bettrage Hotel in Davies Street. Obviously, his grandparents and Harry were not cooking tonight. He was pleased. He did not want them slaving over hot stoves for him.

'The cab's paid for,' Maude said after they had alighted. The uniformed doorman opened the hotel door and the three of them went into the lobby. It was cosy and warm, with red velvet drapes and small armchairs around a fireplace.

It was relatively empty, and James immediately noticed there was no sign of his father and Eddie.

Noting his puzzlement, Maude said, 'The rest will be here any minute, James. Your grandfather told me that Rossi and I should wait here for them, and you're to go up to Room 110.'

James glanced at his mother and frowned. 'Oh, why is that?' His blue eyes pierced hers. 'Why aren't you coming?'

'Your grandparents want to give you your birthday present and, once you have it, we shall all meet and . . .' She smiled at him, and added, 'And start to celebrate your birthday.'

He grinned, nodded. 'Then excuse me for a moment, Mother, Rossi. See you back here, I suppose.'

'That's right,' Maude replied. She and Rossi went and sat down on a small sofa to the right of the hotel door.

It was his grandfather who greeted James when he arrived at

Room 110. Philip was in black trousers, a white shirt and a bowtie, but no jacket. 'James, there you are, my lad,' he said, opening the door wider. 'Come in.'

James did so and glanced around. 'Where is Grans?' he asked.

'She'll be back in a moment or two. In the meantime, I want to show you something.' As he spoke, Philip closed the door and walked into the room. He opened a wardrobe and took out a black frock coat. He showed it to James and explained, 'Your grandmother and I bought you an evening suit as a birthday present, James. And you will wear it tonight, as I will be wearing mine.'

Taken aback for a moment, James stared at the frock coat and then at his grandfather. 'But that's an expensive thing to buy, Grandfather! You didn't have to do this.'

'Yes, we did. We wanted this birthday to be special, and we know you'll have great use for an evening suit in the next few years. So it's money well spent.'

A wide smile spread across James's face and he said, 'Thank you, Grandpa. Thank you so much. Where is Grans? I want to thank her, too.'

Philip chuckled. 'She went to get something, as I told you. But she also wanted to give us privacy so you can change your clothes, get into the evening suit. And, by the way, she made you an evening shirt.'

Philip handed James the frock coat, which had matching trousers, and a white shirt. On top of the shirt, there was a silver-grey silk waistcoat.

'Best go into the bathroom and change into these clothes. Oh, and wait a minute, I have the black bowtie for you.'

Rather overwhelmed by all of this, and still getting over his surprise, James did as his grandfather had instructed and disappeared into the bathroom clutching the clothes. Philip followed him and gave him the bowtie.

Once he was alone, Philip Falconer finished dressing, slipping into a black waistcoat and then his frock coat. There was a mirror on the inside of the wardrobe door. He glanced at himself, saw he looked fine, and turned away. A moment later, there was a light tap on the door.

'It's me,' Esther said. 'Can I come back in?'

'Yes, yes. James is in the bathroom changing his clothes.'

'Was he surprised?' Esther asked, looking at her husband warmly, her eyes twinkling. 'I bet he was.'

'Very much so, and I think he's really happy with the suit. I didn't get a chance to mention that the other men will be wearing evening suits.'

'You can explain that when he comes out,' Esther said, and then looked at the bathroom door as it opened. James was standing there. After a moment he walked into the room, his face lighting up when he saw Esther.

'Thank you, Grans, for the suit . . . how do I look?'

Esther could not speak for a moment, genuine astonishment registering on her face. The elegant frock coat had turned him into another person, someone she didn't know. He had not been born an aristocrat, but he looked like one, as if he had just stepped out of a stately home. She stared at Philip and let out a long sigh.

Philip said, 'I know what you're feeling, Esther, because so am I.'

'Is something wrong?' James asked swiftly.

'No, everything is absolutely right!' Esther answered, walking over to him, giving him a hug. 'Happy Birthday, James! And you look wonderful. The frock coat suits you; it seems to give you a certain maturity.'

Philip added, 'You're a handsome devil, my lad, and I'm happy and relieved the suit fits you so well. A friend of mine works at a gentleman's establishment in Savile Row, and for years he's been making things for me. It was Tony Fletcher who handmade the suit and waistcoat for you. He's done a superb job.' Taking

James's arm, he led him to the mirror on the wardrobe door. 'Take a look at yourself.'

James did so, and was actually as startled as his grandparents had been, for a moment not recognizing the image staring back at him. The evening suit did change him somehow, did make him look more grown-up. He turned to them, his face glowing, and said, 'Thank you again . . . you both spoil me. I don't know how to thank you enough.' He knew it must have cost a great deal, even if his grandfather's friend had given him a favourable rate.

'You've worked hard up in Hull and done so well. You deserve it,' Philip said. 'You've made us proud.'

James said, 'But what about Dad and my uncles? Aren't they going to look out of place tonight? Won't they be a bit upset—'

'Not at all,' Philip cut in. 'Your father and uncles will also be wearing evening suits. These ready-to-made clothes, flooding the market these days, have been a godsend to men, and one company now sells an evening line. A longer jacket and narrow trousers. They each bought one, and they'll be wearing bowties as well.'

For a moment James was speechless. He went back to the mirror, stood staring into it. His eyes took in the whiteness of the linen shirt with the small stiff collar, the black silk bowtie against the stark white, and the silvery sheen of the grey silk waistcoat. Perfection, he thought, how they blend so well together. He liked the satin lapels on the frock coat and the way it flared out at the hips. That was why it was called a frock coat, he supposed.

He shot his shirt cuffs down, saw how well the new gold cufflinks that the Venables family had given him worked, and then glanced at his feet, relieved he had worn black shoes tonight.

Suddenly, he turned around and asked, 'How did your tailor friend manage to make everything fit me so well? It's almost a miracle. I never had a fitting.'

Philip began to chuckle. Esther said, 'I wrote to your Aunt

Marina and asked her to get a tape measure and measure one of the suits you took to Hull. She sent me the longest list of measurements I've ever seen. But Tony was appreciative, I can assure you of that.'

James started to laugh and so did they. Then he went and hugged each of them again. Gazing at Esther, admiration filled his face. 'You look beautiful, Grans,' he said. He noted the happiness on her face, her shining silver hair piled high on her head, the elegant purple silk gown, very tailored, long sleeved, and with a small train. 'I'm so grateful to you, Grans, and you, too, Grandfather. What a wonderful couple you make. But then you are Falconers.'

THIRTY-THREE

There was no sight of his mother and sister in the lobby. None of the Falconers, in fact. As he glanced around, James decided not to say a word. He would let the surprise be just that.

The gift of the evening suit from his grandparents had taken him aback. He was touched and grateful to have received it. He smiled inwardly as he thought of his grandfather's comment that he would need it during the next few years. He could only hope that was true, because then it denoted success.

A few heads turned and people looked at them as they crossed the lobby. James and his grandparents were striking in appearance and their clothes were elegant, and so they drew attention. As they headed towards the corridor which led to the main restaurant in the hotel, James assumed that this was where they would be dining. It was called Quadrille, and Philip knew the head sommelier. His grandfather had taken him there when he went to talk to him about wine several years ago.

But James knew he had guessed wrongly when they walked

past the entrance to the restaurant. A moment or two later, Philip stopped in front of a closed door.

Stepping forward, his grandfather knocked on the door, immediately opened it, and led Esther and James inside. Everyone, who had been totally silent, waiting, cried, 'Happy Birthday, James!'

Indeed, he was surprised. His grandparents had hired the small private dining room of the hotel, and there they were: the remainder of Clan Falconer. His parents, siblings, and two uncles. How smart the men were, and even little Eddie, now almost fourteen, was in a new dark suit, white shirt and black bowtie. The room was lit by gas lamps, and small oil paintings hung on the walls, giving it a welcoming and luxurious atmosphere.

James couldn't help it. He clapped his hands, laughing with happiness, and then turned and hugged Esther and Philip.

'Thank you! Thank you so much,' he said to them, his blue eyes sparkling and slightly moist. 'And you really and truly have surprised me . . .' Staring at his beloved family, his gaze loving, he said, 'How wonderful it is to be with my ilk. To be a Falconer is to be the best.'

'No, we're better than the best,' his father said, and came over, hugged him and stepped back, staring at him. 'You look astonishing in evening dress – quite the toff.'

Glancing at Philip, his father added, 'It's true. You can always spot a bit of pure Savile Row, Dad. James is wearing a superb piece of impeccable tailoring. Tony's a genius.'

'He certainly is,' Philip said. 'Considering James never had a fitting.'

'But Tony did have every measurement known to man,' Esther exclaimed, laughter in her voice. 'Marina didn't miss an inch of the jacket she found in James's room in Hull. She even included the length of a flap on the pocket. Which obviously Tony didn't need.' Everyone laughed.

His uncles George and Harry came and greeted him. Philip

motioned to the two waiters at the end of the room, standing near the bar. They came over with glasses of champagne and fruit juice for Eddie and Rossi.

After toasting James and saying 'Happy Birthday' yet again, Philip led the family to the other end of the room. He waved his hand at the table. 'The hotel's done a beautiful job, just look at this table. The flowers, the candles . . . everything is perfection.'

Esther came and stood next to him, her eyes roaming over her family. 'Your grandfather and I wanted to do something special for your eighteenth birthday, James, rather than waiting until you were twenty-one.' She shrugged. 'Who knows what might happen in three years! We wanted to give you a special dinner. Then we realized we wanted it to be private – just us, the family. Philip had the idea of hiring a private room here, where his friend is the sommelier. He told us it's becoming quite popular to do this. What could be better?'

'Your surprise is wonderful,' James interjected. 'Thank you again for doing this, going to all this trouble. This must be the smartest dinner anyone's ever had!'

After chatting to each other for a while and drinking a second glass of champagne, the family sat down at the round dinner table. The menu was composed of cold vichyssoise soup, which Eddi wrinkled his nose at, rack of spring lamb, new potatoes and peas. The food was thoroughly enjoyed, the wines commented on, and then they settled back, wanting to relax, talk and catch up before dessert was served.

It was Esther who suddenly asked everyone to be quiet, explaining she had something special to tell them. The room was instantly quiet. All eyes were focused on her.

'Now that we've toasted dear James, I want to propose a toast to George. So please lift your glasses to congratulate him on his wonderful promotion at his newspaper.'

'Oh, Mum, really, don't make a big fuss!' George protested. Nonetheless, he looked happy and was smiling.

'Congratulations!' They toasted him and sipped.

It was Rossi, seated next to him, who asked, 'What is your promotion, Uncle George?'

'I've been given a new job, sort of, and a new title. I will now have the by-line of Deputy Royal Correspondent.'

Maude exclaimed, 'George, that's marvellous! That means you are covering the royal family, presumably?'

'Yes, at least many of the events they attend. When the Prince of Wales travels, I shall be in the press corps. Perhaps even when he takes trips abroad, I'll be going along.'

'You won't be writing much about Queen Victoria,' Rossi announced. 'She doesn't travel anywhere. She's always stuck in Scotland, at Balmoral.'

'That's true, yes,' George answered. 'But, in a way, it's because of the Queen that I got my promotion.'

'Really!' Eddie cried. 'Do you know the Queen, Uncle George? What's she really like?'

Laughter erupted. A moment later, when everyone was quiet, George turned to his nephew. 'No, I don't know the Queen. I can't claim to know any of the royal family. But last year I wrote a story about the Queen's Golden Jubilee. There was an enormous reaction from the public, a lot of letters from readers, and my editor was also pleased with it . . . touched, he said. Hence his decision to assign me to cover them.'

Maude said, 'I remember reading it. It was touching, that's true . . . I think you made the Queen appear to be more . . . real, more like ordinary people.'

George nodded. 'I know what you're getting at, Maude. I think I showed her being . . . a mother as well as a queen.'

'Some mother!' James exclaimed, and then stopped abruptly.

Looking across at his uncle, he said, 'I'm afraid I missed that story, but I'd like to know what you wrote, Uncle George.'

'Then I shall tell you.' George glanced around the table. 'Is that all right with everyone else?'

They all agreed and looked at George with bated breath, wanting to hear the story, even those who had read it in *The Chronicle*.

George said, 'Last June, June the twenty-first in 1887, to be exact, I was in Westminster Abbey for the Queen's Jubilee. There were nine thousand people, if you can believe that, all squeezed in together. Many of them were in specially made wooden galleries built up against the walls. I was on the ground floor, being part of the press group. The Queen sat in the Coronation Chair and she was all alone. I was disappointed that she wasn't in her crown and robes of state. She would have been more like the Queen and Empress she is. But no, there she was in her mourning black dress and bonnet, trimmed with white lace. Anyway, as the service progressed, I saw that the Queen was very involved and quite affected by the ceremony . . .' George broke off, sipped his red wine, and continued.

'The person standing closest to her in the abbey was her heir, the Prince of Wales. To me he seemed anxious about her, kept looking at her intently and very warmly, I thought. Once the ceremony was over, the Prince was the first member of the Queen's family to walk forward. After bowing to her, he kissed her hand. And then, much to my amazement, and everyone else's, I think, she leaned forward and kissed him on the cheek. A journalist friend told me that this was very unusual, that she had broken protocol. But, anyway, she did it on the spur of the moment. I believe it was prompted by great emotion. Then, to top it all, she kissed all of the other princes and princesses with genuine affection. Never been done before, and perhaps never again.

'When I got back to the paper, I wrote a story that was about a Queen who was a mother. As I read my notes, I began to see so many little links into that angle. The end result? Readers loved it, and – most importantly – so did my editor.'

'I read the story myself and was moved by it,' Philip said. 'And rather a proud father that day, George. As for this promotion, you deserve it. Congratulations again!'

'Thanks, Dad,' George said, and looked across the table at James. 'Why that odd comment about the Queen?'

'I think she's treated the Prince of Wales very shoddily, and I don't believe for one minute he caused his father's death. Prince Albert died because he got ill and probably wasn't given the correct treatment by doctors.'

'I agree with James,' Rossi announced.

'You always do,' Eddie muttered.

James said, 'I have a lot of admiration for Bertie and many of the things he's done for the country. You'll see one day, when he comes to the throne, he'll be a good king; if not, in fact, a great king.'

'Oddly enough, I tend to agree with you, James,' George replied. 'About Bertie being a good king; although there are those who won't. Unfortunately, there have been too many scandals . . .'

Esther cleared her throat and looked at George, frowning, and then her eyes shifted to Eddie. 'Shall we think about dessert? We ordered something special: strawberries Romanov. Before we have the birthday cake.'

'One of my favourites,' James said, smiling at his grandmother. 'I'd love to have that before my cake, and thank you, Grans.'

There was some discussion at the table about the extra dessert before the cake. Then George said to James, 'Interesting, isn't it, about Victoria? How her progeny sits on the thrones of Europe?'

'It is. But what has always intrigued me is that two Danish princesses, sisters, married two kings. Alix married the Prince of Wales and one day will be the Queen of England, and her sister,

Minnie, married the late Tsar of Russia, whose son Nicholas is now the Tsar.'

George sipped his wine for a second or two, and then remarked somewhat sarcastically, 'And let's not forget that the Queen's eldest daughter Vicky married the Emperor William's son and heir, Fritz. They've had a son who one day will be Kaiser himself. And he's very anti-English, even though he's the eldest grandson of our Queen.'

'That's food for thought,' James answered. He could see his grandparents were not really interested in politics, and so he changed the subject to speak about the theatre, mentioning that he wanted to see Lillie Langtry's new play.

Whilst they waited for dessert to be served, George excused himself, left the table and returned a few seconds later with a package in his hand.

His brother Harry got up when George returned to the table, and it was Harry who spoke. 'We wanted to get you a useful birthday present, James. But because you are you, we thought it ought to be something . . . really nice. And this is our choice.'

He handed the present to James. He and George then said, 'Happy Birthday!' in unison.

James opened the package, still looking somewhat startled, and then exclaimed, 'Oh my goodness, a pocket watch! What a marvellous gift.' He was beaming as he held the watch in his hands and showed it to the rest of the family. Rising, he went to his two uncles and hugged them.

'I'll help you to put it on later,' Philip said, smiling at his grandson.

Eddie, never one to be overlooked, announced to the table, 'Dad and I gave James two cravats and two silk hankies for his top pocket. You did like them, didn't you, Jimmy?'

'I did, very much, and thanks again, Eddie, and you, too, Dad.'

Rossi exclaimed, 'And Mother and I made James two beautiful linen shirts.'

'Yes, they are very smart, and thank you both,' James said, looking from Rossi to his mother, who was sitting next to him. 'I do believe I have been well and truly spoilt. And I shall never forget this birthday.'

THIRTY-FOUR

lexis always smiled to herself when she arrived at the boutique and saw the name: Madame Valance, Atelier. It made the designer sound like a middle-aged doyenne, when in fact she was a young woman of about thirty.

Walking into the boutique on a sunny Monday morning with the promise of summer on the horizon, Alexis smiled at the receptionist sitting at the mahogany desk. 'Good morning, Lettice, I'm meeting Miss Trevalian.'

'Good morning, Miss Malvern. Miss Trevalian hasn't arrived yet. Please take a seat.'

'Thank you.' Alexis sat down in one of the chairs and continued to think about Jacqueline Valance and her clothes. They were always beautifully handmade, as *haute couture* had to be, but also creative and youthful. Although she wasn't trying to compete with Charles Frederick Worth, the great designer of this era, whose creations were favoured by society women, she was becoming more and more popular.

The French designer was making Claudia's wedding gown, and today was the last fitting. Claudia had asked Alexis to be present, wanting her opinion. After the fitting, Alexis was going to be measured for her own wedding gown, which she had strong opinions about, knew what she wanted.

The small bell tinkled as the door opened and Claudia came rushing in, looking slightly flushed. 'Sorry I'm late,' she exclaimed, and went to kiss Alexis. She then crossed to the desk. 'My apologies to Madame Valance, Lettice. Will you please let her know I am now here?'

'I will indeed, Miss Trevalian,' Lettice said, standing up, retreating into a back room. A moment later, she returned. 'Madame wishes you to go upstairs to the main salon, please.'

'Thank you,' Claudia said, and she and Alexis climbed the wide staircase together. 'I don't know why, but there was such a lot of traffic today. The streets are clogged.'

'I know. But then it's Monday, and that's always a busy day. People coming back from their country homes, deliveries to shops after the weekend.' Alexis reached out and squeezed her hand. 'Do relax. Don't be anxious. I'm sure the gown is beautiful.'

The two women sat down together on a low seat in the salon where the clothes were fitted. It was a medium-sized room, the walls, doors and woodwork painted a soft dove grey. There were many wall sconces, which filled the salon with bright light, plus four cheval mirrors for the clients to see themselves wearing the latest garments.

Within a few seconds, Madame Valance arrived, dressed in her usual long black skirt and matching blouse, with a white cotton coat on top.

Alexis called it the doctor's coat, because that was what it resembled. In fact, it was worn to protect the delicate fabrics and the light colours which the designer was using for her creations. Most *haute couture* designers wore them out of necessity, not wishing new pieces to touch their own clothing.

After Jacqueline Valance had greeted them in her cheerful

manner, she said, 'If you will come with me, Miss Trevalian, Jeanette and I will help you into your gown.'

'Of course.' Claudia rose and followed the designer into the adjoining dressing room.

Alexis glanced around, noting, yet again, how plain and simple this salon was. Not a painting in sight, no bric-a-brac and no vases of flowers. She understood why. Madame wanted a neutral setting, so that her designs were the only thing on view.

Ten minutes later, Claudia returned to the salon, holding up the sides of her wedding gown. Alexis caught her breath, and exclaimed, 'Oh, Claudia, you look beautiful and the gown is . . . divine.'

Claudia beamed at her, walked into the middle of the room, where she was helped up onto the large square platform by Jeanette, who began to arrange the skirt of the gown.

When Queen Victoria married Prince Albert of Saxe-Coburg-Gotha in February of 1840, she had worn a white satin gown with a flounce of Honiton lace. In wearing white, she had started a tradition without knowing it, and now many brides wanted to be married in a white gown.

White silk had been Claudia's choice of fabric. Panels of white lace were inserted down the front and the back of the skirt. At the back the panel grew wider as it reached the hem, became a long lace train, eight feet long, stretching out behind the dress. The bodice was made of the white silk, as were the long sleeves, and the trim on the bateau neckline, as Madame called it, was of white lace.

'Please, Miss Trevalian, will you turn slowly so that I can make sure the hem is correct, completely even.'

After doing this twice, with Jeanette helping to move the train carefully, Madame Valance announced, '*Et voilà!* It is finished! I have nothing more to do except try on your veil.' Reaching out, the designer took hold of Claudia's hand, Jeanette the other. They helped her to step off the platform.

Jeanette went to retrieve the veil and Madame led Claudia to one of the cheval mirrors. The veil was short. It fell down over the front of her face to meet the bateau neckline, and at the back it stopped at the waist so that it did not hide the lace panel on the back of the skirt, which turned into the long train at the hem.

'I made this band of roses to hold the veil in place, for the moment,' the designer explained. 'I know on the day of your marriage, you will be wearing one of the Trevalian diamond tiaras.'

'It is rather a simple one, actually,' Claudia said. 'It belonged to my grandmother, and I know it will be perfect with the gown.' Smiling, she added with genuine sincerity, 'Thank you so much, Madame Valance. You have outdone yourself, created something truly beautiful for my wedding day.'

'My pleasure, Miss Trevalian. Now, Miss Malvern, let us sit down and talk about the gown you would like for your wedding day. It is in September, is it not?'

Alexis nodded, her face full of smiles. 'That's correct, and I want a gown of cream satin, but very plain and tailored: sleek is perhaps the best word. And no lace trim, only a lace veil, as long as you want.'

'Cream? Not white? That has become the tradition.'

'I know. But cream suits me better because of my pale complexion. People won't notice, not really. They'll think it's white.'

'Ah yes. Perhaps you are right. What style do you want? Narrow, full, in between?'

Madame rose, went to get a sketchbook, and the two of them then sat talking whilst Claudia changed her clothes.

Madame made several rough sketches quickly, showing them to Alexis. They had their heads together, bent over the sketchpad until Claudia joined them.

After a little more discussion about Alexis's wedding gown,

and when her measurements had been taken, the two young women finally took their leave and went downstairs.

As they went out onto Curzon Street, animatedly chatting to each other, a tall young man, obviously in a hurry, bumped into them, almost knocking Claudia down to the ground. He caught hold of her arm just in time and firmly held her up, apologizing most profusely.

He was so nice about it, saying he had been clumsy and apologizing again, that neither of them were angry. With a small, gracious bow he took his leave and hurried away.

Once he had gone, Alexis looked at Claudia and asked, 'Are you all right? He really did bump into you rather hard in his haste. He was right; he was awfully clumsy.'

'I'm fine, truly, Alexis. I must say he was nice about it . . . and rather tall and handsome, don't you think?'

Alexis couldn't help laughing. 'I suppose he was, now you mention it. And polite, delightful manners. Now, shall we go and have some lunch?'

'That would be lovely, let's do that. Oh, but what about your work? Don't you have to go back to the office?'

'I went there at seven o'clock this morning and accomplished quite a lot,' Alexis said.

'You're just like Papa! You two early risers are made for each other.'

'And in every way,' Alexis answered.

THIRTY-FIVE

As a well-liked journalist, as well as a regular at the Quadrille, which was around the corner from his flat, George Falconer was given one of the best tables when he arrived at one o'clock on Monday.

Longden, the head waiter, who was something of a family friend, welcomed him warmly. As he led him across the room, he said, 'I'm happy and relieved your nephew's dinner was such a success on Saturday night. I hope everyone enjoyed it.'

'Indeed they did. It went without a hitch, couldn't have been better. The food was delicious, the wine superb. Thank you very much . . . I know you oversaw everything.'

'Nothing less for your father. He's a good friend of mine, and he's been a good friend to this hotel over the years.'

Once George was settled on the banquette, facing the room, Longden said, 'I know Monday's your day off, so can I offer you a glass of champagne? Or something else, perhaps?'

'I won't have any alcohol, but thank you. Water will be fine. My nephew is joining me. I don't want to encourage him drinking at one in the afternoon, even if he has turned eighteen.'

Longden chuckled and inclined his head. 'The waiter will come with water and the menu.'

'Thank you.' George now glanced around the restaurant and his eyes settled on the wall opposite him. He found he couldn't look away. Two lovely young women were facing him, and one of them was so stunning that his heart skipped a beat. She looked right back at him and quite boldly. Immediately he reached into his pocket, took out his notebook and opened it. Just to avoid her steady, somewhat curious gaze, he looked down at a page.

Surreptitiously, he glanced across the room, but the stunning woman had turned sideways and was talking to her companion. Nonetheless, George picked up the menu and ran his gaze down the page to resist gaping at her.

He wasn't really reading; his mind moved from the beautiful woman to his nephew. Every adult member of the family had thought James looked older at the dinner. But that wasn't what was different. His face was exactly the same; it hadn't aged a day. What had changed was his demeanour. There was something about the way he moved and spoke that made him seem more mature. Although he laughed a lot, had been happy last night, George had detected a new reflectiveness, a seriousness present in him. It struck George that James now seemed to have a lot more knowledge about the real world in general, and not all of it good.

A small sigh escaped him as he thought of how cosseted James had been by his parents and his grandparents. Just as he, Matthew and Harry had been protected when they were growing up. Despite being in service, with very little to spare, his parents had made sure he and his brothers had been well fed, well clothed and well loved.

That was the way the Falconers were . . . everything was always for the family; giving them the best they could, ready to shield them, to take the bullet, if necessary.

George was certain that it was the assault on James and

Denny – and Denny's subsequent death last August – that had changed him. Out of the blue, real life had hit him hard. It had taught him that wickedness, evil and cruelty abounded, and pain, suffering and sorrow could be the norm on occasion.

George remembered that he had once told his brother Harry that the world was not always an easy ride; that it could be more like mounting a bucking stallion in a Texas rodeo and endeavouring to stay in the saddle. He had warned him to be aware that danger could lurk round any corner.

As a journalist with many connections, George had dug a little into what inquiries Scotland Yard had made after the brutal attack on the two boys. Unfortunately, they had drawn a blank; their bafflement remained. The crime had never been solved. But George knew there had to have been a reason for the attack; he knew that instinctively. One day he hoped they would succeed in finding out why it had happened and who the perpetrators were. Somebody would be made to pay.

James's injuries had been considerable. He had been truly lucky to heal so well. In George's opinion, his survival was something of a miracle. His physical injuries aside, James had been deeply upset by Denny's death. He had tried hard to comfort Jack Holden and his daughter Nancy. All in all it had been a traumatic time for him, and it had marked him.

When George's mother had come up with the idea of getting James out of Camden Town and taking him to Hull, George had encouraged it as an excellent notion. Once in Hull, even though he was living and working with relatives, James had been forced to stand on his own two feet. So, naturally, James Lionel Falconer had changed. He had grown up. And very, very fast. That was the difference in him.

The arrival of his nephew intruded on George's meandering thoughts. As James walked across to the table, accompanied by Longden, George noticed how people stared at the handsome young man. Especially the women in the restaurant. Women would fall at his feet, that was a given. But George had a hunch that James wouldn't be distracted from his goal. Ambition and success first. He had his feet on the ground and his head ruled his heart.

'Sorry I'm late, Uncle George.' James apologized as he sat down. 'I rushed here from Fortnum and Mason and tried a shortcut, but the streets are overcrowded today.'

'It's the nice weather, I think,' George replied. 'But you're not that late, James. Relax, I've plenty of time. It's my day off.'

'It was nice of you to invite me to lunch, Uncle George. By the way, I love my pocket watch.'

'Harry gave me the same one a few years ago. Then I gave an identical one to him. It's just the right size, a nice timepiece. So why were you at the posh shop? Pretty expensive, isn't it?'

'Just looking around, memorizing things. Then I walked across the road to Burlington Arcade to study the shops there.'

Staring at him, perplexed, George frowned and asked, 'But why? I thought you were going to work with your dad. Are you interested in retailing?'

'Yes . . . that's what I want: to own an arcade and a shop like Fortnum's. I'm going to be a merchant.'

'Very ambitious . . .' George paused and said, 'Don't look across the room yet, just keep talking to me. There's a beautiful woman over there. I think she's trying to get your attention.'

'Are you sure, Uncle George?'

'Positive.'

'What is she like?'

'Gorgeous. Older than you, though. With raven-black hair.'

'Oh, I wonder if it's Mrs Ward.' As he said this, James swivelled his head, looked across the room. It was Georgiana Ward, seated with another woman who James thought might be her sister.

Giving his uncle a quick glance, James explained, 'She is a close friend of Great-Aunt Marina's. I met her in Hull. She told me she was moving back to London.'

'Do all the women in Hull look like that? If so, I might just move there. To hell with Fleet Street,' George replied in an amused tone.

'I think I ought to go and speak to her. Just to be polite,' James said and got up. 'Excuse me for a moment.'

Walking confidently, James crossed the restaurant to the women's table. Smiling, stretching out his hand, he said, 'How nice to see you, Mrs Ward.'

'And you too, Mr Falconer.' Turning to the woman with her, she continued, 'Deanna, I would like to introduce James Falconer, Marina's great-nephew . . . he's the young man who suggested Clarence could sort out my problem with those shares. Mr Falconer, this is my sister, Mrs Wilson.'

Deanna Wilson stretched out her hand and said, 'How do you do?' James shook it, smiled back, and answered, 'Mrs Wilson.'

Mrs Ward asked, 'Are you in London for your birthday?'

'Yes, that's right. My grandparents gave a family dinner for me.'

'How long are you staying?'

'Until the weekend. I'm so glad we got a chance to say hello.' With another wide smile and a small bow to both women, James returned to his uncle's table.

George said, 'Welcome back. Let's order lunch and then you can tell me all about Hull. And perhaps that charming friend of Aunt Marina's too.'

James picked up the menu. He decided to have potted shrimp and grilled sole. His uncle ordered the same. The waiter filled their glasses with water and departed.

'So, where is Mr Ward?' George now asked, eyeing James, riddled with curiosity. He had noticed the adoring look on the woman's lovely face.

'Preston Ward is dead and we're just friends, so don't look at me like that.'

'How am I looking?'

'Like the cat that got the cream, Uncle George. At Uncle Clarence's request, I helped Mrs Ward with her books – she had inherited her husband's shipping business. Then she had problems with some shares she wanted to sell to her brother-in-law. I suggested she talk to Uncle Clarence. He managed to get her the best solicitor and accountant in Hull. And that's all there is to it. I hardly know her. I'm surprised to run into her, to be honest.'

'I believe you,' George answered, and he did. On the other hand, he felt Mrs Ward might have different ideas, from the way she had looked up at his nephew.

The two of them talked about other things as they demolished the potted shrimp. It was whilst the waiter was deboning the grilled sole that George said, 'Did you know that your great-grandfather Falconer, my grandfather, had a shop in Kent . . . a grocer's shop. If you want to be a merchant, you're just following in his footsteps, James. Retailing must be in your blood.'

At exactly four o'clock that afternoon, James climbed the steps to Mrs Ward's house in South Audley Street, lifted the brass knocker and dropped it once.

Almost immediately the door was opened by Sonya, who bobbed and opened the door wider. 'I think Mrs Ward is expecting me,' James said confidently.

'She is, sir. She is waiting for you in the parlour. I'll take you upstairs.'

James couldn't help smiling to himself. Georgiana Ward had known he would come and visit her after bumping into her at lunch in the Quadrille. How well she knew him.

Sonya showed him into the room and disappeared down the stairs. As he walked across the floor, Georgiana stood up and hurried forward. She came immediately into his arms, holding onto him slightly. 'What took you so long?' she asked. 'I thought you would be here an hour ago.'

'I had to go somewhere with my uncle first,' he explained. 'I finished my business with him as soon as I could. Also, I wasn't sure whether you were expecting me or not.'

'I couldn't say anything in front of my sister. Nor did I know what you wanted.'

'The same as you, I think,' James answered cautiously. He studied her for a moment then took her arm and led her over to the sofa. 'Let's sit and talk for a few moments.'

As she lifted the teapot from the tray laid out in front of them, Georgiana said in a low voice, 'I can't stop wondering . . . how do you think Albert found out about us? Or was it a good guess, because you came every Thursday to do my bookkeeping?'

'Perhaps that alerted him to us. However, I believe he hired a private detective to follow me and dig up some scandal. He's certainly too lazy to have done it himself.'

'But why? I don't understand,' she said, frowning, truly baffled.

'According to what I've been told by my aunt and William, Albert has always been a troublemaker, and envious and jealous of others. William was his victim when they were children. Anyway, his hatred for me stems from my uncle's friendship and affection, and the fact that Uncle Clarence offered me a job with the shipping company.'

'So he wanted to destroy you, so to speak?' A brow lifted.

'Exactly. However, he is so loathed, disregarded by everyone – except his wife, I suppose – that no one believed him.' James reached out and took hold of her hand. 'They gave us the benefit of the doubt. And it had nothing to do with you, Georgiana. Just me.'

'I understand. How long can you stay with me today?'

'I'm afraid I do have to leave shortly. I am meeting my grandparents soon. There's no way I can let them down. But I am free tomorrow afternoon, and all day on Thursday.'

She made a *moue* with her mouth, then smiled at him. 'So I will be able to be with you for a little bit this week. We can make up for lost time, my dearest James.'

Thirty-Six

Courtland Priory was a Georgian house, pure Palladian in style. It stood on a rise above velvet-smooth lawns, which fell away to a large artificial pond, where its mirror image was perfectly reflected in the water.

Sebastian had explained that this was a Georgian invention; a vanity, really, but a skilful and clever way to display another view of the house . . . showing off, in a sense, he had added.

Ever since Alexis had first visited the house, she had discovered many things which both amazed and intrigued her. She had grown to admire Sebastian more than she already did in the way he cared for and looked after his homes. They were perfect.

She was well aware that it was he who had taken this grand stately house and made it comfortable to live in, without destroying its overall grandeur and importance.

'Papa got rid of some of the clutter,' Claudia had explained to her on her first visit, some months ago now.

'Once Grandmama and Grandpapa had died, and it was his, out went the potted palms in brass pots, the unimportant bric-a-brac, and the endless cushions. Papa got the staff to store a great deal of furniture in the attics. You know he likes a spacious feeling.'

Alexis had completely understood, since she had Goldenhurst Farm in Kent as a reference, regarding his taste. She knew Sebastian enjoyed space, light, lovely paintings on the walls, plus total comfort with overstuffed chairs and sofas.

This, his family estate in Gloucestershire, was vast by comparison with Goldenhurst, composed of arable and grazing land, forests, smaller woods and meadows. It was an agricultural estate.

Not far from the Palladian house were the ruins of an ancient priory, where monks had lived and worked centuries ago and from which Courtland Priory took its name.

A river ran through that part of the estate, and the story was that the monks had fished in that river for their meals and had tended garden plots, growing vegetables for themselves.

The Palladian-style house, built by one of Sebastian's ancestors in the 1700s, stood in the centre of the Great Park, which flowed down to the small village of Courtland. This was as old as the house itself, built for the people who had worked for the Trevalians in some capacity, then and now.

The village was charming. Apart from the cottages, it had a church, a church hall, a school and a post office. Every cottage had a front and back garden, and a cellar. The villagers kept the entire village pristine at all times. They were proud of Courtland Priory and their own little plots.

It was seven o'clock in the morning when Alexis slipped out of the house and wandered along the path to the ruined priory. She wanted a little exercise and fresh air before the day began.

The house was already bustling with activity. Extra staff had already arrived and were preparing for this very special day. Claudia's wedding day.

Sebastian had many guests staying at Courtland, as well as Cornelius Glendenning's parents and siblings.

There was going to be a luncheon after the wedding ceremony, and then a small supper for the two families that evening. Quite a long day, Alexis now thought as she sat down on a large, flat stone and leaned against a partially ruined wall. Her thoughts were entirely focused on the wedding, hoping nothing would go wrong.

It would actually take place at noon. That was when Claudia would walk down the aisle on Sebastian's arm as he escorted her to the altar; there Connie would be waiting with his brother Oswald, who was his best man. His two other brothers were among the ushers.

Alexis could only imagine what the expression on Connie's face would be when he first caught sight of his bride in her exquisite white gown, long lace train and diamond tiara. She was quite certain he would be speechless.

In September, it would be her turn to walk down that same aisle in the Trevalian family church, which she could see in the distance.

It was rather beautiful, larger than she had expected. She had been impressed by the soaring ceiling and the interior, especially the many stained-glass windows which filled the church with brilliant light. Ancient family banners hung from the walls, dating back centuries, and were a potent reminder of the family history. Many Trevalians had been soldiers – doing their duty for king and country; patriots all – as well as bankers.

Yesterday she and Claudia had watched from the back of the church as gardeners had carried in masses of blue and white flowers arranged in urns and vases. The gardeners had placed them all over the church, in windows, niches and on the altar, which created an amazing effect. Interspersed amongst the urns were tall white candles, taper-like in style, and held in heavy silver candlesticks.

When she had glanced at Claudia, she had immediately noticed the look of awe on her friend's face. She herself had been filled with amazement at the finished effect. It was quite unique; the interior of the church had become an indoor garden. The mingled scents of roses and other flowers had floated on the air, obliterating the mustiness of the ancient church.

Now, sitting on the stone slab, she glanced around, looked up at the clear blue sky and took in the natural beauty of her surroundings. She realized, with a small shock, that Courtland Priory, this grand stately mansion, would soon be her home for the rest of her life.

Today was Saturday 9 June. Sebastian and she would become husband and wife on Saturday 29 September. Not too far away . . .

An unexpected rush of laughter filled her throat. She, who had proclaimed she would never marry, could hardly wait for the day when she would become Mrs Sebastian Trevalian.

Neither could her father, Henry Malvern, to whom she had confided her secret. Several months ago he had met Sebastian formally and had given them his blessing. Her father had been invited to attend Claudia's wedding and was staying here at Courtland. She had noticed last night how well he had hit it off with Lord Reggie and Lady Jane. This had pleased her.

Rising, walking back to the house, she couldn't help thinking that it was quite a crowd staying over. No wonder Sebastian had hired so many outside staff from the village. They were really needed. With a little jolt, she realized that, once she was his wife, running Courtland would become her duty. But he would guide her.

As soon as she was back in her bedroom, Alexis began the process of getting dressed for the wedding. Her gown was hanging in the cupboard, and she took it out, looked it over intently. It had been newly pressed by Ellen, her maid here, and was ready for her to step into after she had done her hair and used some cosmetics on her face.

Her silk gown was by Madame Valance. It was beautifully

cut and tailored, with a straight skirt at the front, a flare at the back from the hips down that became a small train. A square neckline and long sleeves added to its overall elegance. It was the colour that she loved the most: a soft, lavender-lilac, with just the faintest hint of pink. Pleased with it, she put the hanger back in the closet and went into the bathroom.

As she stood in front of the mirror, brushing her luxuriant auburn hair, it suddenly struck Alexis that today was a dress rehearsal for her . . . for her marriage with Sebastian in just a few months. This brought a smile of happiness to her face. Soon she would start a whole new life with him.

Alexis, her father and Sebastian's sister Thea were the last to enter the church before the bride. As they came in, Thea exclaimed, 'Oh my word! What a sight! The church looks marvellous, and it smells divine. Where's the mustiness gone?'

Walking down to the front row of pews on the right side, where the Trevalians always sat, Alexis explained, 'It's been obliterated by the fragrance from all of the roses and other flowers. Claudia and I saw the gardeners bringing in the urns yesterday. They created quite a spectacle, didn't they? They arranged everything to perfection.'

Thea nodded. Henry Malvern said, 'The light is extraordinary in here. From all of the stained-glass windows, of course. What a lovely aura they impart.'

'Rainbow hues,' Alexis murmured, as she followed her father and Thea into the first pew, sat down and glanced around. Lord Reggie and Aunt Jane were right behind her in the second row. She noticed other friends of Sebastian's, smiled and nodded.

Several minutes later, Miss Allerton, the church's pianist, started to play. Everyone stood up as Sebastian and Claudia arrived at the top of the nave.

Behind them were Lavinia and Marietta in pink silk brides-maid's dresses, each sister holding the bottom of Claudia's train.

Alexis reminded herself that this eight-foot-long train had to be detached from the hem of the gown, once the family photographs had been taken. A clever device had been invented by Madame Valance. Hooks and eyes held the train in place, and later would be unfastened so that the bride could enjoy her reception without getting her feet entangled in the lace train. That would be removed, folded and taken away.

The moment Sebastian began to lead Claudia down the aisle, Alexis fixed her eyes on him and never left his face. As they drew closer, her heart missed a beat. She felt a rush of intense love for this man. Tall, slender, elegant in every way, he looked very much the proud father. He also looked unusually handsome this morning in a dove-grey morning suit, worn with a white shirt, grey silk cravat and a white silk waistcoat.

And, of course, he stood out, since every other man present wore the traditional morning suit composed of a black frock coat with grey pinstriped trousers, white shirt and grey waistcoat. All the men had a white rose on their lapels.

There was total silence in the church except for the music, as father and daughter proceeded to the altar. Alexis turned slightly in order to look at Cornelius. She smiled inwardly. He was staring at his bride in amazement: mesmerized by her stunning beauty, Alexis had no doubt.

The diamond tiara holding the long veil in place glittered brilliantly in the bright sunlight coming in through the windows. The diamonds on her ears sparkled. Alexis knew they were a wedding gift from Connie. The single strand of diamonds around her neck was from Sebastian. It had once belonged to Claudia's mother.

Once they reached the altar, Sebastian took Claudia's hand and put it in Connie's, then stepped back. Everyone sat down. Sebastian joined Alexis in the front pew. He glanced at her, reached for her hand and held it tightly.

Leaning closer to her, he whispered against her hair, 'I can't wait to be standing where Connie is right now.'

Because the vicar had started speaking, she could not answer him, so she simply squeezed his hand and kissed his cheek. A faint smile played around his mouth. He too sat back and listened as his daughter and her fiancé took their vows and within minutes became man and wife. His daughter was a married woman now, and he was pleased with her choice for a husband. She was starting a whole new life and he wished her nothing but happiness.

The reception was in full swing when the bridal couple and their families finally arrived in the pale green dining room after being photographed.

Because there were a hundred guests altogether, the furniture had been removed, except for chairs placed against the walls. Waiters walked around with silver trays offering canapés, champagne, water and white wine.

A quartet at one end of the room was softly playing the popular songs of the day, intermingled with classical pieces. The chatter was high, old friends mingling, other people introducing themselves to those they didn't know, being cordial and friendly on this special day.

Although the long train had been taken off her wedding gown and her veil had been removed, Claudia still wore her tiara. She looked starry-eyed with happiness.

Leading Connie by the hand, she brought him over to Alexis, who stood with Lord Reggie and Lady Jane near the French doors which opened onto the terrace. Sebastian was nearby, speaking with the famous trial lawyer, Laurence Tomlin, who was his cousin from his mother's side of the family.

Cornelius smiled at Alexis, and started telling her about their honeymoon plans. They were going to Paris and then on to Monte Carlo on the Riviera.

'I'm afraid I haven't been to Monte Carlo,' Alexis said. 'But my father has taken me to Paris several times. I've given Claudia the names of some of the nicest bistros I know. You'll enjoy them, and you should visit some of the museums, particularly the Louvre.'

Connie began to speak about his love of art, especially the Impressionist school; as she listened to him, Alexis warmed even more to this fine, upstanding young man. She had liked him from the moment she had met him. He was first rate. Honourable, kind, rather charming in a quiet, understated way, and totally sane, with his feet planted on the ground. Claudia called him the no-nonsense chap, and Alexis understood perfectly what her friend meant.

Now she changed the subject. 'Sebastian told me that you've really settled in well at the bank. I sincerely hope this move to work with your father-in-law is going to be successful.'

'Oh yes, I'm sure it will be, Alexis,' Cornelius said confidently. 'Good position. Learning a lot. He's a great boss. An outstanding mentor. I'm a lucky man.' He leaned into her. 'To be truthful, I'm very glad to be a part of the Trevalian family.' He gave her a sly grin, whispered, 'Happy and relieved to be away from my very competitive brothers.'

Alexis couldn't help laughing, and she nodded. 'I fully understand. You like your independence, just as I do. Incidentally, speak to the concierge at your hotel, ask about Impressionist exhibitions. I think there is one on Monet coming up, also another on Renoir—' She broke off as Sebastian strolled over and took hold of her arm somewhat possessively.

Smiling at his son-in-law, he said, 'Sorry to interrupt old chap, but I need to speak to Alexis. Alone.'

'I understand, sir,' Cornelius replied, and turned to Lady Jane and Reggie, joining in their ongoing conversation with Claudia.

'Is there something the matter?' Alexis asked worriedly, observing the serious expression on Sebastian's face.

'No, but I do need to speak to you. Alone.' He led her through the crush of family and guests, out into the main entrance hall and into the library. Once inside he closed the door and locked it.

She frowned and asked, 'Why are you locking the door?'

'I just want to speak to you and I don't want anybody barging in here. Come and sit down on the sofa with me.'

She did as he asked.

After a moment of silence, Sebastian took hold of her right hand and looked at the emerald ring. 'Why is this on the wrong finger?'

Rather perplexed, she said, 'Because we are secretly engaged. It can't be on the left hand.'

He sighed deeply and shook his head. 'Oh Alexis, everyone knows we're together, so don't be so silly. There's no secret about this situation.'

She did not know how to answer him, but she understood he was annoyed, even though he wasn't allowing that to show.

When she did not respond, he continued, 'Some time ago, Claudia suggested you ought to tell me that I should announce our engagement at her wedding. You said you couldn't do that, and she let the matter drop. Why did you respond so negatively to the idea?'

Alexis bit her lip, and a sudden flush rose from her neck to flood her face. She wondered why she had. She didn't really know. It had felt wrong; had prompted that strange feeling of foreboding. She explained her feelings to Sebastian. 'I see. So there was really no reason, was there?'

'No,' she agreed, now noticing the stern look in his translucent grey eyes. It occurred to her he might even be hurt. She couldn't bear that, and silently chastised herself for not thinking through how it might appear to him.

Glancing at her swiftly, half smiling, he removed the emerald ring from her right hand and put it on the third finger of her left. 'There it stays,' he said. 'Please.'

She did not answer him, looked down at the ring and said softly, in a loving voice, 'It is magnificent, Sebastian . . . thank you.'

After a moment of silence, he said, 'I would like to announce our engagement at the end of the luncheon today. Don't say a word to me about stealing Claudia's thunder . . . she's got thunder surrounding her at this very moment, and enjoying it thoroughly.' He smiled at her.

Alexis gave him a long, loving look, and reached out to stroke his cheek. 'Of course, darling. I suppose I have been a bit over-cautious.'

'You have. But I will correct that later when I tell the world that we are engaged and getting married in September. Here at Courtland.'

During the luncheon, there were speeches and toasts, and more speeches, teasing and jokes. At the very end Sebastian stood up, looked down at Alexis sitting next to him, and brought her to her feet. The guests looked up at him, expectantly.

'I want everyone to raise their glass to somebody else today. Please toast my future bride, Miss Alexis Malvern. We are engaged to be married in September. Here's to Alexis.'

'To Alexis!' the guests repeated and raised their glasses. A moment later clapping broke out when Sebastian brought her into his arms and kissed her.

THIRTY-SEVEN

'**C**an I speak to you for a moment?' Henry Malvern asked, hovering in the doorway of his daughter's office.

'Come in, Papa. Don't stand there,' Alexis replied.

Smiling, he walked over to her desk and sat down in the chair opposite. 'I know you're often at Haven House, but I do wish you wouldn't go to Whitechapel for a while. The newspapers are full of stories about those two women being murdered—'

'Yes, I know,' Alexis cut in. 'They're calling the murderer Jack the Ripper, because after he's strangled them to death, he carves them up and mutilates their bodies.' A small shiver passed through Alexis. Her face was grave as she added quietly, 'And Scotland Yard doesn't have one single clue about his identity.'

'Please, darling, do stay out of that part of London for the time being,' Henry pleaded, obviously extremely troubled. 'There's a killer on the loose.'

'Papa, please, I do have to go with Claudia now that she's back from honeymoon, and before my own wedding. In fact, we've an appointment there today with Madeleine Thompson, the woman who runs Haven House for us. She herself is upset. Even though the abused women are quite safe living at Haven House, they are naturally afraid too. But I do have a solution, I believe.'

'A solution for their fear?' Henry asked, his dark brows coming together in a frown. 'How can you do that?'

'By putting a man in the house. By that I mean a caretaker, who will make them feel more secure. Actually, Claudia and I have decided to hire a married couple to do this caretaking job. Two people will provide Madeleine with extra help, which she really needs. I do believe a kind married man will make the women feel less vulnerable.'

'Are you telling me that the house is . . . full?' Henry sounded astonished as he asked the question.

'Unfortunately, I am telling you exactly that, Papa. I'm afraid a lot more women have arrived on our doorstep lately.'

'Men are abusing women more than ever,' Henry announced sharply, a hint of anger in his tone.

'Probably. But there's something else involved, in my opinion. Now many people know about Haven House, and they are not so shy about coming to us for help the way they used to be.'

'Do you need more money? I'll give you a cheque immediately,' her father volunteered, wanting to help and proud of her dedication to the charity she had started.

'How nice of you to offer, but money is not a problem. Sebastian invested the funds I had in donations, and he's done very well for me, for the charity.' There was a momentary pause before Alexis added, 'I am going to Haven House this afternoon, Papa, with Claudia. We always go on Wednesday. Josh will take us in the carriage, and please, believe me, those murders are taking place in an entirely different section of Whitechapel. In the slums. The two victims were prostitutes, poor souls.'

Henry nodded and stood up. 'All right, if you feel it's your duty to go and make Haven House safer, then you must do that. Knowing Josh will be with you makes me feel better.'

'I understand. Claudia will be in my carriage today. We'll be fine, Papa.'

Later that Wednesday afternoon in early September, when Alexis and Claudia arrived at Haven House, they knew at once that Madeleine was extremely uneasy about the situation.

Sitting in her office, she explained, 'I know Jack the Ripper has killed women in the poorer area of Whitechapel, but that doesn't seem to pacify the women staying here. They seem to think he could very easily break in and kill them all in their beds.'

'But they are not prostitutes. They're mostly abused wives,' Claudia pointed out in an even tone, not wishing to sound challenging.

'Yes, I know that, and so do they . . .' Madeleine's voice trailed off. The expression on her face was one of total misery. She now announced, 'I want one of you to talk to them today, or both of you perhaps. Please.'

'We will do that,' Alexis agreed. 'We'll have tea and a talk shortly. But I do think we must think in terms of hiring a care-taker – better still, a married couple. Two additional people will help you enormously, Madeleine, and a kindly man on the premises permanently will be reassuring to everyone.'

'That makes sense. But where will we house them? What I mean is, where will they live and sleep? We're pretty full up.'

'In the cellars. When I restored this house originally, I did ask for plumbing to run down there, if you recall,' Alexis said. 'However, the cellars have become storage units lately. I think one of them must be emptied, given a fresh coat of whitewash, and I'll manage to furnish it. Somehow. And swiftly.'

Claudia exclaimed, 'I'd forgotten about the cellars! We can

make a nice little flat out of one of them and perhaps keep another area for storage. Aunt Thea will certainly give me some chairs and sofas. She's redecorating. We can afford to buy a bed. Let's do it!'

Madeleine looked from Claudia to Alexis and thought: how clever they are. Always pulling tricks out of a hat. Money. They have that readily available. Whoever said it was the root of all evil was entirely wrong. Money talks.

Madeleine said, 'All of the women who are strong enough will be pleased to help empty the cellars. Maybe we can use one cellar to store a few things. So, when shall we start?'

'Tomorrow!' Alexis exclaimed. 'I'll send a painter down early on Monday morning to whitewash the walls. The furniture will soon follow. Within a few days.'

'Where will we find a couple?' Claudia asked, sounding anxious. 'What if we can only find a man, not a married couple?'

'I suppose that depends on the man and his capabilities, his experience. I shall put my thinking cap on, and so should you, Claudia. Maybe someone on our staffs will know a person looking for a good job that comes with shelter and food.' Glancing at Madeleine, Alexis now continued, 'What about you? Do you have any ideas?'

'I do, yes, as it so happens,' Madeleine answered in a more cheerful voice. Now that these two clever women were here and in command, it gave her a sense of security. 'My brother Terry has a friend, a man he's known for many years. His name is Don Onslow. He's been widowed for a number of years. Recently, he left his job in a machine factory and is looking for lighter work. Terry speaks well of him.'

'Since your brother knows him and has spoken up for him, we would like to interview him, wouldn't we, Claudia?' Alexis stared at her friend, gave her a hopeful look.

'Certainly. Recommendations from people we know are preferable. Would you get in touch with your brother, Madeleine?'

'I will. When would you like to interview Mr Onslow?'

'As soon as possible, don't you think, Alexis? Before you go to Gloucestershire for the wedding. Tomorrow morning? Are you available?' Claudia asked.

'I have a business appointment at my office, but I can change it quite easily.' Glancing across at Madeleine, Alexis said, 'Can you arrange this quickly?'

'I will contact my brother this evening. He doesn't live far away.'

'Very good. And I'm assuming you do agree that a trustworthy male presence in the house would do a lot to alleviate any worries the women have.'

Madeleine nodded. 'I do, yes. You'd better explain you're looking for a caretaker. Reassure them they're really safe here. That Jack the Ripper isn't going to come a-calling.' There was a hint of relief in Madeleine's voice as she said this. Alexis and Claudia exchanged glances, pleased that she had calmed down.

As they rode back in the carriage, heading in the direction of Grosvenor Square, Alexis said, 'I do think the newspapers are having a bit of a field day with all these stories about the murders. And calling him Jack the Ripper. A lot of women are afraid of venturing out at night, wherever it is they live.'

'Yes, I'm inclined to agree with you. On the other hand, two murders in one week, both identical, do make it look as if there's a crazy man on a possible rampage.'

'I must agree. I think highly of Scotland Yard, Claudia. They'll soon identify him, I'm certain of that, and get him under lock and key. And everyone, especially in the East End will be relieved.'

Changing the subject, Claudia said, 'I thought your wedding gown looked beautiful when you had the last fitting on Monday. Madame Valance is the best. So, when are you going to look at the tiaras at Courtland?'

'This weekend. Your father suggested we spend Saturday afternoon in the vaults. He wants me to choose one then, something
to do with the earring he wishes me to wear.' Alexis glanced at
Claudia. 'There must be a large selection of tiaras, from what
he said.'

'Yes, you see they've been kept in the Trevalian family for the
last hundred years, passed down from bride to bride. It's quite
a treasure trove. Just wait and see. You'll get a great surprise.'

George Falconer sat at his desk at *The Chronicle*, staring at
some of the headlines of competing newspapers. All of them
were lurid, as he had expected they would be. A small shudder
of distaste ran through him.

It was Wednesday afternoon on 12 September, four days after
the second murdered woman had been found: Annie Chapman.
And it was thirteen days since the body of the first woman had
been discovered, on 31 August: Mary Ann Nichols.

Identical murders, grisly and horrific – the women had been
strangled and then horribly mutilated, hence the nickname given
to the murderer . . . Jack the Ripper. He had ripped them apart
with a scalpel or carving knife, or something else that was very
sharp indeed.

Although George was now on the desk for his newspaper,
thrilled by the promotion and new opportunities this afforded
him, he was still interested in every bit of news, even these grisly
murders. He was most especially intrigued since he had a good
friend at Scotland Yard.

He glanced at his timepiece and saw that it was almost six
o'clock. Locking his desk drawer, he picked up the column he
had written that afternoon. It was about the Prince of Wales
and the royal yacht, *Osborne*. Prince Bertie had welcomed on
board his hated cousin William, heir to the German throne after

his father Fritz, the present heir-in-waiting. The visit had been last month, and in all probability arranged by Lord Salisbury, always on the ready to foster English–German relations through the two royal families, blood cousins all.

It was what George called a 'think' piece, the kind of story his editor liked. After quickly rereading it, nodding his head, knowing it would resonate in certain circles, he left his office. Walking down the corridor, he went into the editor's empty office, placed the pages on his boss's desk, and left the building.

It was nice weather. Since he liked to walk, stretch his legs after a day at his desk, he went up Fleet Street and into the Strand. It was there that he hailed a hackney cab and gave directions to the driver. He preferred that to taking the Inner Circle railway that ran under London's streets now.

When they arrived at Scotland Yard, George jumped out of the cab, paid the driver and hurried into the building that he knew so well. Within seconds he was sitting in the office of one of his closest friends, Detective Inspector Roger Crawford, who had greeted him warmly.

'I thought you were now the expert on our fanciful royals,' Roger declared, laughter echoing in his voice. 'Don't tell me you couldn't resist digging into this Jack the Ripper mess?'

'I'm curious, of course,' George admitted. 'But have no desire to dig into it. However, I do have the true instincts of a genuine newspaperman, and I just wanted to give you a tip.'

'I'll take any tip from any bugger standing around to give me one,' Roger exclaimed. 'So what is it?'

'I truly believe there will be more murders. I just feel it in my bones, and I've heard the same from a couple of others in the newsroom,' George confided in a voice that was almost inaudible.

'Jesus! Don't say that, George! This is one lousy case and it will be hard to crack. No evidence, nothing left at the scene of the crime. No witnesses. Nobody saw anything. Dead of night.

Everything quiet. Can you believe it? Not even a small cry, never mind a scream. The whole thing is a mystery.'

'You're baffled, Rog? Am I right?'

'I am. But it's not just me. It's every bloody copper in this building.'

'Were the women killed because they were prostitutes? Or doesn't that mean anything in the long run?'

Roger Crawford shrugged, his expression gloomy. He was a brilliant detective, known for his in-depth investigations. For him to be baffled alarmed George.

'If you don't have a clue, then who does?' George asked.

'I just told you . . . nobody. Not at this moment anyway. We've talked to neighbours, people who live in the area, pub owners . . .' Roger stopped and lifted his hands in the air. 'I'd be happy if you jumped on the wagon . . . you were always good at sniffing things out. Help me, George.'

'Not this time. I wouldn't be any help. Besides I can't. Another journalist has this beat.'

'Aye, and he's on holiday,' Roger shot back.

'Come on, Rog. Let's go to the pub and have a pint. I'll give you a few of my thoughts.'

THIRTY-EIGHT

'You look wonderful, Sebastian,' Lord Reginald said, beaming at his best friend. 'In good nick. The rest here has done you good.'

'It has indeed. I was beginning to feel worn out and, as you know, I've been schooling Cornelius in all of our methods at the bank. That's been hard work. He's good, though, no doubt about that in my mind. I have great faith in my new son-in-law. He's clever and, I might add, very loyal.'

'Glad to hear it. Shall we go and sit over there in the ruins?' Reggie suggested. 'I feel a bit puffed out. It was quite a walk you brought me on.'

Sebastian nodded, and the two old friends walked across to the ruins of the priory, sat down on flat slabs of stone, leaning against a partially ruined wall. Reaching into his riding jacket pocket, Reggie took out a packet of cigarettes, offered it to Sebastian, who declined.

'I've caught cold and when I smoke I cough. I don't want all the women fussing over me this weekend.' He grinned. 'Especially Alexis.'

'I know what you mean . . . they love to mother us, or so it seems to me. Anyway, old chap, you and she will soon be tying the knot, and I can't wait to witness it.'

'Neither can I.' Sebastian started to laugh. 'Can you imagine, I never thought I would ever find the right woman, but I did, and so unexpectedly.'

'That's the way it goes. You're just walking along, minding your own business, and you suddenly get hit by a train. Wham! And you're a goner.' Reggie struck a Swan Vesta, put the flame to the cigarette, and took a long drag. 'That was your lucky day, Sebastian.'

'It was. Thanks for agreeing to be my best man, Reg. I really do appreciate it.'

'I would have been as mad as hell if you'd asked anyone else,' Reginald declared, sounding indignant.

'Who would I have asked?' Sebastian threw him a puzzled look.

'Doug, Francis or Malcolm, our three little friends from our Eton days. Tra-la, tra-la.'

Grinning, Sebastian exclaimed, 'That's something I can't possibly visualize, although I did invite them to the wedding and they are coming.'

''Course they are. They wouldn't miss it for the world. And they'll be eaten up with envy when they set eyes on the bride.'

'Speaking of my bride, I have created a Trust for her which will come into play once we are married. As I explained last night, you are still executor of my will, alongside my sister Thea. I've had to make some changes to it because of my marriage. However, it pretty much remains the same, except that I had to make provision for my future wife. I want her to be totally secure financially if something happens to me.'

'I understand you completely, but you've also got the consolation that she's her father's heir. His only child. The Malvern Company will be hers one day. She'll be very, very rich in her own right.'

'I know, I know. But I felt I must do the proper thing. After all, she is going to be Mrs Sebastian Trevalian.'

'Claudia inherits Courtland, doesn't she?' Reggie said.

'Yes, as my oldest child and heir, she gets everything. Well, almost. Her sisters have Trusts. Let's move on . . . I have studied those papers you sent me before I left London. I really think Marcus Whitely has made you a terrific offer for the newspaper company. I would take it if I were you. I doubt you'll do better, get a higher offer.'

Reggie nodded, looking pleased. 'I'm glad I have your blessing. I don't have a son to inherit. I'm in the same boat as you . . . only daughters. Frankly, I want to get rid of the lot and go off and have a bit of playtime. I'm tired.'

Unexpectedly the heavy clouds darkened and a drizzle started. Within seconds it turned into a heavy shower. Both men jumped up and set off down the path, heading towards the house. They began to run when the shower became a heavy downpour. They were both sodden to the skin when they rushed into the front hall, their clothes dripping rain onto the highly polished marble floor.

Sebastian sat in his bath, hoping to get warm and to ease the ache in his bones. He had understood exactly what Reggie had meant when he remarked that he was glad he was selling his company, that he was tired. He had been feeling the same way for the last few months. But, after all, he was in his forties now.

There had been the fuss of his daughter's marriage; all that planning, training Cornelius, and, of course, making the changes to his affairs, a necessity since he was about to embark on marriage.

Marriage to Alexis. Here at Courtland. It would be a lovely occasion, surrounded by family and just a few friends. A small affair, but one he was looking forward to, and then the trip to Paris. He really couldn't wait.

He drifted with his thoughts, dozing in his tub, until at last he roused himself. He got out, wrapped himself in a large bath-robe, and went into the bedroom to sit in front of the fire. He couldn't help wondering why he had been feeling so chilled lately. It's the cold, he thought. I caught a cold. It's nothing; it will go away. Colds always do after a few days.

Sebastian stood on the terrace, looking out across the park. It had turned into a lovely evening. The rain had stopped, the dark clouds had fled, and the sky was pale blue, tinged with pink around the edges of wispy white clouds.

The air was fresh, and there was the smell of wet grass floating in the air. He took several deep breaths, relieved that he could breathe properly again.

When he was dressing for dinner, he had been overwhelmed by a coughing attack; at one moment he had thought he might choke.

Thankfully he was fine now. But he must watch himself, get rid of the cold. It was 12 September and on the 29th he was getting married. He must be fit and well for this important event in his life.

A smile flickered when he thought of Alexis. She was busy in London this week, having fittings for her trousseau at Madame Valance's atelier. Aided and abetted by Claudia and Lady Jane. How lucky he was to have found her, this quite extraordinary young woman.

'There you are,' Lord Reginald exclaimed, walking onto the terrace, stopping next to Sebastian and following his gaze.

'The park looks at its best tonight, especially in this light.' Reggie glanced up. '"Red sky at night, shepherd's delight. Red sky in the morning, shepherd's warning . . ." So at least we know it won't rain tomorrow.'

Sebastian nodded. 'What a soaking we took. I hope you had a hot bath . . . I don't want you to catch cold.'

'No, I didn't, like Melbourne, who once told Queen Victoria that he never took a bath, if you can believe that. But actually, I do usually bathe frequently, unlike most people in this country. I'm told that many are afraid of water, think it opens our pores and exposes us to dangerous diseases. So they clean themselves with cotton towels and avoid water like the plague.'

Sebastian started to laugh. 'I know, but I need a good hot soak some days. It takes away the aches and pains. To change the subject, I was thinking about Whitely's offer for your company earlier and wondering if you really do want to sell to him? Or anyone else, for that matter? I mean, what would you do without the newspapers?'

'My God, how extraordinary! I've been thinking about that exact same thing. It occurred to me I might be at a loss, not know how to pass my time . . . Unless you retired from the bank, and then we could go travelling the world, having fun.'

Shaking his head, grimacing, Sebastian exclaimed, 'I could never retire. I must run Trevalians as long as I'm able to do so. I've started training Cornelius early, because I want him to take over one day, and need him to be aware of everything. He's good, thank God. I was extremely lucky Claudia picked a man who came from a banking family. She had the good sense to choose one with his feet on the ground, and who doesn't mind working hard.'

'The thing that worries me is *The Chronicle*. I've managed to have the best editors, who have kept the paper on the right track. There's not a hint of the tabloid press there. It's a fine newspaper, and I'm proud of it. I wouldn't want it to change.'

Sebastian nodded. He took hold of Reggie's arm. 'Let's go inside and have a glass of champagne before supper, and talk some more.'

They went into the library. As he usually did, Sebastian stood in front of the fire, warming himself. Despite the fact it was a mild evening, the fire wasn't throwing out much heat. Mr Kingsley, the butler at Courtland, walked forward. 'Good evening, sir. What can I serve you, Your Lordship?'

'I'll have champagne, Kingsley, since I spot a bottle ready and waiting. Thank you.'

A moment later the two old friends were clinking glasses and Sebastian picked up their conversation. 'I thought *The Chronicle*'s coverage of those frightful Whitechapel murders was excellent. Any new developments?'

Reggie grimaced. 'Nothing. It's very strange. The police are baffled. Apparently they haven't been able to pin down any suspects. But my money's on the Criminal Investigation Department of the Metropolitan Police. They'll solve it.'

Reggie chuckled when he realized Sebastian was puzzled, if only momentarily. 'That's the official name of the department known as Scotland Yard, which is actually the name of the street and the building where they are housed. At the moment. They'll soon be moving over to a new building on the Embankment.'

Sebastian nodded, sipped his drink. 'I didn't know that.'

Reggie went on, 'Centuries ago, the street called Scotland Yard housed a palace where the Scottish kings stayed when they visited London. Bet you didn't know that either, eh?'

'No, I didn't, and I wonder who else does?' Sebastian eyed his longest and dearest friend in amusement. 'I always said you are full of an enormous amount of strange information—'

'That nobody has any use for?' Reggie interrupted.

'Well, I wouldn't say that. What you've just told me is rather interesting, since I like hearing new things about English history.' Sebastian paused, finally said, 'Going back to the murders, they've been awfully violent, haven't they?'

'Yes. Even seasoned policemen were sickened by the way the women's bodies were mutilated, ripped apart – so I'm told by my editor. Hence the name "Jack the Ripper" . . . Whoever thought of that, though? It's a bit lurid, I think.'

'I was worried about Alexis and Claudia going to Haven House in Whitechapel, but I soon realized that it's not anywhere near the district where the murders took place. They went there this afternoon, I believe. They always go on Wednesday. I suppose they wanted to reassure the women there.'

Reggie nodded and, after a few swallows of the champagne, he threw Sebastian a questioning look. 'Were you going to tell me not to make a deal to sell my newspapers?'

'Not exactly. I was going to retract my rather hasty response to you earlier. I now believe you should think it over. There's no hurry, is there?'

'None at all. I shall take your advice, mull it over.' A reflective look settled on his face. A second later he said in a low voice, 'I do love *The Chronicle*. My paper.'

The two men had supper in the Chinese dining room. Medium in size, it was painted scarlet. It was a favourite of both men. The walls and ceiling were painted scarlet, which had been given a coat of lacquer to make them shine. A chandelier created from Chinese lanterns hung down over a round ebony-wood table, surrounded by Chinese chairs made of the same black wood.

Framed paintings of Chinese landscapes on the walls and other pieces of chinoiserie-style furniture added to the unique effect. As in all the rooms at Courtland Priory, a fire blazed in the hearth, but again Sebastian noticed a chill. The flames didn't seem to be warming the walls of the old house this evening.

'I always feel as if I'm cosy and safe inside a small red box,' Reggie said, looking across the table at Sebastian.

'That was my intention,' Sebastian answered. He ate an oyster, explaining, 'These oysters are from Colchester, by the way, and the best fishmonger.'

'That's how they taste. Jolly good choice on your part . . . I'm glad the season has started. Incidentally, what did Douglas Manfield say about us not going to join him at Templeton Hall for the grouse last weekend? Was he put out?'

'I'm not sure. Worried maybe. He was short of guns when we dropped out. However, I think he managed to invite a couple of other guns at the last minute. I just said I was up to my neck with planning the wedding and that you were busy with me. I let it go at that. I didn't say anything about our growing aversion to shooting down blameless little birds for no real reason.'

'I'm glad you didn't! He would've thought we'd turned into sissies.'

Sebastian stared at Reggie, taken aback, and they both laughed, not caring at all what their old Etonian friend thought about them.

After the oysters, Kingsley and one of the maids served roast beef with mixed vegetables, and the dessert was lemon syllabub, a delicious mixture of cream, sugar, lemon and white wine.

Later that evening, as they sat by the fire in the library, sipping cognac, Sebastian suddenly leaned forward. 'I'm glad you were able to spend this week here with me, Reg, especially since I didn't particularly want to have a bachelor night. These few days with you are much more important. Thank you.'

'No thanks required, old chap, it's my pleasure. Once a chap gets married, things do change. Jane went along with it quite happily, knowing how lives evolve in different ways. Anyway, she's busy with the bride and happy I'm here with you.'

Sebastian smiled at the thought of Alexis. After a moment, he said, 'I've never quite understood about bachelor nights. It seems to me it's just an excuse to go out and behave badly. And who needs that the night before getting married? A thick head must be something of a burden on the wedding day.'

A silence fell between them for a short while. It was Reggie who broke it when he murmured, 'Can you imagine, we've been best friends for over thirty years? And not once have we had a quarrel.'

Grinning at him, Sebastian exclaimed, 'That's absolutely true. But there have been moments when I've wanted to punch you on the nose.'

Reggie burst out laughing. 'And I've felt the same about you. The thing is, we never did it.'

THIRTY-NINE

Lord Reginald Horatio Carpenter, hereditary peer of the realm, publishing tycoon and generous philanthropist, who helped the poor and needy, was a man of many talents. He was extremely clever and could usually solve most problems facing him, whatever they were.

But not at this moment in time. His closest and dearest friend, Sebastian Trevalian, was just that little bit cleverer. At least in hiding the fact that he was ill, which is what Sebastian had done for the last two days since Reginald had come down to stay with him.

As he walked towards the stable block at Courtland early on Thursday morning, Reginald wondered how he was going to outmanoeuvre Sebastian and get Dr Sedgewick over to the house as soon as possible. He knew the doctor, who lived and worked in nearby Cirencester, and who had treated the Trevalian family for years.

Last night, at supper, Sebastian had looked well enough and had appeared perfectly normal. He had been elegantly dressed as always. But Reginald was certain his friend had suppressed a bout of coughing by excusing himself and leaving the table for a moment or two.

Later that evening, unable to fall asleep, his mind on the sale of his newspapers, Reginald had heard Sebastian coughing once more. Dismayed and worried, he had left his bed, and gone out into the corridor to stand outside Sebastian's door. He had wondered whether to go in and see if his friend needed help. In the end he had decided against intruding, aware how private Sebastian was.

When Reginald arrived at the stable block, he saw the head groom saddling up Brilliant Boy, the stallion Reginald had ridden yesterday.

'Good morning, Smiley,' he called, hurrying across the cobble-stone yard. 'I've decided not to ride today. I should have told you earlier.'

The groom swung around, saluted Reginald. 'Morning, sir. Not a problem, Your Lordship, just wanted to be prepared in case you were up for a good gallop before breakfast.'

Reginald stroked the horse's nose, patted his neck. 'He's a wonderful stallion,' he announced, taking a step back, his admiration for the horse showing on his face. He had been around horses all his life and knew a piece of great horseflesh when he saw it.

Smiley said, 'The best we have in the stable, sir. If you asks me, he could've been trained to race . . . he's a racehorse, in my humble opinion. Look at his fabulous legs, his flanks. Gorgeous bit of stuff.'

As he spoke, Smiley went back to the horse, began to unbuckle the saddle. Looking across at Lord Reginald, the groom asked, 'What about tomorrow, sir? Might you be up for a trot then?'

'Yes, indeed. And perhaps Mr Trevalian will join me, Smiley. We'll probably go out together.'

'Oh, I do hope so, Your Lordship! Mr Trevalian didn't ride at all when he was here last weekend. Under the weather, mebbe.'

Reginald inclined his head slightly, knowing better than to discuss his host with an employee, or with anybody for that matter. Bad form, totally beyond the pale.

Reaching out, he smoothed his hand over the glossy, dark brown coat of the horse, and said to the groom, 'You certainly keep him in fine fettle, Smiley. Good work indeed. Very good grooming.'

'I try, sir, and Brilliant Boy is worth it. He's got breeding, stamina and heart. What more can you ask for from a horse?'

'You're absolutely correct, Smiley,' Reginald replied, strolling out of the yard, making his way to the Great Park, walking along the grove lined with ancient oak trees. He breathed deeply of the fresh air on this wonderful sunny morning.

That was another thing he had noticed. Sebastian had had trouble breathing towards the end of supper last night. Reginald came to an abrupt stop as he thought through the implications of that. His friend might well have caught cold, as he insisted he had, but it was now more. Instinctively, Reginald believed it might have something to do with Sebastian's chest or his lungs.

Damn it, Reginald cursed under his breath. I'm going to tackle him at breakfast and insist he sends for the doctor.

His mind now made up, Reginald swung around and walked back up the grove, determined to take charge of Sebastian's health. He was getting married at the end of the month. He had to regain his full health by then. That was an imperative.

As he strode along, Reginald couldn't help wondering why he had been such a coward, not speaking out at supper last night. Or going into Sebastian's bedroom when the coughing had been so harsh, very loud in the late hours. So loud and hacking, he had heard it across the corridor.

He had been foolish, and he cursed himself for that. Stand tall, his father had always said to him. Stand tall and speak your mind. Stand your ground. You are from a long line of soldiers who have fought wars and died for their country. Heroes all.

So many times his father had said that to him.

But his father hadn't been a solider. He had been a skilled businessman who had made a lot of money. Just as he had himself.

His ancestors had indeed been heroes. One great-great uncle had even been at Waterloo in 1815. An officer in the British infantry, fighting against French hussars and Polish lancers. But they had won that bloody and horrific war – and it had been thanks to Wellington, he had no doubt.

Reginald paused, took out his timepiece and saw that it was only seven thirty. Sebastian was usually an early riser. However, he suspected he would not be in the dining room yet. The coughing attack had lasted quite a long time during the night.

Once the Palladian mansion came into view, Reginald sat down on a wrought-iron garden seat, sighing to himself. Having made up his mind to speak to Sebastian as soon as he could, his thoughts turned to the days ahead.

Tomorrow, their few days of masculine companionship in lieu of a bachelor night would be over. Alexis and the family would come to Courtland: Sebastian's three daughters, son-in-law, and sister Thea. And, of course, his own Jane.

A smile crossed Reginald's face when he thought of his wife. He was going to tell her she was like a fabulous racehorse, with her breeding, stamina and heart. She would like to hear that, would be amused at being compared to a horse.

His wife would arrive tomorrow, and he was relieved she was coming before the others, who were to arrive on Saturday morning in time for lunch. She would help him make Sebastian see the sense of consulting a doctor. Jane was a true diplomat by nature, smoothing the way, courteous, always calm, cool, and in control. He could barely remember a time when she had raised her voice. Yes, Jane could help to put things right. She would get Sebastian to toe the line and get medical help.

Because the week before his wedding would be busy, Sebastian had decided to have a celebration dinner this coming Saturday. In the afternoon, he was going to show the diamond tiaras to Alexis. Reginald remembered this now, and knew he had no option but to get the doctor to come today. With this thought in mind, he now jumped up. He hurried back to the house, intent in his purpose.

Much to Reginald's surprise, Sebastian was walking across the front entrance hall when he came in through the front door.

They met in the middle of the hall, embraced and greeted each other. Sebastian looked him over, and said, 'So you didn't go riding this morning after all?'

'No. I did go down to the yard, spoke to Smiley, and saw Brilliant Boy . . . what a great horse he is.'

'I know. I was lucky there. A great buy. Perhaps we can go out together early tomorrow morning? Before Jane arrives?'

Reginald was about to agree and changed his mind, thinking of his father's words. He said, 'No, that's not possible. And you know it, Sebastian. Come into the library. I wish to speak to you privately and alone. Before breakfast.'

Sebastian stared at him, frowning, and then inclined his head. 'Let's talk.'

Once they were inside the library, Sebastian took the lead, speaking before Reginald could say a word.

'I'm not well, Reggie, and I know you know it. You've spotted it, despite my efforts to hide it. Am I correct?'

'Yes, and I—'

'Let me finish,' Sebastian cut in. 'I caught a cold. Last week, I think. And now it seems to have gone into my chest. I have a feeling I might have bronchitis. Dr Sedgewick has treated me for that before. I thought I should go into Cirencester to see him. After breakfast.'

An enormous wave of relief swept through Reginald, and he exclaimed, 'I'm so glad you've seen the sense of getting medical attention. Today's the thirteenth. You've exactly sixteen days to get back into good shape before your wedding.'

'Don't think I haven't thought of that, Reg. It never leaves my mind, as a matter of fact. And Alexis has eyes in the back of her head. She'll spot something's wrong when she gets here on Saturday . . . if I'm not careful.'

'I couldn't agree more. Let us go into the dining room. After breakfast we can go into Cirencester.'

'I'm so glad you intend to accompany me.'

'Whatever makes you think I'd let you go alone?' Reginald said. Taking hold of his friend's arm, he walked Sebastian out of the library, saying a silent prayer all would be well.

FORTY

Sebastian and Reginald sat in the brougham, the spacious carriage that Sebastian preferred. His head driver was taking them into the ancient town of Cirencester at a quick trot.

Neither man had eaten much breakfast, both anxious – in their different ways – to set off to visit the doctor.

At one moment Reginald said, 'I hope Sedgewick can see you and that his surgery is not crowded out with patients.'

'I'm sure everything will be fine,' Sebastian responded. 'Anyway, last year he took on two associates, Dr Leith and Dr Palmer, who have opened a small private infirmary across the street. They've become . . . a sort of team, actually. It's a clever idea, and I have told them so.'

'So what you're saying is that one of them will be available to see you immediately.'

'That's right. The other two are excellent doctors, but Sedgewick has looked after the family for years now. He has all my records, knows my history, my tendency to catch cold.'

'I'm sure that's all it is,' Reginald said, wanting to be positive and reassuring.

'I don't feel too bad this morning, and I didn't cough much last night,' Sebastian volunteered.

After these short exchanges, both men fell silent, preoccupied with their own thoughts. They had always been comfortable with each other, no matter what, ever since their boyhood.

Within twenty minutes, Hamm brought the carriage to a standstill outside the building where the doctor's office was housed. The two men alighted and walked inside. The doctor's receptionist looked up and smiled when she saw Sebastian and a companion entering the office, walking towards her.

'Good morning, Mr Trevalian.'

'Good morning to you, Miss Maeve,' he answered, and added, 'This is Lord Carpenter, a close friend.'

Reginald said, 'Good morning, Miss Maeve.'

The receptionist smiled, greeted him in return, then said, 'I don't believe you have an appointment, Mr Trevalian.'

'No, I'm afraid I don't. But I would like to see Dr Sedgewick if he is available.'

'I will go and tell him you are here, sir,' she replied, and went down the corridor.

Within seconds, Miss Maeve Streeter returned. 'If you would come this way, Mr Trevalian, Dr Sedgewick can see you now.'

'Thank you, Miss Maeve. His Lordship will come with me.'

'Yes, sir.' She led them down the corridor and into the office of Dr Archibald Sedgewick, who stood up when the two men entered.

Walking forward, he shook Sebastian's hand, greeted him cordially, and Sebastian introduced Reginald.

'Lord Carpenter is my oldest and dearest friend, and I would like him to stay while you examine me, Dr Sedgewick. If you have no objection, that is.'

'None at all, Trevalian. Please, take a seat, both of you, and we shall talk for a few moments.'

The two men sat down in front of the doctor, who was behind

his large desk, and Sebastian confessed, 'I haven't been on top form in the last few days. I caught a cold.'

The doctor nodded. 'I know you're prone to them. So explain how you feel. That's the only way I will be able to understand what else might be wrong with you. I wish I had a way of seeing inside you, Trevalian, but I'm afraid I don't. Please tell me about your symptoms.'

'Last weekend I was here at Courtland and began to feel poorly. Chills, sneezing, a light cough. I also felt . . . I think "listless" is the best word to use.'

'What other symptoms have you had this past week?' the doctor asked, frowning slightly, leaning forward over the desk, studying Sebastian's face, his eyes probing. 'You must have other problems or you wouldn't have come to see me.'

'The other day, when I was shaving, I felt a stabbing pain in my ribcage. It went away, but it came back the day after. Also, I've had several coughing attacks that have been hard to bear. Very debilitating, in fact.'

The doctor nodded. 'Have you been spitting up anything? Blood? Sputum?'

'Last night I did spit up sputum, but no blood. Sometimes I get an attack of the chills. I become icy cold, but they usually disappear after a while.'

'Have you had trouble breathing?'

'A few times, and a sharp pain in my chest.'

Dr Sedgewick rose. 'Would you come behind the screen, Mr Trevalian? Please take off your jacket, waistcoat and shirt. I would like to listen to your heartbeat, examine you thoroughly and take your temperature.'

Sebastian did as he was asked, stretching out on the bed where the doctor indicated he should lie down. A moment later, Dr Sedgewick reappeared with his stethoscope around his neck.

After listening to his heartbeat and taking his temperature, the doctor began to press his hands on Sebastian's chest and abdomen. 'Do you feel any pain under the pressure of my fingers?' he asked.

'No, I don't,' Sebastian said, answering truthfully. But, as he sat up on the doctor's instructions, he had a brief bout of coughing, which swiftly abated.

Sebastian dressed as quickly as he could, wanting to know what the doctor had discovered, if anything. Like all doctors, he kept a straight face, never displayed any emotion whatsoever, so it was impossible to read him. The odd thing was, now that Sebastian had seen the doctor, he felt better. But then, wasn't it always like that? He smiled to himself.

Once he was back in the chair, sitting in front of the doctor, Sebastian gave him a long stare and asked, 'Do I have bronchitis?'

'No, you don't. When you have bronchitis, only the air passages are infected. I believe there is an infection in your lungs. You have pleurisy. There's a bit of a fever in your system and your temperature is hovering at just over 101 degrees. However, that is relatively normal. Nonetheless, we must watch this. Hopefully, it won't go any higher.'

Sebastian frowned. 'What is pleurisy, Dr Sedgewick?'

'An infection of the lining of the lungs.'

'Can it be treated?'

'Yes, to a certain extent, but sometimes it does precede pneumonia.'

Sebastian gaped at the doctor. He felt a cold chill run through him. 'Oh my God, not . . . not pneumonia!'

'Let us see if we can treat the pleurisy, prevent anything else from developing. I am going to give you a strong medicine for your cough. I will need to get an analysis of your sputum. Miss Maeve will give you a small glass container for that. If you would attempt to cough before you leave, please. She will show you to the anteroom.'

'Yes, I will be glad to do that, Dr Sedgewick. You know I'm

getting married on the twenty-ninth of September. I hope I will be better by then.'

'I understand, and let me just add that your fever is low-grade, but I do want you to take better care of yourself. No rushing around the estate or lifting heavy objects. As much rest as you can have will do marvels for you.'

Reginald had met Jane Cadwalander when she was sixteen, married her when she was eighteen, and welcomed the birth of their first daughter when she was nineteen. And so he considered he knew her very well indeed, since she was now thirty-seven.

He knew she was bursting to tell him something important. He read this in her eyes and in her demeanour. But his wife had arrived just when he and Sebastian were finishing lunch, and Sebastian had insisted she join them for coffee.

Finally, at last, Sebastian excused himself and went to his bedroom to rest, following Dr Sedgewick's orders, which had been given with some forcefulness yesterday.

It was Friday 14 September, and Jane had been expected in time for afternoon tea. But here she was. Early.

Now that they were alone at the table, Reginald leaned closer and murmured, 'I know you have something to tell me. You're practically bursting at the seams. So what is it?'

'I can't tell you here,' she answered and, pushing the chair back, she stood. 'Come along. Let us go to our rooms. I can only tell you in absolute privacy.'

'If it's such a state secret, perhaps we should go outside, where only the birds can hear. In a house, walls have ears, you know, as well as servants.'

Jane started to laugh and led him out of the dining room and up the main staircase. As usual, they were staying in the Parisian Suite, a set of rooms composed of a bedroom, sitting room, and bathroom. The main rooms were charmingly decorated with pieces of French furniture, along with comfortable sofas and chairs. The suite was spacious, airy and overlooked the gardens. Sebastian never allowed any other guests to occupy it. It was always kept for them whenever they wanted to come.

'So, tell me,' Reginald said, once they were inside the suite. 'You look about to pop.'

'I am about to pop . . .' She led him into the bedroom and indicated he should sit down on the sofa. 'For your own safety, just in case you pass out,' she explained.

He stared at her, obviously more puzzled than ever, and then sat down on the sofa as she had requested.

'You said I looked about to pop. And oh, am I going to pop, Reggie! In about six months.'

'I'm not following you,' Reginald said frowning.

Jane began to laugh, hurried over to join him on the sofa. Taking hold of his hand, she placed it on her stomach. 'Babies are going to pop out of here in about six months. I'm pregnant, darling! Three months pregnant! And the thing is, two will pop. The doctor says I'm carrying twins.'

For a moment Reginald was stupefied, unable to say a word, and then he took hold of her and hugged her to him, hanging onto her as if for dear life.

At last, he said, 'Oh my God, Jane. I can't believe it. You're pregnant! And with twins. Oh my God, one might be a boy.'

'They both might be boys,' Jane pointed out. 'Who knows? I'm just so happy, and I know you are.' When he was silent, she asked carefully, 'You are happy, aren't you, Reggie?'

'I am. Of course I am. I'm over the moon, darling. Why didn't you tell me before? You must have known something.'

'I did, but I am fully aware that I'm a certain age and I didn't dare tell you until I was absolutely sure I was carrying them safely. My doctor told me yesterday that I'm in excellent health, that I shouldn't have any problems carrying them to full term.'

Yesterday I was at another doctor's, Reginald thought, a sudden worry sweeping through him. But he's going to be all right. Sebastian's going to be fine. He wanted to tell Jane, confide in her about Sebastian, but he had promised he would not tell a soul. And he would keep that promise he had made to his best friend.

Rising, pulling Jane to her feet, Reginald led her over to the open window and put his arm around her shoulder. Mustering all of his strength, he said in a steady voice, 'I am thrilled about the babies, Jane, and I'm going to look after you very well, take great care of you, my darling.'

She turned to face him, staring at him. After a moment, she said, 'You're troubled about something, aren't you?'

'Not at all. Just utterly and completely taken by surprise by your stupendous news. Jane, just think: I might have a male heir at last.'

'I know you are . . . I just feel it in my bones. And in my belly.'

FORTY-ONE

Almost at once, Sebastian knew it had been a mistake to bring everyone down to the vaults. They were vast and endless, and very, very cold. He ought to have checked again yesterday and had paraffin heaters brought down to warm them up. Too late. Here they all were. He and Alexis, Jane and Reggie, and Claudia. The rest of the party, his sister Thea and his two other daughters, hadn't wanted to come to view the tiaras; nor had Cornelius, who had his head in bank papers in the library.

A moment later, Alexis hurried to his side, and said, 'It's like the Antarctic down here, Sebastian. I think we'd better go to the room where you put the tiaras, pick one and leave.'

'Yes, we must do that at once. It's bloody icy down here. You're right about that.'

Turning around, he said, 'Reggie, Jane, Claudia, let's make this fast. Alexis and I are very cold, so you must be too.'

'We are,' Jane exclaimed, answering for everyone. They were all freezing. 'Lead the way, Sebastian.'

He did. They went through three more vast vaults and came

to one with an open door. 'In here,' he said. 'I took the pieces out with Kingsley the other day . . . it didn't seem as cold then.'

'Oh my goodness me!' Jane cried when she saw the six tiaras lined up on a black velvet cloth spread across a long table. 'How wonderful they are! And so many!'

She took hold of Alexis's hand and they hurried across to the table, followed by Sebastian, cheering up when he saw the look of awe and anticipation on Alexis's face. She turned, smiled at him, was obviously impressed.

Claudia was fast on their heels, and said to Alexis, 'Remember this is the one I wore for my wedding in June. You mustn't choose that. So let's put it aside.'

'You're quite right,' Sebastian said. His eyes swept over the other five. He reached for the one which was his favourite. It had belonged to his mother and it was elaborate without being ostentatious. It rose to a higher point at the front. He thought it was stylish, and said so, looking at Alexis as he spoke.

'This is my favourite. I would love you to wear it . . . it was my mother's. But in the end, it must be your choice.' He picked it up and started to walk towards her, carrying the diamond tiara carefully. Unexpectedly, it slipped out of his hands and dropped to the floor with a crash.

'Oh, Sebastian!' Alexis cried, running to the tiara, bending down and taking it in her hands. She saw at once that some stones were missing. Claudia came and knelt next to her and they soon found the three missing stones which had adorned the front peak of the tiara.

'What a clumsy fool I am,' Sebastian exclaimed, angry with himself. 'I suppose my hands are cold . . . that's the only explanation I can come up with.'

Alexis remained kneeling, feeling a strange sense of foreboding settling over her. Eventually standing up, shaking this odd sensation off, she walked to the table and carefully placed the tiara down on the black velvet cloth.

Sebastian said, 'It can be repaired quite easily. I will send Kingsley to the jeweller's in London on Monday. It will be repaired in time for the wedding, have no fear.' He glanced at Alexis and smiled. 'Unless there is another one you prefer.'

'No, no, that's the one. Your mother's tiara is perfect for me. Thank you, Sebastian.'

'Then let us take it upstairs. You carry it, Claudia. Do you have the three diamonds that fell out?'

'Yes, I do, Papa. Here in my hand. Not even damaged.'

'You can't damage a diamond,' Sebastian answered.

Reginald said, 'I'd better bring the red leather box in which it will need to travel.' He went to the table, picked up the box and followed the others out of the tiara vault. Turning off the light and closing the door after him, he was relieved to move out of the icy cellars.

That evening, Sebastian sparkled at the dinner table. He was amusing, witty and kept the conversation flowing. The men looked handsome in their dinner suits and the women beautiful in their elegant gowns and jewels. No one made mention of the broken tiara, and Sebastian had put it out of his mind. He had dismissed it as an unfortunate accident.

Much to his relief, he had warmed up after a hot bath and an hour in front of the fire in his bedroom. Although Alexis had fussed about his feeling cold, she had blamed this on the vaults. She had no idea he had pleurisy. Only Reggie knew that, and he was sworn to secrecy. Sebastian was trying to rest as much as he could.

It pleased him that his two daughters, Lavinia and Marietta, were so friendly with Alexis and excited about being bridesmaids once again. His sister Thea was also being charming to his future wife. And why not? Alexis was an exceptional young woman.

Alexis sat facing him tonight at the table, because it no longer mattered if they gazed at each other constantly. After all, they would be joined in wedlock in two weeks. Man and wife. After their honeymoon in Paris, they would be starting a new life together. And a family. He was happy, a contented man. He felt well, in good health. The cough had vanished and so had the frequent pain in his ribcage.

All's well that ends well, he thought, as he fell asleep that night, his arms wrapped around Alexis, the greatest love of his life.

A few days later, Jane and Reginald were walking towards the terrace when they saw Sebastian sitting there, obviously waiting for them. It was almost time for lunch. It was Tuesday 18 September, and they had one more day here at Courtland. Everyone else, including Alexis, had left after the weekend.

Raising her hand, waving, Jane cried, 'Coo-ee!' and she and Reginald increased their pace.

Sebastian stood up, smiling, and walked towards them. Unexpectedly, he tripped and fell. He lay in a crumpled heap on the terrace, not moving, and when they reached him, Reginald was certain he was unconscious. A rush of fear filled him and his chest tightened.

'Stay with him,' Reginald finally managed to say in a shaky voice. 'I'm going to get Kingsley and one of the footmen to help me lift him.'

Jane nodded, kneeling down by her husband's friend, unable to speak, frightened by the pallor of Sebastian's face, his stillness. He hardly seemed to be breathing. She bent over him, felt for a pulse on his wrist and was thankful she found one.

Within minutes, Reginald returned with the butler, Maxwell, Sebastian's valet, and Peter, one of the young footmen. The four men carried Sebastian into the house and up to his bedroom. They placed him on the bed.

Turning to Maxwell, Reginald said, 'Please undress Mr Trevalian and put on his nightclothes, and then get him into bed as best you can. Perhaps you should stay to help, Peter. I shall return in a few minutes.' He glanced at the butler. 'Please come with me, Kingsley.'

'Yes, sir,' the butler answered in a low, concerned voice. 'What happened to Mr Trevalian?' he asked as they went down-stairs.

'I'm not sure, Kingsley.' Reginald paused, then added, 'I think he tripped and fell. I want you to go into Cirencester right away to see Dr Sedgewick. Ask him to come here at once. Is Hamm available?'

'No, Your Lordship. He's gone to London to fetch Miss Malvern. If you remember, she went to London yesterday to pick up her trousseau and her wedding gown.'

'I had forgotten for the moment. Then take another driver and go as fast as you can.'

'Yes, sir, right away, Your Lordship.'

Jane was waiting in the doorway of the library and hurried forward into the entrance hall when Reginald returned. 'Has Sebastian gained consciousness yet?' she asked anxiously.

'He hadn't, but we had better go upstairs to be with him. I've sent Kingsley to Cirencester for the doctor.'

'There's something wrong with him, isn't there?' Jane said, putting her hand on her husband's arm, looking up into his grave face. 'Something bad . . . Sebastian is ill, isn't he?'

Reginald nodded and suddenly tears filled his eyes. He swallowed them back, nodded. 'He has pleurisy. I'm the only one who knows, so keep that to yourself. I thought he was getting better, put perhaps he's not, Jane.'

Jane was stunned, and her face had gone sheet white. 'Pleurisy always becomes pneumonia, Reggie, didn't you know that?

Sebastian must have pneumonia. I'm relieved you've sent for the doctor. Oh my God, that's a deadly disease.'

Reginald stared at her and silently led her upstairs.

When they went into Sebastian's bedroom, Reginald was relieved that Maxwell and Peter had obviously managed to undress him, get on a nightshirt, and put him properly into bed.

Turning to the valet, Reginald said, 'Thank you, and thanks to you too, Peter. I see you've managed to make him comfortable.'

'We did our best, Lord Carpenter,' Maxwell said. 'But he is still unconscious. His breathing is a bit more even, and he does have a stronger pulse now.'

'That's such a relief,' Jane interjected. 'His pulse was very faint earlier, when he first tripped and fell on the terrace.'

'I've sent Kingsley to fetch the doctor,' Reginald told them. 'Now all we can do is wait, and hope that Mr Trevalian regains consciousness soon. In the meantime, Lady Jane and I will stay with him. I would appreciate it, Maxwell, if you would ask the housekeeper to send up a pitcher of water and some glasses, and to prepare a beef broth.'

'I'll go and speak to Mrs Farsley straight away, sir.'

The two men left and Jane went to the bedside and looked down at Sebastian. She choked up. Tears were threateningly near the surface. Gently she moved a strand of his fair hair away from his forehead, then went and sat down on the sofa.

She glanced around and saw that her husband was staring out of the window, and she knew that he was filled with dread.

Dr Sedgewick arrived at Courtland an hour later. Considering the time it took to go to Cirencester and come back to Courtland, Jane and Reginald knew the doctor had left his practice immediately. He had understood it was an emergency.

As Reginald explained how Sebastian had fallen, and how they had managed to get him into the house and up to bed, there was an unexpected change in Sebastian.

Dr Sedgewick spotted it as he stood at the bedside. Sebastian moved an arm and then a leg, and slowly he came awake, blinking in the sunlight pouring into the room.

'That is a huge relief,' the doctor said to the room at large.

'What happened to me?' Sebastian asked in a low, hoarse voice, barely able to speak.

'You fell outside on the terrace, Mr Trevalian,' the doctor explained. 'But I don't believe anything is broken. And now I'm going to examine you. I want to see where we stand.'

Jane and Reginald walked forward, towards the bed, so that Sebastian could see they were there in the room. Then they went to sit on the sofa together. They were both relieved to see Sebastian with his eyes open. And hearing his voice had given them hope.

After a few seconds, Jane and Reginald slipped out of Sebastian's bedroom and walked across the corridor to their suite. They left the door open in case Dr Sedgewick needed them. Jane excused herself and went into the dressing room.

Once alone, she stared at herself in the mirror and saw that she looked extremely pale and tense. After pinching her cheeks to bring colour to them, she straightened her golden-blonde hair, smoothed the sides and settled the curls on top of her head. Unexpectedly, her large blue eyes filled, and she choked up again, but steadied herself, blinking the tears away. Reggie needed her, and certainly Sebastian did. But she was terribly afraid for him. Pneumonia was such a ghastly disease and always hard to beat.

Taking a deep breath, straightening the collar of her dress,

Jane pushed a smile onto her face and went to join her husband, feeling she looked a little neater, more put together.

'Are you all right, Reg?' she asked, going up to him, putting an arm around him.

He looked down at her, half smiled. 'As long as I have you, I'm fine. I am worried about Sebastian though, very worried, Jane. He's been much better, so good on Saturday. That fall on the terrace startled me – shocked me, actually.'

There was a knock on the open door, and when Reginald saw Dr Sedgewick standing there, he immediately beckoned him to come into the room, walking over to escort him in.

'What is the verdict, Doctor?' he asked, keeping his voice steady.

'It is pneumonia. Which is what I expected, it is usually preceded by pleurisy. As I explained last week, that's an inflammation of the lining of the lungs covering the area of his pneumonia. It disappears as the pneumonia progresses. Mr Trevalian has a temperature in excess of 103 degrees, and a fever, at the moment. He has to be carefully watched.'

'But he was so well on Saturday night; he didn't cough, or seem to have any symptoms,' Reginald said, shaking his head, a puzzled expression on his face.

The doctor nodded. 'That sometimes happens if a great effort is made by the patient to suppress the pain. Though sometimes the symptoms of pneumonia are naturally milder, and a person can carry on without too much effort.'

'Is that what has happened in Mr Trevalian's case?' Jane asked.

The doctor shook his head. 'Mr Trevalian is seriously ill. I don't think he tripped up. I think he collapsed. Before I left Cirencester, I asked Dr Leith to join me here as soon as possible. I expect him shortly. I want another opinion, you see.'

'I understand,' Reginald murmured, and he looked across at Jane. 'Perhaps we can offer Dr Sedgewick a bite of lunch. Could you arrange that please, Jane?'

She nodded. 'I will go downstairs and speak to the housekeeper. I also want to find out what time Alexis is expected back from London with her gown and trousseau.'

Alexis arrived at three o'clock, not long after Dr Leith had come out to Courtland to consult with Dr Sedgewick. Jane hurried out to greet her in the entrance hall and swiftly led her into the library.

Alexis instinctively knew there was something wrong. 'What is it? What's the matter?'

'I'm afraid Sebastian has been taken ill, Alexis. The doctors are with him now.'

'Taken ill? But what with? What's wrong with him?' Alexis had turned deathly white and her green eyes were filled with sudden fear. She began to shake inside.

'It seems he didn't feel well last week, before you and I arrived, so he went to see Dr Sedgewick in Cirencester, who diagnosed him with pleurisy. The doctor gave him medicine, which controlled the cough, and also took a sample of the sputum for analysis. It's become pneumonia.'

Alexis was speechless. She just stood there gaping at Jane, and then she flew out of the library across the hall and up the stairs. She had to get to Sebastian at once.

Both doctors looked startled as she came rushing into the room. Taking control of herself, she slowed down, calmed her reeling senses, before going over to the bed, looking down at Sebastian.

Recognizing Dr Sedgewick, she asked, 'How is he?'

'Holding his own, Miss Malvern; resting.'

Sebastian said in that same low, hoarse voice, 'Alexis . . . are you here?'

'Yes, I am, darling. Here to look after you.'

Now he was staring up at her, his translucent grey eyes loving, fixed on her face.

She sat down in the chair, took his hand in hers. 'I will help you to get better, Sebastian, I promise.'

A small smile flickered around his mouth and his eyes remained riveted on hers. He said softly, 'I waited for you . . . wanted to see you again . . . my greatest love . . . ' After a long moment gazing at her, he closed his eyes.

Alexis remained sitting by the bedside, holding his hand, her heart full. When his hand went slack in hers, she sat up straighter. 'Sebastian,' she said softly. 'Sebastian, open your eyes, look at me.'

When he did not respond she stared at the doctor, a frightened expression on her face.

Dr Sedgewick stepped up to the bed on the other side, took hold of Sebastian's hand, felt his wrist, seeking a pulse. He spent some moments standing motionless, then bent down closer to Sebastian again before straightening up.

His gaze went to Alexis. He said in a gentle voice, 'He's gone. I'm so sorry, Miss Malvern. He's passed away.'

'No! No! That can't be!' Alexis cried.

But it was.

PART FIVE

The Way It Is
London/Paris
1888–9

FORTY-TWO

'I need to talk to you about Henry Malvern,' Matthew Falconer said in a low voice, looking intently across the large wooden kitchen table at his eldest son, who was newly back at the family home. 'A great tragedy has occurred. Mr Sebastian Trevalian, Miss Alexis's fiancé, died suddenly about a week before their marriage. She has become gravely ill.'

James sat up straighter in the chair, a look of mingled surprise and sadness crossing his face. 'When did this happen? Was it recently?'

Matthew nodded. 'In late September. While you were still in Hull. Mr Malvern took her to see several different doctors in London. But they realized they couldn't do anything to help her. Mr Trevalian's unexpected death had sent her into shock, and she's been sent away now to a doctor overseas.'

Matthew looked across at his brother George, who was sitting with them at the big oak table in Matthew's kitchen in Camden Town, the three of them enjoying a tot of whisky late in the evening. 'What's his name again, George?'

'Dr Freud. Specializes in nervous disorders. She'll be away for months,' George replied. 'Not in a good way at all.'

'What a terrible thing to happen . . . Miss Alexis must be heartbroken. I feel so sad for her. And for Mr Malvern.' Turning to his father, James asked, 'Has he gone to the Continent with her?'

His father shook his head. 'Mr Malvern came back a few weeks ago and I ran into him at the market, got talking,' Matthew explained. 'He's very down, very troubled by all this.' He fiddled with his pipe on the table in front of him. 'However, to get to the point, James, he's agreed that you can go in and see him. On Monday morning. At his offices in Piccadilly.'

James was rendered speechless for a moment and sat gaping at his father, taken by surprise. 'I can't believe it!'

'You must. It's true. 'Course, I've been singing your praises for months on end, hinting for the past year that you'd like to work for him. As you well know, he's always been interested in us as a family, impressed by the way I've run the stalls, made them successful. So, my lad, you've got a chance, and it's up to you to seize the moment.'

'I will, Father. It's always been my dream to work for Mr Malvern at his Piccadilly office. What a great opportunity this is, you're right about that.' James held his father's gaze, his eyes excited.

George said, 'That's not all. After you and I had looked at those three flats when you were here in May, I took the one in Half Moon Street. Close to Piccadilly, certainly good for me, and could be now for you. I've discovered I can shoot right down to Fleet Street in no time at all. A room is ready and waiting for you, James.'

James seemed startled, glanced at his father. 'You've agreed I can live with Uncle George?'

'I have, and your mother too. We want to give you every opportunity to make good, son. And it's much easier than travelling up to Piccadilly every day from Camden Town. But we expect you to spend Saturday and Sunday at home with us, Jimmy. We've missed you, and so have Rossi and Eddie.'

James began to laugh. 'I only got back last night, and everything's already planned out for me in the best way.' He held his hands out to the fire that was dying down in the grate.

'Don't expect that to happen too often,' George interjected, his voice serious. 'Look at Henry Malvern and his daughter. Life often has a way of knocking you back down . . . You can move in whenever you want, either tomorrow or on Sunday.'

'Sunday might be best,' Matthew said. 'Saturday is such a busy day at the market.'

'I'll come and help you on the stalls, Father,' James said.

'Not on your life, my lad! No more stalls for you. You're on the rise, aiming high. And, anyway, if I let you do that, your grandmother will have my guts for garters.'

Later, when he was alone in the small bedroom he now shared with Eddie, James could not help thinking about Alexis Malvern, and how tragic her life had become. He also remembered Georgiana Ward speaking about a friend of hers who was involved in mental health. When he saw her he would ask her if she had heard of this doctor called Sigmund Freud. He couldn't help wondering how the doctor could help Miss Alexis and cure her. No doubt Mrs Ward would be able to explain.

He moved around his bedroom, looking at all the things he had collected over the years. Small things, mementos of special occasions, his few pieces of good clothing, and his evening suit. Everything was neat and tidy, just the way he liked it to be.

He had truly been surprised that his parents had agreed to him sharing Uncle George's flat. They hadn't been too enthusiastic about it when it was first suggested last May. No doubt the fact that Eddie was growing up and was sharing his room at the Camden Town house was part of it. Actually, it would be much easier for him to walk down Piccadilly for fifteen minutes than walk across London from Camden Town. He was well aware it took an hour from here to the Strand, and an extra half an hour would have to be added to get to Malvern House, the office building.

There was a tap on his door, and his sister Rossi poked her head around the door. 'Can I come in, Jimmy?'

He smiled and beckoned for her to join him. 'Thanks for keeping my room in perfect order,' he said, going over to her, giving her a huge hug, holding her close.

'Mum and I have made some new cotton shirts for you, James. They're in the drawer. I think it's wonderful that you're going to see Mr Malvern. Are you excited?'

'I am, yes,' he replied, smiling and sitting down on the bed.

Rossi went and sat in a chair near the table he used as a desk, and said, 'You will be here at weekends, won't you? I've missed you.'

'I've missed you too, and Eddie. He's grown up all of a sudden, though he's as cheerful and cheeky as ever. But I wouldn't have him any other way.'

They sat and chatted for a while about family matters, and then they went downstairs together to help set the table for supper.

James set off at eight thirty on Monday morning, heading down Half Moon Street and into Piccadilly. He was glad he had left his uncle's flat early, having returned there the previous evening in preparation for his appointment with Henry Malvern. Piccadilly was a busy thoroughfare, full of traffic: horse-drawn buses, hansom cabs, and private horse-drawn carriages. People crowded the pavement, men and women hurrying to work, warmly wrapped up on this cold December day.

He smiled to himself as he worked his way in and out through the pedestrians, thinking that it looked like a sea of black top hats. Chimney pots, he called them. All the men were wearing one, and he wondered if he ever would. He wasn't wearing any kind of headgear. Perhaps he ought to; he would ask his uncle.

Because of the crowds, it took him a good twenty minutes to make his way to Malvern House; he finally arrived there at a few minutes before nine. There was a uniformed commissionaire in front of the building, who showed him inside. Walking over to reception he announced he had an appointment with Mr Henry Malvern, and was sent upstairs to another floor. A young woman was sitting behind a desk. He introduced himself.

Within seconds, Mr Malvern came walking out into the area, smiling. 'There you are, Falconer! Good morning.'

'Good morning, Mr Malvern.'

After giving James a quick glance, noting how smart and well groomed he looked, Henry Malvern indicated James should come with him to his office.

James was impressed the moment they walked inside. It was a spacious room with windows overlooking Piccadilly, furnished with a large desk and a chair on each side. Against the opposite wall, there was a seating area composed of a sofa and several chairs arranged around a low table.

'Take the chair in front of my desk,' Henry Malvern said, walking around and sitting down to face James. 'I am sure your father told you about the tragedy that befell my daughter, didn't he?'

'Yes, he did, Mr Malvern, and I am so terribly sorry. It must be something awful to bear, losing your fiancé just before the marriage – or at any time, in fact.'

'It was a tremendous shock for her, and for me. And for

everyone else, actually, because the illness came out of nowhere. He caught cold and succumbed to a sudden attack of pneumonia.'

'Oh no, that's the worst disease!' James exclaimed. Pneumonia had always a big worry in his family, particularly as his mother Maude had always been so prone to winter colds. He sat up straighter, and added, 'I hope the doctor in Vienna will be able to help her, Mr Malvern.'

'Doctor Sigmund Freud is one of a new breed of doctors; he analyses patients, speaks to them at length, draws them out so that they, the doctors, can fathom what is causing the mental disorder. Then they have to treat it. Doctor Freud has become quite renowned in just a few years. Mr Trevalian's sister, Mrs Rayburn, is with my daughter, and will remain with her throughout her stay in Vienna . . . Now, let's get down to our business, Falconer. I understand from your father that you've spent a year in Hull, and also that you want to work for me. Tell me about it, would you? What experience have you had in business?'

James did so, explaining how he had learned a lot about wine over the years from his grandfather, and how he had worked for his Great-Uncle Clarence Venables in his shipping company. He also mentioned that he had been to France several times.

'All that is wonderful experience for you, Falconer, and will serve you well in the future. And it could be useful here. As you probably know, we have an import-export company, under the overall control of my brother Joshua, with an office in Paris and wine warehouses and two ships in Le Havre. Our cousin, Mr Percy Malvern, takes care of things for us across the English Channel, so we don't need anyone in that part of the business at the moment.'

He paused and sat back in the chair. 'The position I need to fill involves looking after our arcades. We have two in London and several in nearby towns. Does that appeal to you?'

'It certainly does, Mr Malvern,' James answered without

hesitation, excitement echoing in his voice. 'I happen to love arcades, and I'm sure I will enjoy the work. What exactly would I be doing?'

'Helping me with Miss Malvern's duties. They're too much for me with everything else that's going on. Supervising, helping those who rent the space from us, checking them against other arcades, making comparisons. My daughter was always keen to be sure the windows were well dressed, were appealing to the public, and that there weren't too many shops selling the same items in one arcade. I have made a list of her duties, and you can study it. There is one other thing. I hope you won't mind making trips to the North.' Henry raised a brow. 'To Leeds and Harrogate.'

'No, of course not, Mr Malvern. I really do want to work for you, and I have, for a very long time. Do you have arcades in Leeds and Harrogate?'

'Yes, we do.'

James nodded, looked thoughtful for a moment, before saying, 'But not in Hull, and that is where an arcade would flourish,' he stated with confidence.

Henry Malvern was taken aback for a moment, and then asked, 'Why do you say that?'

'Because Hull is called the City of Gaiety, and it is just that. They have dances and balls, big fancy suppers, and do a lot of entertaining. The women love clothes and jewellery.' He gave a small shrug. 'It was just a thought, that's all, Mr Malvern.'

Henry nodded and said, 'Be sure to tell me your thoughts all the time, Falconer. I want this company to grow. And you seem to have a fertile brain.' He stared intently at the young man, thinking how bright he was. He said, 'I believe I've made a good deal in seeing you. How would you feel about working here?'

'That I've made a good deal, too, Mr Malvern.'

Henry Malvern stood up. 'Then you're hired. Let me introduce you to a couple of young men who will be your colleagues, even though they are in different departments.'

Picking up several sheets of paper, he handed them to James, and then the two of them went down the corridor, James's head spinning at the speed events were unfolding. Malvern knocked on one of the doors, opened it, and went inside. 'Good morning, Parkinson, this is a new member of our staff. James Falconer. And this is Peter Parkinson, who works in the property department.'

The two young men shook hands, and then Henry Malvern moved on to the next office, where he introduced James to Marvin Goring, who was involved in overseeing the warehouses.

Once these introductions were over, Henry opened a third door along the corridor and showed James inside. 'This can be your office. Nice little space, plenty of light. Make it your own, Falconer, and study those lists. There is stationery and the like in the drawers; anything else you might need, just ask. I am going to leave you to your own devices for a few days, and then I will take you to the two arcades and introduce you to those retailers who rent from us.'

'Thank you, Mr Malvern.'

James stood until Henry's footsteps receded down the corridor, then sank down onto the desk chair. He wanted to pinch himself. Finally, his dream was starting to come true.

FORTY-THREE

After the quietness of Malvern House, the noise in Piccadilly was overwhelming, and James reeled slightly as he came out of the building. Horses' hooves, metal wheels on the road, organ grinders, and the cries of the newsboys hawking the evening editions of the newspapers; all mingled together to create a huge cacophony of sound that assaulted his senses.

But as he stepped out in swift strides, weaving in and out through the crowds of pedestrians, James soon adapted to the noise of this great metropolitan city. London. The centre of the world, his grandfather called it. His city.

He had studied Mr Malvern's notes for part of the day and had instantly understood that, despite the many practical demands of the job, one of the most important things about it was to make sure the windows were cleverly dressed. It was the shops' windows in the arcades that pulled in the customers who spent money. So the tenants could pay the rent. As for the quality of the products, he knew that was just a question of judgement. How thankful he was that he had spent time wandering through the floors of Fortnum and Mason over the years, looking at their top-notch goods, noting the different weaves of cashmere, wool, gabardine, leather, suede, velvet and silks. He had a good eye, and his fingers were sensitive. He easily recognized what he was touching and its true quality.

The fact that he had a job with Mr Malvern and was actually earning money amazed James. Today his life had changed; it would never be the same. He was on his own, standing on his own two feet, in control of his life, his fate, and whatever the future held.

He smiled to himself, knowing how lucky he was.

The two men, Parkinson and Goring, had each stepped into his office to welcome him properly at different times during the day. They seemed nice enough, had been friendly. He was aware how much he was going to miss his cousin, William Venables, who had become his closest friend and confidant, not to mention his great-aunt and great uncle. How good the Venables family had been to him over this year he had spent in Hull. And he had learned a lot from Great-Uncle Clarence. He knew he had a friend for life in him.

Hull. That had been a brainstorm on his part, suggesting an arcade in the City of Gaiety, but he was sure he was right about how successful one would be. He had noticed that Mr Malvern's dark eyes had sparkled at the mere mention of this. He tucked that idea at the back of his mind. He must formulate a plan. One was already ticking away.

At five o'clock, Mr Malvern had strolled into his office, welcomed him again, and asked him if he would be willing to visit their two arcades tomorrow morning, chatting and checking James had understood the notes. James assured him he knew what to look for and would be happy to accompany Mr Malvern to acquaint himself with the two properties.

With a nod and a smile, Mr Malvern had said goodnight and left, having told him to go home whenever he wanted.

James's thoughts veered to another matter altogether as he

walked along Piccadilly, enjoying the cold, fresh air after being inside all day. Georgiana Ward. He had written to her in the first week of November, announcing that he would be returning to London at the end of the month. She had written back and suggested they have supper at her house on Wednesday 5 December. At six o'clock prompt. He had replied instantly. And he would be seeing her in two days.

He frowned at the people hurrying past with scarves over their mouths. Recently London had been plagued by fogs, mostly created by coal dust and fumes from homes and from the expanding Underground railway. James had only been back since Thursday night, but he missed Hull's sea air. The fogs were something of a menace and caused a lot of ill-health in the city, as well as leaving dirt and filth everywhere.

It suddenly struck him, as he walked towards Half Moon Street, that Mrs Ward was the only friend he had kept in touch with in London, other than his family. He made another mental note to make a point of going to see Jack Holden, Denny's father, on Saturday or Sunday, when he was in Camden Town with his parents. He should pay his respects.

When James opened the front door of the flat and went in, he was delighted to see the lamplights flaring, the fire blazing up the chimney, and his uncle sitting in a comfortable armchair in front of the fire. Naturally he was perusing one of the competing newspapers.

'Here I am, Uncle George,' James said, slipping out of his overcoat, hanging it on the coat stand, and walking into the small, comfortable parlour.

George looked over the top of his newspaper and smiled, 'How did it go, James? How was Mr Malvern? Offered you a job, did he?'

'To answer the first part of your question first: Mr Malvern is just the nicest man, as Father had told me he was. Plain-speaking, to the point, but kind. And, as to the second – yes, he *did* offer me a job! Tomorrow he's going to take me to see the two arcades they own in London. Oh, and he told me I might have to travel to the North occasionally, to Leeds and Harrogate, where they own arcades. I don't mind that at all, since I can easily do a hop, skip and a jump, and land in Hull for Saturday nights on the town.'

His uncle chuckled and put down the paper. 'You've got it all worked out, I see.'

'Not really. But I would visit William. He and I became really good friends. He's genuine and trustworthy, and I miss him already.'

'I know what you mean. A good pal is worth his weight in gold, take my word for it. And hard to come by.'

James sat down in the other chair and warmed his hands. 'It's turned nippy tonight. But there's no fog, thank God.'

'Thank God twenty times over! Damn near unbearable. I don't know why this blasted government doesn't do something about our polluted air.'

'But what could they do? I don't think anyone knows.'

'I've no idea either. Some say stop using coal, and whatever else causes the atmosphere to become dangerous. Actually dangerous. Well, the two of us can't mend the world, but we can go out and enjoy ourselves. It's my day off, James, got any plans?'

'No, I haven't. Nobody to make plans with.'

'That's true. So, you're coming with me. I'm going to have dinner with my best pal, and you're tagging along.'

'Who is he, your best pal?'

'A copper, and a bloody good one at that.'

* * *

George Falconer, a creature of habit, had booked a table at the Bettrage Hotel, preferring the hotel's less formal brasserie for supper.

He and James walked through Mayfair to Davies Street where the hotel was located, chatting amiably about family matters in general.

As they headed to the front entrance of the hotel, they saw there was something of a fuss going on, with several porters and a large pile of luggage outside the front door.

Instantly, George came to a stop, put his hand on James's arm. 'The arrival of two posh ladies,' he murmured. 'Let the porters get the trunks in first, the ladies will follow, and then we can enter.' George grinned. 'The young one is rather a looker, I must admit. The mother's not bad either.'

'How do you know she is the mother?' James asked.

'They look alike, don't you think? The older woman is slightly plumper.'

The trunks were being hurriedly rolled inside on a form of long barrow, and then the ladies went into the hotel.

Stepping out, pulling James forward, George steered his nephew in through the front door after the women. In the bright lights of the hotel's foyer, the women were truly visible, and they were indeed very good looking, elegantly gowned and bejewelled. In a low voice, George said, 'Americans. And no doubt buccaneers.'

James frowned at his uncle. 'What are buccaneers?'

'I'll explain when we get to our table,' George said, his voice low, his eyes following the two women who were standing at the desk of the concierge, talking to him animatedly.

The maître d' of the brasserie greeted them warmly as they entered. 'Good evening, Lomax,' George said. 'I would like to introduce you to my nephew, James Falconer.'

After the two men had greeted each other and shaken hands, Lomax said, 'The inspector just arrived a few seconds ago, Mr Falconer.' He steered them over to a round table in a far corner of the restaurant, which was George's preferred place to sit. It gave him an overall view of the entire room, which as a journalist was important to him. He could see who entered and left with ease.

George quickly introduced his friend Detective Inspector Roger Crawford to James, and the three men sat down. Looking at each of them, George said, 'How about a bottle of champagne? It's a little celebration for me tonight.'

'Sounds good,' the inspector said.

James simply nodded. He'd drunk champagne before, of course, but only on a handful of occasions, with his great-uncle. His parents only drank on rare occasions.

George looked at Lomax. 'Don't bother to send the sommelier over with the wine list, Lomax. Get him to open a bottle of my favourite champagne.'

'Certainly, Mr Falconer. Straight away.'

'I would have liked to have a look at their wine list,' James murmured, as the maître d' walked off.

'You can see it later,' George answered. 'That's not a problem.'

Roger Crawford asked, 'And what is the celebration for, George? Don't tell me you've found a woman and got engaged.'

'No such luck,' George answered. He leant back in his seat and announced, 'I am celebrating the commencement of my nephew's career. James started proper work today. His future as a successful merchant prince has just begun.'

Roger looked across at James and smiled, liking the look of this handsome young man, who had warmth and charisma, and who had walked in as if he owned the world. He certainly owned the room. All of the women diners were glancing at him surreptitiously. 'So you have gone into retailing, have you?' he asked pleasantly.

'Yes, I am now working for Mr Henry Malvern, owner of the Malvern Company. He has several arcades in London, amongst many other things, and I'm working with him, making sure they run smoothly.'

'Sounds like a big job,' the inspector replied, raising an eyebrow. 'Malvern must have great faith in you.'

George said, 'My brother Matthew has owned four stalls in the Malvern Market for years. He has been lobbying Henry Malvern for some time to give James a job. Today Malvern did just that.'

'The penny's just dropped!' Roger exclaimed, and stared intently at James. 'You were one of the two young men who were violently attacked on Chalk Farm Road, about a year and a half ago. I am right about that, aren't I?'

James said, 'You are, sir.' He paused for a moment. 'My friend Denny was in a coma and never came out of it. He died.'

'Yes, that was a terrible affair. It's all coming back to me now.' He looked at George. 'You came to me about it and we were never able to solve it . . . a cold case.'

George nodded. Changing the subject, he said, 'What's happening with the Jack the Ripper case? Three more women brutally murdered, but no news from Scotland Yard. Another cold case?'

Detective Inspector Roger Crawford shook his head, his expression one of deep concern. 'Maybe. We have nothing. Not a clue. Although I have a couple of theories. I—' He stopped speaking abruptly when the waiter arrived with a bucket of champagne.

'I'll tell you what I know after we've toasted your nephew, George.'

FORTY-FOUR

Once the waiter had poured the champagne into crystal flutes, the three men raised them and clinked glasses. It was George who said, 'Congratulations, James, on your first job. I wish you much success.'

'Much success,' Roger echoed. 'And I'm absolutely certain you'll have cartloads of it. You've got everything going for you.'

James thanked them and took a sip of the champagne. He knew from his grandfather's wine lessons that this was the best there was.

Roger settled back in his chair and, after a moment, he said quietly, 'Going back to our previous conversation, I hate to admit this, but Scotland Yard is baffled, none the wiser about Jack the Ripper. Five women have now been murdered in Whitechapel. The first two were Mary Ann Nichols and Annie Chapman. Then there were three more victims: Elizabeth Stride, Catherine Eddowes and Mary Jane Kelly. The murders all took place between late August and November of this year. They were all prostitutes and they were brutally murdered, then mutilated with some savagery. But you know all this, George.'

The inspector paused, shook his head. 'And not one clue was left behind. All we found were their bodies and their blood.' He sat back, his worry suddenly apparent.

'So what you're saying is that this is truly a mystery,' George murmured. He sighed, went on, 'You must all in the police force be feeling frustrated. I can understand that completely. Also, there are so many ridiculous rumours circulating, it makes my blood boil. People are idiots.'

'We are trying to ignore those crazy stories, George. The public are hugely inventive, imaginative, I'm afraid. They say it's a famous surgeon who's the killer, a famous actor, a famous painter. They even suggest that Jack the Ripper is a member of the royal family, if you can believe that!'

Shifting in his chair, the policeman added, 'No one knows who he is, but I believe the murders were committed by a man who was strong, and possibly someone who actually did know how to use a knife with skill and precision. But that's all I know.'

George asked, 'Do you think it's the same man? Or could there be copycats?'

His friend did not answer. He sat staring into his glass of champagne, watching the pale golden bubbles rising. He and his colleagues had discussed this very same idea at the Yard and were without any answers. He had a few theories of his own, which he did not share with anyone at work. So he would not voice them tonight. Even though he had known George for ten years or so, knew he was trustworthy and his word was his bond, Roger felt that caution was the best policy at the moment: the less said the better.

After a long moment, he looked up at George. 'Your guess is as good as mine. Rich man, poor man, beggar man, thief – take your pick.'

James had been watching the inspector while he talked. He saw the worry behind the brief smile, the anxiety in the police-man's eyes, and, understanding he wanted to move away from these awful crimes, he changed the subject. Putting his champagne down and looking at his uncle, he asked, 'Please explain to me what you meant by buccaneers.'

Starting to chuckle, George said to Roger, 'When we were arriving at the hotel, two lovely, rather fashionable women – obviously Americans and rich – were also entering with loads of luggage. So how would you describe the buccaneers to James?'

'Being a journalist, I should think you'd have better words to use than I do, George.' The inspector glanced at James. 'Buccaneers are beautiful, very rich and clever American girls who come over here looking for a husband. An aristocratic husband. They want the title; he wants the money that comes with her. An extremely large dowry. If they're lucky, they will find the right man and fall in love. If not, they make the deal if the man is willing. So she gets her title and he gets the much-needed money.'

James was puzzled and asked, 'Why would an aristocrat do that? Why do they need the money? They're rich.'

'Not all of them,' George shot back. 'Stately homes are suffering; the aristocracy is in trouble, and all because of failing crops, failing agriculture. And the cost of keeping up those estates is eye-watering . . . Now, I see the waiter heading this way with the menus. We can talk about this later, James.'

His nephew nodded and accepted a menu, as did the other two men. James was intrigued, determined to find out more. He knew Georgiana Ward would explain it to him.

After glancing quickly at the menu, George said, 'I'm definitely going to have the Colchesters now they're in season.' Both Roger and James ordered the oysters as well. For the main course James selected the mutton; Roger and George decided on boiled beef rib.

'That's what I like about this place,' the inspector said. 'They make the comfort food I grew up on.'

'I suppose everybody feels the same,' George commented. 'This place is always busy.' He hesitated, then said, 'I don't want to spend the evening talking about the Ripper case, but I just wanted to add that we keep our Ripper stories at a decent level, avoid lurid headlines, Roger. We just don't want to alarm the public. Nor do we want to criticize Scotland Yard. We know you're all doing your job.' He gave Roger a knowing look.

'I've noticed that, George. I think your proprietor is a very reasonable man. *The Chronicle*'s the best paper, in my opinion.'

'Thank you. Lord Carpenter is also clever with political stories. He walks down the middle of the road and keeps a clear head. No partisanship. I'm also happy he's no longer considering selling the publishing company. We were all worried about that when we heard rumours, I can tell you. But we're secure once more. He's said he's not selling, and he'll continue to be in the driver's seat.'

The following morning, James was up, dressed and out of the flat long before his uncle had woken. After a swift walk down Piccadilly, dodging through the crowds, he arrived at Malvern House in less than fifteen minutes.

Once he was in his office, he sat down at the desk and made a list of what he would focus on later that morning. He and Henry Malvern were going to the arcade in Kensington, and he couldn't wait to see it.

He took out the small notebook he kept in his jacket pocket. He opened it, made the notation 'HULL', and then scribbled a few lines about his ideas for an arcade in the City of Gaiety.

James looked around him. He was at the office before anyone else; he couldn't wait to begin. The barrow boy had taken his first step on the road to retail. His first proper day in his first proper job. How exciting it was. And certainly he knew it was a day he would never forget.

FORTY-FIVE

After staring in through the window of the largest antique jewellery shop in the arcade for several minutes, James looked at Henry Malvern and said, 'It's too cluttered. You can't see the wood for the trees. The displays don't make sense: bracelets are here, there, and brooches everywhere. No real order. It's a muddle.'

Henry Malvern rocked back on his heels. He looked at James and nodded. 'I couldn't agree more,' he said, obviously pleased with his comments. 'My daughter was always helping Margie Stillman to keep some sort of order, and a pattern. In Miss Malvern's absence, Mrs Stillman has gone . . . wild, in my opinion.'

James's attention was now caught by a beautifully designed diamond bracelet. He said, 'Mr Malvern, please look at this piece!' He glanced at Malvern and went on, 'Next, look over there, on the right side of the window. There's a diamond brooch which is very similar in design. In the middle of the window, there's a pair of diamond ear clips that seems to go with the other two pieces. Don't you agree?'

After peering in the window for a few minutes, Henry Malvern nodded. 'I believe you are correct, Falconer. But what are you getting at?'

'They ought to be grouped together,' James replied. 'Because I'm sure it's a suite, which certainly makes the single pieces much more valuable. Oh, how I'd like to get my hands in this window! To redo it.'

His employer nodded. 'You can try, but you must go rather carefully with Mrs Stillman. She can be very touchy and she's convinced she has the best window in the arcade. Remember you're the new boy, and this is her store.'

'I will take care,' James promised.

Together, the two men went into the shop.

'Good morning, Mr Malvern.' The young woman behind a small counter smiled warmly. 'I shall go and fetch Mrs Stillman right away.'

'Thank you, Yvonne.' Turning to James, Malvern said, 'Walk around, take a look; you'll see a lot of treasures in here. Truly rare pieces.'

James did as Mr Malvern suggested, moving through the main room of the shop, taking everything in swiftly and with appreciation as he gazed in numerous cabinets with glass doors. The problem was the same as the window. Muddle. And more muddle.

It took James only a few minutes to realize that other sets of matching jewellery had been separated rather than grouped together. Before he could point this out, Henry Malvern was greeting a woman in a black silk dress who was undoubtedly Mrs Stillman.

She was an elegant woman, probably in her early forties, and attractive. But the most striking thing about her was her hair. It was pure silver and abundant, piled in curls on top of her head. It gave her a regal look, especially since she had perfect posture and walked gracefully.

'I am delighted to meet you, Mr Falconer,' she said, walking towards him and offering her hand.

Taking it, James looked at her admiringly, staring at her intently. 'It is my pleasure, Mrs Stillman.' Releasing her hand, but still gazing at her, he added, 'And I must commend you on your taste. I don't think I've ever seen such a fantastic collection of diamond pieces in my life. All of them are truly outstanding.'

'How kind of you to say so, Mr Falconer. I've been lucky in some instances; have come across them almost accidentally,' she replied, smiling at him. Her sparkling eyes filled with pleasure at his compliments.

'More good taste than luck, I would say,' James answered. 'I can't help wondering where you buy?'

'Here, there and everywhere,' she answered, and stepped away, going closer to one of the glass-fronted cabinets.

Her smile was intact and James realized she wasn't being evasive, only vague because she probably couldn't remember exactly where each piece had come from.

James inclined his head. 'While staying with relatives in Hull, I have been lucky enough to attend some auctions and estate sales, and before that with my father around London. It's truly amazing the things you can find in these places.'

'I enjoy the country estate sales myself,' Mrs Stillman confided. 'I've found wonderful jewels where least expected.'

Walking across to the front of the store, James said, 'I was just pointing out some pieces in the window to Mr Malvern, a moment ago. I wonder if you'd mind getting them out, Mrs Stillman, if it's not too much trouble. I want to know if I'm as knowledgeable as I think I am.' He gave her one of his wide, slightly flirtatious smiles.

'It's no trouble at all.' Mrs Stillman hurried forward, opening the curtained glass partition that protected the contents of the window inside the store. 'Which pieces exactly, Mr Falconer?'

'The diamond bracelet on the left, the ear clips in the middle, and the brooch on the right. Thank you so much.'

Turning around, James walked down to Henry Malvern, who

had seated himself in a chair. 'I think I'll be able to work with her all right,' he murmured in a low tone.

'I'm absolutely certain of it,' Henry Malvern said in a dry tone. 'Flattery will get you everywhere, Falconer, as you no doubt already know.'

James merely smiled and went to look in a large cabinet, the contents of which took his breath away. He actually gasped. The glass shelves held a variety of diamond tiaras that were so magnificent they were blinding.

A moment later, Mrs Stillman was standing at one of the counters in the shop, where she had placed a black velvet cloth. On it she had put the ear clips, the bracelet and the brooch. 'Do come and look, Mr Falconer, and you, too, Mr Malvern.'

They joined her. James gazed down at the pieces, which were spectacular. Grouped together it was obvious the three pieces were indeed a suite. The working of the diamonds into a diagonal crisscross pattern was repeated on the ear clips and on the brooch. Wonderful workmanship!

He turned the bracelet over and soon found the jeweller's name: Cartier. Swinging around, filled with curiosity, he said to Mrs Stillman, 'I'm wondering about this beautiful suite. Wherever did you come across it?'

'Those pieces I remember very well,' she answered. 'It was an estate sale at Waverley Hall, not far from Bath. The Dowager Countess of Waverley had died, and her son held a sale of her jewels. There are some other similar pieces I also bought at that particular sale. Now, where did I put them?' She glanced around, obviously at a loss for a moment.

James believed they were the items he had seen in one of the cabinets, and he said, 'I do believe I noticed them over there in that large cabinet.'

'Oh yes, you're right.'

Within seconds, she returned holding a necklace, ear clips and a magnificent ring. 'These were also part of the Waverley collection,' she explained.

As she spoke, he had a brainwave, and knew how he was going to get that window not only in order, but make it outstanding. 'Let us group all of these pieces on the velvet. I think those you're holding may also be from Cartier. Are there any more pieces of the dowager's collection? Have you sold any?'

'No, I haven't. There may be a few smaller items, but I would have to hunt them out.'

'I think you should certainly do that, Mrs Stillman, because I've just had an idea that's going to make you a lot of money,' James announced.

Margie Stillman simply gaped at him. 'A lot of money,' she finally repeated. 'But how?'

'Yes, do tell us how, Falconer,' Henry Malvern said in a slightly clipped tone. James suspected he was trying his new boss's patience and overstepping the mark.

'Show is better than tell, I think,' James murmured, and looked at Mrs Stillman. 'Do you have a tray I can use? I'd like to spread the black velvet on it, then arrange the diamond pieces on top.'

'I do have a show tray I sometimes use in the window. It has tiny legs that flip down. I shall go and get it.'

Once she had disappeared into the back room, Henry Malvern said, 'Why did you tell her that? You're raising her hopes. We have to be careful what we say to those who rent from us.' His voice was tetchy.

'I understand that, Mr Malvern, and please trust me. She just doesn't understand exactly what she's got here. Has no idea of their value. Let me carry on and then perhaps you'll realize what I'm aiming at.'

Henry Malvern merely nodded, but he also pulled out his pocket watch and frowned. Mrs Stillman had returned with the tray. She flipped down the small legs on each corner and placed the tray on the counter.

'Thank you,' James said. He removed the diamond pieces from the black velvet, then draped this cover over the tray.

Henry Malvern and Mrs Stillman watched him as he placed the diamond necklace on the black velvet exactly in the centre. Then he put the pair of ear clips within the circle of the necklace, and next he added the large diamond ring between the ear clips. The diamond bracelet, which had first caught his eye in the window, he placed just outside the circle made by the necklace, and the second bracelet on the outer side of the necklace. 'There you are – a magnificent display! What about calling it The Famous Waverley Diamonds from the Renowned Collection of the Dowager Countess of Waverley?'

His audience of two looked startled.

James went on, 'I must find a good calligrapher who will write those words on a white card. That will then go on the tray.' He glanced at Mrs Stillman. 'Which you must put in the middle of the window.'

Henry Malvern, taken by surprise for a moment, now exclaimed, 'That is rather an extraordinary idea, Falconer, but clever. And I do understand where you're going. You want to draw instant attention to the pieces in the window.'

'I do, Mr Malvern. I can guarantee the whole set will be sold within days . . . a week at the most. Probably to an American woman. There are a lot of them here in London these days, and they are rich.'

Margie Stillman was clever enough to understand that this unusual, good-looking young man had come up with a clever idea. But she now said swiftly, 'What about the other jewels in the window? The tray will take up quite a bit of space.'

He agreed with her at once, and said, 'But I'll help you work out a plan, don't worry about it. Now, can I discuss those tiaras? They make a fabulous collection. Why are they all in the back?'

'I didn't know how to place them in the window, and they

take up so much room. Anyway, not many women are interested in tiaras these days.'

James couldn't help thinking about those American girls whom his uncle had called buccaneers. Might they not want to start looking the part before gaining the title? James thought for a moment before saying, 'I'll have to put my thinking cap on.'

Once they had taken their leave of Mrs Stillman and were moving on down the arcade, Henry Malvern paused for a moment, looked at James. 'How do you know so much about jewellery, Falconer? It seems you're quite the expert.'

'No, I'm not really. I only know about Cartier because my father could always spot pieces by them at the estate sales he went to. He often took me with him when he hired a horse and cart and went to the country. That's where he bought the simpler stuff for our stalls. He taught me well.'

'Well, you certainly impressed me. And Mrs Stillman, I might add.'

'I couldn't tell you who else designs jewellery,' James said with a laugh. 'But I do think she will take a bit of guidance from me, with any luck.'

They toured the Malvern Arcade looking at other windows, and Henry Malvern asked James what he thought of them. For the most part he said they were all too crowded with goods. Too many shoes, too many handbags in the leather goods window. All needed to be redone.

As it happened, the only windows James had been impressed with and which gained his praise were the ones showing women's clothing.

It was with some pride that Henry Malvern told him that they had been created by his daughter. It was Miss Alexis who had always dressed the fashion windows herself. James saw the sadness that crossed the older man's face as he spoke.

FORTY-SIX

When he arrived at Uncle George's flat at five fifteen on Wednesday afternoon, James found it in total darkness. His uncle was on the late shift at the newspaper this week and wouldn't get home until after one in the morning, once the newspaper had gone to press.

After lighting the gas lamps in his bedroom, James quickly took off his jacket, trousers and waistcoat and went to check his white shirt in the mirror. It was perfectly clean so he kept it on. A moment later he took his only other suit out of the cupboard, dressed quickly, smoothed a comb through his hair, and looked in the mirror. Neat and tidy, he thought, and left the room.

A few minutes later he was pulling on his overcoat, all set to go to supper with Mrs Ward. Before leaving he went back and turned off the gaslights in his bedroom. He double-locked the door when he left the flat.

As he walked down Half Moon Street and entered Curzon Street, his thoughts focused on Georgiana Ward. He had not seen her since May, when he had been in London for his birthday. He was looking forward to this evening, being in her company.

His mind turned to his grandparents, thinking how generous they were, how extremely good to him. His mother had told him that they had saved up for a whole year to pay for his special birthday party and to buy him an evening suit.

She had gone on to explain that the hotel had given Philip a special price for the dinner, because over the years he had steered so many people in the hotel's direction. These were the foreign friends who came to visit Lady Agatha in London and needed a hotel room. So his grandfather had guided them to the Bettrage Hotel.

As for the evening suit, Tony had given his grandfather a decent price for the very same reason. Philip had suggested the Savile Row gentlemen's establishment, where Tony worked, to those friends of Lady Agatha looking for impeccable tailoring.

All this, his mother had told him in confidence. They wanted to give him the very best – to set him on the path he dreamed of, and they had made sacrifices with love, to lift him into another world . . . She had added that one good turn deserved another, that friends must always help each other out, and he should never forget that.

James knew she was right. But he found himself in a strange position in the city that he knew so well – his training and transformation left him caught between his upbringing and his ambitions. William, his one good friend, was in Hull. The only other adult friend he had was Mrs Georgiana Ward. Anyway, he didn't have much time for leisure. His job was all-consuming, and he was focused on it. He would still be working his way through the two London arcades that the Malvern Company owned next week, never mind going out of town, and as far as Leeds and Harrogate in the North. These trips were planned for January.

It was a cold night, and already quite dark as he headed up towards South Audley Street. When he came to Shepherd Market, he noticed several ladies of the night huddled together trying to keep warm, hoping to ply their trade. But the street was quiet. Icy winds kept most men in front of their firesides at home with their wives.

Crossing Curzon Street, to avoid the huddle of women, James hurried on, hunched down in his overcoat. It was a good coat, and warm. He did not have many clothes, but the few things he had were well made. Turning up his collar, he wished he had remembered to bring a scarf. He plunged his hands in his pockets and marched on.

Five minutes later he was using the brass knocker on the front door of Mrs Ward's house, noticing it was in the shape of a hand.

It was Sonya who opened the door and guided him inside. After greeting him in her usual genial way, she took his overcoat, then led him upstairs to the parlour.

Georgiana Ward was sitting in front of the fireplace when he entered the room, and she immediately rose, glided across the floor to greet him. He thought she looked more beautiful than ever. Her raven-black hair was swept up, the top of her head crowned with a mass of curls. She was wearing a low-cut purple silk gown which enhanced her dark-blue eyes, turned them to violet. Her smile was welcoming.

She immediately came into his arms, and he held her tightly, then leaned down and kissed her cheek.

'Your nose is icy cold, James. It must be a bad night.'

'It is. And very windy.'

Laughing, moving away, going to a small side table, she said, 'Your nose feels like Polka's.'

On hearing her name, the little dog jumped out of her basket by the fireplace and came racing over. James smiled and leaned down, tousled the dog's head. 'Hello, old friend.'

Georgiana said, 'I'll never forget that storm, James, how you saved us both.'

'I won't forget it either,' he murmured, throwing her a flirtatious look.

'Would you pour us a glass of champagne, please? Or perhaps you'd prefer a glass of whisky? I know you like it.'

'Not really,' he shot back. 'Only on stormy nights mixed with tea, and only when I'm with you.'

He stepped up to the table, filled crystal flutes with champagne, and together they walked over to the fireplace. He handed her a glass once she was seated, stood next to her, and they clinked glasses.

'Here's to our reunion,' she said, gazing up at him, her eyes telling him she felt exactly the way he did. He knew it was going to be a passionate night.

Sitting opposite her, he said, 'I'm very happy to tell you I have a job.'

'So soon!' she exclaimed, a startled expression flitting across her face. 'Now why do I say that, knowing you the way I do? Of course you lost no time. Where are you working? What are you doing?'

Trying to make his explanation short, he told her about his father's working relationship with Henry Malvern, his father's stalls at the Malvern Market, and how Mr Malvern had always liked his father and admired his work ethic.

'So when Mr Malvern spotted me at the stalls in May the day I went to help Father, Mr Malvern came over to speak to me. I told him about working for Great-Uncle Clarence, learning about shipping. After I'd gone back to Hull, my father boasted a bit, I suppose. Eventually he let Mr Malvern know I would like to have a job at the Malvern Company. Once I came back to London, Mr Malvern agreed to see me at his office.'

'And so he gave you one. He's a smart man, James. He spotted talent when he saw it.'

After a long swallow of champagne, James leaned towards her and said in a quiet voice, 'Unfortunately, he really needed me. His daughter, Miss Malvern, had a nervous collapse . . . he said he needed more help. You see, she worked in the company.'

There was a deep frown on Mrs Ward's face when she asked, 'A collapse?'

'Yes.' James explained exactly what had happened, that Miss Malvern's fiancé had suddenly died. And that, in the end, Mr Malvern and the dead fiancé's sister, Mrs Dorothea Rayburn, had taken Miss Alexis to Vienna to be treated by Dr Sigmund Freud. 'Have you heard of him?' James finally asked.

'I certainly have!' she answered, her interest obviously aroused.

At this moment, Sonya appeared in the doorway and said, 'Supper is served, madam.'

'Thank you, Sonya. Please tell Mrs Mulvaney we will be down in five minutes.' Sipping her champagne and looking over at James, she said, 'Dr Freud opened his clinic about two years ago and he has been extremely successful. He treats mental disorders . . . people who have suffered traumatic incidents.'

'But what kind of doctor is he? I don't understand.'

'He's a psychiatrist. The simplest way to describe his work is to say he induces his patients to talk about what has occasioned their "nervous disorders". Somehow he persuades them to do so in great detail. At least, that is what my friend the professor tells me.'

'Like unburdening yourself?' James asked.

'Exactly. And what a terrible shock for Miss Malvern, hard for her. I remember reading the obituary in *The Chronicle*. Sebastian Trevalian was a well-known banker – famous, even – and something of a socialite. How tragic. What a truly sad story.'

'Did you know him?'

'Goodness, no, I don't mix in those circles,' she said with a small laugh. 'Although my sister Deanna does. Leonard, her husband, is from landed gentry, but not with a title.'

'Oh, there's another thing I want to ask you about,' James exclaimed, a sudden eagerness in his bright blue eyes.

'Then you must ask me over supper. I think we should go down.'

Together they went downstairs to the dining room, which was painted in soft greens, with deeper green mouldings and doors. There were marvellous oil paintings of exotic birds, all with vivid and colourful plumages, hanging on the walls. A fire blazed in the hearth and tall wax candles on the dining table and sideboard gave the room a lovely mellow glow.

'Good evening, Mr Falconer,' Mrs Mulvaney said as she showed him to his chair opposite Mrs Ward at the round table. The polished wood was covered with crystal goblets and silver tableware. There was a bowl of flowers in the centre of the table. It all looked elegant and inviting.

Mrs Mulvaney disappeared into the kitchen, and James glanced around yet again. 'It's a lovely room, Mrs Ward. You are so skilled with decor.'

Shaking her head, half smiling, she said, 'I do wish you would stop calling me that, James, and most especially . . .' She paused, dropped her voice, 'When we are in bed making love.'

'I promise. I'll start tonight.'

She looked at him for a long moment. Her unique violet eyes reflected desire and a yearning for him. Nothing had changed.

A moment later, Mrs Mulvaney returned with a tray, which she placed on a nearby table. 'Hot vegetable soup, madam. For a cold night.'

'It smells delicious, Mrs Mulvaney,' Georgiana murmured.

The soup was hot and tasty and warmed James through. He suddenly remembered he had been so busy that he had not had time to eat lunch.

Over soup, James related the story about running into the two American women at the Bettrage Hotel and how his uncle had called them 'buccaneers'. But he had not really explained what this meant. He added that Uncle George had mentioned they were rich American girls who came over with their mothers, hoping to marry an aristocrat who needed money.

'I always thought aristocrats were rich, that they owned England,' James finished.

'Indeed they do,' she answered. 'Because they own the land, many of them own thousands and thousands of acres. But they have always depended on agriculture and farming for their fortunes. They usually own the many farms on their estates, which are cultivated for them by the local farmers. However, the crops have been failing for some years now, due to various things.'

'And so that's why they need rich American brides.'

'It is. Amazing really, but the girls are beautiful, dressed in gorgeous clothes from Worth in Paris. They are usually highly educated, more so than the English girls, in fact. And of course, their fathers are multimillionaires and can afford to give them a large dowry.'

James nodded. 'Is it love? Or a deal?'

Georgiana Ward chuckled. 'Right to the point, James, as usual. Both, I suppose. Some do make genuine love matches, others settle for a deal. But in many instances it appears to work.'

After the soup, Mrs Mulvaney served sliced beef with roasted potatoes and fresh vegetables. James enjoyed this special supper and the excellent wine she had chosen.

After supper, Georgiana and James drifted upstairs to the cosy parlour and sat down in front of the fire. James had poured them a cognac each, and he was relaxed, comfortable and felt content. She had always made him feel that way, ever since their first sexual encounter during the storm in Hull. He was at ease in her company. There was no pressure.

They chatted amiably about a few things, and he complimented her again on the charm and beauty of her house. She appeared flattered and smiled at his comments.

Quite unexpectedly, she changed their idle conversation into one a little more serious, when she said, 'I will be in London until Christmas, James. Then I am going to stay in the country for a few months. With Deanna and Leonard. She is not at all well. My other sister, Vanessa, is genuinely worried about her.'

'I'm so sorry to hear that,' James replied at once, his voice sympathetic. 'Does she have an illness that is . . . well, incurable?'

'I suppose it is . . . she has a heart condition.' A long sigh escaped her, and she added, 'What I'm saying is that I will be here through December, but in the New Year, I will not be in London for quite a while.'

This news saddened him, but he pushed a smile onto his face. 'I understand you have duties, loyalties. So, Mrs Ward, we must make the best of the next few weeks. However, I just want you to know I will be eagerly awaiting your return. In the spring? Or will it be the summer?'

'Somewhere in between, I think.' She looked at him intently, her head on one side, her eyes flirtatious. 'Will you really wait for me to come back?'

'I said I would,' he answered swiftly. 'I doubt I could find anyone like you . . .' He let his sentence slide away, put the brandy balloon on a small table, rose. He strode across the floor, closed the parlour door, and locked it.

'Why are you doing that, James? We can easily go into the bedroom. Nobody would come in there.'

He smiled at her, taking off his jacket, then his waistcoat, his tie, and slowly began to unbutton his white shirt, his eyes not leaving her face. 'I want to make love to you here on the big sofa in front of the fire. Then I want to take you to your bed and love you again and again and again. You see, I don't want you to forget me, Mrs Ward.'

Georgiana felt desire rushing through her as she watched him shedding the rest of his clothes. She walked over to him, smoothed her hands over his long body, and then turned her back to him. 'Could you please undo my buttons?'

He was silent as he did as she asked, and was surprised to see that the only garment under her dress was an underskirt. The dress fell to the floor. She took off the skirt, turned to face him, and pressed her naked body close. 'Let's go over to that enticing sofa, Mr Falconer.'

'It is you who is enticing. Oh, I do want you so much, Georgiana, my Georgiana. You are mine, aren't you?'

'Forever,' she said, and meant it.

Taking hold of her hand, he led her to the sofa and pressed her down on it. He then knelt on the floor at her side, smoothing his hands over every inch of her. As he did this over and over again, they gazed at each other, captivated, truly entranced.

He said, 'I want to savour you, know every part of you.' A quirky smile played at the edge of his mouth. 'You don't mind if I stroke you, do you, Mrs Ward? I want to take it slowly tonight.'

'No,' she whispered as he began to arouse her further. 'I love your hands on me . . . everywhere, Mr Falconer.'

They laughed then, because they knew they were intent on teasing each other and the serious lovemaking would begin a little later.

But it was sooner than he had intended. He leaned over her, kissed her on the mouth, then on her breasts, and finally his hands roamed down to that dark thatch of hair between her legs. Within a few minutes he was on top of her, taking her to him. And she cleaved to him, and cried out, and a second later so did he.

* * *

James lay on top of her for a short while, enjoying the sense of satisfaction and fulfilment as he remained inside her. It was she who spoke first, and said against his chest, 'I've never been made love to like this . . . my husband was not as sensual and erotic as you.'

'Neither have I,' he answered, and this was true.

He finally slid out of her and walked across the room, retrieved their brandy balloons. They cuddled together, sitting up on the sofa in front of the blazing fire, sipping the cognac, neither of them speaking.

Georgiana put her glass down first, drew closer, and began to stroke him. Instantly his drink sat next to hers, and he was embracing her, kissing her hair, her face, her neck. Suddenly he stood, lifted her up in his arms and carried her into the adjoining bedroom.

As he laid her down on the bed and got in beside her, he drew her to him. Against her cheek, he said, 'Now the really serious lovemaking starts, and I won't stop until you tell me to.'

'I don't ever want you to stop,' was her answer as she gazed up into his incredibly blue eyes. 'You can make love to me as much as you want.'

And he did.

FORTY-SEVEN

When James descended from the railway carriage onto the platform in Hull, the first person he saw was William Venables hurrying towards him, waving, with a huge smile on his face.

James waved back and, as they came together, dropped his suitcase to embrace his friend.

'I am so glad you could make it,' William said as they drew apart. 'It's been a long while since we've seen each other.'

'I know, too long,' James replied, grimaced, and added, 'My fault, I'm afraid, but the last six months have been well . . . extremely busy as far as work is concerned.'

'Your grandmother told my mother that Mr Malvern is keeping you well occupied.'

'That's true, but I'm learning a lot and he's actually a nice man, very fair.'

'Good to know . . . I've got the carriage waiting. Papa is at the warehouse in town, and I said I would pick him up at five. He doesn't know you're coming to stay for Easter, so you'll be a big surprise. Mama and I decided to keep your visit a secret.'

A faint smile crossed James's face as he fell into step with William. They hurried down the platform to the exit. It was Thursday 18 April 1889, and the next day would be Good Friday. Having been in Harrogate and Leeds checking the Malvern arcades, James had taken the opportunity to visit his relatives in Humberside, who were forever inviting him to come and stay.

As they emerged from the railway station, they saw Griff, his great-uncle's driver, standing outside the carriage, smoking a cigarette. Immediately, he dropped the Woodbine and stamped it out.

After giving James a warm and cheerful greeting, Griff put the suitcase in the carriage, and the two men climbed inside. Within minutes, the horses were off at a good trot, heading towards the centre of Hull.

Once they had settled into their seats, William said, 'It's your birthday next month, James, do you have any special plans?'

'No, as a matter of fact, I don't. Nobody does. I told my parents I didn't want a fuss – just to have a family supper. I said the same to my grandparents as well. They spent a lot of money on my birthday last year, and it's not right.' A grin spread across his face, and he exclaimed, 'I can't believe I'll be nineteen. This past year seems to have flown.' He glanced at William. 'Why do you ask?'

'I thought I would come up to town and spend a few days there, but if you're busy with your family, I do understand.'

'But you're family, too. You can join us. Uncle Harry will be cooking in my mother's kitchen, and you'll enjoy his food. Uncle George will give you all the latest gossip running rampant on Fleet Street. You'll have a bit of fun.'

William was smiling and nodding. 'I'd love to come. Maybe I could take you to see a play in the West End, as a birthday treat. I think Lillie Langtry might be in a new one.'

'I'd like that, William. I'll ask Uncle George what's new, and if she's in anything at the moment.'

'So it's settled then?'

'Of course it is. It's something to look forward to. When I tell my grandmother, she'll be so delighted.'

It was not too far to the Venables family warehouse. Soon the carriage was pulling up to the steps which led down into the yard; the warehouse stood on a lower level. It was brand new, built to replace the one which had collapsed after the storm.

'Come on, James, come with me to pick up Papa. The men will be around and they'd like to see you; that I do know. You'll always be their hero.'

There was indeed a flurry of excitement when James walked into the warehouse with William. Within seconds they were flocking around the two of them. Joe, who had always revered James, was right in the front line, grinning from ear to ear.

The noise, excitement and cheering brought Clarence Venables out of his office; when he spotted James, he too was instantly filled with pleasure.

Hurrying over, he cut his way through the workmen and went up to James, shook his hand, beaming. 'What a surprise this is – and such a nice one.' He turned to his son. 'I bet it was you and your mother who concocted this,' he said, laughter bubbling.

'In a way, Papa. When James let me know he would be in Leeds, I suggested he pop over to spend Easter with us.'

After some friendly banter, a bit of chitchat with the men, Clarence said he would go and collect his things. He headed for the corridor leading to his office.

A few minutes later they followed him. As they passed another office, the door opened suddenly. Standing there, staring at them, was Albert, a look of fury crossing his face when he realized James was with William.

He rushed at him, glaring, and punched him hard in the stomach, hissing, 'I'll get you one day, you bastard! I swear to God I'll get you, Falconer. You'll be done for.'

Albert was about to hit James again, but did not succeed.

William, in a rage, stepped in between them. He grabbed hold of Albert and said, 'You despicable little toad, get out of my way. And if you ever go within so much as a yard of James, you'll answer to me. And to Papa. You know what that means!' William swiped a finger across his own throat, and added, 'That'll be the end for you, you loathsome man.'

He pulled Albert into the office, let go of him and left at once. Closing the door behind him, William noticed that James was holding his stomach. He hurried to him. 'Are you all right? Did that idiot hurt you?'

James swallowed and endeavoured to straighten up. After a few minutes, he said in a strangled voice, 'I'll be fine. It was a hard punch, though. I hope he hasn't broken my rib.'

'So do I.' William took hold of James's arm and they walked down to Clarence's office. At one moment, William stopped, and said in a low voice, 'Let's keep this to ourselves. Papa will go mad if he finds out, and it'll dominate the next few days.'

'Silent as a mouse,' James murmured.

Much later that evening, long after they had enjoyed a relaxed evening together and then retired to their own rooms, James got out of bed and went to stand at the window. He stared out at the North Sea and realized how much he had missed this particular view. Earlier, when he had first arrived, his great-aunt had given him the picture she had painted for him.

In the moonlight streaming in through the window, he could see it now, propped up in a chair. It was a marvellous painting, and he had told her he would treasure it always. And he would.

He went and sat in the other chair, thinking about Albert. The altercation had disturbed him more than he had let on. The man's hatred did not frighten him, because he was not easily frightened by anyone or anything. On the other hand, someone who was capable of acting in such a deranged way spelled danger to him, obviously, because that kind of person was unpredictable. He must now be on guard when Albert was in the vicinity. He was an enemy.

His thoughts turned to Georgiana Ward. He had not seen her for months, since December, in fact. They had met for one more supper together, and then in January she had gone to the country to be with her sister Deanna.

When a letter had arrived from her two weeks ago, he had been excited as he opened it, having recognized her handwriting. But her letter had been to tell him that she had put her house in London up for sale.

She had moved permanently to the country, not only to be close to her sister, but for her own safety. The fogs had damaged her health, she had said. She could no longer live in the city. She had written how much their relationship had meant to her, how she would never forget him. She finished by wishing him well, forecasting that he would have a splendid life.

And that was that.

He had understood, but, nonetheless, he also realized that he had now lost his only friend in London, and certainly a woman for whom he had enormous affection and respect.

It was over. He had always known that it would be one day. The age difference and class difference were too disparate. Nevertheless, for all that, he would still miss her, his lovely Mrs Ward.

FORTY-EIGHT

Alexis was seated in the arbour at Goldenhurst. Gazing around the garden, she realized, yet again, how lovely it was on this balmy June afternoon. And how peaceful.

She remembered Sebastian's words . . . listening to the silence. How happy she was she had started to come here, sometimes only for Saturday and Sunday. Sometimes for a whole week . . . And all of her visits were restorative, gave her comfort.

She sighed to herself, thinking how resistant she had been at first. She had come back to London in March.

She was not the same person, though. There was sadness deep inside; she had become more reflective, but she had gone back to work, on a part-time basis. A few weeks after her return, she had started to see her dearest friends: Claudia and Cornelius, Lord Reggie and Lady Jane.

Every weekend, though, she came here. Mostly alone. Because Goldenhurst belonged to her! Lock, stock and barrel. It was Reggie who had told her that. There were moments now and then when she still couldn't quite believe it, or how it had been done, with the utmost attention to the legal details. Sebastian

352

had made sure there could be no misunderstandings on anybody's part about what he wanted.

'But why did he leave it to me before we were married?' she had asked Lord Reggie.

'Obviously he wanted you to have Goldenhurst whether you were married to him or not,' Reginald had answered. 'He once told me that the girls weren't really interested in it, that only you loved it the way he did.' He smiled sadly at her. 'He wrote letters to the girls explaining it – on the day that he gave you your engagement ring. You must understand that Sebastian could do whatever he wanted with Goldenhurst. He had bought it with his own money. It was not part of the Trevalian estate.'

Reggie had nodded his head vehemently, his voice firm. 'He meant you to have it, married to him or not. And you must accept this bequest to honour him, to honour his wishes.'

That day she had been hardly able to respond to the man who had been Sebastian's best friend, who had lately appointed himself her unofficial protector. Her heart was full, and incipient tears had gleamed in her eyes. Reginald had explained that Sebastian had also created a trust to pay for the maintenance of the farmhouse and the land throughout her lifetime. And he offered to go to Kent with her to pay her first visit to Goldenhurst if she so wished. If she needed the support.

In the end, she had gone alone, not sure what her reaction would be. After the first few moments of warm greetings from Broadbent and Mrs Bellamy, and a few tears shared, they had led her inside. Once in the house, she had experienced a sudden and unexpected lightness of spirit, a lift, even a little joy. She knew that his spirit was there. And later, when she went walking around the old farmhouse, looking in rooms and cupboards, Sebastian remained with her. Memories surrounded her. And they comforted her.

Now, looking back to those early months, she admitted they

had been made possible by the unusual doctor in Vienna, Sigmund Freud. Her long stay of six months had been worth it.

Slowly he had made her well, by urging her to face her grief, and every aspect of it, from sorrow and loss, anger and guilt, to acceptance that he was dead.

There had been a lot of talking and mediation and even hypnosis, but eventually his treatments had brought her back to the real world. Aunt Thea had been her rock and had stayed with her in Vienna for the entire time.

Her father had visited Vienna, and Claudia and Cornelius, too, and even Lavinia and Marietta had come. They had given her love and encouragement. And they had grieved together at times.

It was because of the doctor that she had found the courage to do something else at the end of April. One sunny but cool morning at Goldenhurst, after breakfast, she had asked Broadbent to make a bonfire in the place he normally used to burn leaves and dead branches in the autumn. He did so without asking why.

As soon as the bonfire was aflame, Alexis had gone inside and returned, carrying a large white box. Broadbent had hurried to meet her, taking it from her. 'What's in here, Miss Malvern?'

'My wedding gown,' she had told him. 'It was made for him, for Mr Sebastian . . . to see me in it . . . when I became his wife.' Her voice had wavered. 'I have no use for it now. Throw it on the fire, Broadbent. Please.'

He hesitated but, at her urging, finally did so. There was sorrow in his eyes.

She watched as the box and the gown had turned to ashes. Once they were gone, Alexis had nodded, thanked Broadbent, and walked back up the hill to the farm. Relief flowed through her. It was as if it had never existed. A burden had been shed.

Rising now, leaving the arbour, and walking back to the blue garden, Alexis thought of Reginald and his reaction when she had told him about burning her wedding gown. For a moment or two she had seen the flash of shock on his face. Then he had nodded, understanding entering his eyes. 'He didn't see you in it . . . so it had to vanish. As if it never existed.'

They had been walking up this very lawn. She had smiled and tucked her arm through his. 'Thank you, Reggie, for being who you are.'

Jane and Reggie were coming to stay with her next weekend, and they would be bringing the babies. It was in March that Lady Jane had given birth to identical twin boys, and everyone, including Jane herself, wondered how they would know which one was which. Their names were Sebastian and Keir, and Alexis had agreed to be godmother to Sebastian. With them would come two nannies, Lady Jane's maid, and Lord Reginald's valet. Just the thought of all these people made Alexis walk much quicker. She must talk to Broadbent and Mrs Bellamy again about that special occasion. They would need two additional chambermaids and an additional cook. There was planning to do.

As she hurried on, these thoughts whirling in her head, she heard the sound of horses' hooves and wheels rolling over gravel. Much to her surprise, it was her father's carriage that was coming to a halt at the front door.

FORTY-NINE

As Henry Malvern stepped out of his carriage, helped by his driver, Armstrong, Alexis ran forward.

'Papa, what a surprise to see you!'

After embracing her, he said, 'Don't look so worried. Uncle Joshua is still with us; there's no change in his condition.' Henry's brother Joshua had recently suffered a debilitating stroke that had rendered him unable to speak or move. He was showing little sign of improvement. 'We have a business problem,' her father told her.

Staring at him, she asked swiftly, 'What is it?'

'Let us speak about it inside, my dear.'

Broadbent hurried towards them; behind him, Mrs Bellamy hovered on the front steps.

'Good afternoon, sir,' Broadbent said, inclining his head in his usual polite manner. 'I'll take your suitcase, Mr Malvern, if I may?'

'Yes, thank you, Broadbent.' Glancing at his driver, Mr Malvern added, 'Get off to the stable block, Armstrong, that's a good chap. We're staying the night. Attend to the horses, and Broadbent here will arrange your accommodations as usual.'

'Yes, sir.' Armstrong touched his hand to his cap, then greeted Alexis, 'Good afternoon, Miss Malvern.'

She smiled and nodded. 'Mrs Bellamy will give you something to eat. You must be starving.'

Once they were inside the house, Alexis swung around to face her father. 'What is this about? Your sudden arrival here, Papa?' she asked anxiously.

'Falconer has come across something quite terrible. But, if I may, I would like to go to my room, freshen up. Perhaps you could ask Mrs Bellamy for tea and sandwiches. I am a little hungry after the trip. I will only be a few minutes, Alexis.'

Her father mounted the staircase. She went into the kitchen where she found Mrs Bellamy already preparing tea and the small sandwiches they enjoyed, each one filled with something different. 'Oh, my goodness, you're already making tea. That's so good of you,' Alexis said, walking towards the housekeeper working at the central table. 'My father is staying the night, so we will need to have supper for his driver as well, Mrs Bellamy.'

'I have plenty of food in the larder, Miss Alexis. Don't you worry,' the housekeeper answered. 'And I'm sure Armstrong must be a bit peckish, need something to eat now. And a good strong pot of tea. It's quite a trip from London.'

'It is, so please do what you have to do. Thank you, Mrs Bellamy.'

Alexis walked down the corridor and went into Sebastian's room, the one she loved the most, which he had helped to build. The sun was coming in through the large window and a fire burned in the hearth. She seated herself on a chair near the window overlooking the blue garden, waiting for her father, wondering what this business trouble was and how Falconer had found out about it.

Within a few minutes, Henry Malvern came into the room and took a seat near the window next to her.

'What's the trouble?' she asked in her blunt way, going straight to the point.

'Someone is stealing from us . . . we have a thief among us.'
Her father's voice was troubled.

'What do you mean? And how did Falconer discover this,
Papa?' she asked, taken aback.

'I shall tell you the entire story, and I would prefer you to
listen until I have finished. You can then ask me any questions
you wish.'

When she was silent, her father said, 'That is all right with
you, isn't it, Alexis?'

'Yes, Papa. I was simply digesting your words . . . ' There was
a hesitation before she said, 'But can I ask just one question
now, all right?'

He nodded.

'When did you find out?'

'Last night. I was working until about six. As I was leaving,
I noticed that Falconer was still in his office, so I put my head
around the door, told him he should go home. He said he couldn't
because he had come across a problem. In fact, he had been
about to come to my office to tell me about it.'

Henry paused as Mrs Bellamy came into the room, carrying
the tea tray, which she placed on a table near the door. Once
she had arranged everything, she said, 'Tea is served, Miss Alexis,
Mr Malvern.'

'Thank you,' Alexis said, and added, 'We'll look after ourselves,
Mrs Bellamy.'

After pouring the tea, Alexis said, 'Help yourself, Papa, you
must be famished, not having had lunch, I'm sure.'

After eating a smoked salmon sandwich and sipping his tea,
Henry continued, 'I asked him what the problem was, and he
told me someone was stealing from us in the wine division. He
added that he was certain it was happening in Le Havre. I asked
him who it was and he said he wasn't certain. He pointed out
that we were selling as much wine as always, but not taking in
the same amount of money. Much less. You see, he thought that

perhaps Uncle Joshua had got himself into a muddle before he had the stroke. Now Joshua can't tell us anything, poor chap. Falconer said he needed to have an overview.'

Henry took another sip of tea. 'He then suggested that one of us – he or I – ought to go to Le Havre at once to examine the books there.'

Alexis frowned. 'I know you asked Falconer to move over to the wine division after Uncle Joshua had the stroke, but I wasn't sure why. After all, Uncle Joshua has several good men working for him, and Uncle Percy is in France. Couldn't they have just carried on as normal?'

'I suppose they could, but I didn't want them to. I wanted Falconer in there, once you were back at work and overseeing the arcades again.'

'I see. But I still don't really understand the choice of this Falconer chap. He only started here in December.'

'He can run rings round them all. He spent a year in Hull, working in the shipping division of his great-uncle's company. Clarence Venables begged him to stay and run the company with him. I myself spoke to Venables, who gave him the highest recommendation. I'll tell you something else; I always thought his father boasted about him, overdid it a bit. But I was totally wrong. He didn't say enough. Furthermore, his father doesn't know the half of it.'

Sitting back in his chair, sipping his tea, Henry Malvern then put his cup down. 'Falconer has the most brilliant mind of anybody I've ever met. He's all brain. He understands a balance sheet more swiftly than anyone I know, including myself. He sees things no one else does . . . as though he has a demon telling him what to do. He's got a gift for marketing, as you well know. As for retailing, he's a genius.'

Alexis smiled faintly. 'I must admit he certainly had a brain-wave when he decided to invent the famous Waverley Diamond Collection, when even the Waverleys had never heard of it.'

Henry couldn't help laughing. 'Nonetheless, they went along with it, didn't they? And everyone made money.'

'How does he know so much about jewels?' Alexis wondered aloud.

'He doesn't. But he has a knack of spotting Cartier pieces. Apparently, his father could always pick them out when they went to the country estate sales. Matthew Falconer was looking for bric-a-brac, fake jewels, vases, and small items he could sell at the Malvern. Seemingly he had developed an eye for those unique Cartier items. And Falconer learned about them from his father.'

'You have great faith in him, and obviously you believe him that there is a thief amongst us,' she said, staring at her father. She had only met James Falconer a handful of times. Why was her father so in thrall to him?

'I do believe him. I trust him. And he is going to Le Havre to investigate. And you are going with him.'

Alexis gaped at her father, shaking her head. 'No, no, I can't go. I wouldn't know how to help. Anyway, I don't know anything about the wine division.'

'I am aware of that. The arcades have always been your baili-wick. You have to go because you are a Malvern, my partner, my heir, and you therefore have the authority invested in you to sign papers, make important decisions, and act on my behalf.'

Alexis was silent, studying her father, at a loss for words. He had taken her by surprise in many ways.

Henry looked at his daughter, a reflective expression settling in his dark eyes. Finally, he said, 'You, as Alexis Malvern, can dismiss people, hire people, make any decision you see fit. He can't, not really. However, Falconer has the knowledge . . . of the wine shipping business, after a year with Venables. He also has a good knowledge of wines. He was taught by his grand-father about vintages, vineyards and quality. And vintners. It's as if he's got a wine catalogue in his head.'

'So you really do mean it? I have to travel with James Falconer to Le Havre to help him investigate?' Alexis asked, eyeing her father.

'You do indeed, Alexis. As my representative. Actually, I will draw letters of authority for both of you, giving you both the right to act on my behalf.'

'Oh, but then he doesn't need me to go. Not if you give him a letter of authority,' she exclaimed, seeing a chance to get out of the trip.

'It has nothing to do with him, Alexis. I want you to go. In fact, I insist you go. One day the Malvern Company will be yours, and you have to make sure you are helping to keep it safe *now*. You are going with Falconer because I insist.' Her father rarely insisted that she did something, and her thoughts were whirling. Alexis carefully put down her cup and saucer. She was about to speak when her father continued.

'And I also insist that you take Tilda with you.'

'Tilda? My maid Tilda?'

'Yes, your maid Tilda.'

'But why?' Alexis raised an auburn brow, astonished.

'You will be travelling. To Le Havre first, and then I want you to go to the Paris office. So you will need Tilda to dress your hair, help you with your clothes, the normal things she does when you're in London and not here in Kent.'

'Well, yes, I suppose so.' She gave him a long, puzzled look. 'And she would be a sort of chaperone—'

He cut her off when he exclaimed, 'Yes, yes, of course, although Falconer is a gentleman, first and foremost, despite his humble birth. He will protect you with his life from any other man, or any kind of incident. No, you need Tilda to get you into shape.'

'What on earth do you mean?' she asked, looking at him askance.

'I have never known a beautiful woman who turned herself into a frump.'

'What?' she cried.

'Yes, that's right, Alexis. You have become a frump. I don't mind that you wish to wear black and dark colours, because you are in mourning for your fiancé. However, I do think you should attend to your hair and your face. And most especially when you travel to France. You are my daughter, the co-owner of the Malvern Company, and you must look the part. That is vital.'

This barrage of words from her father had stupefied her for a moment or two, and she waited for him to apologize. To her surprise he didn't. Instead he took another sandwich and munched on it, waiting for her to speak.

After a few minutes, she asked, 'Do I really look like a frump, Papa?'

'You do. That bun at the back of your head has to go. You need to have that upswept look with curls on top like Thea and Claudia. It's very fashionable at the moment. And you must attend to your face, the way you did in the past. Also, as I just said, you can wear mourning colours, but the clothes must be the very best. I'm sure you must have gowns that are suitable in London. You do, don't you?'

'I do, Papa. When are you sending Falconer, er, us, to Le Havre?'

'Today is Wednesday. We'll go back to London early tomorrow morning. Friday and Saturday you can prepare. I think you should travel this coming Sunday. How does that sound?'

'Perfectly fine, Papa,' she answered in a level voice, knowing that her father was right. She had to protect the Malvern Company because it was hers. Rather, it would be one day. She fell down into her thoughts.

After a short while, Henry Malvern said, 'By the way, Alexis, you cannot travel abroad with that enormous emerald ring on your finger. Somebody will probably cut your hand off to get it.'

She looked down at the ring and her head came up with a jerk. 'But I promised Sebastian I'd never take it off.'

'I think he'd suggest you do as I say if he knew it might cost you your life,' her father pointed out.

She bit her lip and finally nodded. 'You are right, I suppose.' She twisted the ring, which she wore on her right hand.

Suddenly her father said, 'I've noticed that you haven't worn it on your engagement finger since you returned from Vienna. Why is that?'

Alexis sat back in the chair and looked off into space, and then she eventually brought her gaze back to Henry. 'It was Dr Freud . . . he thought it might be healthier. That was the word he used. If I wore it on my right hand. When I asked him why, he said he didn't want me to be engaged to a dead man.'

Henry was taken aback and strangely amused by Freud's apparent comment, and he couldn't help laughing. Then he apologized to his daughter, who was looking at him in the oddest way.

After a second, she swallowed a smile and murmured, 'Well, he was right, don't you think?'

Later that night, just before she went to bed, Alexis sat down at Sebastian's desk. She had made his bedroom hers, because she had last slept in there with him. And she loved to sit at his desk, remembering him.

In May, one day when she had finally moved into Goldenhurst, she had found his diary pushed way back in the top drawer of his desk.

It wasn't an engagement diary, rather a diary in which he had recorded his thoughts about many things . . . including about the day when he had given her the emerald engagement ring.

Once more she read the account of their engagement evening

and smiled, remembering every second of that night. Then she flipped the pages, as she so often did, and came across an entry she had read many times before.

Sebastian had written it one afternoon when she was sitting reading in a chair nearby, unaware that he was writing about her.

'*I wish I were younger, as young as she is, then we would have so many more years together. I must school her well in the years to come to make sure she knows how to take care of herself properly if I am no longer here . . . if I have passed on. She is a strong woman, clever, and independent. I adore her so very much. I must tell her that if it should be that I leave first, she must live the rest of her life with happiness, live it for me and with me, because I will always be with her as long as she lives.*'

She closed Sebastian's diary and held it close to her heart, then she got up. She went over to her suitcase, placed the diary in it. Then she slipped off her emerald engagement ring and put it in its box. Her father was correct. She could not travel with something so valuable; it would be risking her life, perhaps, since thieves and robbers abounded. She took the box over to her handbag. Once she got home to London, she would lock the diary and the ring in her safe. The moment she returned from France, the ring would be on her finger again and his diary in her desk drawer.

Going over to the mirror hanging on the wall, she looked at herself. She knew that her father was correct. She had let herself go. Sebastian would not like that. She must get herself back together, with Tilda's help. And she would take Tilda with her to France, because she did need her to dress her hair and fasten her gowns. Anyway, she liked the idea of having Tilda for company rather than being alone with James Falconer.

FIFTY

James was happy to return to Le Havre. He had enjoyed the trip he had made with Great-Uncle Clarence and William. Docks, ships and the sea intrigued him.

At the last moment, before they had left London, Henry Malvern had decided it would be a good idea to send Josh, Alexis's driver, with them to help James with the luggage. He had been right. As far as James was concerned, Josh had been, and still was, a godsend.

James had taken them to the Chèvre d'Or, the inn that he knew from his previous visit with Clarence. He had been greeted warmly by Jean-Claude Murat, the proprietor, and been welcomed with a bit of a flourish.

James introduced Alexis Malvern. When she had responded to Jean-Claude in French, he had been both flattered and pleased that she was so fluent in the language. He told her he knew her uncle; he was well aware that the Malverns owned warehouses on the docks – along with two ships – and had done important business in Le Havre for many years.

Once they had been shown to their rooms and unpacked, the

four of them went downstairs to the restaurant in the inn, where plain but good French fare was served. It was bustling and lively in there.

Alexis did not have an ounce of snobbery in her, and she quickly took charge in the restaurant, showing the other three where she wanted them to sit.

They had travelled all day and into the early evening; they were hungry and thirsty. After perusing the menus and ordering their suppers, she asked for the wine menu and immediately handed it to James.

'I think you should take charge and order the wine.' She smiled as she spoke.

He nodded and smiled back at her, quietly pleased. After scanning it for a few minutes, he ordered a good white, a favourite chardonnay of his. It would go well with their food, since each of them had ordered fish.

Tilda and Josh remained relatively quiet during the meal, as James and Alexis made their plans for the next day.

By the time he went to bed, James was bone tired. He fell asleep almost at once. But sometime during the night, a brawl between drunken sailors in the street below his window awakened him. He got out of bed, hooked the wooden shutters together, and closed the window. Perhaps the shutters would help to deaden the noise.

Yet for a while he discovered he still could not sleep; he knew this was because his mind was focused on Alexis Malvern.

He was still unable to get over the sudden change in her appearance. Overnight she had gone from a plain-looking, sad-faced woman to a beauty.

At first he had not recognized her when she had walked into her father's library in their Mayfair house on Sunday morning, just before they were about to set out on their journey.

He hadn't noticed she had such gorgeous auburn hair, now piled in curls on top of her head and on the very edge of her forehead. When he had met her at the office on a few occasions, her hair had been in a bun and under a black hat. Also, she had always been wearing glasses.

Yesterday he had been dazzled by her bright, emerald-green eyes and red hair. That vividness of colouring, set against a face as white and as smooth as polished marble, was unique. He had been full of astonishment.

Because she was in mourning, she had worn a black suit to travel in, but it was well cut, with a long skirt and smartly tailored jacket. A white silk blouse with a jabot had relieved the black. Her hat was the smallest black bowler he had ever seen, perched on top of her head full of curls.

Quite a transformation indeed, no doubt aided by Tilda's skills. Even so, there was no denying that Miss Malvern was a beauty . . . but one he could only admire at a distance. She was far beyond his reach.

Early on Monday morning, James and Alexis set out to go to the Malvern warehouse on the docks. She already knew it was going to be a hot day. She had chosen to wear a long navy-blue cotton skirt with a matching cotton blouse. She put on navy straw hat to shade her face from the sun.

James, fully aware of the weather and the hustle-and-bustle of Le Havre in summer from his earlier experiences, was dressed in a white cotton jacket, white shirt, and black cotton trousers, made by his grandmother last year.

'I'd forgotten how busy it is,' Alexis murmured, and moved closer to James as they plunged into the docks at the heart of the city.

Immediately, he took hold of her arm tightly. 'Stay with me.

Don't let go. There's a lot of shoving and pushing. The crowds are overwhelming and they don't care who they hurt.'

'I understand.'

The two of them struggled through the masses of people: sailors, merchants, seamen, men rolling casks and pushing hand-carts, and longshoremen carrying huge boxes.

People shouted and screamed at each other, while moving at great speed. Alexis clung to James, afraid for a moment she might get trampled underfoot. Le Havre was a mighty seaport that serviced the world. Hundreds of ships were docked as far as the eye could see, flying flags of all nations.

'Here we are!' James suddenly shouted, his voice rising above the noise. 'See your name. Look. MALVERN.' He pointed to a huge warehouse to their left. She saw it, nodded. They shoved their way through the masses to the front door of the largest.

The first person Alexis saw was the only person she knew at the warehouse, other than her uncle. His name was Jacques Armand and he was the manager. She had met him in Le Havre years before.

He spotted them immediately as they hurried over to the huge open door, and his surprise turned to smiles as he rushed forward to welcome them.

He addressed her in English, exclaimed, 'Mademoiselle Malvern! 'ow nice to see you.' He nodded, still smiling. Then he looked at James with great interest.

Alexis said, 'This is James Falconer, Jacques. He works for my father. We've been sent to see Mr Percy. Is he in the ware-house? Perhaps you can take us to him?'

A deep sigh rolled out of the Frenchman. He shook his head. 'Mr Malvern gone. Run like wind.' He raised his hands. 'You will find him at the Paris office . . . perhaps. I 'ope so.'

Whilst Jacques had been speaking to Alexis, James had been looking around, glancing at some of the men in the vicinity. He thought they appeared to be shifty-eyed and nervous, even somewhat worried. He knew they were watching the scene surreptitiously.

Now he intervened. He said in a pleasant tone of voice, 'I would like to speak with you in private, Monsieur Armand. Can we go into your office, please? It also might be a little cooler in there for Mademoiselle Malvern.'

'*Mais oui, mais oui,*' the manager agreed, and ushered them into the depths of the huge warehouse. He pointed to a side staircase, added, 'Up there . . . we sit up there.'

The three of them went upstairs.

'My office,' Armand announced, and indicated they should sit in the two chairs against the wall. He took the one at his desk. 'Glad you came, Mademoiselle, Monsieur Falconer. There are problems . . .' He turned to look at Alexis. 'Mr Percival left. On Thursday. Last week. Said he was going to Paris office.' He shook his head. 'I planned to send telegram to Paris office tomorrow. Now you are 'ere. It is good you are 'ere.'

'What are the problems exactly?' James asked, his eyes narrowing, wondering about the manager. And yet instinctively he felt the man was honest.

Jacques Armand sat back in his chair, closed his eyes, as if weary, and then suddenly opened them. He sat up straighter. 'So sorry, Mademoiselle. I feel very . . . *c'est une mauvaise situation.* But your uncle is thief, stealing . . . stealing your money.'

Alexis gave a small gasp. It was what they had suspected, but never really believed would be true.

'I would like to see the books,' James said. 'I have the authority in a letter from Mr Henry Malvern.' He glanced uncertainly at Alexis. 'But of course, as a Malvern family member and a partner, Mademoiselle Alexis also has the power to do as she wishes. Absolute power.'

'You look at books. He took many papers.'

Rising, Armand led them out of his office and across the hall, opened another door. 'Here he worked . . .' He grimaced, muttered, 'At stealing.'

James spent half an hour looking at the few record books which were in Percy Malvern's desk. They told him very little – actually nothing, because they were old books and of no real value to him. But of course, Percy had taken any papers that would condemn him. Why leave them behind if he was fleeing? And he had fled. There was no doubt in James's mind that Percy Malvern was not in Paris either. Thieves didn't hang around to get themselves arrested.

Returning to Armand's office, where Alexis had been talking to the manager, James said, 'There is nothing there that can help me. But you must know something, Monsieur Armand. You are the warehouse manager; you worked directly with Mr Percy. Please try and help us to understand how he did this.'

The Frenchman nodded, grimaced again. 'I discover it, few days ago, what had been 'appening. Mr Percival selling wine to old customers and taking the money.'

'How could he possibly think we wouldn't find out?' Alexis asked.

'Monsieur Joshua not paying attention, an old man, then a sick man. And in London.' The Frenchman gave a Gallic shrug.

'This must have been going on before Uncle Joshua had a stroke,' Alexis said, staring at James and then Jacques.

The manager nodded, obviously concerned.

James said, 'I won't take the papers in his office. They are of no use to me, Monsieur Armand.'

'*Je comprends.* Please, mademoiselle, go to Paris. To office, they give you advice.' He cleared his throat. 'Trust me. I loyal to Monsieur Henry. I stay. I look after warehouse. My men loyal.'

Alexis looked at James and raised a brow. 'What are your thoughts about this situation?'

'I tend to agree with Monsieur Armand. There is absolutely

nothing we can do here. Percy has fled. Taken certain papers with him. I think we do have to go to the Paris office, talk to them.'

'I agree. And I know Jacques will keep everything going here at the warehouse. You will, won't you, Jacques?'

'Trust me. I work 'ere at Malvern's all my life. Monsieur Philippe de Lavalière, the man at Paris office, mademoiselle. Trust him.'

'We will do that, Jacques. Thank you for your advice,' Alexis said, and then asked, 'Where are our two ships? The *Marie-Claire* and the *Belle Étoile*?'

'At sea, delivering goods to Russia,' Jacques Armand answered.

'Please keep track of the two ships at all times,' James asked. 'It's part of my job, and I shall be doing the same.' He couldn't help wondering if the problem was bigger than they realized. He might have to dig deeper, without overstepping the mark; he certainly didn't want to upset Miss Malvern.

FIFTY-ONE

Alexis and James, along with Tilda and Josh, arrived in Paris late on Wednesday afternoon. Amid the tensions of the thefts, and the threat of a family scandal, it was a relief to be in this most beautiful city after the raucous and overcrowded port of Le Havre.

They went directly to Le Meurice, Alexis's favourite hotel in the city, which was where she had always stayed with her father. It was close to their Paris office, which was also located on the Rue de Rivoli.

Tilda had just finished unpacking for her and had then left to go to her own room, when there was a light knocking on the sitting-room door of her suite.

Wondering who it could be, Alexis walked across the floor and opened the door to find James standing there.

'Is everything all right? How is your room?' she asked.

'Very nice, thank you. I just wondered if we could have supper, to go over the business problems before we go to the office tomorrow.' He hesitated, aware that – as an unmarried woman – she shouldn't be seen dining alone with him.

Alexis thought for a moment. 'I think we should stay here. There's a very nice restaurant in the hotel. If we eat here in full view it shouldn't cause too much talk. Shall we meet at seven o'clock in the hotel lobby?'

James nodded. 'See you then,' he said, and was gone in a flash.

Alexis sat down at the desk and was about to write a telegram to her father, and then changed her mind. Perhaps it was better not to put anything in writing for the moment. In fact, perhaps not at all.

A member of their family had committed a criminal act by stealing from them. It was better told verbally, wasn't it? How sad this would be for her father. Betrayal by his cousin was not a nice thing to hear. And he was already deeply saddened because of the condition of his older brother Joshua, rendered helpless after that stroke. Her father was vulnerable at this moment in time. The company had been built by him on hard work, and he prided himself on his managers' loyalty and honesty. Bad news could wait.

Leaving the desk, she walked across the sitting room, lay down on the chaise, and covered herself with a small blanket Tilda had placed there. Closing her eyes, she hoped to have a nap before going to supper with James Falconer.

In the last few days, she had changed her mind about him in certain ways. She didn't know him well. She had met him several times, but he had always seemed oddly cold, too matter-of-fact to her. But now she realized that he was simply keeping his place, reporting to her as his boss, in a sense, when speaking about the arcades. He had done a good job with them; there was no question about that. He was a hard worker, diligent and disciplined.

On this trip, so far, he had remained respectful, but friendlier, and certainly he had handled himself extremely well in Le Havre. Businesslike, efficient, and pleasant with Jacques Armand. She had found herself trusting his judgement when it came to Jacques.

She herself was quite certain the warehouse manager was honest and loyal; after all, he had worked for them for over twenty years. When Falconer had said he believed Jacques' story about Percy and that he really had only just discovered what was going on, this pleased her, gave her a sense of relief.

It was Tilda who awakened her an hour later. She had dozed for a while, and then fallen asleep. The trip from Le Havre had obviously tired her out today.

Tilda insisted on touching up her hair and persuaded her to change out of the navy cotton dress, which was now badly creased. After washing her hands and face, Alexis put on the grey silk gown Tilda had chosen, much more appropriate for supper in this elegant hotel. Tilda had added a shawl of grey cut-velvet and a matching purse.

'Go out and have some fun with Josh,' Alexis said as she was leaving her suite. 'There are lots of little bistros around here. Enjoy yourself.'

Tilda gave her a small, shy smile. 'He asked me already.'

Alexis smiled back. She went out into the corridor and downstairs to the lobby. James was already waiting for her.

Once he had greeted her, he said with a faint smile, 'Tilda and Josh have gone out on the town.'

The way he said it made her laugh, something she hadn't done for a long time.

'Why are you laughing?' he asked, as he took her elbow and led her into the restaurant.

'I don't know. It was just the way you said it, that's all. And I hope they have a nice time. Paris is unique.'

James insisted on ordering a glass of white wine for each of them, whilst they studied the menu. Oddly enough, without influencing each other, they both ordered country pâté, to be followed by coq au vin.

Over the food, James spoke about the forthcoming meeting with Philippe de Lavalière. Alexis had explained that he ran the shipping division at the Paris office and had done so for several years. He was answerable to Percy Malvern directly.

'So who is he answerable to now?' James asked, frowning. 'With Percy in the wind.'

'You, of course,' she replied at once. 'You are running the wine division.'

'Mostly the London end of it, though. Not France,' he reminded her.

'That's true. I'll need to speak to father. Perhaps he should now be answering to you. Until we replace Percy, find someone to do his job.'

James tried to hide an unexpected smile, but his mouth twitched.

'What is it?' she asked, staring at him.

'I was going to say there might well be a lot of people trained in stealing . . . which apparently was Percy's job. Lately.'

The following morning, Alexis and James walked over to the Rue de Rivoli and into the offices of the Malvern Company. Alexis introduced herself, and then James.

Philippe de Lavalière was a nice looking man in his late thirties. He was delighted to meet them, but surprised and upset when he heard what they had discovered in Le Havre.

'I do not understand this. Not at all,' he said in perfect English. 'Percy Malvern a thief? Stealing from his own family?' He shook his head. 'It is not possible. No, no.'

'How did he behave when he was here a few days ago?' James asked, looking directly at the Frenchman, his eyes narrowing.

'In a hurry. He said he had to visit a friend in hospital. We spoke for only a few minutes. He went into his office and, when he left, he simply said goodbye and that he would see me later. What are you going to do? This is a scandal.'

'I think we must hire a French lawyer, investigate the situation,' James replied. 'For the moment, Jacques Armand is continuing to do his job as manager of the warehouse and he will be answerable to you, Monsieur de Lavalière.'

'Very well. That will work, I am certain.' He paused for a moment, looking at Alexis. 'I reported to Mr Percy directly, Mademoiselle Malvern. To whom shall I report now?'

'I need to discuss that with Mr Malvern. For now, as Mr Falconer runs the wine division at the London office, as you already know, I think it would be best if you report to him.'

Philippe de Lavalière nodded. He studied James for a moment. '*Merci*, Mademoiselle Malvern.' He then addressed James. 'I look forward to passing on my reports, Monsieur Falconer. On a weekly basis.'

When Alexis and James finally left the Paris offices of the Malvern Company, they agreed that the meeting had been successful. They had both been impressed by Philippe de Lavalière, and knew he was honest and reliable. James asked Philippe if he would try to find a good lawyer who might be able to handle the case. The Frenchman said he would do that at once and be in touch.

Out of the blue, Alexis exclaimed, 'I think we ought to talk about this further.'

She and James were on their way back to the Meurice Hotel. 'We have managed to solve our problems. Well . . . for the moment.'

'We haven't caught Percy, though,' James answered, eyeing her worriedly as they fell into step. 'Maybe we should have reported him to the police.'

Alexis shook her head. 'I think we must tell my father everything before we do anything like that. He must make the final decision. He won't want a scandal to damage the family name – or the business.'

'Yes, you're absolutely correct,' James agreed, though underneath he still felt uncertain.

Once they reached the hotel, Alexis said she had some errands to do. In London, single women did not go out without a companion or chaperone. But this was Paris. No one knew her. Besides, she looked old enough to be a married woman; she was dressed plainly and would attract no attention.

'I'll see you in the lobby at seven tonight,' Alexis said firmly. ' We need to talk this over and decide what else needs to happen.'

James nodded. He watched her walking away down the street, and wondered how he would manage to get through this evening with her.

His heart sank. The business meetings were a breeze. But dinner? For the first time in his life, James Falconer had fallen in love. And with a woman who could never be his. Last night he had not been able to sleep, thinking about Alexis, her extraordinary beauty, and his desire for her.

No woman had ever captured his heart until now. He could manage to work with her, that he had proved to himself these last few days.

But he could not be alone with her. The solution was to make sure he avoided social events after tonight. He would celebrate their success tonight, as she wanted, just to please her. After that, he would make sure he was unavailable in his free time.

Alexis felt the need to walk, to be outside in the sunlight, to throw off her weariness, all that hurt that had gathered inside her over months. Without thinking of going anywhere special, she just meandered along. Let go of her worries, pushed aside the pain of loss.

Unexpectedly, she found herself on the Champs-Élysées, and remembered how much she and her father had enjoyed walking down this most lovely avenue. It was one of the many created by Georges Haussmann for the Emperor Louis-Napoléon Bonaparte in the 1860s. He was an architect who had turned Paris into the beautiful city it was today.

Suddenly she came to a stop in front of a familiar shop. It was where her father had bought her one of her favourite dresses as a girl. Drawn to it by nostalgia, she went to look in the windows.

A gown on display immediately caught her eye. It was lavender with a hint of pink. Without another thought she went into the shop.

The young woman who came to help her told her the size of the dress. It was taken out of the window at once. Alexis held it against her body, liked the look of it, and bought it. Just like that. On an impulse. Something she had never done before.

Later, when she was back at the hotel, she wondered why she had been so silly. Obviously she would never wear it, even though lavender was considered appropriate for mourning.

There was a light knock on the door. Tilda came in carrying two of the cotton day dresses she had been ironing.

Instantly she saw the dress on the bed and ran over. She stood staring at it. 'Oh, Miss Alexis! It's beautiful!' she cried, putting the other dresses down, picking up the new one. 'You must wear it tonight,' Tilda exclaimed.

'No, I'm not going to, Tilda. It looks cheap, a bad buy, in haste.'

The young lady's maid shook her head, picked up the dress, and took hold of Alexis's arm. She led her to the cheval mirror in the bedroom.

Posing her in front of it, she held the dress against her body, and said, 'Just look at yourself, Miss Alexis. It is the most unique colour and perfect for you. Lavender with a hint of pink.'

Staring at herself as the maid held the silk dress against her body, Alexis had to agree that it did suit her.

After a little more discussion, Tilda brought Alexis to the dressing table. She began to touch up her glorious auburn hair, redoing the curls on top of her head, smoothing the sides, pulling a few curls onto the front of her forehead.

Tilda, as she dressed her hair, chatted quietly, 'You know, you look like Princess Alexandra with this style, Miss Alexis.'

'She's blonde and she's a Dane,' Alexis answered, not seeing the resemblance at all.

'I know she is, but she's beautiful, and everyone has copied her hairstyle and they copy her clothes as well.' Struck by a moment of true inspiration, Tilda added, 'I've seen her in a gown just like this, long and slender with long sleeves. If it's good enough for the Princess of Wales, it's good enough for you, Miss Alexis.'

Before Alexis could stand up, Tilda insisted on putting a little pink rouge on her lips. She smoothed her thick auburn eyebrows with a small brush. 'There, all done,' the maid said. 'Now, you must put on the dress.'

Reluctant though she was, Alexis stepped into the lavender silk gown, waited for Tilda to button it up the back, and then went over to the mirror.

She was shocked at how she looked, turned to Tilda, and said, 'It suits me and it doesn't look cheap at all.'

'It's perfect on you. It highlights your slim figure; you must wear it. It makes you look younger.'

'But what shoes do I have? And I need a purse,' Alexis said.

'The grey shoes and bag will work with the lavender.' The maid ran to the closet and took them out.

Alexis hesitated at the bedroom door, as Tilda sprayed a floral scent on her. 'Are you sure I look all right?' she asked nervously.

'Beautiful, Miss Alexis. More beautiful than I've seen you for . . . a very long time.'

It was just five minutes to seven when Alexis walked into the lobby of the hotel.

James was standing there waiting for her. He was struck dumb when he first set eyes on her. He had never seen Alexis looking like this, in a light-coloured gown and with a hint of cosmetics on her face. She was so beautiful, even other people were glancing at her in admiration. He managed to say good evening in a low voice.

She looked up at him, smiled, and slipped her arm through his. 'I think we should go in for supper,' she murmured, walking with him to the restaurant.

Once they were seated, she said, 'Earlier, I ordered a bottle of Dom Pérignon.' As she glanced around, looking for a waiter, she saw one coming towards their table, carrying the champagne in a silver bucket.

Once their flutes had been filled, they clinked glasses, and Alexis said, 'To your great success, Mr Falconer.'

Finding his voice at last, he corrected her. 'No, to our success.'

A silence fell between them as they sipped the champagne. Alexis, gazing at him more intently than ever before, realized for the first time how very blue his eyes were, almost unnaturally blue. He was a handsome man. How could his looks have escaped her? Preoccupation, she answered herself. Preoccupation with work and my troubles.

Finally he spoke. 'Why are you staring at me, Miss Malvern? Is there something wrong?'

'I was thinking how very blue your eyes are,' she murmured.

'They've always been blue,' he replied, and then laughed. 'Perhaps you never noticed.'

'I think sometimes I have my head pushed down into the work on my desk; I miss things. I have to change that.'

His eyes were riveted on her face. He took in the vividness of her beauty, the flaming auburn hair, the emerald-green eyes, and the sublime ivory complexion. He wasn't going to walk away from her. That was not his nature. He was going to win her. She was going to be his, no matter what.

Alexis recognized the expression in James Falconer's eyes. Her heart tightened. He wanted her.

'Now you're staring at me,' she said softly.

Their eyes locked and she was unable to look away.

She thought suddenly: perhaps there is a life for me after all.

Acknowledgements

I happened to open last year's novel, *Secrets of Cavendon*, the other day, looking for a bit of research. What momentarily startled me was the list of books I've written. Thirty-two major novels and four novellas. I couldn't help asking myself when I had written them as I stared at the page. Over thirty-nine years, to be exact.

Next year, in 2019, I will be celebrating forty years with HarperCollins, my UK publishers.

During those years I've worked with some great people, all of whom became friends as well as colleagues. I've seen people come and go, but everything has always run smoothly and efficiently, and it was like being part of a large family.

It still feels that way today, and my current team is as marvellous as all of those from the past. My editor, Publishing Director Lynne Drew, is brilliant and insightful. She also agrees with my theory that character is plot. In other words, who and what you are as a person will define your life . . . your character is your destiny. That makes it easy to work together.

Lynne is a great listener, and therefore a special sounding

board for me. Her thoughts, ideas and suggestions help to bolster the plot lines and inspire me to come up with many more. I cannot thank Lynne enough for everything she does for me. She is my friend as well as my editor, and she shows that in so many different ways.

Thanks to Eloisa Clegg and Charlotte Brabbin, other members of Lynne's team, who handle those nitty-gritty things for me which help the wheels turn. Penny Isaac has been my copy-editor forever, it seems, and my thanks to her for always doing such a lovely job. Kate Elton, Executive Publisher, Roger Cazalet, Associate Publisher, Lucy Vanderbilt, Group Rights Director, and Charlie Redmayne, CEO, make up the rest of the team and are an outstanding group to work with, full of encouragement and support for me.

I give my special thanks to PR Director Elizabeth Dawson, who has publicized my novels for many years. Loving and caring, Liz has been a true friend and has shown it twenty-four/seven. I have lovingly nicknamed her 'My Own Florence', and she knows the reasons why and laughs with me about it.

It is important to me that I turn in a perfect manuscript; and it is Linda Sullivan of WORDsmart who does exactly that. She is a wonder, a miracle worker producing those perfect manuscripts without errors and at great speed. My thanks to Linda for her dedication and also her willingness to work all hours so that I can make my deadline. I must also thank our personal PR representative, Maria Boyle, who has worked with Bob and myself promoting his movies and my books for many years. Another great member of the team.

Starting a new series is always difficult, especially my latest, The House of Falconer: *Master of His Fate*, perhaps because it is set in the Victorian era and there was much research to do. My husband Bob, always involved in my work, has been a real trooper whilst I have been writing this new one. No complaints about my long hours and late meals, and there have been smiles for me every day and loving words of encouragement. My thanks to him for being a good sport.

Finally I wish to mention four of my girlfriends in New York, often called my posse, sometimes my women warriors. I think they are all those things and much more. Vicki, Avanti, Wendy and Susan, you have my gratitude and love for always being there for me.